Unexpected Enemy

Ultimate Revenge

Tim Cagle

Brighton Publishing LLC
435 N. Harris Drive
Mesa, AZ 85203

Unexpected Enemy
Ultimate Revenge

Tim Cagle

Brighton Publishing LLC
435 N. Harris Drive
Mesa, AZ 85203
www.BrightonPublishing.com

ISBN 13: 978-1-62183-456-4

ISBN 10: 1-62183-456-5

Printed in the United States of America

First Edition

Cover Design: Tom Rodriguez

To those who turn the other cheek to hide the flames from a distant fire.....

"If you want to test someone's character, give them power."

~ Abraham Lincoln

Chapter One

Monday, October 13

The cemetery was located in Chelsea, a blue-collar suburb north of Boston. The entrance consisted of a dirt road on a hilltop leading to a tree-lined meadow. Weathered fieldstone and granite markers dating back to colonial times formed asymmetrical rows. Most were in disrepair.

Just before eleven, Ann Sorenson drove through the rusted gates. She looked in the rearview mirror as Ricki arrived. After exchanging hugs, they approached a headstone in the last row that looked freshly carved and polished. Ann bent slightly and placed the bouquet of daisies on the grave. A soft gust of wind sent a crimson and gold leaf fluttering past the inscription.

Andrea Curtis Perryman

Born: October 13, 1980

Died: July 10, 2008

"Thanks for meeting me," Ann said.

"The least I could do on your birthday," said Ricki, nodding toward the date on the marker.

"Andi was more than my twin. She used to say we were symbiotic survivors," said Ann, as an image of pallbearers lugging her sister's white casket formed. She could almost taste the tears as she remembered the day Andi found a lump in her breast. The doctor said not to worry; it was fibrocystic disease. She was too young to have cancer. Andrea died a few months before she turned twenty-eight.

Ann ran her thumbs beneath the creases where her eyelids met in a halfhearted swipe to neutralize her tears. A thin lock of blond hair fell in front of her blue eyes.

"Are you feeling OK?" asked Ricki, glancing at Ann's swollen belly.

"Mostly mood swings and nausea. But that all ends in another month," said Ann, visualizing the former office she had transformed into a nursery. She could almost bask in the scent of fresh paint from the periwinkle walls covered with animal decals.

"Thank God Lee Harlow is my doctor," said Ann. "The shots and fertility treatments I went through will soon be worth it all. He's a genius."

Ricki turned and grasped Ann's arm.

"Has he gone over everything with you? The birth and the aftermath?" asked Ricki.

"Trust me. I'm as ready as I can be. I know exactly what to expect when the baby arrives," said Ann, leaning against Ricki's shoulder and squeezing her right hand.

"This child will change a lot of lives and right a lot of wrongs," said Ricki, as she pulled out a black velvet box. "I was going to wait until the baby came, but you deserve this for your birthday," she said, extending it toward Ann.

Ann opened the box and removed a sterling silver necklace showcasing a pendant the size of a *demitasse* cup rim. It sparkled like a freshly minted coin in the morning sun.

"It's called a *shèngli*. It's the Chinese symbol for victory," said Ricki.

The symbol consisted of four characters. Ann was struck by the fact that the first one reminded her of a ladder with rungs that demanded ascent. Just like her journey to motherhood.

"Your baby's birth will be a victory for my brother as well as your sister. I hope you don't mind, but I bought another one for myself," said Ricki, showing her an identical medallion.

"I would expect no less from my baby's godmother," said Ann, stretching to embrace Ricki, who stood half a head taller, after they each slipped their pendants under their tops.

"When is Steven flying back?" asked Ricki.

"Tonight. He's in DC for the day. He said he has a special birthday dinner planned in honor of the baby."

"How is Anthony holding up during the wait?" asked Ricki as Ann looked up and shrugged.

"Like he always does. With dignity and grace."

"Tell him to stay optimistic," said Ricki as Ann's eyes locked with hers and suddenly lit up.

"I just realized I'm a woman with two husbands, and like a matching pair of bookends, neither one is around when I need him," said Ann as Ricki shot her a quick, mischievous smile.

"They're typical guys. Instead of double support, you get twice the aggravation," said Ricki.

"Do you have time for lunch?" asked Ann.

"Rain check. I'm going to be stuck in one of those meetings where you need a penis to get attention, and I don't have time to grow one," said Ricki.

"Maybe you can come for dinner this weekend," said Ann.

"It's a date. We have a lot to go over to get ready for the baby," said Ricki as she gave Ann a quick hug before they each drove away.

An hour later, Ann arrived downtown. It was her first time in the city in a few weeks. So far, the day was perfect, punctuated by sounds from the bustling sidewalks and a fall foliage show. Grinning, she saw herself walking through the floor-to-ceiling glass and polished steel skywalk leading from the Prudential Center to Copley Plaza. It provided a panoramic view of Boston's Back Bay while overlooking chic haute couture boutiques on Newbury and Boylston Streets.

As she left the parking garage, Ann's face contorted as her belly was jolted by a hard pinch, as if her flesh was wedged between the joint of two jagged-edged planks. She had been battling morning sickness and fatigue, but this time the pain was different, worse than the tingle she'd felt earlier at home. She stopped to steady herself and then the inferno in her belly faded and a feeling of normalcy returned.

The morning air was warming, so Ann slipped her silk scarf from around her neck and placed it in her purse. After entering Saks Fifth Avenue, she headed off to the cosmetics section and stopped at the Chanel counter. Convinced that the pain was gone for good, Ann asked to see the Vitalumière Foundation for ultra light skin and then reached for her credit card.

Smiling broadly, she grinned and ran her right hand over her cotton top until the outline of the silver pendant caressed her fingertips. The gift was an unexpected bonus but certainly not a surprise. Ricki was one of only a few friends Ann had allowed herself to make since she moved to Boston. After all they had been through together, she had become an older sister. She grinned and pictured Ricki sitting next to her at the symphony or a Patriots' home game when, without warning, the pain brutally struck again, this time like she was impaled.

Ann bit her upper lip as the fire in her belly sizzled. She quivered slightly before bracing herself against a display case. The clerk was about to run her card when Ann clenched her teeth. Suddenly, she knew it was not a passing bout of indigestion.

"Maybe I should come back for the foundation after lunch," said Ann between breaths as her trembling fingers helped stabilize her body against the top of the counter.

A paroxysm of pain sent her reeling to her left against one of the chrome-and-black vinyl chairs. She dropped down to her right knee in a semi-genuflection, pressed her right hand against the cosmetics case, and brought her left hand to her forehead. The clerk retrieved the phone next to the register and quickly dialed security.

"Ve have a coos-tomer who's eel at ze Sha-nell counter. Zend halp," said the clerk in an exotic accent before sprinting forward and guiding Ann to the closest chair.

Ann's face distorted in pain as the blast furnace in her belly grew. It felt like a white-hot knife was carving a zipper. Another associate joined the clerk before a security officer arrived and announced an ambulance was on the way. Immediately, the woman holding the card looked at Ann.

"Take eet easy, Mees. Damon," she whispered, looking up from the name on the credit card, before it handing it back.

Anxiety spread over Ann as she bristled at the sound of the surname "Damon." Her health insurance was also in that name, but not her drivers' license. What if the paramedics checked, exposed her dual identities, and started prying?

What if her baby was coming? She would be taken to a strange hospital with an unknown doctor and be bombarded with questions that demanded answers. She could not have her baby with anyone except Dr. Harlow.

Ann's mind raced like she was running from a lynch mob. Trembling, she knew she had to find an escape when another wave of agony made her feel like she had been sucker-punched.

I can be at Harlow's office in less than ten minutes, she thought, scanning the store before focusing on a side exit to the street.

"I need to stop at the ladies' room," she said to the security guard.

"It's in the rear of the store. I'll have to get a female officer to go in with you," he replied.

"You can wait in the corridor," said Ann, staring into his eyes with a pleading look.

The guard nodded and half-carried, half-guided Ann forward. Separate doors for entry and exit sparked an idea. Knowing her ash-blond hair and royal-blue hounds tooth blouse were dead giveaways, she slipped into a stall and whipped off her top. Then she reversed it to its muted-color side. After tying the scarf over her hair, she donned sunglasses and barely inched open the exit door. The guard had his back turned and was speaking into his radio.

At that moment, two women moved past her toward the entrance, chattering up a storm as they strolled together. Clutching her stomach with one hand and her purse with the other, Ann stepped out as they passed. Their semi-lockstep movement blocked the guard's view, and less than a dozen steps later, she slipped through the side exit on her way to the parking garage.

After tossing her purse onto the passenger seat, Ann climbed inside and gunned the engine. Instinctively, her eyes were drawn to the groin area of her white maternity pants. A few tiny droplets of blood were growing.

A convoy of cars waited to exit. Ann's pulse soared as she searched for an escape route. Focusing on the deserted monthly parking lane next to her, she whipped the vehicle to the right and sped toward the exit. In a flash, she smashed through the faded yellow-and-black vinyl barrier gate arm, shattering it into multiple pieces, and then fishtailed out onto the street. After hanging a sharp left, she headed for the ramp leading to the turnpike westbound. The clatter of horns filled the air as the cashier ran from the booth into the street and pointed his phone at her license plate.

Ann reached for her cell. Her belly began to swell as though ready to burst.

"Artemis Associates. Judy speaking."

"This is Ann Sorenson. I'm a patient of Dr. Harlow's. I'm in terrible pain and just started bleeding," shouted Ann, swerving to avoid sideswiping a delivery truck.

"Did you call for an ambulance?"

"No. I have to talk to Dr. Harlow."

"He's in surgery. Let me get you an ambulance. Give me your location," said Judy.

"No time. I'm on my way," yelled Ann, ending the call.

Ricki will know exactly what to do, thought Ann, as she decided to text even though she knew there would be no answer. The up and down motion caused Ann to swerve twice as she tried to concentrate. Her message was sent to Ricki's burn phone.

Body on fire… baby coming… going to doctor… get me help!!!

With her heart skipping a beat, she sped through the restricted E-Z pass lane, activating the sirens and flashing lights. Another wave of agony made her glance at her belly, a move that made her drift toward the breakdown lane. Her front wheel struck the rumble strip, and the nail-gun pneumatic sound of tires on uneven metal caused her to swerve into the high-speed travel lane. The bloodstain had grown to the size of a saucer.

Ann merged with the remnants of the morning rush-hour commute and tried to stay steady. Suddenly, a different kind of sticky sensation began to ooze from between her legs. Terrified, she touched the tops of her thighs and watched the moisture soak her fingertips. This time, the droplets had a slight sheen and carried a distinctly sweet smell. She remembered that scent from when Dr. Harlow analyzed a sample of her amniotic fluid—a substance her baby needed to live.

The tollbooth was only a few hundred yards in front of her. Instead of slowing down, Ann gunned her engine and headed for a deserted lane. The collector ducked down as she blew by the booth, which shook for a few seconds as though struck by a hurricane-force wind.

After Ann cleared the exit, she entered the rotary and took the first right. The entrance to the fertility clinic was barely one hundred yards ahead, adjacent to the hospital. Two dozen protesters were carrying signs and placards as they marched and chanted in front.

A uniformed security guard was patrolling beside a set of orange-colored barrel barriers and stopping each vehicle for a mandatory security check. The guard began pumping his hands with palms thrust downward toward Ann as she drifted out of consciousness. The guard dove for cover as she blasted through the barriers, leaving each one in splintered chunks and triggering a full-scale alert. Protesters scattered in all directions like stampeding cattle as abandoned signs flew toward the flanks.

She awoke and then cried out loud as her vehicle headed straight toward a young mother pushing an infant in a stroller. As the car drifted directly toward them, Ann marshaled all of her strength and flung the steering wheel hard to the left as her foot slipped from the brake pedal. Mom and baby were safe, but the swerve caused the vehicle to oversteer and slam into the glass doors. It came to rest inside the vestibule.

The crash sounded like an exploding artillery shell as it wiped out the entire front of the entrance. Shards of glass, clumps of sheetrock, and pieces of twisted metal covered the crumpled hood and windshield. Screams of terror filled the room as memories of the Boston Marathon bombing caused people to panic.

There were two-dozen patients and visitors in the waiting area, and the noise dispersed the crowd. The guard arrived with his gun drawn, speaking loudly into his radio in response to the security alert he had broadcast. His hands shook as he pointed the weapon at Ann who was slumped over the deployed airbag.

"Freeze," he shouted, bringing his left hand up to steady his trembling grip.

Ann inched her door open. The guard's hands relaxed slightly at the sight of her top, which showed him she was in such a panic she had put it on inside out. Her bloodstained white pants told him she was in trouble. She managed only a single step, before collapsing onto piles of crash-formed debris. A quick look at her bruised, sweaty face and distended belly confirmed that she posed no further threat.

"We've got a medical emergency," he shouted.

As the receptionist dialed the phone, three people dressed in pale-blue scrub clothing ran out of the elevator. They were pushing a gurney and led by a woman wearing street clothes under a white lab coat. Her nametag read "Judith Davis, RN."

"That woman is Ann Sorenson. She's Dr. Harlow's patient," said Judith to the guard, removing her phone and dialing the operating room.

The team loaded Ann onto the gurney. They began to collect vital signs before rushing her toward the elevator.

"It looks like she's going into labor," called one of the attendants.

Ann tried to navigate as she was wheeled through the hallway on her way to the second floor. Her face was bruised and puffy from the airbag. With a feeling of joy because she made it to Harlow's office, she watched rows of ceiling tiles rush by. She cried out loud as one final violent stab of pain seared up and across her belly before she again lapsed into unconsciousness.

As the medical team departed the crash site, maintenance workers arrived to fortify the entrance. Outside, the bomb detection unit appeared along with television news reporters.

Chapter Two

At the time of Ann's crash, Dr. Lee Harlow was in the operating room at Boston Memorial Hospital teaching doctors in training when to perform a cesarean section delivery. The first-year obstetrical residents stood at attention like military honor guards. They marveled at how the surgical incision was so precise it looked like an engraving. A former chief resident once described the experience as the medical equivalent of composing with Mozart, painting with Monet, or writing with Chekhov.

Residents were desperate to work with Harlow. Other physicians were too arrogant to speak to those in training and never allowed them to learn from the tough cases. Underlings were left to develop their skills someplace else, usually in the units for the homeless, abandoned or indigent.

Most of the attending physicians had elite, high-powered patients who demanded private rooms, luxurious bedding, and silver tea services. The standing joke among those in training was that upper-class vomit didn't look or smell any different from that found in the back alleys and gutters, even when it was cradled by a silk duvet or collected by a platinum bedpan.

Harlow's voice commanded their attention.

"Now you'll understand why I used a *Pfannenstiel* incision. It gives better access to the central pelvis than a midline. Also, you do not need to close the peritoneum separately, and you can approximate the fascia with a delayed absorbable suture."

The circulating nurse entered the operating theater.

"Dr. Harlow, your office just called. There's an emergency with one of your patients named Sorenson."

Harlow stopped cutting, stood up straighter, and arched his eyebrows.

"What kind of emergency?"

"They said she was bleeding, in terrible pain, and coming in."

"Is the baby all right?"

"They don't know yet."

"Do me a favor. Call them back and tell them to stabilize her. I'll be there right away."

Less than twenty minutes later, Lee exited through the hospital tunnel and arrived at the rear entrance to his office building. He ran his hand over his full mop of salt and pepper hair and wondered what the problem was with Ms. Sorenson. She was one of his more difficult cases, and the joy they both felt when she conceived was indescribable.

Harlow was a tall man, almost 6′4″, and he had to duck as he exited the tunnel before arriving at the rear entrance. He was in his early sixties, and to complement his height, he fastidiously kept his weight just at 200 pounds. Some people, especially star-struck nurses and colleagues, said he was so close in resemblance to the actor William Devane that they could have been separated at birth.

Harlow silently gave thanks for the underground entrance because it was the best way to avoid protesters. They had been absent for years, apparently resigned to the fact that the clinic was too valuable to women's lives to be shut down. For the past few days, however, they had started congregating again, apparently in protest over reported scandals that alleged that fetal body parts were being sold in violation of federal law.

When Lee got to his office, Ruth Oliver, one of the nurses assisting that day, was waiting and holding a medical chart.

"Is Ms. Sorenson here yet?" asked Harlow.

"She just got on the elevator. She was triaged but only has minor bumps and bruises along with severe abdominal pain and bleeding."

"Page me as soon as they get her prepped."

"I already pulled her chart," said Ruth, extending the folder forward.

Harlow scanned Ann Sorenson's records, picturing her as he read the entries. White female, thirty-six years old. Married to a tall, thirty-eight-year-old, strikingly handsome Swede named Steven.

These two remind me of a pair of Scandinavian models for Volvo, thought Lee.

He finished reading just as his cell phone rang. It was Judy Davis.

"Dr. Harlow, Ms. Sorenson is in exam room three. She's going into labor."

"On my way," he said.

As Ann lay on the examination table, she could hear the tearing sounds of her clothing being cut off. Her face was flushed and covered with sweat. A cool compress was soaking her forehead, and she could feel the deliciously cold liquid trickling down her cheeks.

The pain left her bewildered. After all she had been through, what if she was in danger of losing the baby so close to delivery? She silently screamed at nature for making such foolish, whimsical choices. The arbitrary way it picked parents who were unfit, unworthy, uncaring, and downright evil, and blessed them with beautiful, healthy babies.

Ann's breathing became shallow as her anger spiked. Despite all the sorrow, sacrifice, and emotional blackmail inflicted on her mind, nature was now demanding a physical ransom from her body.

At that moment, Harlow stepped into the examination room. He reached for Ann's shoulder, and his voice became calm and soothing as he told her everything would be all right. Her face grew into a tight semi-smile.

"Ms. Sorenson, where are you in pain?" he asked, probing her distended abdomen.

"My stomach feels like it's on fire."

Harlow reached for her hand and gently rubbed it.

"You're going to deliver, and you know what to expect. Don't forget what we talked about and how your ordeal is almost over," said Harlow.

"Will my baby be all right?" asked Ann, as she felt another burst of fire in her belly.

"I promise you he will be," said Harlow as Ruth approached.

"Ms. Sorenson, it's Ruth Oliver. I assisted Dr. Harlow when you came in with your husband a few days ago for your last physical. Try to take it easy. Everything is going to be fine," said Ruth, shooting Harlow a look that said she would take charge of keeping Ann calm.

"Get her prepped and draped, stat, and take her down to the OR. Tell anesthesia not to give her anything until I get back," said Lee, before leaving to scrub.

"I know this is your first child, but you'll soon be home with your son. Your husband was notified and is on his way," said Ruth in a soothing tone that almost sounded hymn-like.

Ann tried to smile.

"His name is Steven, right? Remember how Steven misplaced his keys after you arrived last time and I found them? How he came in to thank me personally?" asked Ruth, smiling broadly.

Ann nodded briefly as she choked back a sob.

"Don't worry. Dr. Harlow has everything under control. In no time your son will make his way into the world," continued Ruth as Ann squeezed her hand hard.

Harlow entered the operating suite a few minutes later, dressed in blue scrubs, surgical cap, and mask. Quickly, he donned a sterile gown and latex gloves before positioning himself at the foot of the table.

Ann's feet were inserted into metal stirrups, spreading her long, tan legs apart. She was covered by a fresh white sheet. The nurse anesthetist was adjusting the drip on Ann's intravenous line. Ruth was scrubbed and gowned, ready to assist.

"Shall I give her some Demerol?" asked the nurse anesthetist.

"Too late. She's ready to crown," said Harlow.

"Ms. Sorenson, the placenta ruptured, and that's why you have so much pain. If we give you any medication, it will slow down the delivery and affect the baby's breathing. You don't want this to take any longer than it has to, right?"

"I just want to get it over with," said Ann, wanting to scream.

"Remember everything I told you. Stay strong," said Harlow as his eyes synchronized with hers.

"She's starting to tear. Let me have a number eleven blade," said Lee, extending his hand as Ruth handed him a scalpel. In one fluid movement, he made an incision at the rear of the vagina to enlarge the birth canal and ease the delivery.

Ann grimaced as she stared at the huge overhead lights shining directly onto her groin. She bit down on her lower lip and turned her head slightly to the right, forcing herself to concentrate on the off-white wall tiles.

"The head is visible. Ms. Sorenson, we need some help here. OK, give us a big push."

The birth was underway. First the head, then the torso and, finally, the small legs. As the baby emerged from the womb, Lee Harlow's eyes grew larger and filled with disbelief. He seemed frozen, unable to move.

For a moment, time seemed suspended. No one spoke, and the look on Harlow's face discouraged questions. Quickly, Lee recovered. With slightly shaking hands, he extended the baby to Ruth, who began cleaning the child with a sterile towel. The umbilical cord was cut and tied. The infant was wrapped in a fresh swaddling blanket.

"Looks like he may have slight respiratory distress," said Ruth, her voice quivering.

"Call Memorial and get a complete work up," said Harlow, grasping the edge of the table to steady himself.

"I want to hold him," cried Ann.

"We have to make sure everything's all right first," answered Harlow. His years of medical training kicked in, and he took charge once again.

Turning his back to Ann, Lee moved to face Ruth, blocking Ann's view, and shook his head from side to side.

"We've got to put this off, Ruth," he whispered, after placing his hands on her shoulders. "I'll get her to the hospital and stall until I can prepare her."

"Are you all right?" asked Ruth as her voice broke.

His stare was fixated on the baby. Ruth tried to engage him several times and finally slightly tugged on the sleeve of his gown.

"Is something wrong?" asked Ann.

Harlow turned and said, "Ms. Sorenson, we have to take the baby to the hospital to make sure everything's all right with his breathing."

"I've waited for this day my whole life. Please let me see him before he goes," cried Ann, grasping her sheets with both hands.

Harlow's eyes clouded as he looked at Ruth, holding the helpless infant and rocking him back and forth. There was no way to postpone the meeting.

Finally, he nodded. Ruth slowly approached the head of the table. Like a repentant child facing a stern parent, she extended the infant forward.

"Just show her the baby. Don't let her hold him," commanded Harlow.

A small teardrop fell from Ann's right eye as she smiled at the white bundle. Tears flowed freely as she reached for the fold of the blanket to lift it away from her son's head. As she exposed the child's face, her smile froze, turning first to panic and then disbelief as she began shaking her head from side to side.

Ann's voice broke as she winced and sobbed while shouting, "No. God, no! Please no!"

"Make sure you keep her sedated," said Harlow.

Ann began thrashing and rolling from side to side. Her cries turned into screams.

"That's not my baby! Where's my baby? I want my baby!" shouted Ann, sounding like a victim of a robbery.

Ruth tried to comfort Ann as Harlow discarded his gloves and gown. Medication flowed freely through the intravenous line. The nurse anesthetist stood beside Ann and gently stroked her hand. Ann was fighting the sedation, and wild thoughts were ripping through her broken heart as she slowly lost consciousness.

"Steven, where are you? They stole my baby! My baby's gone! Help me. Oh God please, help me find my real baby!" cried Ann, lapsing into a state of semi-tranquility.

"Dr. Harlow, her husband's white, isn't he?" whispered Ruth, as if she was trying not to divulge a state secret.

Harlow stared plaintively at Ann. When he remained silent, Ruth decided not to press.

This baby could not be her husband's. Not with their genes, Ruth thought wickedly.

It was a beautiful baby, but someone else was the father, she reasoned, taking a deep breath.

No way this baby came from that blond, blue-eyed, Christain Bale clone she was married to! Not this child with his wispy black hair and Godiva chocolate brown eyes. Definitely not with skin the color of dark mahogany.

Chapter Three

After Ann and her baby were admitted to Memorial Hospital, the delivery team gathered in Harlow's office. A call was placed to his attorney, David Whitney, whose secretary said he was on another line and would call back.

"Dr. Harlow, what do you think happened?" asked Ruth Oliver.

"I don't know. The records show Dr. Bartlett did the IVF. Don't talk to anyone about this. Refer everybody to me, understand?" ordered Lee, focusing on every face individually while each nodded back to him as they rose to leave.

Harlow continued to pace until his intercom rang and David Whitney's voice sounded from the telephone speaker.

"Lee, it's David. What's the emergency?"

"The sky has fallen in over here. I just did a delivery on a patient named Sorenson. She underwent in vitro fertilization several months ago. Her baby was a preemie and he's in neonatal ICU. She's been admitted to Memorial. The delivery was routine except for one problem."

"Go on," said Whitney in the voice of a battle-worn marine used to being parachuted into the war zone *du jour.*

"The baby's black, David."

There was a long pause before Whitney responded.

"Why's that a problem?"

"For Christ's sake, she's white. I told you her name is Sorenson."

"Is her husband African American?"

Harlow threw up his hands and rolled his eyes.

"He looks like an albino in a snowstorm."

"All right, calm yourself. Sounds like someone has some genes they didn't know about," Whitney said. "Or she had an affair and got caught."

"That might be hard to prove. She had trouble conceiving through intercourse."

"Did you cure her problems?" Whitney asked.

"Yes."

"So she could have conceived if she had sex with another man, right?"

Harlow stopped and ran his right hand over his hair.

"It would depend on the quality of her partner's sperm. I'd say the chance was at best fifty-fifty."

"That means one out of two. She kept on screwing her lover and her husband at the same time. A jury will love that story," said Whitney.

"You've got to do something quick," said Lee.

"I can't be there until this afternoon. I have to meet with the Governor's Council."

"We'll be waiting for you."

Harlow absent-mindedly looked at the double-framed picture on his desk. On the left side was a photograph of his mother and father, taken just before he married his wife, Katherine. They each had looks of joy on their faces, even though fate would not let them survive more than a few days after the photo was taken.

In the right frame was his father's favorite quote. It seemed like it had been designed for that moment:

The final forming of a person's character lies in their own hands.

-Anne Frank

He remembered the things his father taught him about how character determines a person's destiny. Those who had it would overcome; those without it would perish.

He also taught Lee that strength is what helps a person overcome a crisis, and tenacity is a direct descendant from character. This was the kind of crisis that demanded such strength. Soon, all involved would learn exactly how acutely their character had been formed.

Ricki did not get Ann's text until early afternoon. A knot filled her stomach as she called back. When there was no answer, she began to reach out to the others. First, she quickly banged out a text to Speed.

<u>something is wrong… she's racing to doctor… thinks baby's coming</u>

He replied at once.

<u>I haven't heard from her… I'm coming to Boston today!!!</u>

A wave of panic spread over Ricki.

<u>NO!!! u can't… we have to follow plan… let me see what's up and I'll get back 2 u</u>

She called Clay. Voice mail. Her phone buzzed with another text, this time from Eddy.

<u>baby in ICU… respiratory distress… unexpected whim from mother nature</u>

With quivering hands, she texted him back.

what do we do?

Clay responded quickly.

we have to talk later tonight… tell clay

She thought for a moment before asking the most important question.

how bad?

It took him several minutes to reply. When he did, it left her weak-kneed.

critical… if he dies, everything changes

Panic struck Ricki as she finished reading the text. If they were caught, it meant exposure and ruin—even prison. Her fingers quavered as she tried to reach Ann. The call went straight to voice mail.

Steven Sorenson arrived at Boston Memorial shortly after dusk. The message from the nurse informed him that Ann had gone into labor and was hospitalized. He had also received a text from Ann but could not reach her. After trying to contact Dr. Harlow without success, Steven returned to Boston.

His thoughts drifted back to Ann and what would happen if something was wrong. He felt a surge of pride as he remembered the struggle she overcame to conceive and deliver the child. This was an unexpected event; he silently gave thanks that Ann was with Harlow and was not stuck in some strange hospital.

After landing, Steven turned on his phone and found two texts from Ricki telling him the baby came early and was admitted to the hospital. She also said the baby had acute respiratory distress. He called Ricki back but got her voice mail.

Sorenson knew the tunnel would be congested, but he hadn't expected the sea of brake lights he found. Thirty-five minutes later, he finally reached the turnpike and headed west. He called

Ann's cell phone several times until she finally answered and told him what had occurred, carefully choosing her words in front of the nurse who was adjusting her intravenous line.

"Are you alone?" he asked, his voice cracking slightly.

"No," she answered, watching the nurse carefully.

"Can you tell me what's going on?" asked Steven.

"They said my placenta ruptured. There were no signs that I was in trouble until this morning."

"How's the baby?"

"Not well. He's on a machine to help him breathe."

"Easy, everything will be OK," Steven offered.

"No, it won't. I have to tell you something. Something that will change everything."

"What?" he asked.

"It's not our baby. It's just not our baby!" shrieked Ann, eyeing the nurse, whom she knew was listening to every word.

Steven paused as he considered the best way to ask his next question.

"How can it not be our baby?"

"Didn't Dr. Harlow call you and tell you what happened?"

"No. I got a call from the hospital telling me you had an emergency delivery and had been admitted."

"You'd better brace yourself," Ann said. "The baby can't be ours. He's… He's black."

"What do you mean?" he asked.

"I can't talk about it on the phone with people around. Get here as soon as you can," she replied, bringing her right hand up to the phone and lowering her voice.

Suddenly, Steven let himself grow agitated.

"How the hell... I mean... I don't understand. How can he be black?" he asked, picturing Ann surrounded by a room full of people, each one trying to decipher their conversation. "Where's Harlow?" he asked, knowing it was time to let his outrage show.

"He's not here. I don't know where he is."

Steven's voice tightened as he responded.

"We can't take this child home if it's not ours."

"Stop it," cried Ann, her face distorted with anger as the nurse again glanced at her. "We need to figure this out together."

Ann choked back a sob and broke the connection. Several minutes later, Steven entered the hospital parking garage and swung his black BMW into one of the last spaces on the roof. He bounded down the stairs two at a time until he reached the information desk. After getting Ann's room number, he proceeded to the maternity ward on the third floor in the hospital's east wing.

Ann was sitting upright in her bed when a text sounded. It was Ricki telling her she could not come by until tomorrow and to stay strong. Ann folded her arms while gently rocking back and forth. Then the door to her room opened, and Lee Harlow entered. A professionally somber David Whitney accompanied him in his dark pinstriped suit and crimson floral tie.

At the same time, a uniformed security guard arrived at the entrance to Ann's room and stationed himself outside. Ann seemed to be in a trance as tears of anger flowed down her cheeks.

"Ms. Sorenson, are you all right?" asked Harlow. When Ann did not reply, Harlow placed each end of the stethoscope into his ears and bent down to examine her.

Without warning, Ann lunged forward and struck Harlow with an open backhand, dislodging his stethoscope. In a fit of rage, she swept everything off her nightstand. Glasses, a pitcher of water, tissues, and a tray containing her uneaten dinner went flying against the wall. Suddenly, she started screaming uncontrollably.

"What have you done with my baby? My real baby?" she cried as Harlow restrained her.

Ann continued to attack Harlow, clawing and scratching at his face. As Steven entered the room, his muscles tensed and hardened as he observed Ann and Lee struggling. When the security guard tried to stop him, Steven pushed him aside. Harlow was reaching for a syringe, and Ann was caught up in David's grasp. Infuriated, Steven threw an overhanded right cross that barely missed Harlow's jaw.

"I'll call every talk show in America and tell them what happened to me, you incompetent fraud," cried Ann.

Harlow recovered and plunged the syringe into the intravenous line in her left arm. At the same time, the guard burst into the room, speaking frantically into his radio. He threw his arms around Steven, wrestled him to the floor, and subdued him. Steven kept leveling punches until other security officers arrived.

"It's about time you showed up, Harlow," raged Steven. "We want an explanation now that you've had the time to think of one."

David Whitney replied first.

"Please calm down, sir. We're conducting an investigation. We won't have an answer for you until we check out every possibility."

"Who the hell are you?" demanded Steven.

"I'm Dr. Harlow's attorney, David Whitney."

"His lawyer? Well, he's gonna need you and Alan Dershowitz before we get done with him."

"It won't do any of us any good to be confrontational, Mr. Sorenson," replied Whitney.

"Of course it won't, Counselor, but you don't have to go home and raise a child that's not yours, now do you?"

Whitney started to reply but Harlow's raised hand silenced him.

"We intend to tell you everything, Mr. Sorenson, but this conversation is not helping your wife. She needs rest. The medication has left her somewhat incoherent. May I respectfully suggest that we step out into the hallway and let her sleep while we talk?" said Harlow.

Steven's emotions began to ebb as Ann tried unsuccessfully to speak coherently. He moved to Ann's side as she squeezed his hand and said, "Go ahead, Steven. I'm so tired now. We can talk about what to do when I wake up."

Steven bent to kiss Ann on the cheek as the medication sapped her consciousness, and she drifted into a deep sleep. After closing the door to Ann's room, Steven let his rage build as the guards led him to Whitney and Harlow. They were standing next to the window at the end of the hallway.

"All right, gentlemen, you talk; I'll listen," began Steven, clenching his fists.

"Mr. Sorenson, we know how upset you must be. I want to assure you that we will do whatever it takes to find out exactly what happened," said Harlow.

"You can investigate all you want, but I'm still suing this place for every dime you've got."

"That's certainly your right," countered Whitney. "But if I were you, I'd make sure I had all the facts first."

"What the hell does that mean?"

David cast a quick glance at Harlow before he replied.

"It means you might be forced to deal with some very unpleasant findings."

Steven edged forward and clenched his jaw.

"Like what?" he asked.

"Maybe one of you has a relative you didn't know about," said Whitney, shifting his feet and then moving his eyes as if he was solving an equation, "or maybe your wife was seeing someone else. I know that's something you didn't consider, but we have to look at every possibil—"

With a massive lunge, Steven broke loose from the guards, sprang forward, and grabbed a startled David Whitney by the lapels of his navy suit coat. The impact was so fierce that it almost toppled the two men over onto the tile floor.

"You evil son of a bitch. I'll rip your lying lawyer tongue right out of your mouth," screamed Steven as Harlow moved to separate them.

"Since you can't get a grip on yourself, Mr. Sorenson, we're going to have you escorted out," commanded Harlow, pulling away from Steven as Whitney tried to free himself. After a moment of struggle, Steven released his grip and the guards maneuvered him away.

"I should have known this is what you bastards would stoop to. Sling mud all over the place and hope no one will notice what you did to my wife," he yelled.

A technician approached Harlow and Whitney.

"Dr. Harlow, the hospital sent me to find you," said the tech, turning to watch Steven as the guards led him to the elevators. "The Sorenson baby is still in neonatal ICU with respiratory distress. They're going to put him on ECMO if he doesn't improve soon. I was also told to give you this report."

Harlow reached into his pocket and removed his reading glasses as the man handed him a sealed white envelope, turned, and left.

"What's ECMO?" asked Whitney, straightening his clothing.

"Extracorporeal membrane oxygenation. It's a machine that breathes for the baby until his lungs clear up."

Harlow opened the envelope, retrieved the report, and quickly scanned its contents. Fear filled his eyes as he looked at Whitney and then turned and stared off into the distance.

"What is it, Lee?"

"The hematology report on the Sorenson baby. They just finished analyzing the blood samples I sent over."

Silence filled the air as Harlow paused. A terrified look spread across his face before he continued.

"The lab report indicates the baby has a lowered T-cell count and a confirmation of HIV antibodies. My God," said Harlow as his voice broke after a short pause. "He's infected with the AIDS virus."

Whitney's abdomen tightened as if a vise had squeezed it, while his legs grew rubbery. "How could that be?" he asked, as a hollow feeling spread through his body.

Harlow looked off into the distance. "Maybe the semen she got during her insemination was tainted," he said, after swallowing hard.

"Could it be a mistake?" asked Whitney.

"They ran the tests twice," said Harlow, shaking his head.

"Does this mean the mother is infected?"

"Of course. That's how the baby contracted the virus."

Whitney began to pace before he spoke.

"This puts us behind the eight ball with the parents, Lee. The husband will be a tough sell, but I've seen tougher ones that a vault full of money calmed down."

"This means the mother is going to die, and so is her baby. How much money do you think someone would take for that?" asked Lee.

"Liability insurance will take care of Ms. Sorenson and her baby."

David Whitney began to tremble slightly as he faced the man who had been his close friend for many years. He began to consider all the options. None were good.

"My investigators will reexamine every event in their past, and we will totally dissect their lives in order to get you off the hook."

"I thought this was about truth and justice," said Lee.

David stared at Lee for a long moment.

"Truth is what your lawyer convinces twelve jurors it is."

"What about justice?"

"Justice is when you win."

"This doesn't sound like you, David. I've always known you to be fair and act in ways that showed you have a conscience."

"I have a conscience, but my obligation is to represent you zealously within the bounds of the law. Just like you have the same ethical duty to each of your patients."

David grasped his old friend by the arm before turning to leave.

"Lee, I promise you one thing. If we find out Ms. Sorenson had a black ancestor or lover, it's my duty to fight them as hard as I can. On the other hand, if the evidence shows the clinic is at fault, I'll make sure this case gets settled quickly. But you have to give me time to investigate."

Lee's face relaxed slightly as David continued.

"When do you have to tell Ms. Sorenson about the AIDS result?"

"No later than tomorrow. She deserves to know as soon as possible. I want to have the test run once more to confirm the findings. Then I'll tell her."

"I'm going with you," said David.

Ricki initiated the conference call just after 9:00 p.m. Speed came on the line first, followed by Clay and Eddy.

"I've confirmed the baby was diagnosed with acute respiratory distress," began Eddy.

"Is it treatable?" asked Clay.

"Yes, by ECMO, I believe," said Ricki.

"Also, oxygen therapy," said Eddy.

"Prognosis?" asked Speed, sounding like he was caught in a trap.

"Time will tell. Keep the faith," said Eddy.

"I can't just sit here. What if the baby dies?" asked Speed.

"We all knew there were risks involved. This is a quirk of nature. You have to let the doctors do their jobs," said Ricki, sounding like a general commanding troops.

"What's our next move?" asked Clay.

"We wait and keep our heads. The baby comes from great genes. There's a lot of courage on both the mom's and dad's sides," said Eddy.

"Let's give the doctors a chance and see what happens tomorrow," said Ricki.

"OK, I'll give it one more day. But if he's still not out of the woods, I'm coming to Boston," said Speed.

Everyone on the call began to protest as Speed asked his final question.

"Is there any one of you who wouldn't do the same thing if it was your son who might die?" he said softly.

Chapter Four

Tuesday, October 14

Ann Sorenson was sipping a cup of lukewarm tea early the following morning. A nurse was adjusting a monitor to the right of the bed. Ann's body was sore from the trauma of delivery, and when her cell phone rang, she sat up in bed so she could watch the nurse without turning her lower torso. When she answered, Steven spoke.

"When can you come home?" he asked.

"I can't get anyone to tell me. I'm leaving tomorrow, whether they release me or not. I'd leave today but I'm too weak."

"Are you alone?"

"No, the nurse is here with me."

Steven's ears perked up.

"What do we do about the baby?"

"I don't know," she replied as a tear fell. "He's still in ICU, so until he gets better, he'll stay here."

"He'll pull through. You have to keep the faith," Steven said.

"Do we need to get a lawyer?" she asked as her voice trembled.

"I'm trying to find someone. I got the name of a law firm on State Street," he whispered. Ann nodded in the nurse's direction.

"No, there's a woman I heard about. Erica Payne," said Ann in a voice that seemed to make the nurse lean closer.

"What do you know about her?"

"She's smart and tough. I don't want a male lawyer after what happened to me," said Ann in a low voice, but one she was sure could be heard.

"I'll call you as soon as I know something," he said.

Shortly after noon, Lee and David entered Ann Sorenson's room. Harlow looked grave, like a wartime chaplain bearing bad news, while Whitney stayed outwardly calm. Silence filled the room as Harlow nodded to Ann, who was sitting in bed with her arms folded. She refused to acknowledge his greeting.

"I've been waiting for you since yesterday, Doctor," she said, her voice a menacing hiss. "I want some answers, and I want them now."

"We'll tell you what we know, Ms. Sorenson," intoned Whitney.

"Damnit," fumed Ann, looking directly at Harlow while pointing sharply in Whitney's direction. "Have you been rendered mute, or is this asshole a ventriloquist's dummy?"

"Let me talk, David," replied Harlow.

"How's my baby?" demanded Ann.

"Not well. We had to place him on a machine to help him breathe. His lungs are not fully developed and can't take the strain of respiration. He's been prescribed a surfactant to help open his airway. He's also on oxygen therapy, and is being treated with antibiotics."

"There's no danger to him from the breathing machine, is there?" asked Ann.

"No. We hope it will let his lungs rest until they can gain the strength to go to work."

"What happens if the device doesn't help?" asked Ann.

"Let's take this one step at a time. If ECMO doesn't work, we'll handle that at the appropriate time."

"When can I take him home?" Ann asked.

"We won't know for several days. He's still in neonatal intensive care. I've asked a colleague, Dr. Carnevale from pulmonology, to take charge of his care," said Harlow.

Ann stared at both men for a moment. Her face took on a mask of rage.

"I want to know how this happened to me," she demanded.

"We don't know yet," replied Harlow, shaking his head.

"I want out of here right away," continued Ann. "When can I go home?"

"Probably the day after tomorrow. You had some slight internal damage during delivery, and there was a tear in the perineum. The baby will be hospitalized indefinitely."

Ann folded her arms in anger and was about to ask another question when Harlow spoke.

"Ms. Sorenson, there's one other thing," he began, his heart pounding.

"What?" she demanded in a tone bordering on a shout.

Harlow's face took on a look like a funeral director about to console a surviving spouse.

"Brace yourself for some devastating news," said Harlow as he paused. "The baby has tested positive for the HIV virus. That means he contracted it from you. We're testing him to see if he has developed AIDS—"

Ann brought her hands up to her face and began to sob wildly.

"Oh God!" screamed Ann, as she began thrashing in her bed. "God no. You evil bastards. I want out of here now. God, please help me. I'm going home if I have to jump out—"

At that moment, the door opened, and Steven Sorenson led an entourage into the room. He was followed by a very attractive woman with a commanding presence. She was sharply dressed in a fitted navy Valentino suit, linen-white silk blouse, and Hermès navy-and-plush-pink scarf. The colors in the scarf matched the *poudrette* stones that dangled from her ears like pendalogues complementing an antique chandelier.

Accompanying her was a tall, thin, young man in a gray pinstriped suit; a short, fortyish man wearing a plaid jacket and gray slacks; and two uniformed police officers. Ann extended her arms toward the group and sobbed.

"Steven, you've got to get me out of here," she cried. "They just told me I have the AIDS virus. First, they gave me the wrong sperm, and now they tell me I'm going to die. They killed me, and they've killed the baby!"

The veins on the sides of Steven's neck bulged like bamboo shoots, and he let out a guttural growl. Pivoting angrily, he stepped toward Harlow. Lee moved back as one of the police officers grabbed Steven and ushered him to the door, wrestling him outside into the hallway. Whitney caught Harlow as he moved backward.

The woman swept her eyes over the room; then she stopped and addressed the group.

"Gentlemen, my name is Erica Payne, attorney for the Sorensons," she said, opening her *Ermenegildo Zegna* attaché case, reaching inside, and extending two documents toward them. "I have a court order requiring you to surrender all of Ann Sorenson's medical records to my custody now. I also have another order for her immediate discharge, so she can be treated at another facility."

Turning to Ann, Payne continued, "Ms. Sorenson, there's an ambulance waiting to take you to Suffolk General Hospital. Do you feel well enough to sit in the wheelchair, so we can get you out of here?"

"I'd crawl on my hands and knees to get away from these despicable people," replied Ann, as her voice broke.

The man in the pinstriped suit walked over to Ann and grasped her arm softly. "I'm Dr. Christopher, Ms. Sorenson. I'm here to take care of you until we can get you transferred. Please let me give you a quick examination before we go."

"I'm Detective Corcoran of the Boston Police," said the man in the Glen plaid jacket. "I'll be conducting an investigation to see if this is a criminal matter. Dr. Harlow, do you have any plans to leave the state?"

Whitney stepped forward to shield Harlow.

"Are you charging Dr. Harlow with a crime?" he asked.

"Who the hell are you?" demanded the detective.

"I'm David Whitney. Dr. Harlow's attorney," Whitney shot back.

"Not yet, but stick around, Counselor, in case he needs you," retorted Corcoran.

"I have to go to my clinic in Martha's Vineyard on Friday," answered Harlow.

"OK, but don't leave the state without checking with me. Understand, Doc?"

"My client understands, Detective," replied Whitney.

Christopher finished his examination as a wheelchair was brought into the room. Ann was helped from her bed, fitted into a robe and slippers Steven brought her, and wheeled out of the room. Payne waited until Ann was on her way to the elevator—until her eyes seemed to grow into small, angry slits—before addressing Harlow again.

"What did Ms. Sorenson mean about contracting AIDS?" Payne demanded.

"Preliminary findings show the presence of HIV antibodies in the blood samples from both the baby and mother," blurted Harlow before Whitney could silence him.

"Don't you test your sperm donors before they give a specimen?" asked Payne, shaking her head.

"There's no need. He is her husband, after all," said Lee in a frustrated tone.

"Why wouldn't you do everything possible to ensure the safety of your patients? You test blood before every transfusion, don't you?"

"That's different," snapped Harlow. "Blood can come from an outside source, but semen is between husbands and wives. It's not unreasonable to presume couples trying to conceive are faithful to each other, so we have no reason to run unnecessary tests," said Harlow as his eyes flashed with irritation.

"Be on notice that Mr. Sorenson will be tested. When he comes up clean, you'd better have a stronger explanation than that one. If you have such foolproof standards, how did the semen get contaminated unless you received it in that condition? Which is something you would have known if you tested it. If that's the case, who the hell's in charge of this place? Vladimir Putin's chief hacker?" asked Payne caustically.

"Spare us the smartass remarks. There's no jury here," said Whitney.

"Here's a fact that's not in dispute. You not only gave her the wrong semen but also managed to find some that would kill her at the same time, didn't you?" asked Payne, looking back and forth, while wearing the look of a sniper ready to empty her rifle's magazine.

Harlow started to respond, but Whitney grabbed his arm.

"Lee, don't say anything else," he said with a stern voice.

An angry look formed on Erica Payne's face.

"That's all right, Doctor. You don't have to tell me now. I'll wait till I get you under oath in front of twelve of your dearest friends and neighbors stuffed into a jury box. Then you can tell the whole world exactly what happened. And I can promise you we won't settle for anything but the truth, the whole truth, and nothing but the truth."

Turning, Erica started for the door. Before exiting, she pivoted back to Harlow and Whitney, and waited until each man looked her directly in the eye. As she turned, the light from the window caught the crown facets of the stone in her right earring before sending out bursts of light mimicking mini-lasers.

"So help you, God," she said and then turned and walked away.

When David Whitney arrived back at his office, Jamie Quintell was waiting for him. She had been his lead investigator for over ten years, even though she was only in her mid-thirties.

Quintell was a short woman, barely 5′3″, with a small moon face and nondescript features. Whitney had also seen her looking lithe and acrobatic in the gym, and dazzling in black sequins and heels. Her best quality was her ability to assume a disguise that would allow her to blend, extract what she needed, and be gone before anyone noticed.

"What did you find out about the Sorensons?" asked Whitney.

"They've lived in a condominium in Wellesley for over two years. Looks like they can barely afford it. She's from a suburb in New York; he's from San Francisco. They met after college. No family to speak of for either one. The only relative we found so far is his brother in Colorado. Her maiden name is Olsen."

"Where did they live before Wellesley?"

"Richmond, Virginia."

"Are you sure?"

"That's what our computer check indicated. Of course, sometimes the info gets processed wrong, so we have to check it out in person."

"Or someone creates a phony profile. What else did you find?" Whitney asked.

"There's no reason for a fake background. They look like the all-American couple, but there are some minor skeletons in the closet. He's got one arrest for operating under the influence, with an acquittal. Also busted for possession of marijuana when he was in college, but it was dismissed because of an illegal search. Nothing showed up on her."

"Where do they work?"

"Ann's a recruiting consultant who works out of her home. Steven's a sales representative for a hardware supply company headquartered in Washington."

"Any drug or alcohol problems?"

"Nothing other than what I told you."

"Either of them involved with anyone else?"

"No."

"Keep checking."

"I will. I also need some background on Dr. Harlow," said Jamie.

David looked up with a contented look of admiration on his face.

"I can tell you he's one of the top doctors in the country. Graduated from Harvard Medical School *summa cum laude* and got one of the four prized obstetrical residencies at Suffolk General. He has a reputation as the leading expert on infertility in the country."

"How long have you known him?"

"Over twenty-five years. My firm represented his wife's family, and I met Lee when I first joined the practice. I became his personal counsel several years ago and have advised him in all his business affairs since."

"How do you think this could have happened?"

David paused for a moment and shook his head.

"I don't know. I've never heard of Lee making any kind of mistake when he was treating a patient."

"Tell me about Harlow the man."

"Why?"

"If he is as good as you say, then he would not have made an error like this. Maybe something in his personal life caused him to get sloppy or preoccupied."

"Dead end, Jamie. Lee Harlow is all warmth and comfort on the outside, but he's a barracuda on the inside. He had to overcome a lot of adversity, and it made him develop an inner toughness that's incredible. He would never let some personal problem interfere with his concentration, especially where a patient's welfare was at stake."

"Maybe he had money problems."

"No. I'm his business advisor. I would have known."

"What kind of adversity did he have?" Jamie asked.

"Lee came from a wealthy family and was a star athlete and valedictorian in prep school. He turned down several Ivy League schools because he wanted to play football at Notre Dame before med school. It was his strong character traits that let him finish Harvard after his father lost everything and died."

Jamie shook her head and looked surprised.

"I thought you said he came from wealth."

"Only until he got to medical school. His father's death came just as Lee completed his second year. So Lee scraped and struggled to borrow money in order to finish school and then worked to build his practice."

"Why did his father lose everything?"

"I don't know the whole story. There was some talk of embezzlement, and Lee's father died in disgrace shortly afterward."

"Couldn't you get the whole story?" she asked.

"Lee would never talk about it. Finally, I stopped asking," replied David.

Quintell looked at David for a long moment before she continued.

"What's Harlow's practice like?"

"Booming. Right after he started to make his reputation, he was so besieged with patient requests that he opened two satellite clinics. One in Nashua, to take care of patients from southern New Hampshire and Northern Massachusetts, the other on Martha's Vineyard to handle the south shore and Rhode Island. Lee spends one day per week at each satellite and the remainder of his time at his clinic."

"Any other doctors with him besides Jack Bartlett?"

"Just Lee's son, Austin."

"I'll start checking everyone out. Right after I finish with the Sorensons."

"You know about Lee's father-in-law, right?" asked Whitney.

Jamie's lips formed an awkward smile.

"Senator Langley Mitchell of the Prides Crossing Mitchells. Been in the senate for four or five hundred years. Do you think this could be political?" she asked.

"Nothing would shock me at this point."

Quintell rose and headed for the door.

"Make sure your people back off Steven Sorenson now. Their lawyer is Erica Payne and all communications have to go through her," said David.

"Do you know her?"

"Only by reputation. We just met at the hospital."

"I'll run a background. From what I've heard about Payne, she's trouble."

"Maybe next time I'll get lucky and draw someone who's shy and obscure like Gloria Allred," said David.

Jamie rolled her eyes.

Chapter Five

Ann began to calm down as the ambulance left Memorial Hospital for the fifteen-minute ride to Suffolk General. As soon as they were en route, her cell phone rang, and she trembled as the distinctive voice sounded.

"Are you all right?" he asked.

"As well as can be expected," she replied. "You know it's dangerous for you to call."

"I'm coming in. I have to check on the baby."

Ann grimaced and shook her head as she answered.

"No, not yet. He's still in ICU. They're hoping the machine he's attached to will fix his breathing problems."

"No one told us the baby was in trouble," he said.

"They didn't know. This just happened out of the blue without any warning."

"I can be there tomorrow."

"I'm begging you, hold off for a while."

"Is he going to make it?"

She paused. "He has some trouble breathing, but everyone says Dr. Carnevale is a genius. The baby is in the best possible hands."

Ann could hear his voice growing more serene as he continued.

"The baby has to survive. No matter what, he can't die."

"He will. Harlow made sure he got us an expert for the baby's respiratory problems," said Ann.

"Speaking of Lee Harlow, how did your meeting go with him?" he asked.

Ann's face spread into a tight grin.

"He came by with his lawyer, David Whitney, just like we knew he would. He stumbled around the fact that the baby has to stay in the hospital for now. Then he finally got the guts to tell me about the AIDS virus," said Ann.

"You're kidding. What did you do?"

"Exactly what I was trained to do. If Steven Spielberg were here, I could picture him saying, 'And the Oscar goes to,'" Ann said as her voice lifted slightly.

"It won't be long until we all get to thank the Academy," he replied.

"As long as our son recovers and the three of us come out of this together as a family," said Ann.

At four o'clock, Lee Harlow sat behind his desk and listened to the sound of a key sliding into the rear door. Rising from his seat, he walked toward the sound just as Langley Mitchell and Lee's son, Austin, entered. Harlow's face took on a scowl as they both followed him back into his office.

Lee's aggravation continued to rise because Langley had entered with his own key. Shrugging, he realized that was part of the price that had to be paid when someone else owned the real estate that housed his practice. Mitchell plopped into one of the chairs in front of Lee's desk like a monarch about to rebuke a subject.

Langley Mitchell was at the end of his seventh term as Massachusetts's senior senator. He was an average-sized man, standing 5′9″ with a slight build. It was said by allies and enemies alike that when he took to the floor of the US Senate, he became a giant. He spoke with a thick Bostonian accent in which the letter "r" is pronounced as "ah," and he seasoned it with English idiosyncrasies because he was convinced it made him sound like an aristocrat.

Langley had just reached his eighty-second birthday, and he was in excellent condition. His face was stern and ruddy, and it was said that he could have been a twin of the actor Edward Herrmann.

Austin Harlow, on the other hand, was short and stocky, and he looked nothing like Lee. He stood barely 5′8″, wore wire-rimmed glasses, and had a full head of dark brown hair. His affect was one of entitlement, as his entire essence seemed to be engulfed by the hugely successful medical practice he would someday inherit. He seemed to be uncomfortable in the presence of Lee and Langley, and projected a sense of fear of his father and unrestrained awe of his grandfather.

"I don't want you barging in here unannounced. You need to call first," barked Lee while pointing at Langley.

"I don't cayah what you want. I have every right to come in here any time I want. Don't forget; it's my name on the deed," replied Mitchell, folding his arms.

Austin looked at each man before he spoke. The hate between his father and grandfather was visible. He decided to play peacemaker.

"I was the one who opened the door, so blame me. Grandfather asked me if I would bring him over," said Austin

Lee looked at his son and did not reply. The senator got right down to business.

"All right, it's time to stop all this caterwauling. I want to know what the hell is going on with this black child," began Langley.

"It's none of your business," said Lee, picking up a patient chart.

He began to read when suddenly, Langley became enraged, leaped to his feet, and ripped the chart out of Lee's hand before slamming it onto the desk.

"Everything that happens here is my business," cried Langley as Lee glared at him.

Austin stepped in between them. The anger was pronounced, like two heavyweight fighters who refused to stop when the bell rang.

"What the hell did you do to this Sorenson woman?" asked the senator.

"Not that it's any of your business, but I made her fertile."

"How did you give her the wrong semen?"

"I didn't. She got her husband's sperm," Lee replied.

"Then why did she have a black child?" screamed Langley. The veins on his forehead suddenly constricted and grew into a faint shade of blue.

"Nature."

"What the hell does that mean?"

"It means she had an African American baby because the semen she received was predisposed to producing a black child."

"Her husband's white, for Christ's sake. How could she have a black baby unless she had a black lovah?" screamed Langley.

Lee continued to stare at the enraged man as he folded his arms.

"Don't you know what this means?" raged Langley. "Scandal and ruin. Everyone associated with the clinic will be tainted by yoah incompetence."

"Especially me. You must know Grandfather is not going to run for another term," said Austin haughtily. "He's going to back me to succeed him."

It was Langley's turn to gloat.

"We were going to wait until the spring to break the news, but we've just learned the governah is ready to announce as soon as I make my official declaration public. So we have to beat him to the punch. We're having a huge campaign event on Novembah seventh and nothing can interfeah with that. So put out all these fyahs and get this scandal under control at once," scolded Langley.

"I don't care if you two decide to run for the Mexican border," said Lee, glaring at the senator.

"This scandal could cost Austin a chance to get my senate seat," said Langley.

"Good. Maybe he'll find some backbone if he has to face a situation that you can't buy your way out of," said Lee.

Langley's face took on a look of triumph as he shook his right index finger at Lee.

"Jealousy. That's what's eating away at you, isn't it? My grandson will continue my legacy while you floundah," he hissed.

"Your legacy will someday be exposed. You might want to take cover when that happens," Lee said as Langley rose and stormed out.

"Sometimes, I wish you weren't my father," said Austin icily, before following his grandfather, leaving Lee staring straight ahead.

That wish might come true sooner than later, thought Lee.

Clay was the first to arrive just before eight o'clock at the Marriott in the town of Andover, thirty minutes north of Boston. He paid cash for the room after making certain that it was on the ground floor and as far away from the lobby as possible. He called Ricki and Eddy, and then ordered three dinners and two bottles of wine.

Ricki knocked on his door fifteen minutes later. Eddy arrived last, followed by the waiter. When they were finally alone, they began to discuss the next phase of their plan.

"Any update on the baby?" said Ricki.

Eddy's face grew somber as he shrugged.

"Too soon to tell. He's holding his own."

"How does this change things?" asked Clay.

"It gives us a new sense of priorities," said Ricki.

"What do we do if he dies?" asked Clay.

"He comes from good stock and he's strong. I don't mean to sound cold, but even if the baby dies, it won't change the fact that he was born," said Ricki.

"My sources confirm that the announcement will come on November seventh. The timetable has been moved up," said Eddy.

"Can we move that fast?" asked Clay.

"Of course," answered Ricki. "This is the leverage we were missing. Our position was much weaker when the announcement was scheduled for next spring. Now we can force immediate satisfaction in exchange for nondisclosure."

"Clay, are you ready to expose Rhodes?" asked Eddy.

"Any time I get the word. Santos found that old bastard in Southern California," he said.

"I propose a toast," said Eddy, raising his glass and touching the others in salute. "To the baby. He is a gift from God, and we will do everything to make sure he pulls through. If he has to leave us now, his purpose here on Earth has at least brought justice to a lot of people."

Clay's face broke into a wide, sinister grin.

"Is Bartlett around this week?" he asked.

"He's been out of town seeing patients and returns tomorrow," said Eddy.

"I think I'll show up in the morning to shake up his world. I'll use the protesters as cover to get right up next to him," said Clay.

Clay swirled his drink around as the ice made a clinking sound.

"Time to let him know what a world of shit he's in," said Eddy.

"Everyone will get exactly what's coming to them. We can't do it in a courtroom because their rules mean you only get a chance at justice. Most of the time it gets stolen by those with the kingdom, power, and glory. Not this time," said Ricki.

All three exchanged satisfied glances.

"I think Harlow has outlived his value," said Ricki. "It's time to make sure he's not around to contradict the Sorensons' version of what went on with this baby's birth."

"Only one thing left to do," said Clay.

"It's time for Lee Harlow to die," said Ricki as they each extended their glasses forward in a toast.

Chapter Six

Wednesday, October 15

Over a dozen protesters were waiting when Lee Harlow arrived at his office at six-thirty the following morning. When he began walking toward the clinic, they raised their signs and started chanting behind a fenced-in area to the right of the rear entrance.

Lee had seen protesters when his practice first opened and sporadically for a few years afterward. At times, antiabortion groups showed up even though Lee had performed less than half a dozen abortions in his entire career. Because his practice was devoted to bringing life into the world, he usually referred the patient to another doctor for an elective abortion unless it was necessary to save the mother's life, protect her from a health threat, or help a victim of rape or incest. In those cases, his duty as her doctor would preclude him from denying the woman the medical care she needed, including the right to terminate her pregnancy.

To the protesters, it didn't matter that Lee was not an abortionist. In their world, no one had the right to interfere with or question God's divine plan for reproduction and life. Harlow had discovered that their views were black and white, and no shade of gray could ever be allowed to seep in.

Harlow began walking faster when a black Porsche pulled into the parking space with a sign in front that read, "Jack Bartlett, MD." A short, handsome man wearing a navy suit and mauve tie exited the vehicle. He was several inches under 6′, with streaked iron-gray patches at the temples in sharp contrast to his full head of coal-black hair. His deep-set eyes sparkled as he surveyed Harlow.

Lee stopped and waited for Bartlett to join him. Their greeting was empty and barely cordial.

"David Whitney called me and said we've got some problems," said Jack.

"Ann Sorenson, Jack. Does that name ring a bell?"

"No. Should it?"

"You covered for me and did the in vitro last February when I was called out on an emergency," Lee said accusingly, pointing his right index finger at Bartlett.

Bartlett's face flushed to shades of scarlet as he grew defensive.

"So what? We cover for each other from time to time."

"She and her husband are white, and she delivered a black baby."

"You can't blame me for that" shouted Bartlett. "She was your patient."

"You did the procedure. Who am I supposed to blame, the stork?"

Bartlett stayed silent as Harlow continued.

"I don't remember anything out of the ordinary. I got the semen from you," said Bartlett.

"And I got it from Lori Wegman, the nurse."

"Have you talked to her?"

"She quit a few months ago. I don't even know where she is."

Bartlett's face took on an inquisitive look, as if he'd just figured out a major brain teaser.

"Maybe she switched the semen."

"That's sabotage. Why would she do that?"

Bartlett folded his arms, shook his head, and looked up.

"How do you know this Sorenson woman didn't have a black lover?"

"Even if she did, she also had a thickened cervical mucus. She could have slept with every black man in Zimbabwe and, unless he was firing hollow-point seminal bullets, she probably wouldn't have gotten pregnant."

As Bartlett and Harlow continued walking briskly past the chanting protesters on their way toward the entrance, Clay suddenly pulled his baseball cap on tighter, dropped the sign he was carrying, and broke out from the middle of the pack. He sprinted forward and leaped over the barrier at the entrance to the parking lot as six or seven others followed.

In an instant, he was next to Harlow and Bartlett. He pushed Bartlett to the side, grabbed Harlow by the jacket, and pinned him against the car. As he began to berate Harlow in a low voice, Bartlett moved next to Lee and grabbed Clay's arm.

"You smug assholes think you're God. You murdered my mother while my father was in Vietnam. There is no place you can run where we won't find you," snarled Clay.

At that moment, the security guard began shouting. Clay let Harlow go and then sprinted to the back of the parking lot. He reached the fence in seconds, bounded over it, and disappeared. By then, the security force had the other protesters rounded up and corralled behind the fence.

Bartlett looked at Harlow with terror in his eyes.

"Who the hell was that?" he whispered frantically.

"I never saw him before," answered Harlow.

"Did you hear what he said? What do you think that meant?" asked Bartlett.

Harlow stared at him for a long moment, watched him squirm, and then turned away.

"He had to be talking about Michelle," he whispered.

"How could anyone find out? Only you and I know what happened," gasped Bartlett as his face grew cloudy.

"Maybe she told someone before she died."

Bartlett brought his hand up and rubbed it over the top of his head.

"If you're right, I'll lose everything and could go to jail," he said.

Harlow grabbed his partner's shoulder.

"Pull yourself together, man. I'm late for a meeting at the hospital. We'll talk about this when I get back. Until then, no one can know what just happened. In case you don't know it, there's no statute of limitations on murder," he replied, as Bartlett nodded vigorously.

Suddenly, Bartlett grabbed Lee's arm and moved in front of him.

"Wait a minute. I can't just sit here and stew. This could mean scandal and ruin. So don't tell me you have to go to some stupid meeting when my whole life is going down the tubes," he shouted.

Harlow reached up and tore Bartlett's arm away.

"I said later, Jack. Go somewhere and come up with a plan to deal with this instead of standing here stamping your feet like some child who can't get his way," Harlow said forcefully before turning and walking toward the clinic entrance.

Shortly after nine, Jamie Quintell turned down Cambridge Street on her way to Government Center. Slipping in through a private entrance next to a large redbrick building, she pulled into her private spot. Whitney's office was located in the heart of the action, directly across from Boston's maze of state office buildings composing the Commonwealth's political command center, and stood adjacent to the city's legal hub, as the Suffolk County Superior Court and Supreme Judicial Court Building was less than a block away.

David was already in the office. Jamie met him in his private suite.

"Give me two minutes," he said, as she sat in one of the richly upholstered chairs in front of his massive walnut desk stacked with rows of documents in neat files.

Jamie remembered joining David over ten years ago. She had moved to Boston from New Jersey almost eighteen years ago to study criminal justice at Northeastern University. Upon graduation, she went with the most notorious private investigator in the East, Jake Erlich, where she received a crash course in surveillance, spying, snooping, and deception. After her training had reached its pinnacle, Jake died in his sleep from a massive stroke, leaving behind an insolvent business. He had blown almost every cent at the racetrack.

With nowhere to turn, Jamie contacted Whitney, whose cases she had concentrated on for the previous six months. David was extremely satisfied with her work and, when Jamie offered to work for him exclusively, he agreed.

Shortly after Jamie and David began working together, David and his wife separated. Jamie hinted that she was interested in him romantically, but he pretended not to notice. Finally, she asked him out and he declined. Embarrassed, he told her he was secretly seeing a woman who was going through a divorce. Eventually, she accepted it, and they began to mesh as business partners, old friends who anticipated each other's moves and shared a deep mutual respect. Sometimes she felt a sense of regret, but mostly, she was content to have a business relationship and hoped that time would help it develop into something more.

As she watched David put the finishing touches on a motion to dismiss, she remembered how he'd shared his background with her over dinner one night. He grew up in Beverly, on Boston's North Shore, the son of a letter carrier whose wife died shortly after David was born. He spoke when he was barely fourteen months and read at two years old. By the time he was three, David was labeled a prodigy, worthy of the finest education money could buy. The problem was there was barely enough money to live, certainly none for a luxury like education.

He sailed through public school in six years, skipping from third grade to sixth. When he graduated from high school at fifteen, there were over thirty-five scholarship offers waiting. That was followed by a preparatory year at Philips Andover, where he received several grants before entering Harvard two months after his sixteenth birthday.

After graduating *summa cum laude*, David finished Harvard Law, and a month later, he married Cortnee Woods, a classmate from law school. Cortnee had two children in three years and then joined a corporate law firm in the heart of the financial district.

David and Cortnee were divorced six years to the day they were married. Cortnee married her lover and moved to California with the boys. David tried to mend his broken heart by taking on more work.

"Where do we stand?" asked David.

"We haven't found anything new you could use against them. Nothing out of the ordinary so far," Jamie replied.

"What did you find out about Erica Payne?"

"She has twelve verdicts over one million dollars. She came from a middle class family. Army brat. Lived all over the world until her father retired as a full colonel. She's a Phi Beta Kappa from Stanford. Divorced for nine years, no children. Forty-eight years old, but looks ten years younger."

"Tell me about Payne the lawyer."

"Went to law school at Duke and started at Dale and West before leaving to form her own firm. Erica is the head of civil litigation. Called the "girl scout assassin" because of the way she schmoozes people until she gets them in court."

"Sounds like she's a real warrior," he replied, deep in thought.

Jamie's eyes lit up as she continued.

"You'll like this story. Several years ago, Payne sued the archdiocese and tagged them for nine and a half million. The bishop was so upset he gave her a prayer of her own based on the 'Hail Mary.' Do you know that verse?" she asked.

"No, I was raised Protestant."

"The real words are 'Hail Mary, full of Grace, the Lord is with thee. Blessed art thou amongst women and blessed is the fruit of thy womb, Jesus.' The bishop changed it to 'Hail Erica, full of waste, the court is with thee; wretched art thou amongst women, and wretched is the loot of thy doom, egregious,'" said Jamie, as David laughed out loud.

"Keep me updated. I've got a call into the general counsel for the malpractice insurer. She'll want a full report on everything you find," he told her.

"Who's the insurance carrier?"

"Eastern Casualty."

"Oh God. Is Rebecca Castle still their general counsel?"

"Yes, it's the princess of pestilence herself. Rebecca of Donnybrook Farm."

"I'll bet Castle has her own prayer written by Osama bin Laden and Leona Helmsley. She and Payne hate each other."

"Maybe, but from what I've seen, I'd rather have Payne's case than ours."

"I've asked my staff to do a complete work up on Lee Harlow. I'll let you know what turns up," she told Whitney.

Dr. Louis Carnevale had just finished pediatric rounds when he was told Dr. Lee Harlow was waiting for him in intensive care. After making two short entries into his final patient chart, Carnevale replaced it and walked briskly to the elevator. Five minutes later, he arrived outside neonatal ICU, where he found Harlow, clad in light-blue scrub clothes, sipping coffee and talking with one of the nurses, Carol Casey.

"Hello, Lee. What brings you to pediatrics?"

"Good to see you, Lou," answered Harlow, rising and extending his right hand. "I need a moment to discuss the Sorenson baby."

"Sure. Why don't we talk in the unit?" asked Carnevale. He walked inside, and Harlow followed, quickly pulling alongside the shorter man.

"What's the baby's prognosis?" asked Harlow.

"He's still in acute respiratory distress. We've got him on ECMO, but so far, it hasn't done everything we hoped it would."

"He's only been on ECMO since yesterday, right?" asked Harlow, as Carnevale nodded.

"If we can buy enough time to let his lungs develop and function on their own, he should be out of the woods soon."

"I came over here to ask you for a personal favor."

"Go ahead. We've been friends for a long time."

"Do everything you can to help this child. I know you would do that for any infant, but I want you to know this one is extra special. Don't let the residents do anything but observe. It would mean a lot to me if I knew you were managing this case yourself."

Carnevale looked into Harlow's eyes and felt his pulse quicken when he realized how troubled they were. He grasped his old friend by the right shoulder.

"You have my word that I'll do whatever it takes to save this baby."

Jack Bartlett was in surgery and did not return for his meeting with Lee Harlow until just after two. Tension filled the air as soon as the two men were alone. Bartlett refused Harlow's offer to be seated and instead stood impatiently in front of the desk with his arms folded over his starched white lab coat and a scowl embedded in his face.

Bartlett had a reputation as a first-class surgeon, but was also known as having the personal skills of a chronically agitated mixed martial arts contestant. Harlow was on his cell phone, and Bartlett grew irritated, his eyes glaring while he surveyed everything in the room. Bartlett spoke first as soon as Harlow finished his call.

"Now that you've given me the honor of granting me this papal audience, tell me what the hell that scene was all about this morning," he said caustically.

"Some nut job," said Harlow, placing his hands on the arms of his captain's chair.

"He talked about the murder of his mother. That can only mean one thing," said Bartlett.

"You don't know that. He never called her by name."

"Jesus Christ, this could sink us!" said Bartlett as he began to pace.

"He could have meant a pregnancy termination. All those protesters think we're running an abortion mill here," replied Harlow.

"Women don't die from an abortion if it's done right," Bartlett spat. "He used the word murder."

Harlow shook his head as a look of disapproval spread across his face. "You're letting your imagination run away because of a guilty conscience," he said.

"Bullshit. I want you to get Whitney to find out who he is," said Bartlett.

Harlow shook his head.

"I don't want David to know about this yet. If this guy makes a specific threat, then I'll figure out a way to get him involved."

"He looked about the right age to be Michelle's son," Bartlett said in an anxious tone.

Bartlett paused as Harlow glanced toward the window.

"Do you think that guy was a legitimate protester or a plant?" asked Bartlett.

Harlow drew his hands together. He looked at Bartlett with an accusing glare. "I think he knew who we were and did exactly what someone sent him to do."

"But why now, for Christ's sake?"

Harlow leaned back and stared at his partner.

"Because we've both got everything to lose now."

Bartlett began to pace again.

"There's no proof it was me who got her pregnant. Still, I did the dirty work because the court hadn't legalized abortion at the time. No doctor would have performed the procedure without putting his whole life at risk."

"That's bullshit. There were doctors who did abortions then. You could have asked someone for help," said Harlow.

"I went to see the chief resident, and he said no one would step up. Don't you remember that was the same time when Ken Edelin was chief resident at Boston City, and he was charged with manslaughter after he performed an abortion? And that was after it was legalized. It was open season on doctors then."

"You could have tried to find an attending instead of a resident to help," snapped Harlow.

Bartlett stopped and ran his hand over his forehead.

"She was married, dammit," he said.

"An attending would have had her admitted to the hospital under a false name, and no one would have known. The case would have been booked as a dilation and curettage, like they did in those days," said Harlow, bringing his hands together and waiting for Bartlett to regain his composure. "I wasn't the father, Jack. It was you," Harlow continued coldly. "And, I didn't kill her. You did."

Bartlett's face took on a look of triumph, as if he'd just found the winning lottery ticket.

"It's my word against hers. The case is cold and she's dead, so there is no DNA or any other way somebody can prove I did it."

Suddenly, he stopped and his face turned into a mask of anger.

"Don't turn into a snitch," he fumed, pointing his wobbling index finger.

Harlow glared at Bartlett with a cold, frozen stare, as if he was being sentenced for a crime he did not commit.

"I have never told anyone about that time, Jack. I always considered it my greatest failure, along with yours. I still believe that I owe Michelle's family a debt that I can never repay."

Bartlett turned away and fell deep in thought before he finally stormed out of the room, slamming the door hard behind him.

Chapter Seven

The clock read almost five when Lee Harlow's secretary told him his wife, Katherine, was waiting to see him. He showed a quick burst of surprise because she had no interest in medicine or his practice and had not been to the clinic for several years. Disdain overtook his curiosity as he rose and went out to get her.

Katherine Harlow was an elegant woman, always looking chic and acting like the daughter of a US senator. In her designer clothing and tasteful jewelry, Katherine knew how to turn on the charm and work a room, making every person she met feel like they were the most important individual in her life. She was in her early sixties, but looked at least ten years younger. She always dressed stylish but subdued because she was convinced it reflected positively on her father's campaign crowds.

When Harlow reached the reception area, his wife was pacing and somewhat agitated. She asked if they could speak privately, and he escorted her back to his office.

"I came to talk to you about this Sorenson woman," said Katherine.

She dug into her purse, pulled out an unsealed envelope, and pushed it toward Harlow.

"I just found this at the front door at home. It must be for you," she said.

Inside the envelope, Harlow found a single sheet of bond paper. In the center was written

"When I was sick, you gave me bitter pills; now I must minister the like to you."

~William Shakespeare, Two Gentlemen of Verona

"What does that mean?" she asked.

"I have no idea. Did you see anyone outside?"

"No. I don't know how long it was there."

They were silent for a moment and seemed deep in thought.

"Level with me, Lee. Is the clinic in serious trouble?" Katherine asked.

"Is that what you're concerned about? The clinic? Not me?" asked Harlow, raising his eyebrows.

Katherine's skin bristled as she slid forward in her chair while grabbing its arms.

"Dammit, you know what I meant. Can you survive this incident?"

"Yes, I can survive. I guess that means you and your father will survive with me. That's what you really want to know, isn't it?" asked Harlow.

Katherine shot her eyes to the left.

"I guess it is," she said.

Both were silent for a long moment.

"Why won't you tell me what's bothering you? If I did something, tell me what it is so I can fix it. You owe me that after all our time together," said Katherine.

"What happened between us has been broken too long to be fixed. The only reason we've stayed together this long is because I have nowhere else to go, and you think it would look bad for your father's campaign if you left me and married Jack," Harlow said.

Katherine looked at him as if to protest and then glanced at the floor.

“There’s nothing between me and Jack,” she said softly.

“That’s what you said when we got married,” Harlow replied.

Lee Harlow was waiting when David Whitney arrived at ten. He picked up the intercom and summoned Jack Bartlett, whose nurse said he would be in surgery all day and was unable to join them.

“I’ve been over all her background records, and there’s nothing unusual in them,” began Whitney, handing Ann’s chart over to Harlow. “The situation’s pretty bleak, Lee. These two aren’t up for canonization, but they aren’t Charlie Sheen and Lindsay Lohan either. Preliminary investigation indicates a jury could come down on you hard unless I can confirm that she had a black lover.”

“I see,” replied Harlow, folding his hands with his index fingers extended.

“You hit the main issue yourself. Even if I can prove she was screwing someone else, it was still questionable whether she could have gotten pregnant without your help and technology.”

“A long shot, but not impossible. I’ll swear to that under oath,” vowed Harlow.

“Of course you will, but they’ll have an expert who’ll claim the opposite. If it comes to that, the jury will hold for them,” said Whitney.

For a brief moment, Harlow thought about the times he had seen Whitney in action inside a courtroom. Harlow acted as an expert witness in half-a-dozen cases and worked with David on several other occasions, suggesting strategies in cross-examination and offering advice on medical facts that should be admitted into evidence. Whitney accepted and refined Harlow’s suggestions, and ultimately destroyed opposition witnesses when they took the stand.

“Tell me about the day of the in vitro,” said Whitney.

"I reviewed the chart and found nothing out of the ordinary," began Harlow. "The husband's sperm was collected at ten past two by a nurse named Lori Wegman. She took it to the lab and processed it. When we were ready to do the IVF, I was called to an emergency, so Jack Bartlett substituted for me."

"How soon after Mr. Sorenson ejaculated was the in vitro completed?" asked David.

"Almost two hours."

"Why wasn't it done immediately?"

"Because the oocytes weren't mature enough. That's the clinical name for an egg."

"When did they mature?"

"Just after four o'clock."

"Is that unusual?"

"No. It almost always takes six to twenty-four hours."

"What do you do until they mature?"

"Put them in an incubator."

"And they stay there until they're fertilized?"

"That's right. The length of time depends on the maturity of the oocyte," replied Harlow. "The research shows the rate of success for fertilization improves dramatically if you delay the introduction of the sperm. We always check them after six hours."

"Don't you have to use the sperm immediately?" Whitney asked.

"No. It lives for several hours."

"Are you sure Lori Wegman collected the specimen?"

"Absolutely certain because that's our customary procedure. After the donor finishes masturbating, he gives the nurse the plastic cup containing his semen. It's then taken to the lab where it is spun down to eliminate all the protein and waste products."

"Why?" asked Whitney, continuing to write.

"So that only pure spermatozoa are mixed with the eggs in the petri dish. After the sperm and egg unite, the eggs that take the seed are then reimplanted into the woman's uterus," replied Harlow.

"How do you know you have the right semen?"

"The nurse escorts the donor, receives and labels the container with his information right there on the spot, and then takes it to the lab. After it's processed, it gets delivered to the surgeon."

"How long does processing take?"

"Fifteen to twenty minutes."

"Could the nurse get the semen mixed up?"

Harlow moved forward and began pushing his fingers together like an accordion.

"Only through complete incompetence or a deliberate act." Harlow paused for a moment before he continued. "In anticipation of your next question, there was no reason for Lori to sabotage this case."

"We'll get to motive later on," said Whitney, without looking up. "What's the procedure for harvesting the eggs?"

"We usually do an ultrasound guided approach because you don't have the added risk of general anesthesia, and there's no incision except for the small puncture sites in the vaginal wall. Then the eggs are injected into small dishes containing culture medium before being transferred to an incubator," answered Harlow.

"Is that the way you did it for Ann Sorenson?" asked Whitney.

"No. I had to do a laparoscopy on her because of the position of her ovary. That means she had to be anesthetized before a small scope was inserted through her abdomen, and the oocytes were aspirated through a small gauge trocar. In laymen's terms, it was like sticking a straw into the bottom of a cup and sucking out the bubbles," replied Harlow.

"What time?"

"Eight-thirty that morning."

"And her husband's sperm was taken to the room for fertilization about two o'clock?"

"That's correct."

"Who has access to the storage area where the sperm is stored?"

"Everyone who works in the lab or OR."

"Including Jack and Austin?"

"Of course."

"Where's Austin today?"

Harlow's face took on a huge scowl.

"My son is taking the day off to spend it with his grandfather. The senator came home early from Washington and has been whining about missing a vote," answered Harlow.

"I need to talk to both Austin and Jack."

"Judy will pull their schedules for you. I think Jack is operating all day tomorrow, and Austin will be with his grandfather. I have to fly to the Vineyard on Friday, so you can brief me when I get back," replied Harlow.

"Have you talked to Jack about his recollection regarding the in vitro procedure?"

"He said it was completely routine."

"Do you have a forwarding address for Lori Wegman?"

"I'll check."

"One more thing. Erica Payne asked you about testing the semen for contamination. Why didn't you run a test for HIV antibodies?" asked Whitney.

Harlow shook his head as he answered. “There was no need.”

“Why not?”

“Because with married couples there is no reason to test. Quite frankly, a husband who has even the slightest suspicion he might have an STD would be the biggest fool on earth if he let his wife become inseminated,” said Harlow.

“That makes sense,” replied Whitney. “But that still leaves the question as to how Ann Sorenson got sperm that was infected. It seems impossible without negligence or an intentional act.”

David grabbed Harlow’s arm gently and looked into his tired eyes as he spoke. “Who do you think was the target? You or Ms. Sorenson?”

“I don’t know. I’m sure I’ve made enemies over the years. If someone is out to ruin my reputation, this case could certainly do it.”

Chapter Eight

Thursday, October 16

After a thorough examination by Dr. Christopher, Ann Sorenson was discharged from Suffolk General Hospital. Although she was still weak, she finally convinced him to release her. It was barely nine o'clock when she was taken by wheelchair to the front entrance. The scent of the crisp autumn air filled Ann's lungs with relief after the troubled time she'd spent confined to a bed.

Although Ann was anxious to go home, she decided to stop at Boston Memorial to see her son. When Ann and Steven arrived, they agreed that Steven would wait for Ann by the entrance to the hospital to give her time alone to bond with the baby. She could feel the soreness in her body as she walked past the bank of waiting taxis that formed to the right of the hospital entrance. She paused before entering, looking past the main building and focusing her gaze on the adjacent Harlow clinic.

A nurse named Carol Casey met Ann as she entered the unit. She was a small woman in her late fifties dressed in light-blue scrubs. Casey told her that the physician in charge, Dr. Carnevale, would be unavailable until later that afternoon. Before escorting Ann inside the neonatal ICU, Casey gave her a blue surgical gown to wear over her clothing.

Her son was lying in an incubator, sleeping soundly. Wisps of short, brown, curly hair covered his head and highlighted his cocoa-brown skin. Ann quickly became overwhelmed as tears formed while she followed the tubes leading from the tiny chest.

"Can I touch him?" asked Ann without looking up.

"It's better if you don't. We don't want to wake him."

"What's this machine doing?"

"Transporting his blood through that first tube," said Casey, pointing to the right side of the baby's chest, "to that cylinder called a membrane oxygenator where the blood receives oxygen and is then returned to his body through that other tube connected to his carotid artery. The machine essentially breathes for him so his heart and lungs can rest and mature."

"How long will he have to stay like this?" Ann asked.

"Until his lungs mature enough to work on their own. Dr. Carnevale will be able to give you a better estimate."

"Is he going to live?"

Casey looked deeply into Ann's eyes before she answered.

"We're optimistic this will help him."

"Not every baby who goes on this machine makes it, do they?" pressed Ann.

"It's helped a lot of children."

"But not every single one, right?"

"No," said Casey after a pause.

"That's what I thought," said Ann, as her voice broke.

Suddenly, she was filled with an overwhelming urge to flee. Turning quickly, she slipped out of the gown, placed it in a hamper, and left the room.

After placing his hand in hers, Steven drove away from the hospital and rode with Ann in silence all the way home. Traffic was heavy, forcing him to concentrate on driving. Ann continued to stare out her window, welcoming the solitude as she thought about her baby lying helplessly in intensive care.

It was just past ten o'clock when Whitney arrived at the clinic for his meeting with Jack Bartlett. Bartlett told Whitney that he had known Harlow since they were roommates in medical school.

"I don't see why I'm so damned important to this investigation," said Bartlett with a condescending tone.

"Because you did the in vitro," snapped Whitney, his patience exhausted from the stress of the past few days. "If the police find evidence of criminal negligence, your ass is on the line big time. So you can either cooperate with me or do this on your own."

Bartlett started to reply and then changed his mind. He took another sip of coffee and muttered softly, "Sorry, old man. It's just with all that's happened, I'm afraid my temper's a little frayed."

"Tell me what you remember about this case," said Whitney.

"According to my notes, after Lee harvested the eggs, he was paged because one of his patients had presented in the ER with a vaginal bleed. He asked me to do the fertilization to avoid a delay," replied Bartlett.

"Was that unusual?"

"No. We often step in for each other if an emergency comes up."

"What happened after he left?"

"The sperm specimen was in the room when I arrived. I introduced it to the eggs and returned the culture to the incubator."

"Did you check the semen to see if it had the patient's name on it?"

"Yes. I checked it."

"What happened next?" asked Whitney, continuing to write.

"We waited for twenty-four hours to see if fertilization had occurred. It had, and I scheduled Ms. Sorenson for transfer of the conceptui the following morning," said Bartlett.

"The conceptui would be the fertilized eggs?" asked Whitney.

"That's right."

"Who did the transfer?"

"Lee. I only did the IVF part."

"How does the transfer occur?"

"Ms. Sorenson was taken to the OR. No incision was required, so anesthesia wasn't needed. He would have placed the eggs into a long narrow catheter and passed them through the cervical os, which is the clinical name for the entrance from the vagina to the uterus, into the uterine cavity."

"How many eggs did she have?"

"Two. The records show only one was accepted. That's a common phenomenon with fertility drugs. They stimulate the ovaries to produce multiple eggs. We transfer as many as we think is feasible in the hope that one will gestate."

"Jack, you've done dozens of procedures since this one. How do you remember this case so clearly?" asked Whitney.

"Because I reviewed my records," answered Bartlett, sliding them over to Whitney and pointing to the bottom of the form. "My notes show that the nurse handled the semen in the usual manner. Then she delivered it to Lee for the in vitro."

"Have you ever met the Sorensons?" pressed David.

"No. I've never seen either one."

"Do you remember the nurse?" asked Whitney.

"Slightly. I know her name is Lori Wegman. I didn't know her well."

"Do you know why she quit?"

"No."

Whitney continued to scan the information in the file as Bartlett waited and tapped his fingers.

"One more question, Jack," Whitney began slowly. "Do you know what Lee's relationship was with Lori Wegman?"

"Are you asking me if he was screwing her?" demanded Bartlett.

Whitney nodded.

"It wouldn't surprise me," Bartlett answered.

"Why do you say that?"

"Let's just say that Lee and I go back a long way. I don't think he's changed one bit."

"Do you know for certain that Lee had an affair with her?"

"As you lawyers say, I don't have proof. But I saw her come out of his office a couple of different times when I was working late. Once, after everyone else had gone, I heard her yelling at Lee before she bolted out and slammed his door. She seemed pretty upset and looked like she was crying."

"Did you hear what she was saying?"

"No."

"Was it before or after the Sorenson in vitro?"

"Before. She quit a short time later."

Moments after Ann and Steven arrived home, Erica Payne pulled into the complex in a silver Mercedes. Although she knew Ann and Steven were both emotionally exhausted, Erica insisted on meeting with them. She knew they each had information that needed to be processed while it was fresh. Other lawyers might have waited a day or two, but much of Payne's success was achieved by the aggressive attention she paid to details.

Her strategy was simple. Erica only took cases in which she believed her client was not guilty, was wronged, or was justified in committing the act. If a defendant was bad, Erica made the victim worse. If the victim was good, she would portray the accused as delusional. If they were both good people, she would arouse pity for her client.

He closest friends knew she'd gone to New York at eighteen, desperately wanting to act in the theater, but could only seize two bit parts in three years. Eventually, the law became her surrogate stage, because every trial let her act as producer, director, playwright, and lead, and the rest of her life became a supporting phase for her starring roles in complex litigation.

Her most notorious criminal trial involved a twenty-two-year-old man who had been accused of sexual assault and murder of a five-year-old-girl and convinced her he was innocent. After a vicious, two-month trial, Erica got an acquittal and became a media star.

Three months later, he was found standing over the body of another dead child with a bloody knife in his hand. DNA testing confirmed that the semen inside the child's body was his. Erica refused to represent him again, resigned from the firm, started her own practice, and never handled another criminal case.

Immediately, she took her courtroom skills to medical malpractice cases and soon developed a disdain for doctors. Many were not the caring, dedicated servants of humanity that the public had been led to accept. Most were overworked and arrogant, and felt they were superior human beings because of their medical skills.

In her first malpractice trial, Erica based her strategy on sympathy for her client, a forty-nine-year-old man who was blinded because the surgeon used an outdated technique. Erica could almost see tears forming in several jurors' eyes as she made her closing argument. However, the jury refused to vote with their hearts, and Erica Payne lost her first malpractice case.

For the next four months, she spent every free moment in a medical library until she acquired a thorough working knowledge of anatomy and physiology. The following week, she flew to Los Angeles where her best friend from college was a neurosurgeon. Erica went to the hospital every day and observed surgical procedures with surgeons of different specialties. It was an education that other lawyers could only dream about.

That was almost ten years ago. Erica had won every one of her cases since.

Steven met Erica at the door and escorted her to the master bedroom where Ann was resting in bed as she sipped tea. Payne smiled at how much better Ann looked than when she was in the hospital, even though her eyes were still red and puffy. Erica grasped Ann's hand softly before she spoke, while Steven carried in two wooden chairs and set them beside the bed.

"How do you feel?" asked Erica.

"Sore. But I had to get out of that hospital. I'm so worried about my son."

"He's getting the best care possible."

"I know, but I still can't believe this happened so fast."

"The doctors will come through. I know this is sudden, but we have to go over your testimony. I need to hear exactly what you plan to say to convince people that you never expected to have a black child," said Erica, removing a digital recorder and activating it.

"I've given this a lot of thought. I think you'll be happy," said Ann.

Erica watched her intently as Steven leaned forward and nodded.

"Make sure you talk about the baby. He's your main focus," said Erica.

"Every time I think of him on that machine, I just want to break down," said Ann.

"The first thing the defense will claim is that you had a black lover. A doctor with a reputation like Harlow's would never make a mistake like this. You slept with a black man who got you pregnant and gave you the AIDS virus," said Erica.

"They have no proof of that," said Ann, frowning and shaking her head.

"They'll try every trick in the book to sway a jury, with or without proof. Let's go over how you'll testify about the day you had the in vitro," said Erica.

"I went to the hospital early in the morning to have my eggs removed. Dr. Harlow called me the next day and said fertilization occurred and to come in the following morning to have the eggs put back in."

"You need to mention that it's usually not successful the first time," said Erica.

"I know. I was told my success was pretty rare."

"Tell me about your time with Harlow," said Erica.

"I told him I would do anything he said to have a baby. He stared straight into my eyes and used his deep, melodic voice to soften the cruelty of his words. He told me I had almost no chance of conceiving, and he probably couldn't help me."

"What did you say?" asked Erica.

"I said I heard he was a genius in his field. He shook his head and said, 'There's no such thing. I keep going when others quit, but that doesn't make me any smarter. It's just that I hate to lose a thousand times more than I love to win.'"

"What did you do?"

"I told him I would never quit until we beat the odds. He said there were other options, like surrogate adoption, but I was determined to conceive on my own. He told me his success rate was barely forty-five percent, and it was still one of the highest in the world. But that meant he could not help almost six out of every ten women."

"What happened then?"

"He said most women come to him month after month and go through all the blood tests and ultrasounds, intramuscular injections and surgical procedures, only to fail time after time, until he had to sit them down and admit he couldn't help." I sat there in silence and looked away. He said, "I don't mean to be harsh, but I won't give you false hope."

"What did you do?" Erica asked.

"I looked at the wall, which was filled with photographs of mothers with newborns and accompanied by inscriptions gushing with thanks. He seemed embarrassed by the display, which showed so many young, pink-faced, joyous women who were holding smiling, frowning, or downright mischievous-looking infants. But his humility told me that deep inside, each photo sparked a huge sense of pride and gratitude in him."

"Why did you want this baby so much?" asked Erica as her eyes locked onto Ann's face.

"This child is the legacy for me and my husband."

"Everyone feels that way about their children. Is that the only reason?"

Ann's eyes flashed as she paused. "No. having my son is a debt I owed to my sister, Andrea, as well as my husband," said Ann, bringing a tissue up to her eyes.

"Tell me about her," said Erica, watching Ann as though she was proctoring an exam.

"Andi and I were abandoned when our parents were killed by a drunk driver just after our ninth birthday. We went from one foster home to another."

"How did she die?" asked Erica.

"The day after our twenty-sixth birthday, Andi found a lump in her breast. The doctor told her she was too young to have cancer. That error cost Andi her life. At the cemetery, I made her a promise that I would keep her alive by naming my baby after her."

"Why was that promise so important?"

"Andrea and I vowed our children would never have to grow up like we did. We would make sure they had a home and all the love we never had. Let me show you how much it meant to us," Ann said, rising and walking to the far wall. After removing a picture, she returned.

"She gave me this when I got engaged," Ann said softly before extending a gold, gilt-edged frame containing an image of children at play surrounded by the famous quote from Alistair Cooke.

Erica looked down at the words and felt her skin tingle.

"It would be a crime against nature for any generation to take the world so solemnly that it put off enjoying those things for which we were designed in the first place; the opportunity to do good work, to enjoy friends, to fall in love, to hit a ball, and to bounce a baby."

"Did you tell Dr. Harlow about Andi?" asked Erica.

"Of course. He told me the risks were overwhelming, and I said the rewards are immortal before I nodded toward the photographs on the wall in his office. I'll never forget his final words that day. He said, 'I get the feeling Andi will be watching us,'" said Ann.

"That's excellent. Now tell me about the treatment you went through," said Erica.

"He said I couldn't get pregnant through normal intercourse because I was allergic to a protein in my husband's semen. It was because of a condition called 'seminal plasma allergy' that came from microplasmic pneumonia when I was in my teens. Strains of the bacterium stayed dormant in my vagina and neutralized the sperm. Injections helped but there was another problem. My cervical mucus was also thickened and formed a barrier to keep the sperm from penetrating because of its low motility. I asked what that meant and he said, 'It's like shooting Styrofoam bullets.'"

They all chuckled before Ann continued.

"I had legions of tests and shots of fertility drugs that would help my body produce eggs. Artificial insemination was performed twice. Each failed. He told me I was not a candidate for gamete transfer, so there was only one option left. He called it in vitro fertilization. He said lay persons called it a test-tube baby."

"That's when your fertilized eggs were implanted?" Erica asked.

"Yes. Harlow told me the difficulty in retrieving my eggs made it unlikely I would get another chance. My menstrual cycle ran, and I was ready to soar when a pregnancy test confirmed the miracle had occurred," said Ann.

Erica tossed her yellow legal pad and pen on top the bed and then beamed at Ann. "That's perfect. Don't change a word," she said.

Payne turned to Steven, who was looking passively at them, as if he was waiting for a decision from the casting director who was considering him for a bit part.

"What's your account of the day Ann was inseminated?" asked Erica.

"I got to Harlow's office a little before two. I had to go into a private room like before and give a sperm specimen. When I was finished, I gave it to the nurse and left," he answered.

"As usual, the guy gets the easy part. I'm surprised they didn't give him a beer and fantasy football betting sheet," said Ann, chuckling as Erica and Steven grinned back at her.

"Do you remember the nurse you gave the specimen to?" asked Payne.

"Not really."

"Do you know what she did with the specimen?"

"I think she went to process it and then deliver it to Dr. Harlow."

"Your reaction to the birth is crucial. You have to make sure not to come across as racist when you talk about how this baby is not yours," said Erica.

"The reason I'm so upset has nothing to do with the baby's race. I would be just as troubled no matter what the baby's ethnicity is. This racism crap has nothing to do with his color. I will look a jury in the eye and tell them I'm devastated because the baby never asked to come into this world and now has received a death sentence because of the acts committed by people from the clinic," said Steven.

"Make sure to tell everyone that you don't blame Ann," said Erica.

"How could I? She's the biggest victim of all," said Steven, slipping his hand into Ann's.

"What if the defense lawyer asks why you just can't give the baby up for adoption and move on?" asked Erica.

Steven and Ann exchanged glances.

"I won't abandon this child because I'm his mother. He has no one else, and the clinic is to blame for why he's going to die," said Ann.

"Those bastards at the clinic made it so he doesn't have a chance to live any kind of life. The child is entitled to justice. It has nothing to do with his race," said Steven.

Erica looked at each of them with pride.

"Outstanding answer," she said as a cell phone rang. Ann picked it up.

"It's Santos," she said to Steven, who rose, took the phone, and then headed for the door.

"I'll take it in my office," he said.

"All right, let's shift to another area," Erica continued after Steven left the room. "How do you feel about African American men?" she asked sharply.

Ann folded her arms and looked as if she was being questioned by the Senate Judiciary Committee.

"What the hell kind of question is that? Am I supposed to say they all have rhythm, or that 'black lives matter'?" she asked, as her voice rose.

"Are you a racist?" asked Erica, pressing the issue.

"Of course not," said Ann, laughing.

Anthony will love that one, she thought, as Erica shook her head vigorously.

"Don't take these questions lightly. The defense will explore your feelings about race. If they can show that you dislike black men, they will try to make your claim a racist one. On the other hand, if you have a romantic history with African American men, they can use that to show you had a black lover."

"Good Lord, black men are just like white men. The issue's not race; it's gender. Any woman who's ever been in a single's bar would swear that all men are lower primates who just hijacked the Viagra truck. I don't like or dislike anyone because of their color. Nobody gets points added for who they are or deducted because of who they're not."

"How does it make you feel to have a black child?"

"Like a mother," said Ann. "That's my son lying in that hospital bed. There's no way I could pretend that I love this child any less because of his color."

Erica beamed as she continued to study Ann for a moment.

"Have you had any other lovers since you've been married?"

"Of course not."

"The defense will claim that if you had a white lover, he carried genes from a black ancestor that could be passed on to your children," said Erica.

"Well, I'm proud to say I've been faithful to my husband."

"Are you strong enough to go through with this?" Erica asked.

"I'll never give up," declared Ann defiantly. "Not after what they've done to me and my baby. I want to make sure they never do it to any other woman."

"The defense will try to paint a picture that you're doing this for the money."

"Let the bastards try," said Ann, leaning forward as her face filled with defiance. "I wouldn't take all the money in the world for what I'm going through. My baby and I will still die."

After a brief pause, Erica shut off the recorder, put it into her briefcase, and then rose to leave.

"That's exactly the way I want you to testify, especially with all those kind words about Harlow," she said.

"Some people could think that Harlow is a victim here also. Especially because of all the good he's done and all the women he's helped. I don't want to turn him into a martyr," said Ann.

"I agree. Just let your story come out without anger. Don't show any bitterness toward him, and a jury will think he seduced you into feeling safe and let you down big time," said Erica as she reached forward to embrace Ann.

"You're the boss, Ricki," replied Ann, using the nickname Erica's father had given her when she was only a baby.

Chapter Nine

At five o'clock, David Whitney drove past the huge stone light posts and followed the winding driveway for almost a quarter of a mile past the rows of evergreens before arriving in front of the elegant, white federal colonial. It was flanked by huge columns and distinguished by black shutters, a widow's walk, and Palladian windows.

The home was accentuated by the splendor of the peaking Fall foliage, complete with striking shades of brown, red, yellow, and purple. It belonged to Langley Mitchell and was located north of Boston in the affluent community known as Pride's Crossing. The property was bought at a foreclosure auction several decades earlier, right after Mitchell's first election to the senate. No other bidders appeared because the auction date was kept hidden. Mitchell declared it a bureaucratic snafu. His detractors claimed fraud.

Austin Harlow escorted Whitney into the parlor. Whitney's irritation sparked as he watched Austin swagger. His affect was one of an entitled young boy trying to be man. He was an only child and became an obstetrician like his father and a reclusive snob like his mother. Although he practiced medicine with Harlow, the two men were strangers.

Katherine was seated in the Chippendale chair next to the fireplace talking to her father, a white-haired man dressed in an immaculate navy blazer, striped burgundy tie, and gray flannel slacks, perfectly creased and tailored. Senator Mitchell and his daughter shared distinctive facial characteristics, clear blue eyes, a prominent chin, finely sculpted cheekbones, and thick, perfectly textured hair. While both carried themselves with a royal air, she reminded Whitney of an aging society matron, while the senator still had the poise of a senior statesman.

Mitchell had served in the US Senate for over forty years, elected as a populist candidate bent on a family values platform. During his first term in the senate, he introduced over thirty anti-crime bills. His efforts resulted in doubling the criminal penalties for repeat pedophiles, and he also pushed through a federal law requiring registration of all convicted sex offenders.

Mitchell had an appetite for power that was so voracious, friends and enemies alike were deathly afraid of him. He stopped at nothing to destroy his enemies, and his memory for grudges was legendary. Some claimed he was still in politics simply because he had not gotten even with everyone yet. He was respected, revered, and hated. Most of all, he was feared.

Katherine was the only daughter of Langley and Marjory Mitchell. Marjory died of cancer when Katherine was only twenty, and Mitchell did not remarry. After Marjory's death, Katherine went through a period of rebellion that culminated in her bringing home Lee Harlow, a young medical student, to Washington to meet her father. As soon as Mitchell voiced his displeasure with her choice of suitors, Katherine smugly announced that she and Lee were engaged. She regretted crossing her father ever since, and never stopped trying to atone for ignoring his wishes.

Whitney had represented the family on several matters. He was not the senator's lead counsel, as that work was parceled out to major campaign contributors. But when high-quality representation on business matters involving the clinic was needed, Whitney and his firm were the top choice.

Whitney walked over and embraced Katherine, kissing her softly on the cheek. Turning to his right, he extended his hand and said, "Hello, Senator. Good to see you again. I'm sorry we have to meet under these circumstances."

"Hello, David," answered Mitchell in a subdued voice. "I must say this entyah business is quite disturbing."

"I can't believe we have to deal with this Payne woman again," said Austin, folding his arms with disgust.

"What do you mean?" asked Whitney.

"She was the attorney for a man who was injuhed in an auto accident with Austin," offered Mitchell. "During his last yeah in college."

"Tell me about it," Whitney said, after opening his briefcase and removing a legal pad and pen.

"Not much to tell. This man was passengah Austin's cah. Austin swerved to avoid hitting a dog and the vehicle turned ovah. The man was paralyzed. It turned out fine, though. He got a huge cash settlement."

Whitney's face grew flush with white patches of disgust as he fought to control the cruel words that sprang to his lips.

"That's not exactly a fair exchange, Senator. Cripple a man for life and have your insurance company toss him a few bucks," Whitney said, folding his arms.

"I don't want to hear any moah about that crash or this Payne woman!" thundered the senator. "This is irrelevant to the matter at hand."

Mitchell glared as Whitney continued.

"How does Payne fit into this case?" asked Whitney.

"We think she still holds a grudge against Austin," replied Mitchell.

"This whole damn debacle comes at quite an inopportune time," muttered Austin in an irritated voice before taking a sip of brandy. "Grandfather has decided to make his big announcement in three weeks instead of waiting until April."

"What announcement is he talking about, Senator?" inquired Whitney.

"I'm stepping down and endorsing Austin for my senate seat. This will be a changing of the guahd, David," said Mitchell, waving his arm in a sweeping gesture toward Austin. "Provided you can keep this Sorenson business quiet. Have you found out what happened?"

"No," replied Whitney, digesting the news. "We're still investigating."

"You have to stop this event from staining the reputation of the clinic. Austin is counting on you," said Mitchell, as his daughter touched his hand.

The senator rose and left the room. Whitney shrugged as he realized he had just been dismissed. After Austin showed him out, Whitney slid behind the wheel of his Lexus and exited the circular driveway just as a white delivery van pulled up to the Mitchell estate. The driver bounded out of the vehicle and headed for the front entrance. He was met by a servant before he could ring the doorbell.

"I have a package for Langley Mitchell," said the driver as the butler warily looked him up and down.

"I'll take it," the butler replied.

In response, the driver thrust an electronic device forward for a signature.

The senator was in his study when the butler approached.

"You have just received this delivery, sir," he said.

As the servant departed, Mitchell fumbled with the package and found a cassette recorder with a tape already loaded. Perplexed, he hit the play button and the sound of two voices appeared. Instantly, his whole body stiffened as he recognized the first voice as that of his former chief of staff. After hearing the content of the conversation, he knew it was a recording from the 1970s—one that he thought had been destroyed. He let it play until the end and paid particular attention to the last exchange as the voice filled the air.

"So that there is no misunderstanding, you will list the official cause of death as heart failure. In exchange, you will be paid ten thousand dollars in cash, and you will report for duty as an assistant medical examiner at the agreed upon facility in South Carolina in one month. Correct?"

"That's right. Tell the senator we have a deal, Mr. Newell."

The voice that replied was a mystery, but that did not matter. The words he'd just heard told Mitchell everything he needed to know.

A huge lump formed in his throat as the tape went silent. With his hands shaking like a Parkinson's patient, he poured himself a brandy before retrieving his address book from his desk drawer and desperately searching for anyone who might be able to help.

Eddy placed the conference call shortly after nine o'clock. Ricki came on the line first, followed by Clay.

"Where do we stand?" asked Ricki.

"Everything is in place," said Clay.

"Incidentally, that was a pretty convincing touch when you fought with Harlow and Bartlett," said Eddy.

"Did you see the look on Bartlett's face as he tried to figure out if I was really Michelle's son?" asked Clay, chuckling.

"You almost see him trying to imagine how Michael would have looked after he aged over the last forty years," said Eddy.

"Is everything all set for the airport?" asked Ricki.

"I'm meeting my contacts at four-thirty tomorrow morning," said Clay.

"This plan is like having surgery to remove a cancerous tumor. It might kill you, or it might let you live the kind of life you want. Either way, the tumor will be destroyed. I can promise you that Langley Mitchell is the biggest tumor I've ever known," said Ricki.

"This reminds me of the first time we met, Eddy. When you identified Roger Newell, and Ricki came up with this plan," said Clay.

"Ann's baby is the key to success. We have to make sure we do everything so that he pulls through," said Eddy.

There was a long pause before the silence was broken.

"There's only one way to do that. We have to stay vigilant. Just like the motto of the marine corps, *semper fidelis*," said Clay.

"Those words had a special meaning to my brother," said Ricki.

"I know. They were the first words he shouted when we finished boot camp and the last thing he whispered before he died in my arms in Iraq," said Clay.

Chapter Ten

Friday, October 17

Just before dawn, two men carrying a long, black vinyl bag slipped out of the rear entrance to the morgue in the basement of Westport Municipal Hospital. They deposited the bag into the back of a dark-colored sport utility vehicle and then drove out of the dimly lit hospital parking lot and headed south toward Providence where they were to meet their contact.

The sky turned overcast and a slight drizzle began to fall. Forty-five minutes later, they arrived at the airport where Clay was sitting in his BMW, waiting for them near the tarmac. The SUV stopped, and the men exited as Clay approached them in the pre-dawn darkness.

"Hope you boys have my packages," said Clay cynically.

"I've got your little one here and the big one is in the back," said the driver, displaying a syringe containing a pinkish substance in a zip lock bag.

"Are you sure this is exactly what I told you I needed?" asked Clay as he studied the bag.

"My guy got it right from the OR after it went into the hazardous waste bin. It came directly from an oral surgery case."

"What about the films?"

"Dr. Painless came through. Now all you have to do is make it snow tooth powder."

"He'll think he's in the Rockies in February. Is the big package the one we talked about?" asked Clay, nodding toward the rear of the vehicle.

"Yeah, it's clean. Dropped off the radar with no ID," shrugged the taller of the two.

"What's the immediate C-O-D?"

"About what you'd expect. They found him in an alley near the South End."

"Help me get the bag loaded," said Clay, walking around to the back of the vehicle.

"Sure, pal. Right after we take care of business."

"Don't you guys trust me?" Clay smiled.

"Yeah, about as much as I trust my ex-wife's lawyer."

Clay reached into his pocket and produced an envelope.

"Here," he said, handing the envelope to the tall man. "Fifteen grand cash for you boys and another fifteen for the doc, just like we agreed."

The man snatched the envelope, opened it, and began counting. When he finished, he silently congratulated himself for telling the doctor he could only get him ten grand. That meant he would pocket a $5,000 finder's fee. Smiling broadly, he turned to his companion.

"OK, let's get rid of this stiff and get back on patrol."

The tall man turned to Clay.

"Anytime you need another package, you let us know. We've got an endless supply," he chuckled.

It was just before seven o'clock when Jamie Quintell arrived in the conference room and reread the report her subordinates had compiled on Lee Harlow. Jamie took notes to use when she met with David Whitney.

The report said Harlow went to Notre Dame on a football scholarship. He was a gifted running back and expected to follow in the tradition of legends like the Four Horsemen, George Gipp, and Heisman Trophy winner Paul Hornung, until he blew out his knee. After college, he graduated from medical school and was board certified as a fellow in the American College of Obstetricians and Gynecologists. He had over thirty obstetrical publications as well as numerous awards for fertility research case studies.

Harlow had what some considered an unyielding code of ethics. He never forgot an unprovoked insult and demanded that everyone, including himself, accept blame for his or her own wrongdoing. He believed that mercy should not be offered unless earned and insisted that proper punishment be administered for a violation of his ethical code. The background check concluded that Harlow's favorite mechanism for overcoming adversity spawned from the ancient Greek saying, "Character is destiny."

The report also showed that Harlow was the only child of Trenton and Alicia Harlow. Trenton owned a surgical instrument company after starting out as a sales representative for a company from Germany. The German instruments were light, precision-balanced, and made of superior steel. It was very tough, grueling work, requiring him to meet with surgeons to demonstrate the instruments and convince them his company made a superior product. For months, doors were constantly slammed in his face. On rare occasions when he was able to see a doctor, his products were completely rejected because resistance to the German instruments was overwhelming.

American companies were ruthless, but Trenton persisted until he made a breakthrough. Word spread quickly about the superior German instruments, and orders began to pour in. Trenton's salary doubled twice in six months. Soon, he was so busy he could not keep up with all the orders.

The next part of her report showed that Trenton became a distributor for the company. He could buy their products and resell them at a profit in the six New England states. A five-year contract was signed, and yearly sales quotas were outlined.

The following year, Trenton made his annual quota in February. The company informed him that no matter how many more instruments he sold, he would be paid no further commissions. Words were exchanged, lawsuits were filed, and the agreement was dissolved.

A month after the case was settled, Trenton formed a new company with an Austrian engineer named Hans Straussman, a man he met in Germany. Immediately, they began making their own instruments in the basement of Trenton's home. Three months later, after scraping together their life savings, they opened a small factory that featured custom-made, specialized surgical scissors, hemostats, and forceps, before eventually expanding the line.

Trenton dreamed of the day when Lee Harlow would join the company. Lee had other plans; he was going to be a surgeon. Trenton was disappointed, but accepted his son's fate. "At least I'll have one steady customer," he joked.

A few days before Lee's wedding, Trenton told him he suspected that Straussman was stealing from the company. Lee offered to postpone the wedding and honeymoon, but his father would not hear of it. While Lee and Katherine were honeymooning in California, they received an urgent message from Alicia that forever changed Harlow's life.

"Come home right away, son," his mother cried. "Your father is dead."

Upon returning from his honeymoon, Harlow learned that Straussman had fled with the company funds and that Trenton's body had already been cremated. Lee went to see the medical examiner who told him his father died from heart failure. When he asked to see his father's medical records, he was told they had been misplaced. They were never recovered and there was a note from Lee to David that he suspected a cover-up occurred. Another note showed David pressed Lee for further details but Lee refused to pursue the issue and no other explanations were provided

After Trenton's death, Lee became withdrawn. Plagued by guilt, he was tortured by the thought that he should have rushed to his father's side. Soon, his mother was forced into bankruptcy. Despite Harlow's pleas for time to reorganize, the banks moved swiftly to foreclose.

Lee tried to help his mother find comfort. He begged her to go to church, to join community groups, and even forced her to go to counseling, but she refused to talk once she reached the therapist's office. On the day before her home was to be auctioned off, Alicia climbed into the bathtub with a bottle of gin and one of Trenton's diamond-tipped scalpels, and then she emptied her veins into the warm water.

The scandal left Harlow on the verge of quitting medical school because he no longer had any financial support. Despite pleas from his wife, Lee refused to ask his father-in-law for help after Trenton's death. Trenton left him something more precious than money: strength of character, which made him persevere. Harlow fought to secure enough grants and loans to finish medical school and complete his training. Then he began to build his reputation.

It took him over ten years, but he repaid every one of his father's debts and vindicated Trenton's name by having it expunged from bankruptcy. And now, like Trenton, everything Harlow went through to build his successful practice was on the verge of slipping away. His name was about to be associated with scandal and ruin.

Jamie finished her notes and went to make a copy for Whitney. She had a deeper understanding of Lee Harlow and what kind of man he was. He was the son of a father who was bullied but not afraid, swindled but not deceived, and killed but still alive in his son's mind.

The cynics might soon say, like father, like son, she thought.

David Whitney dialed Lee Harlow's private office number shortly after 8:15 a.m. Harlow came on the line right after the second ring.

"Hello, David. What's up?"

"Jack said you two were jumped by one of the protesters. Did he threaten you?"

"He was raving about murder and motherhood. I didn't take it seriously," said Harlow.

"One more thing. Jamie is coming by the clinic later today to interview you again," said Whitney.

"About what?"

"Personal things. I thought you'd be more comfortable talking to her than me because we go back such a long way."

Harlow chuckled before he replied. "Bullshit, David. You think someone with a young, new face can get more information out of me than an old friend, right?"

It was Whitney's turn to laugh.

"Something like that," he answered.

"Well, have her come by before eleven this morning. I have to leave for the Vineyard to see patients."

Traffic moved briskly, and Jamie Quintell arrived in front of the clinic at several minutes before nine. She parked, and when she entered the building, she was quickly ushered into Harlow's office. He was talking on the telephone, but motioned for her to sit in one of the burgundy leather Queen Anne chairs in front of his imported teak desk.

Her eyes were drawn to the photographs covering the wall behind his desk. Whitney told her the photographs were put together by the nursing staff because Harlow was too modest to display them himself. Most of the pictures showed women holding babies, although some were of couples posing with more than one child. Each picture was signed, usually by the mother. Jamie smiled briefly as she calculated at least five of the babies in the pictures were named "Lee" or "Leigh."

After turning back to look at Harlow, Jamie studied the rugged face and steely eyes, and began to recall the background information. Harlow and his wife, Katherine, lived in Marblehead, on Boston's North Shore. It did not appear to be a happy marriage. There was no evidence of hatred or abuse, but indifference was the recurring theme of their union.

Quintell was surprised to learn from the reports that Senator Mitchell and Katherine owned the real estate housing each of Harlow's three clinics. Katherine's involvement as Harlow's wife seemed reasonable, but there was no business reason for the senator to be involved. Whitney told her that many physicians put the title to their property in their spouse's name to shield assets from creditors in the event of a lawsuit. But Senator Mitchell's ownership sent up a red flag because Whitney had told her about Harlow's strained relationship with his father-in-law and how Mitchell had stepped in because Harlow's financial situation would not let him obtain a loan for the real estate when he first began his practice.

Jamie surveyed Harlow's desk and was surprised that the only picture he displayed was one of his mother and father, not his wife. Trenton and Alicia Harlow were positioned in a dual frame bound by hinges. She was somewhat surprised at the Anne Frank quote inscribed in the other frame. Harlow's conversation ended, although he continued to make notes before giving Jamie his complete attention.

"I've sent for one of the staff to help you with whatever you have to do," Harlow began, without looking up as he continued to write. "I'm sorry, but we haven't been able to locate a forwarding address for Lori Wegman."

"That's all right. I've already traced her and her husband to Texas. I'll be contacting her soon."

"What can I do to help?" asked Harlow.

"Let's start with some background. Why did you name your practice Artemis Associates?" asked Jamie.

Harlow grinned slightly before he answered. "In Greek mythology, Artemis was the daughter of Zeus and known as the goddess who protected women in childbirth. Some of my patients need every ounce of help they can get. That name never lets any one of us forget why we do what we do here."

"David also wants me to find out everything I can about Erica Payne and Austin's accident so I can see if there is any connection," began Jamie.

"You need to ask Austin. I had nothing to do with that case."

"David wants me to get your impression of the accident."

Harlow studied her carefully.

"It happened the summer after Austin finished prep school. He had six people in his car. They had all been drinking," he said.

"How old was he?"

"Nineteen. Two years under the legal drinking age."

"Where did they get the alcohol?"

"One of the boys took it from his parents' summer home."

"Tell me how it happened."

"Austin was driving to the beach. He was showing off by speeding and lost control. The car hit a tree head on. One of the boys was thrown out and fractured his pelvis. I found out he was paralyzed afterward."

"How was it resolved?"

"I wanted Austin to admit what he had done and apologize to the boy and his family, and then stand up like a man and take his punishment. But his grandfather stepped in and forced the insurer to make a cash settlement. In exchange, Austin pleaded no contest to careless driving, a misdemeanor that was wiped off his record when he turned twenty-one. In my opinion, he got off scot-free."

"Why do you feel that way? Cases like this get settled all the time."

Harlow's eyes turned a shade of dusky gray, and a chilling look spread across his face before he answered.

"Because Austin has to learn the difference between right and wrong, and that his grandfather can't bail him out of every jam he finds himself in. He never expressed an ounce of remorse for crippling that poor boy, and he refused to even go see him in the hospital. I thought that was despicable."

"Erica Payne was the man's attorney?"

"Yes. She was ready to crucify Austin. The senator decided to make Austin his heir apparent and could not have a scandal like that ruining his grandson's political career. He decided to use his political influence with Payne's law firm and squeezed out a settlement in exchange for getting them some government contracts. So Austin traded his character for his grandfather's senate seat. In some ways, I think he received more severe injuries than the victim, even though Austin's wounds are not visible."

"Whatever happened to the boy who was paralyzed?" Jamie asked.

"I'm not sure."

There was a long pause.

"I'll need to see your list of sperm donors," said Jamie.

"What do you need to get started?" asked Harlow.

"A list of everyone, by race if possible."

"We don't keep them by race, but by year in alphabetical order."

"The donors are identified by race in the charts, right?" she asked. Harlow he nodded affirmatively. "Can't the computer flag the African American donors and get me a printout?"

"I don't know. We've never had to do that before," Harlow replied.

He picked up his intercom and had a brief conversation. A moment later, a semisoft knock sounded on his door.

"Come in," he called.

Judy Davis entered the room.

"You wanted to see me, Dr. Harlow?" she asked.

"This is Jamie Quintell. She works with David Whitney. I want you to give her whatever help she needs today. Jamie, this is Judy Davis."

After the two women exchanged greetings, Harlow rose to leave.

"Dr. Harlow, we did find something unusual," said Judy.

"What?" asked Harlow.

"We just found an African American donor named Carl Hartman. When we went to check for his sperm, the receptacle was empty."

"Are you sure?" asked Harlow.

"Yes," replied Judy, in a frustrated tone. "I double checked it myself. It was the right slot. There was nothing there."

"What could that mean, Dr. Harlow?" asked Jamie.

"Maybe he asked to have his semen destroyed. That happens when donors change their mind," said Harlow.

"I checked for such a letter, but his file is missing," replied Judy.

"Could someone have used Hartman's vial and then discarded what was left or put it back in the wrong slot?" asked Jamie.

"That's highly unlikely," said Harlow.

"But not impossible," pressed Jamie.

"No, but someone would have to know their way around here to do anything like that."

"I'll have to check this out," said Jamie. "Do you think you'll be returning tonight?"

"It depends on how fast I can finish. I'll call Judy later this afternoon and let her know how I'm running. If I can't return, Judy has the number of my hotel in Edgartown."

"Do you want me to leave your schedule intact for the rest of next week?" asked Judy.

"Yes. I'm in surgery Monday morning, and then I'm meeting with David Whitney in the afternoon."

After Harlow left, Judy and Jamie went to the deserted administrative office that had been reserved for them. Jamie wanted to start with the records for all the cases on the day of Ann's insemination and the records of all donors who supplied semen to the clinic's sperm bank.

Judy sat behind the computer and logged on. After the screen illuminated, she began to search for the documents that Jamie requested and stopped when she found all that were listed for February 12. The operating room schedule showed there were twenty-one procedures, seven of them in vitro fertilizations. Judy typed the print command and received a list of donors and storage locations.

"Can you tell from this record what the race is of each patient?' asked Jamie after she finished reading.

"No, but I can pull that information from each chart. There are only twenty-one patients listed here. I can dig that out for you right away," said Judy.

"Fine. Now, I want to see the records of the sperm bank."

"I don't think that's programmed by race either."

"How many donors do you have?"

“Almost two thousand,” answered Judy as she continued to type.

Judy began to punch the keyboard harder and shake her head.

“I’m having trouble accessing the files,” she said, repeatedly hitting the enter key.

“Keep trying.”

“Every time I type the command, it says incorrect code,” answered Judy, returning to the menu. “I don’t understand. I know the code is correct.”

The screen suddenly went dark; the index appeared and the words ‘Files have been erased, return to main menu” displayed on the monitor in huge block letters.

“We can’t access the files. Now what do we do?” asked Judy in a panicky voice

“Only one thing we can do,” answered Jamie, her voice taking on a tone of despair. “Cancel all our plans for the next few days.”

Chapter Eleven

The cemetery was located eight miles south of the city, just before the countryside turned into Boston's south shore. The road led to a grassy field, bordered by a wooden fence that needed painting and surrounded by oak trees and wildflowers. Many of the graves did not have headstones; those that did seemed to be encapsulated in a maze of lost lives that appeared to have been forgotten.

Eddy arrived just before ten, entered through the weather-beaten wrought iron gates, and drove for several minutes until he reached the edge of a row farthest from the entrance. He had been there many times but was always overcome by an overwhelming stab of loneliness as he fought to keep his emotions in check. He stopped for a moment and stared at the hundreds of memorial sites before grabbing a bouquet of lilacs and a small bag. It took him less than two minutes to reach the grave.

Eddy stood in front of the headstone for a few moments, concentrating as always on the inscription that read

Michelle Vellois

Wife and Mother

Born: July 7, 1948

Died: January 3, 1973

He pictured Michelle and her elegant, playful laugh and lonely smile. He thought of the son she left behind who was forced into foster care, just like Ann and her sister, Andrea. Michelle's death was the watershed event that changed his life. Eddy's debt would never be repaid, but he could try to soften it. Ann and her baby were giving him a final chance at total and complete redemption. Swallowing hard, he pledged to find a way to make her baby stay alive.

He laid the bouquet on top of her grave just below the headstone. After a final reverent nod, he opened the bag and removed a battery-powered drill and small black velvet box. Eddy extracted a silver pendant from the box. After holding it up against the tombstone, he quickly drilled two holes, inserted anchors, and affixed the pendant with weather-resistant screws.

The silver medallion was a gift from Ricki. In the center was an ancient Chinese symbol known as *sheng li*. Engraved on the face underneath the symbol was a quote from Shakespeare:

"All Losses Are Restored and Sorrows End."

After ensuring that the pendant was secure, he stared at the headstone for a long moment before whispering a soft "Rest in peace." Then he turned and walked back to the car.

At exactly ten-forty, Lee Harlow arrived at the municipal airport in Westover, Massachusetts, twelve miles south of Boston. He drove behind the aviation building onto the tarmac until he came to the company plane, a blue and silver Piper Lance. The airport was small and secluded, and there was no tower. Even the coffee shop had closed over a year ago because of inactivity. He would be alone, unless another pilot showed up.

After parking his car, he did a walk-around inspection and then climbed into the cockpit, tossed his blazer behind the seat, and conducted an instrument check. In less than ten minutes, he was airborne. The weather was ideal for flying, cool and clear with very light winds. He could almost feel the rush he always got from cruising high above the Atlantic Ocean.

Clay watched the departure from his BMW until lift-off was complete. As the plane cleared the runway, he got out of his car and walked to where Harlow's vehicle was parked. With a quick, fluid movement, he slipped a sealed envelope under the windshield wiper, climbed back into the Beamer, and roared away.

An intense feeling of satisfaction appeared. As he shifted to fourth gear, a feeling of euphoria overtook him as he realized the plan was about to head into the final phase. It was time to repay all debts. Suddenly, a huge grin spread across his face.

Like Michael Corleone in the Godfather, *I'm about to settle all family business*, he thought gleefully as he headed north to Boston.

At the same time, Lee Harlow's plane was headed southeast toward Martha's Vineyard. Harlow reached for his radio and adjusted the frequency.

"Bridgeport, this is four-niner-one-two tango, do you read? Over."

"Roger, one-two tango, this is Bridgeport."

"I'm at two thousand feet and climbing out of Westover. I'll be flying south by southeast to Martha's Vineyard. Fuel is satisfactory. ETA is eleven hundred hours. Over."

"Roger. Visibility is ten miles. Traffic is heavy in your area. Advise you proceed southwest avoiding heavy traffic unless you have an emergency. Over."

"Any unusual winds or weather? Over."

"Negative. Winds light and variable. Weather unchanged."

"Roger, Bridgeport. One-two tango out."

Harlow removed his headphones and slid them down around his neck.

He began to reminisce about his father's death. Shrugging, he realized it was probably a natural reaction because the two of them had been forced to deal with similar circumstances that could lead to destruction. Staring at the pale blue sky dotted with crowds of powder puff clouds, Harlow stopped thinking about his past and reflected on his future. He was certain of one thing. He would not let himself succumb to the same fate as his father had.

Slowly, he turned to the man in the seat next to him and a broad smile formed on his lips as he looked out over the azure-tinged horizon and spoke.

"Hold on tight, my friend. The eagle will be landing soon," he said, as the plane began to bank to the left.

Ann Sorenson was sitting at her kitchen table staring out the window thinking about her baby dying. Trembling as she sipped her coffee, she began to wonder how she would deal with that contingency. It was something she had not given any consideration when she decided to get pregnant.

For a moment, she imagined watching him cooing in his crib, joyfully discovering the mysteries of the excitingly strange new world he had finally entered. Suddenly, an image appeared of her and Andrea getting the news their parents were dead. Tears formed as she pictured the scene days later when they were told no one in the family would take them in. An image formed of the nights they spent crying together in a series of foster homes.

Her cell phone rang. Containing her tears, Ann answered. Her body began to quake as she recognized the caller.

"I've been waiting for your call," she began breathlessly.

"How's the baby?"

"No change. He's still hooked up to that machine," she answered.

"Have you talked to the doctors?"

"Yes. They say he has shown a slight improvement. But not enough for them to consider taking him off the device."

"Is he out of the woods yet?"

"No. They say it could still go either way. They should know soon."

"I can't wait any longer. Every second away is an eternity."

"What are you going to do?"

"I'm coming to Boston."

Ann's chest tightened as she shook her head.

"You can't. Not yet. You know it's not the right time," she protested.

"You trust me, right?"

"Of course."

"Then believe me when I tell you that I can't stay away any longer. What would you do if you were in my place?"

Ann grew silent for a long, torturous moment. If she knew her child might not survive, she would rush to his side. His next words send a wave of simultaneous joy and stinging fear throughout her body.

"I want to see him for myself. I'm coming to be with my son."

The clock read almost 5:30 as Whitney sat alone in his office reviewing the reports he'd received from Quintell as he began making his own set of notes. Whitney knew that this case was also about friendship. He genuinely liked Harlow because of his tenacity and compassion, and was especially impressed by the way Harlow treated his patients, especially those who could not be helped.

Much of Whitney's success as a litigator could be traced to his knack for knowing how to pick a jury. Most of his colleagues used jury consultants, but Whitney relied on his own instincts. He knew all the tricks, like picking jurors based on their footwear.

Studies showed that people who wore comfortable shoes tended to be more easygoing, therefore more likely to favor a person they could identify with. He made his clients dress casually in court: a shirt and tie, of course, but never a business suit; sport coats and slacks with comfortable shoes for men; and conservative feminine dresses and low-heeled casual footwear for women. They were advised not to wear any jewelry except for wedding rings.

Whitney reflected on Harlow's easygoing manner and how it camouflaged the intensity of his commitment to his patients' success. Harlow's greatest feeling of pride occurred when one of his patients became pregnant. Whitney remembered being at dinner with Harlow on several different occasions and how exuberant Lee would become after learning of a successful conception. When success occurred, he would always make the same remark, "The eagle has landed," repeating the phrase used by the first astronauts to reach the moon.

To Lee, difficult pregnancies were like the first moon landing—a two phase operation, thought David. *The conception, like the arrival on the lunar surface, was phase one. Delivery, like the actual moonwalk, was phase two.*

The sound of his door bursting open caused Whitney to turn. It was a third-year junior associate whom Whitney had assigned to do legal research on the Harlow case. Whitney was annoyed that the associate had failed to knock and he started to speak. The man cut him off.

"David," the associate said breathlessly, leaning forward and placing his knuckles on the front of Whitney's desk. "Sorry to barge in but something awful has happened. It just came on the news. Dr. Harlow's plane went down off the coast of Martha's Vineyard. His radio went out in mid-transmission, and the plane disappeared from the radar screen. The coast guard is searching for the wreckage now."

Whitney's throat tightened, and a dull pain began to gnaw at his insides as he asked the inevitable question.

"Any survivors?" he asked, his voice breaking.

"None have been spotted."

Jack Bartlett left the clinic just before seven o'clock. The October sun was setting, and he did not see the document under his windshield wiper until he was almost upon the vehicle. Puzzled, he grabbed the envelope and tore it open. Inside was an old photograph. Jack's hands began to shake, and his breathing came out in spurts as he looked over the document.

The photograph was from a Polaroid camera. The model used was big in the 1960s and 1970s, and was a breakthrough at that time in self-development film technology. People could see their pictures instantly and no longer had to take film to a camera store and wait for it to be developed.

Jack's heart raced as he stared at the images in the photograph. Three people, two men and one woman, were facing the camera and smiling, while several others were depicted in the background. The woman stood in the center wearing a huge smile, as each man flanked her and had his arm wrapped around her waist. All three held drink glasses.

Even though the picture was decades old and slightly worn, there was no question as to the identities of the men. Lee Harlow was on the woman's right and Jack Bartlett was on her left. They looked like mischievous teenaged fraternity brothers and seemed to be in the midst of a festive party scene.

Jack put the photo down as if it were red hot. Suddenly, he looked off into the distance and then felt his chest pound as he panicked while rereading the caption on the Post-it note attached to the picture.

"There is no statute of limitations on murder."

Chapter Twelve

Saturday, October 18

Whitney arrived at Lee Harlow's home several minutes after eight the following morning. He had been up most of the night, trying to uncover information on the missing plane. Although the Coast Guard had suspended all search operations at twilight, David asked Jamie to dispatch one of her associates to Martha's Vineyard and to conduct a private investigation. They last talked shortly before 4:00 a.m. when Whitney learned there were no new developments. Annoyed, he finally tumbled into bed and slept for less than two hours before calling Katherine Harlow about meeting with the family just after seven.

Senator Mitchell met David at the door and escorted him into the parlor where Katherine and Austin were waiting. Both nodded without speaking.

"Is there any news today?" inquired Whitney after being seated.

"None," replied Katherine. "The Coast Guard commander called and said they would notify us as soon as something developed."

"This plane crash debacle is about to ruin Grandfather's announcement," muttered Austin Harlow, sipping his coffee.

David stared sharply at Austin, who seemed bloated with arrogance and condescension. He wanted to walk over to the skinny little bastard and shake some sense into him.

"That's a very poor attitude," answered Senator Mitchell sternly. "Keep in mind that your father is lost at sea. You'd better start showing some sympathy, at least in public."

The telephone rang and Austin answered. He became engaged in a short, animated conversation. When it was finished, he turned to the group.

"That was the Coast Guard commander," he began stiffly. "They just found the wreckage of the plane about three miles off the coast of Oak Bluffs. They are towing it in for the FAA to examine. He said a preliminary investigation showed that a clogged fuel line was the cause of the crash."

"Any news on your father?" asked Katherine.

"No sign of the body. They're continuing to search. There's one other thing," continued Austin nervously. "It looks like the fuel line was tampered with. It's possible this was not an accident."

"I can't believe it," said Whitney. "When will they have an official report?"

"I don't know," replied Austin, looking at his watch. "Well, I don't want to be late for my squash game."

"Will you be joining us for dinner?" asked Katherine.

"No. I have two functions to attend tonight, so don't plan on me."

"Aren't you bothered by the fact that someone sabotaged the plane, Austin?" asked David.

Austin thought for a moment before replying. "Yes, I guess I am. It could have been me flying when it went down."

Whitney's anger peaked as he started to respond. Katherine and Mitchell continued to look at Whitney without any emotion, as if waiting for word that cocktails were ready. Suddenly, David's rage spread over him as he rose from his chair and left.

Standing in the shower, Ann Sorenson let the warm mist run over her body. As the water sprayed her face and neck, her heart ached as she thought of her baby. Suddenly, her eyes filled with tears as she pictured him lying in intensive care.

Ann walked to her dressing table and began her daily ritual. When finished, she walked to the closet and selected a navy pant outfit to wear to visit her son. Suddenly, she was overcome by a sobering thought. She had not even given the hospital his name yet.

I'll force myself to stay this time. I just won't look at those tubes connected to his little body, she thought.

When she was fully dressed, Ann walked down the stairs, grabbed her purse, and started for the garage when the telephone rang.

"Hello," she said dully into the receiver.

"Ms. Sorenson, please," replied a deep male voice.

"Speaking," responded Ann.

"This is Dr. Carnevale from Boston Memorial Hospital. I'm afraid I have some troubling news."

Oh God, now what? thought Ann as fear spread over her.

"It's about your baby, Ms. Sorenson. I'm very sorry, but the ECMO is not helping him the way we hoped it would. I think you should come to the hospital as soon as you can."

"Oh no," replied Ann, her voice breaking as tears began to well in her eyes.

"He's had a tough fight from the start. I know that circumstance doesn't help, but his little lungs need more time to function on their own."

"Can you do anything?"

"We've just increased his oxygen intake. There's a very good chance it may work. But I wanted to call and tell you that I think you should get down here just in case."

"I'm on my way right now," said Ann, struggling to recover.

"Ms. Sorenson, there is one other thing," said Carnevale softly. "We'll need to know the baby's name."

"It's Andrew Anthony," replied Ann in a gravelly voice.

After the connection was broken, she whispered inaudibly toward the telephone, "I'm naming him after his father and my sister."

Jamie arrived at Harlow's office in the early afternoon. Judy Davis and two other employees were in the conference room continuing to go through every medical record in order to compile the list of all sperm donors who had been erased from the computer. It was tiring, painstaking work, but it was the only way the information could be retrieved.

"What did you come up with on Maxwell Evans?" asked Jamie.

"His storage spot is empty. I've checked it half a dozen times, and the record states that it belongs in this spot."

"Why do you think it's missing?" asked Jamie.

"This only happens if someone sends a written request to discard it," said Judy. "If not, we keep the specimen indefinitely. There's no letter, so his sample should be there."

The two women stared at each other for a long moment.

"Did you find Carl Hartman's file?" asked Jamie.

"Yes. That one was just a misfiling," said Judy who suddenly burst into tears and began to shake.

Jamie put her arm around Judy's shoulder as the woman sobbed. After a moment, self-control returned, and Judy reached for the tissue that Jamie handed her.

"I'm sorry, but when I got the news about Dr. Harlow, I just lost it. Everybody here is in a state of shock. First, the tragedy of the Sorenson birth, now the doctor's lost at sea. He was a wonderful man, you know. Really kind and caring. We'll all miss him a lot."

"I know but we have to keep on going. Tell me about Carl Hartman."

"I searched for almost two hours before I located his file. It was misfiled under the letter 'C.' There was a letter from Mr. Hartman requesting that his semen be destroyed."

"Explain the symbols on this list," said Jamie after scanning several handwritten sheets containing names and other information.

"That's the list of men we have so far: name; address; personal information; race; blood type; date of donation; spouse; infertility diagnosis, if applicable; and the location of the specimen."

"What do you mean, if applicable?"

"Not every donor has an infertile partner. Sometimes, we get women who want a child who do not have a partner. A few men donate their sperm for random insemination."

"How many donors do you have so far?" asked Jamie.

"Almost fifteen hundred," answered Judy. "Most have infertility problems."

"How many African American donors?"

"Eighty-six so far."

"Why don't I start confirming the names you have?" asked Jamie.

"This number on the far right corresponds to the compartment where the vial containing the semen is stored. Each vial is kept in a large tray in a numbered slot."

Jamie grabbed the list and walked to the laboratory located at the end of the hall. Inside the lab, at the rear, was a large room containing several large appliances resembling commercial freezers. Every appliance contained multiple trays of semen vials, each frozen in liquid nitrogen to render it inactive until thawed for insemination.

She began to check the location of each of the black donors. It took several minutes to find the appropriate appliance, locate the correct tray, and match the information provided to each one. Jamie spent almost an hour and a half completing the task.

At the end, Jamie turned to the name of Steven Sorenson and confirmed the location of his container. Seeing that it contained a vial, she removed it and checked the number. A label showed the vial was out of place. Someone else's semen was in Sorenson's slot.

Jamie's head pounded as she scanned the list for the donor who matched the number on the vial in the slot. The name seemed to jump out at her.

Maxwell Evans. Black male.

Jamie was under strict orders from Whitney to preserve the chain of custody by making sure nothing was moved, so the slots would have to remain intact. She snapped digital photographs of both slots and then replaced the locks on each container and left for Whitney's office.

Shortly before midnight, Clay used his key to open the door to Harlow's Clinic and then disabled the alarm before quickly making his way through the facility to the storage area that housed the donor sperm specimen. Upon arrival, he searched for the semen container of Maxwell Evans with a small, powerful flashlight. After finding the slot where he had been told it was now housed, he removed the vial and placed it in the bag he was carrying.

Without hesitation, Clay removed an identical vial and then withdrew a syringe that was half filled with a murky-looking solution. Holding the specimen upright in front of the flashlight, he injected the contents of the syringe into the vial and placed it back into the slot belonging to Evans.

After slipping the spent syringe back into the bag, he entered the file room and approached the far-right cabinet. In a matter of seconds, he fitted a key into the lock, removed a manila file from the top drawer, and then replaced it with a substitute. He activated the alarm, exited the facility, and drove away with his window half down to bathe his face in the cool night air.

I haven't felt a rush like this since I left the company, he thought.

His mind took him back to his days as a CIA operative and all the covert operations he ran in Western Europe or Southeast Asia, with names like "Hemlock" or "Ligature." As an old sixties protest anthem began playing on the radio, its title became the perfect name for the operation. Images of each current target arose, causing Clay to chuckle as he reached for his phone to text Ricki and Eddy.

Like the old song says, I believe we're on the "Eve of Destruction."

Chapter Thirteen

Monday, October 20

A light rain was falling when Erica Payne entered her office building on Rowe's Wharf, overlooking Boston Harbor, just before seven. She found a small man in his late fifties who looked like an ex-boxer, wearing a dark Tyrolean hat, beige golf shirt, and navy Dockers. He was engaged in an animated conversation with the guard. It was Ritchie Carbone, her private investigator, waiting for her at security with a large white bag containing coffee and donuts.

"So she says my research shows that Native American men have the biggest penises and Jewish men have the most stamina, and then this guy at the end of the bar hops off his stool, comes over and says, 'Excuse me, miss, we haven't met. I'm Geronimo Goldberg'," said Ritchie as the security guard broke into a fit of uncontrolled laughter.

"Mahnin' Ms. Payne," replied the guard, still laughing. "Take George Carlin here with you, OK? It's too damn early to laugh like this."

"Come on, Ritchie. Duty calls," replied Erica, as the guard threw a playful punch at Ritchie's shoulder.

After riding the elevator to the thirtieth floor, Erica opened the office door and deposited her briefcase in her private office while Carbone walked toward the rear of the suite. She grabbed a yellow legal pad and joined him in the conference room.

"What did you find out at the hospital?" she asked.

"Plenty. And it's pretty sad."

"Tell me."

"Well, the records are sealed, so nothing's official. But I got it firsthand that the Sorenson baby is going through a pretty rough time," said Ritchie.

"How are his chances for survival?" asked Erica.

"He keeps improving every day. The nurse I talked to, a woman named Carol Casey, said they should know in forty-eight hours if he's turned the corner. Of course, even if he does, he is still under a death sentence from the HIV virus."

"Anything else?"

"No. I'll stay in touch with Casey. I think she likes me."

"Tell me what you found out about David Whitney."

"He's a blue chipper. Philips Andover and Harvard. But he did it the hard way by winning scholarships and grants to pay for his education. He has a superb reputation. Several appearances before the Supreme Judicial Court making new case law. He's never lost a case on appeal."

"Tell me about Whitney the man."

"He has a reputation as a real gentleman. Good-hearted and kind. He has a fierce sense of loyalty and fights like hell for his clients."

"You sound like we're talking about the Dalai Lama."

"His investigator is Jamie Quintell. She's first rate and looks like one of those Russian gymnasts but has the strength of a heavyweight fighter. They say the only difference between Quintell and a pit bull is distemper shots."

"Tell me about Whitney's weaknesses?"

"Only one. He has a big heart."

"I don't understand."

"He never forgot where he came from. Quintell's the same. They both live for combat, but each has a strong sense of right and wrong. He doesn't practice law by scorching the earth like some of those bastards. David is considered a tough negotiator but someone who will cave in and settle when liability is clear. So Counselor, get ready to take his ass to the cleaners. I predict you'll win in a photo finish."

"Ritchie, remind me to give you a bonus."

Carbone looked satisfied as he sipped his large black coffee.

"Just keep those checks coming," he replied with a huge grin.

It was almost ten o'clock when Jamie arrived at police headquarters in Westover. The detective in charge of Lee Harlow's disappearance was waiting, and they moved to an interrogation room where he gave her the sketchy details he had uncovered so far. Afterward, he showed her the contents of the envelope left on the windshield of Harlow's vehicle when it was parked at the Westover airport. Jamie looked over the photograph as well as a decades-old obituary and death certificate stuffed inside.

The obituary was a photocopy and had a date of January 4, 1973. Her curiosity piqued as she continued to read.

VELLOIS, Michelle, age twenty-four of Charlestown, died suddenly on January 3, 1973, from unknown causes. Loving mother of Michael, age two, and beloved wife of Lieutenant Commander Andre Vellois, who is currently deployed to Vietnam. Burial is private. There are no calling hours.

The accompanying death certificate listed the cause of death as "cervical hemorrhage." The photograph showed a much younger Lee Harlow and Jack Bartlett with their arms around a woman and Quintell made herself a note to ask Bartlett about it. After making her a copy of the documents, the detective promised to share any further developments.

Jamie left police headquarters thirty minutes later and arrived at the airport in Hyannis a few minutes before the next voyage of the Island Queen. After parking, she made her way topside for the forty-five minute ride to Martha's Vineyard. After slipping into one of the red plastic seats, Jamie sat shivering and wished she had worn a heavier wool sweater. Going below was out of the question. The cool sea air was the only thing that kept her from losing her breakfast as a result of being seasick.

As the boat pulled out of the harbor, she opened the manila file and reviewed all the information. The wreckage was recovered three miles off the coast in shallow water. Despite the heavy damage, the investigating team was able to piece together what happened. The fuel line was crimped so that a slow leak developed. In order to keep the pilot from seeing the abnormally quick loss of fuel, the gauge was tampered with to hide the actual reading. Pieces of the line were being saved for her.

Twenty minutes later, they docked, and Jamie walked to the car rental agency located next to the dock. After renting a Toyota Camry, she headed for the airport and arrived twenty minutes later. The wreckage of the plane was located in a hangar at the rear of the landing field. Jamie parked next to the hangar and entered. Then she was directed to a small office to the left.

"Mr. Landis?" she asked, after knocking and being waved in by a red-faced, overweight man in his late thirties, wearing a light-blue shirt and navy Dockers.

"Yeah, I'm Landis," replied the man gruffly.

"Jamie Quintell. I'm here to see you about the Harlow case."

"Sit down. Want some coffee?"

"I'm fine, thanks. I understand your investigation is over."

"That's right. I'm leaving for Washington this afternoon."

"So your results are official then?" asked Jamie.

"Absolutely. My report will be filed tomorrow."

"Could the fuel line have malfunctioned on its own?"

"You mean cut its own throat? Not a chance."

"How do you know the gauge was tampered with?"

"Because the levelor was bent so it would read more full than it was. Had to be done by someone intentionally," replied Landis confidently.

"There's no evidence that someone was a passenger with Dr. Harlow, is there?"

"No, but there is no way to confirm that. Someone could have hitched a ride, bludgeoned Harlow, jimmied the fuel line, and bailed out."

"That means the gauge had to be damaged when the plane was on the ground, right?"

"Yes. That would confirm what we have."

"And you're sure it could not be caused by mechanical failure of some type?"

"Absolutely sure."

"Why?"

"Because we found markings on the levelor that shows someone went to the trouble of tampering with the fuel lines. Probably used common tools like a screwdriver and pliers."

"Will you be doing a further investigation?"

"No. That's not within our function. We just look at the cause of the crash."

"What happens if you find evidence of who's responsible?"

"We turn it over to the police."

"Anything else you can tell me?"

"Yeah. Whoever was out to get Harlow did one helluva job."

David Whitney and Erica Payne were scheduled to meet at half past ten. Late Friday afternoon, Whitney had faxed all pertinent documents to Rebecca Castle, general counsel for Harlow's malpractice insurance carrier, accompanied by an urgent message notifying her of the meeting. Castle called Whitney's answering service early Monday morning, leaving word that she would attend.

At 10:15 a.m., Whitney's intercom sounded. His secretary told him that Rebecca Castle had arrived. Whitney's door opened and a tall, heavyset woman in her mid-forties was ushered in. She wore a masculine-style, charcoal-gray business suit; plain white blouse, and a sour look on her face, as if she had stomach cramps. Her hair was cropped short and was the color of ebony. She carried a leather valise and wore wide-framed glasses that softened the size of her pointed nose.

"We have a lot to cover before Payne arrives, so let's get started," she said curtly without greeting Whitney.

"It's nice to see you too, Rebecca. I see you're still putting off that personality transplant."

"I'm not here to console the bereaved. Tell me what you've got on this case."

"I faxed you a copy of Jamie's report. There's nothing to add at this point. She's still digging."

"Well, it's not sufficient. I've got my own investigators working on this case."

"What have they found?"

"The same things Quintell has."

Whitney rolled his eyes and gave his head a slight shake. "Sounds like money well spent."

"It's none of your concern."

"What do you know about Payne?" asked Whitney.

"I met her several years ago. She's known as a real ballsy bitch. Someone once described her as Lizzie Borden with PMS when she tries a case."

"Is that why you're handling this one personally?"

"It certainly is. If you start thinking with your dick instead of your head, I'm here to protect the company's money."

Whitney felt his chest tighten and his radar go off. It was time to go over the rules with Castle before he threw her out of his office.

"Let's get one thing straight up front. I'm here to protect Lee Harlow and the clinic. You can either work with me or against me; it's up to you."

"Your personal feelings mean nothing to me. I'll work for the best deal I can get for the company, and if you get in the way, I'll nail your ass to the bedpost."

Whitney glared at Castle for a moment when his intercom rang again. His secretary announced Erica Payne's arrival. She was immediately escorted in. Castle remained seated in one of the leather chairs as Payne stood in front of Whitney's desk.

"Thank you for coming, Ms. Payne," he began, extending his hand and studying her carefully.

Erica wore a form-fitting, black *St. John* suit—one that displayed her well-defined curves and long, shapely legs, which were fully accentuated by three-inch, black-and-gold *Gucci* pumps. A string of cultured pearls hung from her neck, and the only jewelry she wore besides her Chopard, a floating diamond watch, was a small twenty-four-karat gold filigree ring on her left hand.

"Let's make it informal, OK, David?" Payne replied, meeting his firm grip with hers as he smiled and nodded.

"I understand you know Attorney Rebecca Castle, counsel to Eastern Casualty," said David.

"We're acquainted," said Erica, extending her right hand, which Rebecca shook limply, like it was a diaper she had to change.

"I wanted to meet with you to go over this case," Whitney began after they were seated. "We're still conducting our investigation into what happened. I won't have an answer for several more days."

"There can only be one answer," replied Payne forcefully. "Your people were negligent, maybe even reckless, when Ms. Sorenson was inseminated. You and I know this is a policy limits case against both the clinic and Dr. Harlow. Incidentally, what are the limits?"

"Five million each occurrence, ten million aggregate," said Castle, evaluating Payne's reaction.

"That's good. I think your clients are going to need it."

"Settlement is premature until I complete my investigation. Your client may not be as clean as you think," said Whitney.

"How's that?"

"We're searching for evidence indicating that she may have been seeing a black man," replied Whitney. "That would certainly explain everything."

"Nonsense. That's a bluff you're trying to run, and it won't work."

Castle sat up straight and gave a slight huff. "I plan to have the husband tested for the AIDS virus," she barked. "If he comes up positive, we'll argue that he infected his wife. My investigators are checking out Steven Sorenson to see if he makes Bill Clinton look like a cloistered monk."

"He was already tested," answered Erica.

"What's the result?" asked David.

"We don't know yet, but it doesn't matter. Even if he tests positive, we'll argue she gave it to him after the clinic gave it to her. Why don't you save all of us a lot of headache and make me an offer? Ten million for the parents and ten million for the baby for both causes of action. Also, I'll be sending a subpoena for a DNA sample from the baby to rule Steven out as the father," said Payne.

Castle and Whitney exchanged glances. Castle brought her hands up and snorted.

"We all know what the result will be. Complete exclusion of any ancestral connection with Mr. Sorenson and this child. I think I hear the words 'gross negligence' and 'policy limits' having a fistfight to see which one gets to be spoken first," said Payne.

Castle seemed to be almost salivating as she cut Whitney off with an impatient wave of her right hand.

"Why don't we also throw in a waterfront condo in Maui for a bonus?" asked Castle, her voice dripping sarcasm. "Nice try, Counselor, but we both know you can only get ten million exposure for the whole case."

Payne brought her hands together as her lips curled into a tight, confident smile.

"We'll let a judge decide that," replied Payne confidently.

"And you'll be pissing your pants in a nursing home by the time this case goes to trial," retorted Castle, throwing down her pen and folding her arms.

"Will you be trying this case, Rebecca?" asked Payne sweetly.

"That's my intention," answered Castle, unfolding her arms and sneering.

"Then this is truly a dream come true. Not only will I cripple your client with a verdict from the stratosphere but also everyone will know it happened because they were represented by Magda Goebbels with a law degree," replied Payne.

"We can't offer the policy limits without concrete proof of exposure. Liability is certainly not clear," said Whitney.

"Then why did you ask me to meet you here?" asked Payne, jerking her thumb in Rebecca's direction. "To help her find new ways to foreclose on orphanages?"

"I need your help."

"How?" she asked.

"I need your word that neither you nor your clients will go public with this case until I have finished investigating it. If liability seems clear, I'll do my best to expedite resolution."

Erica Payne studied Whitney's face carefully before she replied. Her first impulse was to refuse and instead try to use the threat of disclosure as leverage. Why should Whitney help her? What was in it for him?

"Why should I keep my clients in check?"

"Because they may get what they want without a battle."

"Not if I have anything to do with it," snapped Castle.

"What they want is their lives back," said Payne forcefully, ignoring Castle. "You can't give them that."

"It's logical, Erica," replied Whitney, in a sincere tone. "I'm looking out for my clients' interests. They won't settle unless I tell them liability is clear. The last thing my clients need is the publicity that will come from this. I would also like to point out that your client could also do without the public scrutiny. There are a lot of people out there who might like to speculate about a white couple who gave birth to a black baby."

"You're asking for an awful lot and not giving much in return."

"It might seem that way. Actually, what I'm asking is reasonable. If you file suit and go public, the insurer will take a hard line and force you into a battle. Why not wait a short time and let me do my job and see if you can get what you want without legal bloodshed?"

"How about you, Rebecca. Isn't bloodshed part of your daily diet?" asked Payne.

"I want what's best for the company. I'm only interested in pleasing the board. In that light, I'm profit. You're overhead," said Castle, folding her hands together.

"I'm glad you were drawn to the law, Rebecca. But I'll bet it was tough giving up your past life repossessing implanted cardiac pacemakers in indigent patients," said Payne as Whitney coughed to keep from laughing.

"Give me some time, Erica, and we'll work out something fair," said Whitney, trying to quell the stiffening animosity the two women felt for each other.

Payne thought for a moment and made a quick decision.

"Tell you what. We won't go public until November seventh, twenty-one days from now. That should give you enough time to find out what happened. At that time, I will expect a check for policy limits, or I'll be filing suit in front of a television audience."

"I was hoping you'd hold off for ninety days."

"Ninety days is almost a lifetime. Three weeks is the best I can do."

"I don't think we can be done in three weeks."

"Then I suggest you hire more help. It's three weeks. Take it or leave it," answered Payne firmly, meeting his eyes and holding her gaze steady.

"I guess I'll take it," he said reluctantly, as she turned to leave.

After Payne left, Castle rose and looked at Whitney.

"Let me tell you something, Whitney. If you want any help at all with this case, don't ever take sides with the plaintiff against me again," she said in a guttural growl.

"Why are you such a hard ass? Why not try to reason with people?"

"Because I can intimidate most lawyers into settling on terms that are favorable to my client. That's my job and I know how to do it."

"You can't beat a judge or the law, Rebecca, no matter how obnoxious you are."

"Leave that to me. I've got some ideas on how to get this before the right judge. I sure as hell don't want a man on this case. This case would go a helluva lot smoother if you were a woman."

"Why?"

"Because Payne's so busy shaking her perky little ass at guys like you she doesn't know what it's like here in the trenches with someone who doesn't give a shit about her bra size. When she sees she can't pull her usual tricks on me, the value of this case will fall like a wet noodle."

Carol Casey had just finished consulting with Dr. Louis Carnevale regarding the condition of Andrew Sorenson and left for a quick lunch in the hospital coffee shop. When she entered the hallway, a black male in his late thirties was seated in one of the orange plastic seats in the family waiting area. Carol watched him struggle to his feet because of the leg braces he wore. After he stood and his crutches were in place, he hobbled in her direction. With a pang of sorrow, she tried to step around him until she realized that he was addressing her.

"Excuse me, ma'am, I have a question about one of the patients in intensive care," he began.

"Which one?" she replied.

"The infant Sorenson."

"Are you a relative, sir?" asked Carol, looking the man over from head to toe.

"No. Just a family friend."

"I'm sorry, but unless you are a member of the baby's immediate family or we have a release, we can't give out any information."

"Please, I've come a long way to see him. Can't you tell me if he's any better?"

Carol stared deeply into the dark-brown eyes that were imploring her for an answer.

"I'm sorry. We have rules."

"Can't you tell me anything about his condition?"

"I can't."

The man stared at Casey for a moment. His eyes seemed tortured, and his mannerisms seemed to indicate that he was starved for the slightest crumb of information. Finally, he responded.

"OK. I understand. Please take care of him."

"He's getting the best of care. Why don't you wait until his mother comes in? Maybe she can give you some information."

The man nodded slightly and then turned and walked away. Every step seemed an effort as he struggled with the crutches and braces that restricted his movements and confined his ability. As he walked slowly toward the elevator, Casey shook her head and felt a wave of sadness spread over her.

Jamie arrived at Whitney's office later that afternoon at the same time as Paul Sweeney, her associate and led him down the hallway to the first deserted conference room. Sweeney grew up in an inner-city housing project and was an ex-gang banger who now concentrated on body building. Although he stood only 5′10″, he had 220 pounds packed solidly on his stocky frame. His black leather jacket appeared to add to his considerable bulk.

Sweeney and Jamie had worked together for over four years. They met when Sweeney was a confidant and informer for Jake Erlich. Sweeney was an ex-convict and had done time for larceny and breaking and entering. When Jake died, and Sweeney realized his only legitimate source of income had dried up, he approached Jamie and promised to straighten out his life in exchange for a job. After several meetings, Jamie reluctantly agreed. It turned out to be the right decision when Sweeney instantly reformed and became her most valuable asset.

"OK, lay it on me," she began.

"Well, the Sorensons must be phantoms. None of their neighbors know anything about them. It's like they lived there, but were invisible."

"Did you go over their background check?" she asked.

"Yeah. Nothing stands out."

"Could it contain false information?"

"I found nothing to show that. Besides, why would they want to fake it?"

"I don't know. They both traveled a lot."

"Why on earth would they want a baby if they lived that kind of lifestyle?"

"I have no idea. Anything else?"

"No. Tell me what you need done next," he answered, removing a small red notebook from his jacket and taking out a pen.

"Top priority is confirming Lori Wegman's new address."

"I thought we found her in Texas."

"My contact there said she moved across town, and he was trying to get her new location. See if he's got a work number for her."

"I'll get on it right away."

"Next, I want you to make a list of all the senator's enemies. Since he's involved in the clinics, this could be a political act of sabotage."

"Jesus, Jamie, from what I know about Langley Mitchell, I could just bring in the phone book."

"Yeah, I know. Get me the real hardcore list first. We'll start there. What did you find out about that obituary found on Harlow's car that I gave you?"

"Very little. Christ, it was so long ago, so there's no one who's still around that I can talk to. She was the wife of a navy pilot. He got killed in Vietnam. When she died, she left a two-year-old son behind. He went to a foster home and then dropped out of sight," said Sweeney.

Jamie thought for a moment before she answered.

"OK. Keep digging and let me know what you find. That obituary and photo are sending us a message, and we have to find out what it means."

"What else?" asked Sweeney.

"I want a complete profile on Jack Bartlett."

"Why?"

"He was Harlow's partner and stands to gain the most from Harlow's loss. Control of the clinic and all that."

"What about Harlow's son? I thought he would be the heir apparent."

"He's going to run for the Senate. Bartlett will probably buy him out and keep the practice for himself."

"Is that it?"

"One final thing. I want you to check out an auto accident Austin Harlow was involved in several years ago. There was a passenger in the car who fractured his pelvis and was left paralyzed."

"What's his name?"

"Anthony Damon."

"How was Damon connected to Austin Harlow?"

"They went to college together."

"You think someone who's paralyzed could be behind this? That's quite a stretch."

"I know it's thin. Just see what you can find out. We can't rule anything out at this time, so we have to cover all the bases."

"OK, but I'm going to put that one on the back burner."

The intercom rang. Sweeney answered.

"Your DNA expert is on the line," he said, looking up at Jamie.

"Let's hope he found something," she said, reaching for the telephone.

Chapter Fourteen

Tuesday, October 21

Daybreak came shortly after six. Off the coast of the island of Martha's Vineyard, the fishing boats from New Bedford and Providence had arrived, and crews were preparing for the day's catch. The sun peeked out from the overcast eastern sky around ten to eight before climbing toward the heavens as the haze burned off.

The Island Queen left on its first run just before nine o'clock, passing the Woods Hole ferry as passengers waved and horns sounded. It was a magnificent autumn day in New England, and everyone wanted a piece of it.

Along the white sandy beaches, people searched for trinkets. Some wished for man-made treasures, hoping to gain from someone's loss. Others wanted to capture the solitude and splendor of the day, to hide in their concerns for the months ahead when the gales would make the sea come crashing in and the sky would turn into a threatening pewter-gray wall.

Among the people combing the beach in Chilmark was a young family visiting from California. Husband and wife were dressed in warm-up suits and sneakers, strolling slowly near the water's edge, as their six-year-old son ran ahead. The couple were absorbed in each other and did not see the child being drawn toward the ocean. They did not even hear him cry until he did so the second time. Instantly, the father sprinted forward and snatched his son back from the dark-blue bundle lying in the shallow water.

It was a body, bloated and black from exposure to the ocean, with its clothing in tatters. The body had drawn a carnivorous crowd from the time it had been submerged in the sea. One arm and the hand of the other were missing, as well as the entire right foot. The face was swollen and covered with dark patches. To the left of the bridge of the nose was a tremendous gaping hole where something had apparently bitten through.

The man felt the bitter taste of bile at the back of his throat and fought the urge to vomit. Scooping up his son in his right arm, he turned and shielded his wife from the body as he hurried them from the water. Minutes later, after the family had calmed down, he called the police.

David Whitney was waiting for Jamie Quintell when his secretary told him Erica Payne was calling. His heart began to race slightly as he paused for a moment and then picked up the line.

"What's up, Erica?"

"I sent you the DNA report on Steven Sorenson. It completely ruled him out as the father. This child came from another man. I presume you've seen the latest medical reports on the Sorenson baby."

"Not yet," replied Whitney, looking at the file on the left of his desk that he had been preparing to read. "I just got them."

"The baby is still on ECMO. Even if he dies, we intend to hold your clients liable for inflicting him with the HIV virus. I anticipate that I will have expert testimony that will link his premature delivery with the mother's weakened immune system. I don't want anyone to think that the problems with the baby will expire with his death."

"That's arrogance on your part to infer that Dr. Harlow would be that callous," countered Whitney, snatching the file from the upper right-hand corner of the desk.

"It's not just Harlow I'm talking about. Jack Bartlett is also involved, and Austin Harlow may be linked."

How could she have gotten the damn records already? thought Whitney angrily as he picked up the file and opened it.

"You know that the court will not let you speculate about damages if the child dies from another cause," he offered, scanning the documents rapidly.

"C'mon, David. I'll put the mother on the stand, and then you can try to explain what happened to her and her deceased baby. Then I'll cross-examine the nurses and doctors and let them tell the jury about all the tubes and needles sticking out of that tiny body and how he died because his immune system collapsed under the strain of his illnesses. Then we'll let those same jurors decide what that's worth," she replied.

Anxiously turning his Cross pen in circles, Whitney remained silent.

"The price of this case has just risen," she continued. "The baby's infection is a separate cause of action with considerable exposure for your client. That's in addition to the claims for the mother's insemination and infection. That means policy limits of twenty million, not ten. I'm calling to tell you our deal to remain silent is off. Either you offer me the entire ten million in insurance coverage to settle the baby's claim, or I'll be calling everyone I know in the media as soon as we hang up."

"Wait a minute! You gave me until November seventh. You can't go back on your word."

"Your clients have created a walking time bomb with Ann Sorenson. Every minute is an eternity, and she deserves as much time as I can get her to live out the rest of her life in peace. I won't let your clients stall until they can invent some sleazy defense or try to manufacture some dirt on the Sorensons. The deal is off."

Whitney was scanning the documents he held as he considered his options.

"How about a compromise?"

"It had better have several zeroes and a couple of commas in it."

"Give me till this afternoon to investigate what you said. If it's true, I'll recommend that we give your clients five million to settle the wrongful birth of the baby. You agree to continue your silence until November seventh. At that time, we'll either settle the negligence case against the mother, or you can go forward into suit."

"Why should I take only five million?" Payne asked.

"Because you won't have to try the damages part of the baby's case. Damages for an infant are speculative. It's not like a fully functioning adult with an education and work history. You run the risk of a judge issuing a remittitur and reducing your damage award. It's a smart play, Erica."

Payne thought for a moment. Then she made a swift, but calculated, decision.

"That's agreeable with one more proviso. We will not give you a full release for all claims, only for this one. That way, all of our other options stay open against the defendants."

"I'll call you this afternoon before the close of business," he said, hanging up the telephone as Jamie walked into his office.

She briefed him on her meeting with the detective. After seeing the photo, Whitney confirmed that the men appeared to be Harlow and Bartlett. He read the obituary and death certificate twice before shaking his head. He told her he would ask Bartlett about the documents at their upcoming meeting. Jamie told him she would dig out all the information about Michelle Vellois.

"What else is going on?" asked Jamie.

Whitney rose and began pacing before waving his hands in frustration.

"Welcome to my own private version of a Turkish prison cell," he offered as she smiled. "How'd you make out at the Vineyard?"

"Dead end. The FAA claims the plane was tampered with on the ground. There is no evidence that there was a phantom passenger. They think everything has been found and are ready to close the case unless some new evidence surfaces that someone was flying with Lee. I'll keep digging."

"What do you expect to find?"

"Who had a reason to mess with the fuel lines? Was there someone flying with Harlow? Things like that."

"How long do you need?"

"As much time as I can get. I also have to run some personal checks on the black sperm donors to see who may have inseminated Ann Sorenson. I'm also waiting for the profile report on Jack Bartlett."

"You've got to find all the answers within two weeks. I made a deal this morning that will buy us only seventeen more days. Then this whole incident goes public."

"David, I can't do this in such a short time," she protested.

Whitney shook his head, and his face took on the look of a man just handed a death sentence.

"You have no choice. Hire as much help as you need. Just do the job. And call me later this afternoon."

When Jamie turned to leave, Whitney's intercom rang, and his secretary told him Rebecca Castle was calling.

"Did you go over the medical records and reports I sent?" asked Whitney without a greeting.

"I did. The records won't change a thing in this case. If the baby dies from respiratory distress syndrome, I believe we'll be off the hook as a matter of law because we will argue any negligence was superseded by an unforeseeable event, and no one could have prevented it."

Whitney's mind raced as he was overcome by a feeling of disbelief.

"Bullshit. A jury will come down hard and hand you your ass gift wrapped. This is a policy limits case. I think Payne will take five million because she expects another ten for the insemination."

"I don't give a damn what she expects. Offer her five hundred thousand, then we'll talk about the insemination part once the investigation is complete."

"She won't take half a million. She's not a rookie."

"Then she can take a hike. Tell her it's five hundred thou, or she can stuff her scrawny little ass into an *Armani* ball gown and run into court and file suit."

"Will you listen, for Christ's sake? It's a policy limits case. That could mean ten million for the mother and ten for the baby."

"Bullshit. It's a ten-million-dollar aggregate for all claims, end of story."

"Are you that thick, Rebecca? They can file one claim against Harlow and another against Bartlett. They can also file a claim on behalf of the baby for wrongful birth and negligence, and a separate cause of action for Ann Sorenson's infection. Payne is so good she can raise enough hell to convince a judge to let each case proceed separately. If that happens, your company will be on the hook for double the policy limits. That means a full twenty, as in two times ten million, as opposed to a mere ten million dollars."

"Let her try to pull that one and I'll be all over her like body lice," sneered Castle.

"Talk as tough as you want. But if I were you, I'd cover my ass and tell the corporate hierarchy that we've talked her into taking only five million for the baby's claims because she's willing to compromise in order to wrap up that part of the case now instead of prolonging this by going to trial."

"I won't give her one damn copper cent that I don't have to."

"Payne's willing to accept five million for the baby. Either give me the five mill now, or I'll let her go public, and you bastards can see what a jury think he's worth."

"My investigators are still trailing Ann Sorenson. Maybe they'll uncover something."

Whitney threw up his hands in frustration.

"Exactly what do you think they'll uncover? That she didn't have a baby? That he wasn't black? That the genetic research is flawed and Steven is really his father? That she doesn't have the AIDS virus? That the baby wasn't HIV positive? Are you delusional?"

"I'm going to demand a DNA test for the mother," said Rebecca.

"What the hell for? Ann Sorenson is the mother. We've got a room full of witnesses. Do you think she smuggled an infant into the operating room in a Hefty bag and faked the birth? DNA just confirmed Steven Sorenson is not the father. That means it doesn't matter who his relatives are. What do you think a jury will do when Payne tacks on a death sentence from contaminated semen?"

Castle thought for a moment before making a decision.

"OK, offer the five million," she spat. "But make it clear to Payne that we will be doing some negotiating on the rest of this case that will make this exercise seem like a night in Tahiti in a hot tub."

Just before eleven, Jamie arrived at the office of the Dukes County Medical Examiner. After parking on the street in front of the ancient courthouse in Edgartown, she made her way to the last office on the second floor. Entering through the glass-and-wood door, she found the sparse reception area deserted and, after calling out, listened as a voice said that the secretary was out sick and for her to enter.

Jamie opened the door and passed into the coroner's office. Behind the oak desk with the hand-carved sign that read Burtram Weiss M.D., sat a short, elderly, gray-haired man wearing a navy suit and yellow polka-dot bowtie. Looking at her over the top of his glasses, he returned the manila file he had been reading to the left-hand corner of his cluttered desk. Files were strewn across the desktop, while several more were piled on top of the black filing cabinets in the corner.

"What can I do for you, young lady? I hope you're looking for a job as a filing clerk," said Weiss, moving his hand in a sweeping direction across his desk.

"I'm Jamie Quintell. I called about meeting with you to discuss the death of Dr. Lee Harlow."

Weiss looked up and stared at Jamie after removing the black-framed reading glasses that rested on the bridge of his nose.

"What's your interest in the Harlow case?" he asked in a no-nonsense tone.

"I'm a private investigator working with Dr. Harlow's attorney, David Whitney. Mr. Whitney is handling the resolution of Dr. Harlow's business affairs and putting the estate through probate."

"What do you want to know about the case?"

"First of all, Doctor, don't be offended, but the preliminary word showed that the body was unidentifiable. Are you sure the deceased is Dr. Harlow?"

An indignant look spread across Weiss's face, as if he was being interrogated about his alibi.

"Absolutely sure."

"What makes you so certain?"

"The facial features were severely distorted. And with no hands left on the body, we couldn't get fingerprints. But we matched the dental records precisely to the deceased. Even though I felt the records confirmed the victim's ID, just to be certain, I called in a dentist who reviewed my findings and concurred with my assessment. The body we found is Lee Harlow's. I've asked the family for his medicals records just to tie up any loose ends but as far as this office is concerned, the dental records are a positive identification."

"Where are the dental records?"

"In the file with my report."

"Can I see them?"

"The file is somewhere in the stack waiting to be put into storage. When my secretary gets back to work, I'll have her send you a copy of everything."

His tone told Jamie it was useless to press the issue.

"I understand there was also evidence of a blow to the back of the head."

"That's correct. Probably not hard enough to kill, but certainly one that would render the victim disabled for a period of time. He could have gotten it the day before and recovered though."

"Did you find a weapon?" pressed Quintell.

"No."

"Could he have struck his head when the plane crashed?"

"It's possible. Except there was no sign of blood and nothing to indicate that he hit his head anywhere in the plane. But I couldn't rule it out definitively though because of the time both the plane and victim sat in the water."

"Anything else?"

"Yes, there were traces of barbiturates in the decedent's body."

Jamie's eyes opened as wide as they could.

"What do you make of that?"

"I'm not sure. He could have taken a common sleeping pill, but that doesn't seem likely if he were going to fly a plane. That's a mystery, and I don't have an answer," answered Weiss matter-of-factly.

"How do you explain a head injury and barbiturates in his system?"

Weiss began to fidget slightly.

"Maybe he hit his head before flying and tried to get some pain relief."

"But barbiturates are not used for pain, right?"

"That's correct."

"And he wouldn't take one to sleep if he was flying?"

Weiss picked up his glasses. He stuck the end of one of the vinyl arms between his teeth and began to gnaw.

"Unlikely, unless someone slipped it in his coffee," said Weiss with a touch of irritation.

"Would a body usually decompose in salt water in just the short period of time that this one was submerged?"

"Certainly. The ocean is only about forty-five degrees this time of year, and the salt would break down the tissue and account for the discoloration. What was puzzling was the huge hole in the face on the left side."

"Describe the wound, please," said Jamie, writing furiously.

"It looked like a fish bite of some type. Like a small shark targeted the left eye and cheek, and took a chunk out of it. I examined it carefully, and it almost looked like parts of the wound were very symmetrical, like someone cut them out with a surgical instrument."

"Can you confirm there was a surgical excision?"

"No. My professional opinion is that it only looked symmetrical. I could never testify that it was. There's no question in my mind that some kind of fish did the extraction."

"What do you make of these findings, Dr. Weiss?"

"I'm still ruling the cause of death as trauma, secondary to a plane crash. Every one of my suspect areas can be explained. I'll turn over the evidence to the district attorney, even my inconclusive findings, and it will be her job to decide if there's criminal activity, not mine."

"Have you heard the plane was tampered with?"

"I was told something to that effect. It won't change my opinion," declared Weiss adamantly.

"Why not?"

"Because that's up to the FAA. If they ruled the plane was sabotaged, that's their job. If Dr. Harlow died because his plane had engine failure, that coincides with my findings. Now, if you'll excuse me, I have a full afternoon left," said Weiss in a dismissive tone.

"Are you planning to call a coroner's inquest?"

"No. The matter of Lee Harlow's death is closed," he answered firmly.

"Dr. Weiss," replied Jamie, rising and shutting her briefcase. "You may have closed the case, but as far as I'm concerned, until I see the dental records myself, it's still open."

"You do whatever you want. Last time I checked, it was my decision alone to close the case. It doesn't go to a committee, and even if it did, you don't get a vote."

After Erica Payne returned from court, her secretary buzzed and said Ritchie Carbone was on his way in. She had no sooner replaced the telephone when her door opened and Carbone entered.

His eyes seemed to be filled with excitement, like a child breathlessly waiting to tell a parent about a new discovery.

"I'm glad you're sitting. I've got a hot scoop for you."

"Am I going to like this?"

"I don't think so. I just left Carol Casey at the hospital. She told me a black man on leg braces was asking questions about the Sorenson baby. He told her he was just a family friend, but seemed pretty upset when he couldn't get any information."

"Any idea who he was?" asked Payne, with a slight hint of apprehension in her voice at his reference to leg braces.

"None. I asked around and no one remembered seeing him. Of course, it's a busy place, and everybody minds their own business, so that doesn't mean much."

"What exactly did he want to know?"

"The usual stuff. How's the baby? What's the prognosis? When will he be released? Casey didn't get a name, of course."

"Ritchie, we have to know exactly what we're up against."

"I'll start digging right away."

As he left the office, Payne's secretary entered. She was carrying a large manila envelope, which she handed to Payne.

"This just arrived by messenger," she said.

Payne reached for the envelope. After briefly scanning the return address, she deftly slit the flap with her antique letter opener and removed the documents. Quickly, she read David Whitney's cover letter and the enclosed exhibits before focusing on the attached cashier's check. Erica's body trembled slightly as her eyes swept the contents of the check made out to Ann and Steven Sorenson and Attorney Erica Payne, and listed the amount as five million dollars.

"Do you want me to deposit that in your escrow account?" asked the secretary.

"No, I'll do it. I have to go to the bank," answered Payne. *This is one deposit I want to make personally*, she thought. *It's a down payment on a new beginning for all of us.*

The October afternoon sun pulled behind the huge gray-and-black cloud cover when the silver-and-blue state police cruiser arrived at Harlow's clinic. Out stepped two detectives: one a lieutenant from the Boston Police and the other from the Massachusetts State Troopers. Both were tough, seasoned cops who were now supervisors, but they had spent some time in the roughest neighborhoods and back alleys. Years in those environments had taught them to evaluate every situation in street terms.

They went inside and asked for Dr. Austin Harlow. The security guard grabbed a red-and-white federal express envelope before he led the detectives to Austin's private office.

The Boston detective had drawn the case assignment on the day that Erica Payne called and requested a criminal investigation. After accompanying her to the hospital, he had stayed on top of the events since then, trying to piece together the parts of the puzzle that were difficult to assemble. When Lee Harlow's plane went down off the coast of Martha's Vineyard, he partnered with the trooper, who was assigned to the case to coordinate the Commonwealth's interests.

The guard led them to the elevator. Austin Harlow was waiting when they arrived. Without a greeting, he shoved a file in their direction and was given the federal express envelope.

"Those records will be used to reconfirm the coroner's identity of the body they found. Are you sure that's Dr. Lee Harlow's complete medical file?" asked the Boston cop, as Austin nodded his head.

"It's everything except dental records for the past thirty years. His dentist retired and moved to Florida, so my father got his dental records from him last year. They were stored in his private file before we sent them to the coroner's office as soon as the plane went down."

"What's the dentist's name?" asked the trooper.

"Harry Jacobs. He's in the Naples, Florida, area."

The detectives nodded and left. When they were out of sight, Austin opened his envelope from Federal Express. Inside was a single sheet of bond paper. In the middle was written an ancient quote of the English poet and philosopher Lord Byron:

"The beginning of atonement is the sense of its necessity."

Austin stared for a moment before crushing the document and tossing it into his trash can.

I'll remember it on the next Yom Kippur if I ever decide to convert, he thought caustically.

David Whitney arrived at the conference room just after five o'clock. He had been in Federal District Court most of the day, arguing motions on an antitrust case. Whitney tried to obtain a substitute so he could devote his time to the Harlow matter, but the case had been his from the start, and he was the only lawyer in the office who was capable of effectively handling the motion session.

Whitney was irritated as he walked into the room and found Jamie waiting. Absent-mindedly, he nodded as she began.

"The coroner says the body is Lee Harlow's but I'm still skeptical," she said.

"Why?"

"The body was badly decomposed. They're using dental records to make the ID."

"When will they have a definitive answer?" asked Whitney.

"Later today."

All eyes turned to the door of the conference room that suddenly burst open after a quick knock sounded. Standing in the doorway was a new first-year associate.

"Sorry to barge in, David, but I thought you'd want to know," the man began as unbridled excitement made him pause for breath. "The medical examiner issued a positive identification of the body on the Vineyard. It's Lee Harlow."

David Whitney felt the tightening in his throat as he received the news that he had feared would be coming at any moment. His long-time friend was dead.

"There's more," the associate said, swallowing hard as Whitney lifted his eyes to stare. "The D.A. called a press conference and said there is evidence he was hit in the back of the head. The police are launching an investigation into whether or not he was murdered."

Ricki called the special operator and waited to be connected. In less than a minute, Eddy came on the line, followed by Clay several seconds later. Ricki spoke first.

"A major crisis. Speed's in town, and he was seen."

"How do you know?" asked Eddy, his voice tight and concerned.

"I just found out that Carbone is hot on his trail," answered Ricki.

"Was he identified?" asked Eddy, his voice somber.

"Not positively," replied Ricki.

"Find him, Clay," ordered Eddy. "Keep him under wraps at all costs."

"How's the baby?" asked Ricki.

"No change," replied Eddy. "At least he's stable."

"We have to move soon, regardless of the baby's condition. The announcement's coming, and we have to use that leverage," said Ricki.

"I think the baby has an even shot to come out of this fine. Carnevale has all my confidence," answered Eddy.

"Anything else?" asked Ricki.

"Sweeney is still snooping around. He's been through everyone in Wellesley and Newton. I found out he's also made inquiries in Virginia," replied Clay.

"Clay, are you sure we're covered there?" asked Eddy.

"Absolutely. I've got a plant and multiple phony computer entries that will keep him going in circles for a long time. Once he finds out about the deception, I'm convinced we'll be gone and done with everything."

Chapter Fifteen

Wednesday, October 22

A light rain was falling, shrouding the day with grayness. At ten o'clock, the memorial service for Lee Harlow was underway at St. Peter's Episcopal Church in the town of Marblehead. As per Harlow's wishes, his ashes would be interred alongside his parents in the family mausoleum in Wellesley. Because of the power and influence of the Mitchell family, along with Harlow's national reputation, the turnout far exceeded the capacity of the church, and many were left on the streets after all pews were filled.

The bishop, a pious-looking celebrant with over thirty years' experience, gave a brief homily, followed by Senator Mitchell, who read a prayer. Lee Harlow was then eulogized by his longtime colleague, Jack Bartlett, who went out of his way to give a touching speech, relishing the spotlight and visualizing his future now that Harlow was out of his way. He spoke fondly about their days in medical school before dwelling on their final years of practice and how they helped hundreds of couples achieve the ultimate satisfaction of bringing a child into the world. When he finished, many of Harlow's former patients were crying.

With the service concluded, Jack Bartlett and Lee Harlow's family, along with David Whitney, retired to the home of Senator Mitchell. It was less than an hour's drive, and the entourage arrived shortly after three. They gathered in the drawing room next to the formal study.

"I'm sorry we have to discuss business at a time like this, but every second counts," began Whitney, looking into the eyes of Katherine, Senator Mitchell, and Austin Harlow, respectively.

"I don't understand the urgency," snapped the senator. "What the devil's so important that it couldn't wait?"

Whitney stared at the senator for a long moment and decided this was not the time for confrontation.

"We've got some big problems with the Sorenson case, Senator. The baby is in critical condition. If he dies, the plaintiff's attorney will claim that his immune system was weakened by the virus, which compromised his breathing and led to his death. If she finds an expert witness who agrees to testify, we could be in serious trouble," replied Whitney.

"That's why we have malpractice insurance," broke in Austin Harlow. The others nodded.

"The insurance will cover most of this, but you must be aware that if the damages exceed the coverage, all the property in Lee's estate could be at stake."

"There's ten million dollars' worth of coverage. How can they get more than that?" asked Mitchell.

"Simple. If we make liability doubtful, they will probably take less. If it becomes clear that someone at the clinic is at fault, ten million won't be enough."

"Wait a minute," said the senator. "Lee's practice was incorporated on your advice. I thought if someone formed a corporation, their assets would be safe, and they could not be held personally."

"That's usually true, Senator, but not for professionals like doctors. Lee could not escape liability for the things he did in his practice just by incorporating. His corporation only gave him tax breaks and did not provide a shield against lawsuits," said David.

"Isn't there any way around that?" asked Mitchell.

"If Lee had nothing in his name, then any judgment would be moot. It's the trying-to-get-blood-out-of-a-stone theory."

"As far as I know, Lee kept very little in his name," said Katherine.

"There is one thing that concerns me. The company holding title to the real estate for all three clinics is owned entirely by you, Senator and you, Katherine," Whitney said.

"That's the way we wanted it, David," said the senator. "No way Lee Harlow would evah be anything other than a very handsomely paid employee of ours. He didn't have that proverbial piss pot and couldn't get financing, so I had to front the money to buy the property. That's why the title is in mine and Katherine's name. He came into our family with nothing and, if it weren't for me, would still be struggling in obscurity."

"The corporation also has insurance," said Whitney.

"Is that in addition to the malpractice coverage?" asked Katherine.

"Yes," replied Whitney.

"So let the insurance companies fight over who pays. Just keep them off my back," said Mitchell huffily.

"Unfortunately, Senator, I told you that you could be held liable for personal negligence committed if you failed to follow the rules regarding corporations. I hope all your records are up to date and within the strict letter of the law, because the Sorensons have a real shark for a lawyer."

"You told us a corporation would shield us from personal liability," said Mitchell.

"Ordinarily, yes, but not this time. Against my advice, you and Katherine guaranteed the notes for the clinic real estate personally. That act exposes both of you to personal liability until the notes are paid."

"We had to guarantee them to get the loans," cried the senator. "Even with my influence, no bank would lend us several million dollars for the clinic without our signatures. The bankers would open themselves up to criminal liability."

"Better them than you, Senator," replied Whitney quietly.

"My God, David, how could you let this happen?" wailed Katherine.

"You insisted on doing these things your way. You and your father said you didn't want Lee to have any power since it was your name and money that made the clinics possible."

"Can't I transfer the assets now?" asked Katherine.

"No, that would be fraudulent conveyancing," answered Whitney sternly. "Our only hope will be to find that no one was negligent. If not, I'll have to make a deal. I'm confident there are enough corporate assets, particularly the real estate, that we can combine with the insurance policies to get you out of this mess."

At two o'clock, David Whitney arrived at the headquarters of Partners Insurance Group in the heart of the Boston financial district for his appointment. He made himself comfortable in one of the sleek, black leather chairs until a secretary escorted him down the hallway to the huge conference room. Three middle-aged men, all wearing navy pinstriped suits, white button-down shirts, and red patterned ties, were in the room when Whitney entered. The man to the left stepped forward to greet him as introductions were made.

"I'm somewhat curious as to why we could not have discussed this matter on the telephone," began Whitney after they were seated.

"We have to go over this in person, Mr. Whitney," replied the general counsel, "in order to ensure that you are given proper formal notice of the company's position."

"It should be quite simple," countered Whitney, sensing danger. "Your company holds the corporate business insurance for the officers and directors of the Mitchell Realty Corporation, the owner of the real estate housing Dr. Harlow's three clinics. There is a claim I've come to discuss, one with significant exposure to you, the insurer, and, under the terms of the policy, you must have notice. I could have done this by registered mail, but you gentlemen insisted on this meeting."

"There's a good reason for that," replied the chief executive officer. "We no longer insure the corporation."

"That's ridiculous," countered Whitney. "You've held all their business insurance for almost twenty years now. I have copies of the policies in my briefcase."

"You're partly correct, Mr. Whitney," replied the corporate vice president. "We did have the corporate insurance for many years."

"What do you mean did?" asked Whitney, sounding irritated. "If you are trying to weasel out because of some obscure clause subject to a dual interpretation, let me tell you—"

"That's not it, sir," interrupted the CEO. "The reason we no longer insure the corporation is simple. The premiums have not been paid in almost three years. I have copies of the cancellation notices and other correspondence."

"I can't believe that," sputtered Whitney as he was handed a stack of documents that he quickly scanned. "Who did you send this to?"

"Dr. Lee Harlow," replied the general counsel.

"Why didn't I get copies?" asked Whitney. "You knew I was his counsel."

"Because we received a letter from Dr. Harlow telling us you were no longer his business attorney and to correspond with him directly."

"I have a copy of the letter here," he said, offering a copy to Whitney. "It's signed by Dr. Harlow."

"I don't believe it. Lee wouldn't do that," protested David.

"See for yourself," the man replied.

Whitney stared at the letter in disbelief. It confirmed what he had been told. Quickly, he searched for the signature and found it scrawled at the bottom of the second page. David Whitney had seen Lee Harlow's signature hundreds of times over the years and recognized it instantly.

That's why he knew the one on the letter was a fake.

It was almost four o'clock when Jack Bartlett finished the last of his three scheduled deliveries and walked into the surgeons' lounge to dictate the cases for transcription. Afterward, he showered and shaved before heading back to his office for afternoon patients. Bartlett was aggravated because he was supposed to be in Nashua that afternoon. Since the corporate aircraft had been lost, he didn't have time to make the three-hour round-trip drive and instead rerouted all the southern New Hampshire patients into Boston.

The thing Bartlett missed the most was the actual flight time to Martha's Vineyard or Nashua. He'd loved flying since he was a boy and spent four years as a navy fighter pilot before he went to medical school. He still told anyone who would listen that his greatest accomplishment in life was not being a doctor; it was making pinpoint landings under adverse weather conditions in a storm-tossed aircraft carrier.

Soon after he joined the practice, Bartlett talked Lee Harlow into purchasing the aircraft. Harlow had balked at first, but then Bartlett agreed to help him obtain his private pilot's license. Once Harlow was airborne and soaring past the horizon on wings accenting the splendor of flying, he was hooked.

Austin also learned to fly, so each of them could use the plane whenever they were scheduled to see patients in Nashua or the Vineyard. It helped their practice tremendously, allowing a huge expansion of medical services because travel became much easier. Bartlett grumbled silently as he made a mental note to find out when the insurance company planned to provide a replacement aircraft.

A smile crossed his lips as his thoughts shifted from the downed aircraft to the clinic and what his new role would be. Even though Austin was Harlow's son, Bartlett was senior by virtue of his experience and expertise. His smile faded to a determined frown as he told himself he could win the clinic away from Austin in a fight. Katherine had told him about the upcoming senate campaign. He would wait until after the election and persuade her to intervene on his behalf with the senator when Austin Harlow was safely tucked away in Washington.

I know how to play dirty, thought Jack wickedly. *And I won't hesitate to kick that little bastard out on his ass.*

Reflecting on how lucky he was that Harlow had died, Bartlett hummed softly as he walked briskly through the passageway toward the clinic. He was not sorry about Harlow in the slightest. All he could think about as he unlocked the rear door to his office was how Harlow's passing had boosted his personal situation.

Once inside, he removed his suit coat and replaced it with a freshly starched white cotton lab coat with his name embroidered in navy thread over the left breast pocket. He spent the next twenty minutes catching up on paperwork. When his intercom sounded, Bartlett's secretary told him his first patient had arrived. He ordered her to send the patient to the last exam room and quickly reviewed her chart. Several minutes later, he left his office, stopped to get his nurse assistant, and then walked down the hallway to find his patient.

"Hello, dear," called Bartlett in a condescendingly syrupy tone after knocking briefly and entering, followed by the nurse.

"Hello," the patient said, smiling. She was thrilled to talk about the upcoming birth of her third child.

"How are we today?"

"Excited. How was my last bloodwork?"

"Perfectly normal. Are you having any problems?"

"I tire easily and my breasts are pretty sore."

"Nothing to be concerned about," said Bartlett, "just part of Mother Nature's plan. Go ahead and get dressed, and we'll see you next month. Nurse, will you make sure this chart gets filed?"

Bartlett turned and left the room. As he entered the hallway, he was confronted by three men and a shaken Judy Davis.

"Dr. Bartlett, I tried to keep them out, but I couldn't," began Judy, visibly upset.

"What's the meaning of this?" demanded Bartlett. "Who are you and who do—"

The tallest of the men moved behind Bartlett, grabbed his left arm, and started slipping on handcuffs as his partner spoke.

"Dr. Bartlett, we're agents from the Federal Bureau of Investigation. You're under arrest for insurance fraud. Anything you say can and will be used against you. You have the right to an attorney. If you cannot afford an attorney, one will be appointed for you. Do you understand these rights as I just explained them?"

The color drained from Jack Bartlett's face as he opened his mouth to speak but could not. Suddenly, his bowels and bladder were loose from the sheer terror he felt, and he had to squeeze his muscles tightly to retain control.

"Doctor, I'm asking you again, do you understand what I just told you?" asked the lead agent, sounding official.

"Yes," stammered Bartlett. "I mean, what's going on—I didn't do. I don't understand—"

"This is a search warrant," the agent continued, holding up a folded document. "We will be confiscating your files."

The agent jerked his head in the direction of the entrance, and the other agents guided Bartlett toward the door.

"Wait a minute," pleaded Bartlett. "Don't take me out like this. I promise I'll go with you."

"Sorry, you have to go in like this," answered the lead agent.

"All right, then, please take me through the back door. I have several patients waiting. Pregnant women who would certainly be upset if they saw their doctor being led out like some criminal."

The lead agent paused and made a quick decision.

"All right," he said, nodding toward the rear. "Take him out the back."

One agent escorted Bartlett to the rear exit as the others filed the first of three large cardboard boxes with records. As Judy went to call David Whitney, all four men disappeared from sight.

The knock at the hotel room door sent waves of fear through Ann Sorenson. She leaped up from the bed, and seconds later, the bathroom door opened, and a black man wearing leg braces hobbled into the room. He glanced at the entrance and gave her a look of fear.

"Who the hell could that be?" Ann cried as she took his arm.

"Maybe room service wants to clean up," replied the man, casting a quick glance at the table filled with dirty dishes, glasses, and other remnants of their dinner.

"Who is it?" called Ann after rushing to the door.

"Open the damned door!" commanded a man's voice.

"Oh my God," cried Ann as both she and the man recognized the voice of Steven Sorenson.

"Go ahead," called Ann's companion in a defiant tone. "Let him in."

Ann released the safety lock and opened the door. Steven was standing there with an angry look on his face. He brushed past her and burst into the room. For a long moment, he put his hands on his hips, stared at the black man, and seethed. He looked angry enough to strike them both.

"Dammit, what the hell are you doing here?" he raged, taking an ominous step toward the man.

"I came to see the baby. He might die."

Steven threw up his arms in frustration.

"You can't see the baby. We could lose everything. He's getting the best medical care, and there's nothing you can do to help."

"I couldn't stay away."

"You have to. And you have to get out of here. I'll take you to a motel out in the suburbs. Some place where you won't be seen. Start packing."

"I have to see my son in case he dies."

Steven threw up his hands in a gesture of frustration.

"OK, Speed, we'll try to figure a way to do that. But you have to promise to stay out of sight," he said.

Turning to Ann, Steven spoke in an exasperated tone.

"Dammit, can't you talk some sense into this husband of yours?" he yelled.

Ann stared at Steven for a moment before forming a sinister smile and answering.

"I'll try, but he's almost as stubborn as you are, Clay."

Chapter Sixteen

Thursday, October 23

David Whitney entered the US District Court House at 9:30 a.m. for Jack Bartlett's arraignment. He'd tried to arrange bail with a judge the previous evening, but was denied. That meant that Bartlett was forced to spend the night in the Suffolk County jail.

The charges included 155 counts of insurance fraud, all involving medical procedures allegedly performed on phantom patients, some over three years old. Whitney tried without success to gauge the strength of the government's case, but the US attorney's office refused to disclose the source of their evidence until the arraignment. The assistant prosecutor would only tell Whitney that the chief US attorney herself would be prosecuting the case if it finally went to trial. Whitney took that news with apprehension. The head prosecutor only handled the big cases—those that led to career enhancement.

The case was not called until mid-morning. Bartlett was brought into the prisoners' dock with three other men, looking disheveled and unshaven, dressed in orange inmate coveralls. Whitney returned Bartlett's pleading look and gave a tight smile of encouragement.

"United States versus Jack Bartlett," called the clerk before turning and handing a manila file to the judge.

"Who's here for the defendant?" barked the judge.

"David Whitney from Carrington, Kaplan, and Whitney."

"I'll hear from the government," ordered the judge.

"Your Honor, this is a case of alleged insurance fraud," began the chief assistant US attorney. "The defendant is a physician who practices in Newton and Edgartown. We have evidence showing he has submitted fraudulent claims for patient services in excess of two million dollars over the past three years."

"What's the evidence, Counselor?" asked the judge, peering down over her glasses.

"The claim forms themselves," answered the US attorney, raising a huge cardboard bankers' box. "And sworn affidavits from over one hundred patients who say they were never treated as the claims indicate."

"What's your source for these allegations?" asked the judge.

"An anonymous informant."

"Objection," called Whitney. "Without corroboration, that's insufficient for probable cause."

"How does the government respond?" asked the judge, peering at the prosecutor.

"Your Honor, the informant described the allegations with adequate particularity. We sought our warrant with specificity, and all counts that we filed were substantiated by what we were told. This was not a fishing expedition, as defense counsel would have the court believe, but was so exact, it bordered on a confession by the accused," replied the chief assistant US attorney as he sneered at Bartlett.

"Any bail recommendations?" asked the judge.

"In light of the amount involved and the multiplicity of charges, the defendant is a prime candidate to flee. He is a licensed pilot and could easily charter an aircraft. The people request no bail and remand."

The judge turned, removed his reading glasses, and addressed Whitney.

“What’s your response, Mr. Whitney?”

“These charges are totally unfounded, Your Honor. We assert the total innocence of Dr. Bartlett and intend to defend vigorously. My client denies all these charges and is convinced they must stem from a bureaucratic nightmare. I am confident an investigation will exonerate him. I am asking that he be released on his own recognizance.”

“I can’t do that, Counselor. The charges are too severe,” said the judge.

“Dr. Bartlett is one of the most highly respected physicians in the Commonwealth. He has deep roots in the community and is not a risk to flee. He owns a home in Weston and one in Wellfleet. I must beseech the court to set a reasonable bail in order for him to continue to attend to his patients as well as help in his own defense,” continued Whitney.

“What do you consider reasonable, Counselor?”

“Twenty-five thousand dollars. Plus my client will surrender his passport,” said Whitney, hoping to entice the judge.

“We’ll add a zero to those conditions. Bail is set at two hundred and fifty thousand dollars with ten percent surety. The defendant is also ordered to surrender his pilot’s license along with his passport.”

The call from Memorial Hospital came in just before eleven on Ann Sorenson’s cell phone. She clasped her hands together with a twinge of fear as she answered it.

“This is Dr. Carnevale. I have some wonderful news. Andrew is doing much better.”

Ann brought her hand up to her face and squeezed her lips to keep from shouting. Tears began to fall, and her entire body trembled as he continued.

"The ECMO machine and increased oxygen intake seem to be doing their jobs. I'm optimistic that he may be well enough to go home in a couple of days."

"That's fantastic," cried Ann, shoving her fist skyward. "When do you think he can be released?"

"Let's plan on Thursday. I will call you that morning just in case we decide he might need an extra day."

"I don't know how to thank you, Doctor," said Ann.

"Raise a strong, healthy son. That's all the thanks I need."

Jamie Quintell was sitting in Whitney's conference room poring over reports when Whitney's secretary told her that he was back from court and a messenger had just arrived with a document from her DNA expert.

"Bring it in right away," said Jamie, feeling the tension spread over her body.

Seconds later, the secretary entered and handed a large manila envelope to Jamie, who tore open the outside flap, removed several pages, and began to read. She was halfway finished with the first page when she looked up.

This has to be wrong, she thought, shaking her head.

After completing the first sheet, Jamie hastily placed it on the bottom and continued to read furiously. When finished, she walked to the end of the room and snatched the telephone from its cradle. Rapidly dialing Whitney's extension, she suddenly stopped and replaced the receiver. She could not tell him on the telephone.

This report would change everything. The worst part was that the findings had been confirmed repeatedly. She had to deliver the results to Whitney personally.

Quickly, Jamie walked down the hallway to his office, knocked, and entered just as he finished a call.

"Remember I told you Steven Sorenson's sperm vial was out of place at the clinic and in its slot we found sperm belonging to a black man named Maxwell Evans?" asked Jamie hesitantly, as Whitney eyed her with arched eyebrows.

"That could have been a filing mistake," he interrupted. "It doesn't prove anything."

"I had it checked. This is the DNA profile, and it shows that Evans has a 99.8 percent chance of being the father of Ann Sorenson's baby."

Whitney felt like a huge knife was twisting its way through his chest.

"Holy shit. There goes the whole case."

Jamie paused and felt her insides churn.

"There's more. They found traces of the AIDS virus in the semen."

Whitney was silent for a moment as he stared at Jamie while digesting the disclosure.

"Castle will have a seizure when she gets the news," he said finally. "Ann Sorenson is about to became a very rich young lady."

After Jack Bartlett posted bail, he and Whitney agreed to meet at 6:00 p.m. Whitney made a quick stop at this office before driving to the Registry of Deeds for Middlesex County, located in Woburn, a Boston suburb northwest of the city.

Since he'd received the news about the absence of corporate insurance coverage, Whitney had been nervous about the exposure of the realty corporation owned by Katherine Harlow and her father. He was also beginning to worry about whether or not they had committed any acts that could leave them open to personal liability.

If they had run the business without strictly following the corporate laws, a court could find that their acts were outside the corporate veil of security, which meant their shell of invulnerability could vanish before the wrong judge. A man like Senator Mitchell, with so many years of public service, surely made his share of enemies who would like nothing more than to see him fall from power. The bench was the perfect place to make that wish come true.

The Registry of Deeds would give an up-to-date summary of all transactions regarding the real property on which the clinic was located. It would also confirm that the real estate was not encumbered by any tax liens, judgments, or other types of attachments that could cloud the title to the property in case it needed to be liquidated or mortgaged.

Whitney parked in the garage next to the Registry and walked inside the relatively modern building. He glanced briefly at the crowd of people searching records as he dropped his briefcase off at an empty table before moving to a computer terminal and pulling up the Grantors' Index, a complete list of all property owned in Middlesex County. In no time, he located the name of the Mitchell Realty Corporation and was led to the volume containing a record of the deed to the clinic in Newton. Whitney breathed a quick sigh of relief as he saw the copy of the document he had accepted as the attorney for the corporation almost twenty years ago.

With anticipation, he continued to scan the documents until his eyes froze at the entry in the margin. It showed a mortgage on the property dated the previous week and listed the appropriate book and page number where the original had been recorded.

That's impossible, thought David. *The mortgage was paid off five years ago.*

Whitney continued to search until he located the mortgage. His heart began to pound as he read. A loan was taken out for two-and-a-half million dollars, almost the exact value of the property. Whitney scanned the document until he came to the signatures of Katherine Harlow and Langley Mitchell. Neither signed the document in their corporate capacity, but as individuals. In addition, each personally guaranteed the loan. That meant if the mortgage was not paid, Katherine and Langley would have to pay off the debt with their own funds.

A sickening feeling passed over Whitney as he moved to retrieve the printed documents. Although Whitney was not as familiar with their signatures as he was with Lee Harlow's, again, he was reasonably sure of one thing.

Each had been a forgery.

At four o'clock, Ritchie Carbone was waiting when Erica Payne arrived in her office. Exasperated after a long day in court, she waved to him briefly and then beckoned for him to join her in the conference room. He patiently spent time rereading his notes until she finished reviewing her messages. Then he proceeded with the latest update.

"I got a lead on the black man Casey saw."

"What did you find?"

"I had an artist draw up a composite. She made a positive ID, and so I started searching the area around the hospital."

"Find anything?"

"Plenty. A security guard remembered the guy. Said he'd never forget the sight of him walking with those leg braces. Then I started canvassing the hotels and restaurants around the hospital. I got lucky at the Holiday Inn in Government Center. The desk clerk definitely remembered him. So did a doorman. Said he was sure he saw the guy driving away in a white van with Canadian plates."

"Is he still at the Holiday Inn?" asked Payne as her pulse quickened.

"They said he hasn't been seen since last Friday night. So I guess I'm back to square one."

"Are you going to keep digging?"

"Bet your ass I am. I bribed the desk clerk to get me a list of guests and matching vehicles. Cost me two big ones. Nothing matched what we have. So far, he hasn't found any record of a van with Canadian plates. That's taking a lot longer."

"Keep me posted on everything you uncover."

"Don't worry. If this guy's around, I'll find him."

Jack Bartlett arrived at David Whitney's office at six o'clock sharp. After he was seated in the conference room, Whitney appeared with two cups of black coffee. Bartlett could barely contain his anxiety and started to speak before Whitney could motion for him to sit down.

"David, these charges are bullshit…" Jack began as David waved his hand to cut him off.

Whitney put his hand on Bartlett's shoulder and interrupted.

"Take it easy, Jack. We'll get to that in a moment. Right now, we've got other problems to discuss."

"Like what?" asked Bartlett in a fearful tone.

Whitney slid the obituary and photo the police found at the Westover airport parking lot toward him. The color drained from Bartlett's face as he picked them up.

"Where did you get this?" he finally stammered.

"They were left on Lee's car the day his plane went down."

Bartlett dropped the documents as he recalled finding the same photo under his own windshield wiper. He rose and began to pace. His eyes darted around the room, and he seemed on the verge of losing control. Then he returned to his seat, picked up his briefcase, removed the photograph, and handed it to Whitney.

"I was going to keep this quiet but I guess it doesn't matter now," said Bartlett.

"Keep what quiet?" asked Whitney as he glanced at the picture.

"Someone left that on my car a while back."

"This is the same woman in Lee's photograph. Who is she?" asked Whitney.

Bartlett stared straight at Whitney for a long moment before he replied.

"Her name is Michelle Vellois. The same one in the obituary. But you already figured that out, didn't you?" asked Bartlett in a voice that was almost inaudible.

"Tell me about her," said Whitney.

"That was taken when we were in medical school. Lee and I got invited to a birthday party for one of the residents, and we met Michelle there."

"Who took this picture?"

"I don't know. The nurses all pitched in and bought this guy a Polaroid camera for a present. Everybody kept taking pictures all night."

"What's the link with this obituary and the photograph?" asked Whitney.

Bartlett brought his hands together and stared straight ahead.

"God, David, she's part of something I thought was buried forever."

"Looks like she just resurfaced," said Whitney.

Bartlett sat back in his chair. Suddenly, he rose, walked to the window, and stared at the traffic crawling through the street below.

He bit down on his lower lip to try to maintain calm before speaking again.

"Michelle Vellois was a navy wife," began Bartlett. "She married Andre at twenty and followed him through his military training. A year later, Michael was born. Michelle and Andre were in Pensacola then, while Andre was training on jets. Then Andre was sent to Vietnam, and Michelle came home to Boston to live for the thirteen months he was on tour. The party in that photo was held two months after Andre deployed. I think she was attracted to me because I was a former navy pilot. She wound up having too much to drink at the party and I slept with her."

"Did you know she was married?"

Bartlett paused and turned away again. "Yeah, Lee told me."

"How did you justify sleeping with her if you knew she was married? Especially since you were a naval aviator? How could you do that to a brother officer and his wife?" asked Whitney.

Bartlett looked as if he had just been indicted for war crimes when he turned back to Whitney.

"Her husband was gone and she felt abandoned and depressed, and she'd had a few pops. I found out Lee also had sex with her earlier that evening. He claims she got tipsy and came on to him. He also swore he didn't know she was married. I watched them go into the bedroom and figured she was just an easy lay, so I went after her later."

Whitney's face took on a look of disgust.

"What the hell were you thinking? Damn, Jack, that's rape. No consent because she was too intoxicated."

Bartlett brought his hand up and ran it over his hair. His fingers were trembling.

"I know, but we were stupid and drunk. Lee told me that after she sobered up a little, she started feeling really guilty and freaked out about going to bed with him. Then she started slugging drinks and smoking some grass." Bartlett paused. "It didn't seem like a big deal to me with the sexual revolution in full force and all that," he said, finally, while staring at Whitney with a blank look in his eyes.

"You were a board certified asshole, Jack," Whitney said as he glared at Bartlett.

Bartlett's eyes began to form tears. His hands kept shaking, and drops of sweat appeared on his forehead.

"I know. She sobered up a little in the middle of things and started calling her husband's name. After I was done with her and got up to leave, she realized I was a stranger and really lost it. She started screaming, and Lee had to help me subdue her. I gave her an injection, and we let her sleep it off. When she woke up in the morning, I managed to convince her that nothing happened between us."

"Why didn't you take the blame for what you'd done?" asked Whitney, sounding angry.

"I convinced myself it would just go away. Maybe I was jealous because Lee was dating the daughter of a US senator, and I wanted to hurt him. A month or so later she showed up pregnant and held Lee responsible. I knew I could have been the father, but I never came forward and told her or him."

"What happened next?" asked Whitney.

"Well, it was 1972, dammit. Right before Roe versus Wade was decided, so abortion was still illegal and shameful. I agreed to perform the abortion. Lee wanted no part of it and tried to find an alternative. When I did the procedure, I tore a blood vessel in her cervix. Two days later, I found out she bled to death."

"How do you know the abortion caused that?"

"Lee and I went to the coroner's office and checked the death certificate. It said cervical hemorrhage. Lee said he felt like an accomplice to her murder. We had a huge fight. He said even a life with an impediment is better than death, and it drove a wedge between us."

"What happened next?"

"Lee was furious because I did the abortion in her apartment. He said if she had been in a hospital, a doctor could have saved her. I said there was no way a hospital would allow an abortion because I had no license and it was against the law."

"What did he say about her husband finding out if she kept the baby?"

"He knew it would ruin her life. But Lee said Andre wasn't due home until a month after the birth. Michelle could have given the baby up for adoption."

"Did anyone find out?"

"If they did know back then, no one could trace the abortion to us. It became the tie that bound Lee and I together, so to speak. The following week, we got word that Andre had been shot down."

"What happened to her son, Michael?"

"He became a ward of the state and was sent to an orphanage. I was told he died in a fire."

"Did you or Lee ever try to make amends for what happened?" Whitney asked.

"What could I do to make up for it? Lee was so upset he changed his medical specialty from neurosurgery to obstetrics. That's why he went into infertility research. He devoted his career to bringing new life into the world after he said he helped cause her death."

"Who do you think left these documents on Lee's car?" asked Whitney.

Suddenly, Bartlett's face clouded over as if a light bulb of fear had exploded.

"Lee and I got jumped by a protester outside the clinic the other day, and he mentioned that we'd killed his mother decades ago. My guess is that it was her son."

Whitney was silent for a long moment as he watched Bartlett's eyes while he spoke.

"Did you ever try to find out what happened to Andre?" asked Whitney.

"Yeah. We lived in panic for a long time that he would return and try to avenge Michelle's death. Lee even got a private detective involved, but the PI told us his military sources confirmed Andre was dead or captured in Cambodia. Finally, we gave up and got on with our lives."

Suddenly, Whitney rose from his seat.

"I think I know what's going on, Jack," he said.

Bartlett gave him a puzzled look.

"Either Michael Vellois or Andre Vellois is still alive," said Whitney. "And one of them has decided to get even with the men who killed their wife and mother."

Bartlett looked up and his eyes met Whitney's. They both had the same thought.

"Too much has happened for this to be the work of one man," Bartlett stammered as Whitney nodded. "What if they're both alive?"

Chapter Seventeen

Friday, October 24

Dawn was breaking through the cloud-filled sky when David Whitney arrived at Logan International Airport the following day for his chartered flight to Martha's Vineyard. An hour later, he was headed east for the Registry of Deeds in Edgartown.

Whitney parked on the street in front of the Dukes County Registry of Deeds just before nine o'clock, several minutes before the building opened. Impatient with waiting and doing nothing, he began to pace up and down the street past the row of waterfront restaurants and specialty stores.

A moment passed and then another. Glancing at his watch, he read 9:01. His mind becoming reengaged, Whitney turned and walked briskly back to the Registry five doors down the street. He was the first nonemployee inside the antiquated brick building.

Once again, Whiney headed straight for the Grantors' Index. He sat down behind the first public computer terminal and then quickly scanned through the pages until he found the listing for Harlow's clinic. After locating the proper book and scanning the correct page, he began reading the margin notes used by Registries of Deeds to cross-reference all related documents.

Whitney's body tensed as he focused on the last entry. Furiously turning pages, he searched for evidence of a mistake, something that would justify the entry. The only thing he found was more bad news.

The clinic on Martha's Vineyard was sold the previous week. After carefully surveying the recorded deed, Whitney examined the signatures. Once again, he was certain they were forgeries.

His mind began to furiously process the details of the transaction. The buyer of the property was listed as the Srotiart Corporation. Along with the forged deed transferring ownership, there was a mortgage recorded for $1.5 million—the total value of the property. That meant that after the transfer, the property had no equity.

All of the mortgage documents had been signed by a man named Andre Vellois, who was listed as president of the corporation. Whitney sat up straight as he remembered that surname on the obituary and his conversation with Bartlett. David printed copies and then retrieved his briefcase. As he was ready to close out of the index, a notation on the bottom-left corner of the page suddenly caught his eye.

Whitney's pulse raced as he ripped through the book to the page number in the referenced notation. Stunned, he read the entry and desperately tried to make sense of it. The page showed there was another mortgage on the property for the exact same amount, $1.5 million, which had been recorded ten minutes after the prior mortgage and dated the day after Lee Harlow's plane went down.

That meant two different banks lent the Srotiart Corporation a total of $3 million for a piece of property worth only half that amount. The attorney for each bank was Robert Smith. Whitney thought it was strangely coincidental that each bank had an attorney with the same name.

It looked like the second Robert Smith missed the first mortgage when he recorded his documents. Since no mortgage was found, he thought the property was unencumbered, or free from liens, and allowed his bank's loan to go through. Now, with both mortgages recorded, one, if not both banks, would be stuck with a bad debt, and the conveyancing attorneys would be exposed to claims of legal malpractice, bordering on fraud.

This is crazy. Some lawyer has made a huge mistake, thought David. He shuddered as his mind immediately supplanted professional negligence with criminal conspiracy.

What if it's the same Robert Smith representing both lenders? he thought. *That means it's out and out larceny! Smith's in cahoots with the borrower and finessed two different banks for a loan at the same time. They stole the damn money like they had masks and guns.*

That meant discovery of the fraud wouldn't occur until the monthly mortgage payments failed to be tendered. Criminal investigations would not commence until the borrower defaulted. By then, it would be weeks too late to stop Andre Vellois and his lawyer, who were probably already lying on a sun-soaked beach, collecting compound interest, and laughing all the way out of the bank.

Whitney knew that someone had gotten away with some very clever acts of outright fraud. Someone named Andre Vellois, as in the husband of Michelle, whose life ended in homicide so long ago.

The clouds disappeared and the sun was perched high in the sky when Ritchie Carbone reached the garage next to the Holiday Inn in Government Center. After parking in one of the last slots on the bottom level, Ritchie climbed the stairs and headed for the attendant's booth. A man in his early fifties, with coal black hair streaked at the temples and a thick salt-and-pepper moustache, was watching a small-screen television when Ritchie reached the booth.

"Hey, pal, got a minute?" asked Ritchie.

"I ain't goin' nowhere until six."

"I'm trying to locate someone. Maybe you've seen him."

"You a cop?"

"Naw. PI."

"Well, Mr. Magnum, I'm real sorry; my memory has faded worse than my oldest pair of Levis."

Smiling, Ritchie reached into his shirt pocket and produced a twenty.

"Will this bring it back?"

"Maybe just a little," replied the attendant, snatching the bill. "But everything's still real blurry."

"Gettin' clearer?" asked Ritchie, shoving another twenty forward.

"Damn, like I scrubbed it with Windex," said the attendant, pocketing the other bill and grinning as he turned down the volume on the television.

"I'm trying to locate a black guy who was pretty crippled up. Stayed at the hotel last week. Had to use leg braces and crutches to walk. Maybe drove a van with Canadian plates. Seen anyone like that?"

"Yeah. You couldn't miss him. He had a helluva time moving around even with those crutches. Looked like he was hurt pretty bad."

"When did you see him last?"

"Friday. He came out here with another guy who was helping him with his bags."

"What did the other guy look like?"

"Damn, I'm real sorry. That cloudy front just moved in again."

"Jesus Christ, gimme a break. Look, I only got sixty bucks left. Will that get me the whole story, or am I gonna have to take out a mortgage and get Trump to co-sign?"

"For another sixty, I'll tell you my life history as a bonus."

"Right now, I just wanna know about the other guy with the black man."

"He was about six-three. Blond, good looking. Drove a black Beamer. Real sharp."

"Why do you remember him so well?"

"He asked me to help with the black guy's luggage. Plus, he gave me ten bucks just for carrying one bag. I remember the car because my kid brother used to have one just like it."

"Anything else you remember about this guy?"

"Just some letters on his license plate."

"Are you shitting me?"

"No. This job makes me notice license plates. Just to get rid of the boredom. I remember his plate had the word 'Rae' in it."

"Why would you remember something like that with all the cars you see?"

The man's face softened, as if he was remembering his first kiss.

"Because I was in love with this babe named Kayla Rae. Everyone called her Rae. She had an ass made in heaven and moved it like one of those acrobats in the circus. She had lips that made you believe she could suck the seams off a basketball through a piece of ziti, and all the while, you felt like she was just enjoying a jelly donut. So I guaran-damn-tee you I'll never forget her name. When I saw it on his car, it stuck."

"What else was on the plate?" Ritchie asked.

"Christ, who do I look like, Seigfreid or Roy?"

"Do you remember anything at all?"

"Just some numbers."

"Before or after 'RAE?'"

"Hell, I don't know. Who could remember that?"

"Hear any names used?"

"Just one. The black guy said something about following the white guy to the Mass Pike and called him Clay."

"Clay? You sure?"

"As sure as I can be for a hundred bucks."

It took Jamie Quintell less than thirty minutes to check the records at the Registry of Deeds in Nashua, New Hampshire, before heading back to Boston. Traffic was snarled, and it was almost five when she reached Government Center. Once inside, she found Whitney in the conference room alone, reviewing documents that now filled four large accordion files. Briefly looking up, Whitney grunted a short greeting as she entered.

"What did you find in Nashua?" he asked.

"Bad news. All the real property owned by the clinic was conveyed several days ago. The deed was to a company called Srotiart Corporation. Someone named Andre Vellois signed all the papers. Something else that's strange. The property has two mortgages. One used to finance at the time of closing and another for the same value right after it."

Whitney sat up straight and let out a short gasp.

"Damn. Was the lawyer's name Robert Smith?" asked David, leaning forward.

"Yes. How did you know?"

"Because I found the exact same results."

"What banks did you find in Edgartown?"

"Northeast Federal and East Coast Commercial."

"Same in New Hampshire. It's funny that both mortgages were recorded on the day Lee Harlow's plane went down. It looks like Mr. Vellois and his lawyer pulled a real fast one on some mortgage lenders," said Jamie in a voice that almost had a tone of admiration.

"Did you copy all the documents?"

"Of course," she replied, opening her briefcase and removing a file. "The thieving bastards charged me a buck a sheet, but I got them all."

"Ever heard of this guy Vellois before?"

"Just what you told me about his wife, Michelle."

"Are you familiar with Katherine Harlow's signature?"

"I've seen it once or twice. Why?"

"I've got a specimen of hers here. Compare it to the signature on the deed," answered Whitney, shoving the papers at Jamie.

Jamie looked at the two signatures for a moment and then studied them very carefully. She placed her hands on the table and leaned forward to get a closer view.

"The one on the deed is a forgery," she declared flatly, as Whitney nodded.

"Run a trace on all these signatures. Make it a top priority."

"Anything else I need to know?"

"I finally got Paul's report on Jack Bartlett. Seems he left his practice in California under questionable circumstances. One report said he was on the verge of being indicted when he agreed to surrender his license and leave the state. I had it checked out and his status is listed as voluntary resignation."

"What do they claim he did?"

"Insurance fraud."

"You're kidding. What did they have for evidence?"

"I'm told it was some documents his lawyer could have explained. That's why they let him resign instead of being prosecuted."

"Does the evidence show Jack did it?"

"Probably. He certainly needs the money, David."

"For what? He does pretty well practicing medicine."

"Bartlett's got a major league gambling problem. He built up quite a tab and then tried to skip out on some markers with the big boys in Las Vegas when he headed east. A couple of their emissaries paid him a visit and managed to give him a little character guidance that convinced him to square up."

"Maybe he's reformed."

"Not so. Paul confirmed that he still has the problem. He spends most of his time at the tribal casinos in Connecticut."

"Are you checking that out?"

"Definitely. Incidentally, David, did you ever get a copy of Harlow's dental records from the coroner?"

"No. I called Weiss and he claims he can't find them. He says he's still looking and will send us the information when the records turn up."

"Damn, how long will that take?"

"It doesn't matter, Jamie. That's a dead end. Positive ID, remember?"

She shook her head as a wave of stubbornness floated over her.

"I don't care. I won't be convinced until we see the records and get our own dentist to make a positive confirmation."

It was almost twilight when David Whitney arrived at the clinic for his meeting with Jack Bartlett. Bartlett was seated behind his desk thinking about his situation. The more he thought, the angrier he became.

I'm losing patients left and right. I might as well take the rest of the year off, he fumed.

Bartlett began complaining as soon as Whitney entered.

"Dammit, all my patients are bailing out on me. If this keeps up, I won't have a practice left by next week. How can you let those sons of bitches get away with this? Why can't you get these trumped-up charges dismissed? What the hell kind of lawyer are you?" shouted Bartlett, throwing up his arms in a fit of rage.

"Listen, you pompous asshole, I'm the only thing keeping you out of jail, so don't get me aggravated, understand?" shouted Whitney, his patience exhausted. "Either you cooperate or go find yourself a new attorney."

Bartlett looked deeply into Whitney's flashing hazel eyes and knew he had pushed too far.

"I'm sorry, David. I'm at my wits' end over this thing. Tell me what you want me to do," said Bartlett.

"I want you to stop whining and help me find some answers. I'm trying to save your practice, Jack, because of how I felt about Lee. I'm used to dealing with one crisis after another, but I've been hit in the face by so many ax handles since the Sorenson baby was born, I don't know what's coming next."

"Can I help?" offered Bartlett.

"Do you know of anyone who had a monstrous grudge against Lee or his family?"

"Not really. Of course, the senator's been in Washington for a long time, so I'm sure he has enemies."

"I don't think anyone's out to get the senator. But Lee and Katherine are another story. Someone has been forging documents that have put Lee's estate and Katherine in severe jeopardy."

"How do you know they're forged?"

"Because I know both their signatures," answered Whitney, studying Bartlett's reaction. "You were roommates when he married Katherine, right?"

"Yeah."

"What was his relationship with her family?"

"They never accepted him, and he always resented them. Then there was that business about Lee's father and how he died."

"Tell me the details."

"Well, you know Lee grew up with considerable wealth," began Bartlett, folding his hands over his knees. "Right after Lee and Katherine got engaged, Trenton's business began to crumble. There was a scandal about embezzlement and bankruptcy. The old man was crushed because that was a time when insolvency was considered shameful. Lee went to the senator on the eve of his wedding and begged him to help his father. The senator refused because he didn't want his name tainted. Then, Lee's father died and his relationship with the senator became so hostile he vowed to never ask the senator for help again."

"Why did the senator think he would be linked to Trenton?"

"Guilt by association, I guess."

"Tell me about Trenton's death."

"Well, Trenton died mysteriously while Lee and Katherine were on their honeymoon and the body was cremated before they returned. It was rumored that the cause of death was suicide. Lee was convinced that someone was hiding something because he couldn't believe his father would take his own life. Then he found out that Senator Mitchell claimed it was a routine heart attack instead of suicide to avoid a scandal. Lee never forgave him. But, since Mitchell made it possible for Lee to get financing for the practice, Lee let it slide even though I suspect it continued to eat away at him."

"Why did the senator allow Lee and Katherine to marry if he disapproved?"

"Because Austin was born seven months after the wedding,"

"You mean Katherine was pregnant when they got married?"

"Absolutely. The senator was pretty straitlaced about matters like that."

Whitney paused as Bartlett began squirming and flexing his fingers. He decided to move on.

"You two became partners about nine years ago, right?"

"You drew up the papers for us. Why are you asking me about that?"

"Because Lee never gave me any details on why it happened. I left the financial details blank so Lee could fill in the figures himself. You know how he was when he didn't want to talk about something. Lee just said that you were joining him, and he wanted a partnership agreement drawn up. Tell me how you two decided to associate."

"I was practicing in Southern California and wanted to get away from all the nuts and weirdos out there, and come back East. I called Lee, and he said he needed some help, so he brought me into his practice."

"How did he treat you then?"

"Like he always had. Our relationship changed about four years ago."

"When did you become a full partner?"

"As soon as I joined the practice," replied Bartlett, as Whitney raised his eyebrows.

"How much did it cost you to buy a partnership?"

"One hundred thousand dollars," answered Bartlett sheepishly. "The senator managed to convince Lee that my medical reputation was worth the price of admission."

"You mean you came into a multimillion-dollar practice and only put up a hundred grand? It should have been worth at least a million and a half. Why would Lee agree to that?"

"I'm sure the senator pressured him to do it."

"But Lee and the senator hated each other. Why would Lee do anything for him?"

"He probably did it for Katherine," answered Bartlett, sounding uncomfortable.

"Something doesn't add up here, Jack, and you're making me drag it out of you. It would be a helluva lot easier if you just told me."

"I was going through a bad time. My wife and I split up, and my practice was on the skids. Katherine helped me out because we were old friends. That is, we were good friends before she married Lee."

"Is that all you're going to tell me?" quizzed Whitney.

Bartlett paused and began to shuffle back and forth.

"I think Lee suspects that I had an affair with Katherine."

"Did you?" asked Whitney, looking directly into Bartlett's eyes.

Bartlett stared straight ahead for a long moment.

"Yes," answered Bartlett, looking away.

"When did Lee begin to suspect you two?"

"Not until after I moved back and went into practice here. That's when he changed."

"How do you know?"

"Lee caught us at their home one afternoon. We weren't in bed or anything like that, but he knew I wasn't there for tea."

"Is it still going on?"

Bartlett looked away again, and Whitney had his answer. Suddenly, he thought of the question that had to be asked.

"How long have you and Katherine been seeing each other?"

"Off and on since Lee and I were in medical school."

"Jack, could you be Austin's father?" asked Whitney carefully after putting down his pen and folding his arms.

Bartlett was silent for a long moment before he replied.

"I don't know. Neither does Katherine."

Chapter Eighteen

Monday, October 27

David Whitney was reviewing his case files when Erica Payne returned his call shortly after nine o'clock.

"I need you to agree to extend the deadline for going public on the Sorenson case," began Whitney.

"Why would I do that?"

"Because our investigation is progressing slower than we anticipated. I'm sure we can have everything wrapped up in thirty days."

"Not a chance. An extra month won't change the facts or buy your clients the miracle they think is waiting for them."

"This is in your clients' best interests too," he said.

"How?"

"This will be the last extension. When it's up, I'll either make you an offer or invite you to go public and file suit."

"I can do that right now. What difference will thirty days make for my clients?" she asked.

"Waiting might make us going to war moot," he answered.

"In your dreams. That baby could still die, and he and his mother are HIV positive. Thirty days won't change that," she said emphatically.

"If you go public, we'll dig in our heels and refuse to settle," said Whitney.

There was a long pause.

"That's certainly your choice if you want to play it like that. But there's an election coming up and hundreds of new patients who will be needing medical care from the clinics, so if your clients want to watch all of that disappear like a bad dream, then get ready for a battle."

They spent almost another half hour with Whitney trying to convince Payne to extend the deadline. She flatly refused to reconsider the terms of their agreement, and continued to remind him of what his clients had at stake compared to hers.

Finally, frustration forced him to give up, and they agreed to a settlement conference for Thursday of the following week. There was no doubt in his mind that he should be offering the entire policy value, ten million dollars, plus whatever assets Katherine and the senator might be forced to surrender in order to end the case. That meant a battle on two fronts: one with Rebecca Castle, and the other with his clients.

The biggest reason Whitney knew the case had to be resolved was because a jury could turn its collective rage against the doctors into a $20 or $25 million windfall. Plus, they could tack on several million dollars more for punitive damages.

Whitney turned at the sound of his private line. He picked up the receiver and a distinctly feminine voice began to echo in his ear.

"Mr. Whitney, this is Lizzie Emerson from the *Boston Globe*. I'm investigating the circumstances of Dr. Lee Harlow's death. There are rumors that something disastrous happened at the clinic before Dr. Harlow's plane went down. We have reports that a patient of his was inseminated with the wrong sperm. As Dr. Harlow's lawyer, will you give me a comment?"

Whitney felt a cold chill as he digested her words.

"My only comment is that you are fishing for a story that doesn't exist," he said.

"So you're saying there is no truth to the rumor about a negligent insemination?" she asked.

"No, I'm saying you're pissing into the wind because you think every potential story is a reincarnation of the movie *Spotlight* where you can invite everyone at the Globe to link arms and sing, *Auld Lang Syne*," barked Whitney before slamming down the phone.

The US Airways flight carrying Jamie Quintell landed at San Diego International Airport a few minutes before three o'clock. Grabbing her carry-on bag, she arrived at the Hertz counter ahead of the rush. Fifteen minutes later, Jamie was headed north on the freeway toward the town of Vista.

Traffic was gridlocked as Jamie found herself trying to follow her GPS and change lanes at the same time. It was almost a quarter past five when she finally found the yellow ranch. After parking in front of the house, she walked briskly up the front steps and rang the bell. Immediately, a tall, thin, African American woman who appeared to be in her early forties answered the door.

"Yes?" inquired the woman.

"Are you Kenesha Evans?" asked Jamie.

"Who are you?"

"My name is Jamie Quintell. I'm a private investigator from Boston. I need to talk to you about Dr. Lee Harlow."

"What about him?"

"Were you a patient of his?"

"Well, I was a patient at his clinic. Dr. Bartlett treated me there."

"We have a situation that may involve you and your husband. It's urgent that I find Maxwell Evans as soon as possible."

Kenesha's face began to flood with anger.

"What is this, some kind of sick joke?"

"Ma'am, please. I have to speak with him. It's life and death."

Tears began to well up in Kenesha's eyes.

"You can't speak with him. He's dead."

Jamie took a step backward as though a knife was ripping through her body.

"I'm so sorry. I didn't know."

"Why did you come here?"

"Because a woman just gave birth to a baby, and the tests show that he was probably the father."

Anger began to surface as Kenesha replied. "Now wait just a damn minute," Kenesha exploded. "If you're trying to claim Max was unfaithful and shake me down for money, it won't work."

Jamie shook her head vigorously from side to side.

"Ms. Evans, I swear it's nothing like that. The records show your husband donated his semen for your insemination, and somehow, another woman got his sperm by mistake. I'm trying to find out how it could have happened."

Kenesha felt her anger ease as she looked into Jamie's eyes. They seemed sincere.

"Maybe you'd better come inside," she said.

Ten minutes later, Jamie sipped her tea and smiled sadly at Kenesha, who was pouring a cup of coffee. They were in the small, pristine kitchen seated at a wooden breakfast table next to a bow window overlooking the majestically maintained flower garden in the back yard.

"Dr. Bartlett told us that Max's semen was going to be destroyed because the risk of our having children was too great."

Jamie had a puzzled look on her face, as if she was trying to solve a riddle.

"What kind of risk did you run for having a child?"

"Well, Max worked at Suffolk General Hospital in Boston before he took the teaching position at San Diego State University and we moved out here. One of his friends, a geneticist at Suffolk General, did a genetic profile on each of us after we decided to go for infertility treatment."

"What did it show?"

"Max had a recessive gene that could cause Huntington's disease in the baby."

"That results in nerve problems in someone's brain, right?" asked Jamie.

"Yes. We discussed it with Dr. Bartlett, and he advised us not to conceive because the risk was too great of passing the condition on. He told us Max's semen would be discarded right away," said Kenesha.

"Why were they storing his sperm at the clinic before you knew about the genetic problem?" asked Jamie.

"Dr. Bartlett said it was a good idea to have a specimen in storage in case Max became impotent through injury or something like that. He recommended we keep it frozen so we could consider taking a chance on other options, like a surrogate mother. He said they usually stored a patient's semen until all the procedures were done, just to be prepared for an unforeseen event."

"So after you found out about the recessive gene, you decided to stop with your fertility treatments?"

"That's right. They were supposed to destroy Max's semen then. I know Max sent a letter to the clinic."

"How did your husband die?" asked Jamie.

"Heart attack. The doctor said his coronary arteries became completely occluded, and he died suddenly," said Kenesha, reaching up to wipe away several tears that had formed.

"What kind of work did he do?"

"Biomedical engineering. He was trained as an electrical engineer and was responsible for approving all the electrical devices used in the operating room."

"Are you from Boston originally?"

"Yes. I grew up in the South End."

Jamie looked at her for a long moment, trying to decide if she should disclose the devastating news about her husband's semen. Finally, she made a decision.

"I have something else to tell you."

Kenesha looked deeply into her eyes as Jamie continued.

"I'm afraid both the mother and baby were HIV positive. We tested the semen, and it contains the AIDS virus. You probably need to get tested right away."

Horror spread across Kenesha's face.

"Oh God, you're telling me Max was HIV positive?"

"The sperm showed the virus was present."

"It can't be true."

"We did the test three times. Each time it was positive."

Kenesha began to cry softly as Jamie reached over to touch her hand and whispered, "I'm really sorry this happened."

"That semen was almost three years old," said Kenesha. "If Max had the virus then, there's no doubt I have it now."

Chapter Nineteen

Tuesday, October 28

It was after 9:00 a.m. the following morning when David Whitney finished reviewing the reports Jamie Quintell had submitted. His intercom rang, and he was informed that Katherine and Austin Harlow had arrived for their meeting, accompanied by her father. Closing the file, Whitney grabbed a legal pad and walked down the hallway to meet them in the conference room. He had barely gotten through the door when a grim-faced Senator Mitchell started asking questions.

"David, what the hell is going on? Who's responsible for this mess?"

"How could you let this happen, David?" hissed Austin Harlow.

"Yes, how could you?" snapped Katherine.

Whitney stopped and threw up his arms for calm, like a referee signaling a time out.

"Look, folks, either you give me a chance to respond, or we can scream at each other all day," replied Whitney. "Frankly, I'm just as outraged as you are, but I don't have the luxury of blowing up at anyone. So you can either help me solve this puzzle before the whole world collapses, or we can take turns playing 'I'll get you at recess.'"

Senator Mitchell folded his arms in a manner shared by those used to being coddled, not scolded, as Austin Harlow moved behind his mother's chair.

"What can we do to help?" asked Katherine.

"Try to think of who might be out to destroy you," said Whitney, matter-of-factly.

"Why do you think it's a conspiracy?" asked the senator.

"The clinics have been sold through fraud."

"Good God, how could that happen?" asked Katherine as the others gasped.

"I'll be filing suit to void the sales even though the banks will object," said Whitney.

"I'll deal with the damned banks," said Mitchell.

Whitney continued, "We also just found whose semen was used on Ms. Sorenson."

"How do you know it's the right sperm?" asked Mitchell.

"The DNA profile matched."

"Is the donor black?" asked Katherine fearfully.

"He is," answered Whitney.

"My God," the senator responded.

"Do any of you know someone named Andre Vellois?" asked Whitney.

"No. Why do you ask?" replied Katherine.

"He's the person who was involved in all the real estate transactions. Are you sure that name does not ring a bell? Maybe by a different first name?"

Everyone shook their heads, but Whitney was sure the senator flinched when Vellois'ss name was mentioned. Finally, after a series of denials, Whitney decided not to press the issue until they were alone.

"Senator, Katherine, I need to know each of your financial positions before we proceed," continued Whitney.

"Why?" demanded Senator Mitchell.

"Because if the clinic has no assets, then you both face personal liability in the Sorenson case as owners of the real estate."

"Dammit, man, I thought that's why people formed corporations," thundered the senator.

"Senator, we've been over this before. They must perform their company duties in a corporate capacity or forfeit their protection. I've found that no corporate conditions statements have been filed in years. Someone also filed articles of dissolution for the corporation over a year ago," said Whitney.

"What does that mean?" asked Katherine, suddenly grabbing the armrests on her chair and looking as if she had just received an eviction notice.

"It means the corporation no longer exists," replied Whitney.

"I thought you said these documents were all forged," exclaimed the senator, his face turning red. "Why can't you go into court and have everything declared illegal?"

"We can, Senator, but that means reporters and television cameras. Do you want to face that right now with this Sorenson cloud hanging over our heads? The publicity could be a killer," counseled Whitney.

All were silent as they began to fidget.

"There's more bad news about your real estate corporation. I found evidence that corporate funds were co-mingled with your own. That's a red flag to someone suing you."

"What do you mean?" asked the senator.

"Did you lend Lee two hundred and fifty thousand dollars last spring?" asked Whitney, holding up a document.

"Yes. He said he needed it for new equipment. Why?" replied Senator Mitchell.

"Did you write the check out of your own account?" pressed Whitney.

"Of course. After Katherine and I signed the note, the bank gave us a check we each had to endorse. We ran it through our joint account. I don't see the problem," said the senator.

Whitney shook his head as they all looked confused.

"You can't do that. Erica Payne can argue that your act of co-mingling funds means the corporation is a shell. If she can convince a judge she's right, you will both be on the line personally," Whitney replied.

"We're all being destroyed!" cried Mitchell.

"Not yet. Give me some help here. What's your financial situation?"

"I've got about one million in assets and another million, five hundred thousand in my campaign fund," said the senator hesitantly, leaning forward and folding his hands over his knees.

"Katherine?" asked David.

"A few hundred thousand in assets, plus the trust fund from my father."

"How much is in the trust?" asked David.

"Over a million," replied Katherine, as her voice trembled.

"What about Lee's life insurance? You haven't received the proceeds from that policy yet, have you?"

"He's only been dead a few days, David," said the senator gruffly. "With everything that's happened, how could anyone have thought of cashing in Lee's life insurance policies?"

"I'll take care of that for you right away. He had five million dollars in key man life insurance through the corporation. That amount hasn't changed over the years, has it?"

"That was your recommendation, David, and we made sure it was followed," answered Mitchell.

Whitney was about to reply when the intercom rang. After reaching for the telephone, he had a short conversation and instructed, "Put him on."

The color drained from Whitney's face as he listened silently for several minutes. Finally, he said, "Get me a complete report by the end of today."

"What was that all about?" demanded Austin.

"That was Martin James, my accountant. I've had him auditing the books of the three clinics. He found over two million dollars in deposits missing."

"I don't believe this," shrieked Mitchell.

"There's more," continued Whitney, staring straight ahead. "He also talked to the IRS. They intend to make a claim against the clinics for unpaid taxes. They've given us thirty days to come up with one hundred and seventy-five thousand dollars in back taxes and employee withholding, or they will shut everything down."

Jamie Quintell's flight landed at the Dallas-Fort Worth International Airport later that morning. She walked to the first taxicab in front of the terminal and gave the driver her destination of Central Texas Medical Center. It took her less than ten minutes to reach the facility.

"You'll need to fill out the forms on the clipboard and make sure you put your insurance information down," said the receptionist without looking up, as she continued to sort several stacks of patient charts while answering the phone at the same time.

"Excuse me," replied Jamie. "I'm here to see Lori Wegman."

The receptionist pointed toward the rear as she sorted. "She's in the rear of the clinic."

Jamie entered through the first door on the right. Passing several cubicles filled with doctors, nurses, and patients, she came to a small desk with a young Asian woman sitting in a wooden chair talking on the telephone. Jamie waited until the conversation finished, and the woman looked up at her.

"I'm looking for Lori Wegman," said Jamie.

"She's with a patient, but should be right out," replied the woman, before grabbing a medical chart and heading down the corridor.

Several minutes later, a tall, thin, dark-haired woman in her late thirties came to the desk. She was wearing light-blue scrubs.

"I'm Lori. Are you looking for me?"

"I'm Jamie Quintell. I need to speak with you for a few minutes about Dr. Lee Harlow," Jamie said, watching as Wegman flinched slightly.

"Who are you?"

"I'm a private investigator. Look, this is kind of complicated. Could we go somewhere private for a few minutes?"

"Is Dr. Harlow in trouble?"

"Dr. Harlow's dead, Ms. Wegman. The evidence suggests he was murdered. I'm investigating what happened to him," replied Jamie.

Lori's eyes grew larger and then filled with tears.

"Wait here. I'll take my break now and get someone to cover for me."

Several minutes later, they were alone, sitting in a secluded corner of the nurses' lounge.

"How did he die?" asked Lori, as she dabbed at her eyes.

"Plane crash a few days ago."

"I didn't see it on the news," said Lori.

"The coverage has been sketchy because it's still being investigated."

"What do you want from me?" asked Lori, clutching her coffee cup.

"Information. Did you know a patient of Dr. Harlow's named Ann Sorenson?"

Lori thought for a moment. "Vaguely. Why?"

"Everything started with her. She was inseminated by Dr. Bartlett through an in vitro procedure. She and her husband are both white. She had a baby several days ago, and he is black. The tests show she got semen from a black man named Maxwell Evans. Do you remember anything about this case?"

"Not much. We had a lot of patients, and I didn't get to know many of them personally. Why are you singling me out?"

"The records show you handled the semen washing and transfer from the donor to Dr. Bartlett."

"That was my job. I didn't do anything wrong."

"No one's accusing you. I need to know what you remember about the day of the procedure. Ann Sorenson is in her early thirties. Very pretty. Someone who might stand out."

"Wait a minute, is she married to a tall, good looking guy with blond hair?" asked Lori.

Jamie nodded.

"I remember him a lot better. He made a few jokes when he gave me his sample. Like why didn't I come in and help him, you know? The usual guy stuff."

"She was inseminated last February twelfth. The records show you were responsible for the insemination procedure."

"I remember handling his sperm a couple of different times. But I don't remember anything about that day standing out."

"Did Dr. Harlow get called to an emergency?"

"I'm not sure. Wait a minute. He did, but it was canceled, right?"

"That's not in the record."

"Well, I remember it was canceled because Dr. Harlow came back from the hospital and told me he would get the semen from the father. He said they were personal friends. That stands out because I never saw him do that before. After he collected the semen, he had it spun down before he gave it to me. I delivered it to Dr. Bartlett."

"And you say that was unusual?" asked Jamie, continuing to write.

"Our procedure was to stay with the donor until he ejaculated and then make sure the sperm was processed and delivered so there would be no chance for a mix up. I remember this case now, because it was the only time Dr. Harlow ever handled the sperm before I delivered it."

"Are you sure about this?"

"Absolutely. I remember every time something out of the ordinary happened because it was so rare. That's why I'd never forget him collecting the sperm for me."

"Did you ask Dr. Harlow why he collected the sample for this case?"

"Not after he told me he was friends with the husband. There was no need."

Jamie moved on to a different topic.

"Why did you move to Texas?"

"Because my husband and I both got new jobs down here."

"What does he do?"

"He's a software designer," said Lori, sounding angry. "He wanted to come down here because he was contacted by Mr. Vellois and offered a job here in Texas."

"Mr. Vellois?" Jamie asked, feeling her spine stiffen. "What's his first name?"

"Andre."

"Have you ever met him?"

"No. Right after we moved, Mr. Vellois sold the company. My husband got a nice severance package but had to find a new job."

"Do you know where Vellois went?"

"I don't think he went anywhere. My husband said he still lives in Palm Beach, Florida."

Jack Bartlett arrived at David Whitney's office at half past one. He was escorted to Whitney's office and entered with obvious annoyance. Folding his arms, Bartlett glared at Whitney who continued working on a document.

"I don't understand, dammit. What do you mean the clinic is broke?" spat Bartlett.

"The auditors' findings show someone cleaned out all the receipts and took off with them. I talked to the police, and they are investigating to see if you had anything to do with it," said Whitney.

"Why the hell am I a suspect?" demanded Bartlett. "Where's the evidence that I did it?"

"You're already under indictment for fraud, Jack. It's not a huge leap to add embezzlement."

"That's ridiculous. I told you I don't recognize most of the patients on the list that I supposedly submitted fraudulent claims on. I sure as hell haven't been fudging the books at the office either. I have no reason to."

"What about your gambling problems?" questioned Whitney. "Trying to welsh in Vegas?"

Bartlett looked as if he had just been caught burglarizing a home.

"How did you find out about that?"

"Answer my question, Jack. Did you take the money to cover your losses?"

"I swear I didn't. I quit gambling when I left California."

"You've been seen in the casinos at Mohegan Sun on several occasions."

"I only go there to be around the action. No one told you they saw me in a game, did they?"

"No. But the report says you're pretty well known there."

"Of course I am. But the people in Las Vegas made sure no one in Connecticut will take my marker, and most of my salary goes to pay back what I still owe. But I swear I'm clean."

"If I found out about your past, you can bet the prosecution will. This doesn't help your case."

"David, I've been set up this time. Patients here are canceling in droves. Thank God we've still got Nashua. There's only been a small spread in the New Hampshire papers since I was arrested. I can still see most of my patients there, but I don't know for how long."

"Hang tight, Jack. I'm trying to work this all out. I should have some answers next week," replied Whitney.

Chapter Twenty

WEDNESDAY, OCTOBER 29

It was just after 8:00 a.m. when Senator Mitchell arrived at David Whitney's office. Mitchell was taken to the private conference room, and Whitney continued poring over papers, delaying his meeting ten minutes longer, before leaving to meet the senator.

"Thank you for coming in so early," Whitney said.

"I don't understand why you wanted to see me alone," snapped Mitchell.

"Someone is out to destroy everything. Not just Lee Harlow, but everyone who was connected with him."

"How does that involve me?"

"This could be part of an old political debt started by someone with a grudge against you. Someone who's vicious and has a gigantic score to settle. Can you think of anyone like that?"

Senator Mitchell folded his arms and thought for a long moment.

"I have many enemies, like everyone else in public life. I can think of a dozen men who would like to have my scalp hanging from a pole. But that doesn't mean they would construct a conspiracy of these proportions to do it."

"Tell me about when you and Lee met."

"Katherine first met him when he was in medical school. She brought him to my home in Washington on Thanksgiving weekend. I did not approve of the relationship, but she was a headstrong girl. I knew if I protested, she'd marry him to spite me. So I disapproved passively and hoped their fling would run its course."

"That was during your first term in the Senate, correct?"

"Yes, I won a bare-knuckled brawl against Grant Donovan when the seat became vacant. The people have continued to send me back for seven terms," said the senator, nodding his head and flashing a wide grin proudly, as if he'd just received a reward for gallantry.

"Just stick to the facts and save the rhetoric for CNN," jabbed Whitney.

Mitchell's face flushed.

"Tell me about Lee's father."

"Trenton Harlow got caught with his hand in the till. He came to me before the wedding and asked me to bail him out."

"What was the trouble?"

"Trenton claimed that his partner, a man named Hans Straussman, had been embezzling from their company and left Trenton holding the bag. He was going to be forced to declare bankruptcy and face criminal charges. Trenton swore he was innocent and begged me to use my influence in Washington to have the criminal investigation dropped in exchange for him liquidating all his assets and filing for reorganization. I refused."

"Why?"

"Because I never believed Trenton was innocent, and I didn't want some damned reporter linking me with a cover up."

"Did you check out the claims about Straussman?"

"No."

"Why not?"

Mitchell hesitated and looked at the floor before he answered. “I couldn’t take a chance on there being a scandal,” he said.

“What happened to Trenton?”

“He committed suicide,” answered Mitchell hesitantly. “Shot himself in the head. It was gruesome. The crazy fool drove down to the entrance to my house, stopped, got out of his car, and blew his damn brains out on the front lawn. My chief of staff, Roger Newell, was a witness. Of course, we had to keep that quiet to avoid an investigation so we got the medical examiner involved in the cover-up.”

“I thought the coroner ruled Trenton died from a heart attack.”

“He did.”

“Why would he do that?”

“Because I convinced him it would be good for his career.”

“You mean you blackmailed him, right?”

“I prefer to think I had him do a more thorough evaluation,” said Mitchell.

“How much money did Trenton need?” asked Whitney.

Mitchell shifted uncomfortably before he answered. “Thirty thousand dollars,” he said finally.

“You mean you couldn’t help him out for a measly thirty thousand dollars?” asked Whitney.

“We’re not talking about some bum you met at a bus stop here, Senator. This was your son-in-law’s father.”

“I couldn’t have helped without my reputation being stained.”

“What happened to Newell?”

Mitchell paused for a moment before answering.

"He died from cancer a few years ago," he said, as his voice took on a slight vibrato.

"Senator, we're both men of the world, so let's not bullshit each other. You pushed Trenton over the edge. He wasn't a member of your political party, so don't tell me that wasn't a factor."

Mitchell didn't respond for a long moment. Whitney folded his arms and let him fidget.

"I suppose there's a grain of truth to that. I've regretted it ever since," began the senator. "I tried to talk to Lee about it, but he always refused to discuss the matter after Trenton died."

"Sounds like Lee had a reason to destroy you."

"Probably," countered Mitchell smugly. "But he's dead, so I guess his revenge will have to wait for the next life."

"Are you sure you've never heard of this man Andre Vellois?"

"Never. It's not a common name, so it's one I would remember," replied Mitchell before looking away.

Whitney continued to press but Mitchell remained defiant.

"All right. Here's what I want you to do," commanded Whitney. "Call in all the favors you have in Washington and see what they can dig up on Andre Vellois. We are almost out of time."

While waiting in Whitney's office, Jamie scanned the report she'd received earlier that morning about Andre Vellois. There was no record of a social security number or driver's license in Vellois's name. The Srotiart Corporation linked to Vellois was chartered in the Cayman Islands and listed a registered agent in Palm Beach, Florida. Srotiart was not registered to do business in Massachusetts or New Hampshire. Technically, all the real estate transactions had been illegal.

There were no records of any tax filings or identification numbers issued by the Internal Revenue Service for Srotiart. The company maintained no bank accounts in Massachusetts or New Hampshire, but did have one in Palm Beach. Accounts were suspected in the Cayman Islands. There was also suspicion that an account had been established in Zurich. As Jamie finished the report, there was a knock at the door. A secretary entered with a small, frail-looking man in his late sixties who was wearing a tweed sport coat and navy bowtie.

"Jamie, your handwriting expert, Mr. Dixon, is here. You said to bring him back when he arrived," said the secretary.

"Yes. Thanks. Come in, please."

Dixon shook Jamie's hand weakly and then sat in the leather chair next to hers.

"You said this was urgent, so I changed my schedule for you," he began.

"I appreciate that," said Jamie, knowing her appreciation would be calculated precisely when she received his bill for services. "Here's what I need your help on."

Jamie shoved two stacks of documents toward him as he reached into his briefcase and removed a handheld magnifying glass.

"I want you to compare the signatures on these documents and see if they match. Start with the signatures of Lee Harlow. Then compare those of Andre Vellois."

Slowly, the expert began to study the documents, making notes on a yellow pad as he continued. Several moments passed. He put the magnifying glass down and turned to Jamie.

"All right, what do you want to know?"

"Are the signatures of Lee the same on all the documents?"

"No. They are close and a good attempt at forgery, but easy to spot under the glass."

"So if I told you this letter had an original signature, then the one on this other letter would be a forgery," continued Jamie, pointing to the document on the table, while handing Dixon the letter to the insurer canceling the clinic's insurance coverage for corporate officers and directors.

"Most definitely," he replied, after examining the letter briefly.

"What can you tell me about the other signature?"

"It is quite an interesting script. Look at how the letter 'l' in Vellois appears. Also, the particular curvature of the letter 's' and the way the letter 'e' is opened so far."

"What does that tell you?"

"Two things. First, these signatures were all made by the same person," he said, picking up the documents and reexamining them for a moment.

"Well, what's the second?"

"Andre is a man's name, correct?"

"As far as I know. Why?" Jamie asked, puzzled.

"I'm convinced these signatures were all made by a woman."

Chapter Twenty-One

Friday, October 31

Jamie joined David Whitney at his office shortly after seven o'clock. He walked into the conference room carrying two cups of coffee, placed one in front of her and then sat in the chair on the opposite side, and took a huge gulp from his cup.

"The shit keeps getting deeper, David," began Jamie. "I did get a lead on Vellois, but it looks like a dead end."

"I've talked to the loan officers at the banks about Robert Smith. They claim all the mortgages were arranged through Washington law firms retained by the senator, and Smith was a local lawyer used by them to handle the transactions."

"Did you find an address for Smith?"

"None was listed on any of the documents. I asked the loan officers to search their files and get back to me. I also called the Massachusetts Bar Association. There are thirty-one Robert Smiths listed."

"Do you want me to run a check on each one?" Jamie asked.

"Absolutely. See what you can dig up."

"What else did the banks tell you about the mortgages?"

"Not much. I couldn't get specific without arousing suspicion. I'll wait until we resolve this on Friday and then launch a full-fledged investigation. That way, the senator can make his announcement after we settle the case and I get an agreement for confidentially."

"I'll see what I can find out about Smith, but I'm not optimistic."

"Anything on Lori Wegman?" Whitney asked.

"We found her at a hospital in Texas. I talked to her. She swore she did everything right and denied any romantic involvement with Lee. She claims she gave Steven Sorenson's semen to Lee, who delivered it himself for the insemination."

Whitney frowned.

"Did you confirm that?"

"Not yet. But it was Harlow's clinic, and he could have easily pulled it off without anyone knowing"

"Why did Wegman move to Texas?"

"She said she got a new job, and her husband was offered a position by a man named Andre Vellois."

Whitney's eyebrows arched as he looked at her.

"Did you get a positive ID on Vellois?"

"Not yet. I tried to talk to Lori's husband about him but he was pretty aloof because he's still upset about moving to Texas for a job that lasted less than three months. I did get him to agree to look at a photo in case we come up with one."

"What's your plan now?" asked Whitney.

"This morning I'm driving to Manchester, New Hampshire, to see what I can find out about Michael Vellois. Then I'll call my contact in Palm Beach to check on Andre."

"You don't expect to find Andre in Florida, do you?"

"Of course not," declared Jamie. "But Srotiart Corporation is supposed to have an office there. Also, I need to drive over to Naples and interview Harry Jacobs."

“Harry Jacobs? Isn’t he Lee’s dentist?”

“Yeah. It still bothers me that Lee had his own dental records. That’s pretty unusual, and I want to check it out. What’s up for you today?”

“I have to call Erica Payne and tell her I’m recommending that the insurer offer the policy limits. I don’t see any alternative, no matter what you uncover.

“Why are you offering to settle if you know there’s some kind of criminal conspiracy?”

“Because that doesn’t change the fact that someone was negligent.”

“What about Castle?”

“I’ll convince her.”

“How, by staking her to an ant hill?”

“If I have to,” Whitney shrugged.

“What if Erica won’t take the policy?”

“I don’t expect her to. I’ve been preparing Katherine and the senator for the possibility of having to come up with some of their own funds. They appear to be cash poor and will have to liquidate assets to make up the difference. At least, this will keep Erica Payne quiet.”

“Is that possible after all that’s happened?”

“I’m finding evidence that Jack’s case is a bureaucratic mistake. Katherine and the senator have been victims of fraud and embezzlement. Lee’s death is still a mystery, but nothing that would bring the clinic down,” replied Whitney.

“I’ll be in touch as soon as I get back,” Jamie said.

“One more thing. Can you run a check on Hans Straussman, Trenton Harlow’s former business partner?”

Jamie’s face lit up. “Why?” she asked.

"I have a feeling the senator is hiding something."

"I'll get someone to start digging."

Twenty minutes later, Whitney called Rebecca Castle. He was kept on hold for several minutes before she answered.

"Did you get the DNA reports?" asked Whitney.

"Yes. I'm having my people go over them."

"That's fine, but don't expect anything to change."

"I don't care. I'm getting confirmation from my own experts," Castle said.

"I want to offer Payne the policy of ten million."

Whitney heard a huge, guttural growl come from the phone and pictured Castle in the throes of a seizure.

"I want to be chairman of Hillary and Bill Clinton's foundation. Let's make a bet as to which one happens first," she hissed.

"Are you offering anything to Erica?"

"Yeah. Tell her we'll pay five million."

"Five million is bullshit, and you know it."

"It's more money than this bimbo ever dreamed about. I'll make it in cash. Hundreds and fifties. Insist on Sorenson being there. Spread it out on the table so she can stare at it. She'll want it so bad she'll be wetting her pants."

"Sorry, that's not my style," Whitney said.

"Guess that's why you're where you are and I'm up here," smirked Castle.

"If Payne sues you, I'll be a witness for the plaintiff!" Whitney exploded.

Castle sneered and then chuckled.

"Try to imagine how little I care. Let her sue. I'll tie the case up in court for five years and keep the money in an interest-bearing escrow account."

Whitney was not able to reach Erica Payne until he arrived at Logan Airport at several minutes past eleven o'clock. Her secretary came on the line twice to inquire if he would like a call back, but Whitney politely informed her each time that he would wait.

"Hello, David. I was expecting your call," said Payne finally.

"I've discussed the case with the insurer, and we've made a decision," began Whitney.

On the other end of the line, Payne shook slightly and felt her body grow tight.

"We are willing to offer five million dollars in this case. Of course, you must sign a confidentiality agreement."

Erica was silent for a moment as she contemplated Whitney's offer. She had received over a million dollars several times in her career, and it always produced a sensation of euphoria. She began to smile as she remembered a friend of hers who once said that as a lawyer goes through the aging process, settling a case is almost better than the most exotic, steamy sexual encounter.

There's only one big difference, she thought sardonically. *In settlements, size sure as hell matters*.

Stifling a chuckle, she continued, "We'll agree to the confidentiality, of course. But the money's significantly short."

"Short? Five million dollars is short? Are you out of your mind?" asked Whitney.

"A jury won't think so when they hear the facts."

"C'mon, Erica. We've already paid you for the negligence toward her baby. New medical treatments make death unlikely for decades. Your greed is showing now."

"David, we're both consenting adults, so let's cut the bullshit and stop the Academy-Award performances. I'll forego my outrage at the insulting offer, and you can stop pontificating about how tort reform is close at hand."

"What's the bottom line?" asked Whitney.

"Policy limits plus some of your client's assets. I'll recommend fifteen million dollars to Ann Sorenson. I can't guarantee she'll accept, but I'll push it strongly."

I know I can bring a settlement in for thirteen million or less, thought David. *That will be the easy part. Getting the money from the senator will be the real coup.*

"That's outrageous," said Whitney, pleased he had called his shot so accurately.

"So's what you did to Ann Sorenson."

"I need some time to talk to my clients."

"Thursday afternoon at five o'clock. Otherwise, I'll be on the evening news," warned Payne.

"That's extortion."

"In negotiation, it's called leverage."

At the same time that Whitney placed his call to Erica Payne, Jamie drove north to Manchester, New Hampshire. She crossed the Amoskeag Bridge before heading east past Notre Dame College, until she reached the address she found for St. Lucy's Home for Children. It was an old two-story house built a century earlier, but it looked like it had been remodeled several times since.

After parking on the street, Jamie walked to the entrance and rang the bell. It took several rings before an elderly woman answered. She was bent over slightly and walked with a barely noticeable limp.

"Hello, I'm Jamie Quintell. Is this St. Lucy's Home for Children?"

The woman shook her head and grew a sad look.

"Not any more. The orphanage closed many years ago. This is a private home now."

"Where would I find the records for St. Lucy's?"

"Why do you want them?"

"Who are you?" asked Jamie.

"June Burelle. I knew the owners of the orphanage many years ago."

"I have a client who was separated from her brother, and I want to find him."

"When were they separated?"

"In 1974," replied Jamie, growing annoyed.

"When in 1974?'

"July," Jamie lied. "Look, I don't want to be rude but—"

"Oh. That's too bad. You won't find any of those records," interrupted June, shaking her head.

"How do you know?"

"I used to work here. We had a fire and everything was destroyed. All the records too."

"Are you sure there are no records anywhere?"

"The newspapers might have something. What was the brother's name?"

Jamie thought for a moment and decided to take a chance. "Michael Vellois," she blurted.

June reached out to take Jamie's arm.

"I'm so sorry, miss," she said gently as she stroked the back of Jamie's hand. "But I remember that time like it was yesterday. Michael was one of the children who died in the fire."

Jamie felt her whole body tremble as she stared at Burelle.

"How can you be so sure?"

"Because I saw it."

Jamie stared into the woman's sad, tired eyes for a long moment. Watching tears glisten at the corners, she was struck by the fact that it still provoked such an emotional response, even so many years after it happened.

Finally, she mumbled her thanks, walked to her car, and drove away, headed for the main offices of Manchester's leading newspaper, the *Union Leader*, to see what she could uncover about the fire.

As the woman watched Jamie leave, a sad smile covered her face. She turned and walked back inside where Clay was seated at the table, looking out the bay window and watching Jamie drive away.

"Well, I said what you wanted me to," she whispered softly. "I hope you got your money's worth."

"It was perfect," Clay said with a smile as he pressed ten new, crisp one hundred dollar bills into her left hand and then headed for the door.

Whitney arrived at LaGuardia Airport on the 11:30 shuttle and took a taxi into the heart of Manhattan. He reached the corporate offices of National Insurance Company, located on the Avenue of the Americas, fifteen minutes before his appointment.

He rode the elevator to the fortieth floor and was escorted into a private office for his meeting with the vice president of operations. An average-sized man in his sixties, who was nattily dressed in a navy suit and demure red-striped silk tie, rose to meet him.

"Good afternoon, Mr. Whitney."

"How do you do, sir?" offered Whitney, extending his hand. "Thank you for seeing me so quickly."

"What can I do for you?"

"You should have received copies of pertinent documents by e-mail this morning, regarding the recent death of one of your insureds, Dr. Lee Harlow. I'm the attorney for the estate, and I've come to collect the proceeds from his life insurance, as the estate may encounter some debts that will require an immediate influx of cash."

"I see. This will be on an additional policy with our company, of course."

"I don't understand," replied Whitney, as a sinking feeling rose in the pit of his stomach.

"Well, Mr. Whitney, I'm sure you are aware of the transfer of Dr. Harlow's life policies when he assumed his new corporate title."

"What are you talking about? What new corporate title?" asked Whitney.

"As chief of medical operations with Srotiart Corporation. All of his insurance was transferred at that time."

Whitney looked like he had been punched in the stomach.

"Dr. Harlow never was involved with a business entity other than his clinic," snapped Whitney. "If someone said he was, it's a lie."

"I'm sorry, but that is not true," the man countered as he handed a document to Whitney. "As you can see, this letter was signed by Dr. Harlow himself, authorizing us to change his business insurance. He also signed a change of beneficiary form to name the Srotiart Corporation as the new recipient of any insurance proceeds."

Whitney studied the documents before he replied, "All right, we'll have to straighten this out in court. I'll have to get an injunction preventing you from releasing any funds until I can determine if this document is a forgery."

The vice president shifted uncomfortably before he replied, "It's too late. We paid the proceeds on this policy last week."

"Dammit, man, how could you do that? Now we'll have to sue you to recover what rightfully belongs to my client."

"We paid that policy on good faith. We had a certified copy of the death certificate and a letter from the corporation making formal demand for the policy. It was our obligation legally to pay the proceeds under the circumstances. If you bring litigation, we will have no alternative but to countersue."

"Who signed the letter from the corporation?"

"An attorney named Robert Smith. He picked up the check himself."

"Describe him."

"Tall, fortiesh, rugged looking. He was very professional, and his credentials were all in order."

"Who did you make the check out to?" asked Whitney, dreading the answer.

"Why, the president of the company, of course. Mr. Andre Vellois."

Chapter Twenty-Two

Monday, November 3

The eastern sun rose into a fiery burnt orange ball, signaling the beginning of another perfect weather day in southern Florida. The sky was cloudless, while the temperature hovered in the mid-eighties with light winds blowing across the beach.

After her first full night's sleep in several days, Jamie was showered and dressed at a quarter to eight before taking the elevator to the hotel lobby to meet her contact: a local private detective named Mickey Cornette. He was recommended to her as the best investigator in Dade County by one of David Whitney's old classmates who now practiced in Miami. Jamie did not have time to do a thorough background check on Andre Vellois or his company and decided to let Cornette do the preliminary inquiry.

Mickey was sitting in one of the wingback chairs in the hotel atrium. He was short and unshaven, with thinning hair and stocky limbs. He wore a colorful island shirt, a pair of white shorts, and black high-top sneakers without socks. Cornette looked like a tourist who was still wide-eyed at the eighty-degree temperatures in November.

Jamie walked over and introduced herself before accompanying him to the restaurant. As they were seated, Cornette refused a menu and quickly ordered a huge breakfast, while Jamie settled on coffee and a bagel. Immediately, they got down to business.

"What did you find on Vellois?" asked Jamie, sipping her coffee.

"Not much," replied Cornette after stuffing the remnants of a biscuit into his mouth and buttering another. "Son of a bitch is a mystery man. No records here in the States. Just the stuff in the Caymans. He could be a front."

"For who?"

"Hell, there's lots of nominations. Used to be the syndicate. Today, you can pick from drug dealers, arms merchants, or money launderers, not to mention your basic old-fashioned hoods with a score to settle."

"Did you know that Vellois was a navy pilot who was shot down in Vietnam?"

"Yeah, that's the prevailing theory, but I think it's bullshit," declared Cornette as he speared the last bite of sausage and mopped up the rest of his eggs before popping the mixture into his mouth.

"Why?"

"Because every time the CIA wants to ice a guy, they make him a war hero of some kind. That's a great cover if somebody wants to move on and not leave a trace."

"How do you know he was in the CIA?" Jamie asked.

"I called the psychic hotline, kid." He laughed.

"You've already confirmed that, haven't you?"

"That's why I get the big money."

"How can you find out what happened to him?"

"Usually, it's easy. As long as you've got plenty of dough and can find someone on the inside who's willing to talk."

"Do you have any contacts in Washington?"

"Bet your ass, I do," said Cornette.

"Any suggestions on how to get around the bureaucracy?"

"I need ten grand today if you want the real info by tomorrow night."

Jamie let out a short whistle and then pushed her hands together.

"That's pretty stiff. How do I know you can get me what I need? Will you tell me how you do it?"

Cornette grinned as wide as a canal.

"Remember that old movie *The Cincinnati Kid*?" he asked.

Jamie shook her head from side to side.

"Well, Edward G. Robinson played this card shark, Lancey Howard. He was explaining how he once bluffed this young big-shot gambler out of a huge five-card stud pot, and afterward, the gambler asked Lancey how he knew he had him beat even though the guy had three jacks showing. Ol' Lancey rubbed his chin, looked him in the eyes, and said to the poor bastard whose bankroll he had just scarfed up, 'Son, all you paid was the looking price. Lessons are extra.'"

Jamie chuckled and stared back.

"So I guess that means the official word Mitchell got from the Pentagon was free, and he was still overcharged. The truth is gonna cost me a helluva lot more."

"You catch on fast," he said, smiling as he drained his coffee.

"I'll have David Whitney wire it to you right away," said Jamie.

"I can trust you, right?" demanded Cornette. "I have to front the cash so my ass won't be waving out here in the wind. Tell me now if your people can't handle that much action."

"I'll give you one of my credit cards if that will seal it."

"Naw, no card," Cornette said, grinning as he fired off a text. "I like your face. It's trustworthy, and you're not some sleazy lawyer."

Jamie took out her phone and texted Whitney. When she finished, Cornette had a huge grin on his face as he nodded and said she should consider it a done deal.

"Find anything on Srotiart Corporation?" asked Jamie.

"They've got an office over on Lakewood Road. I bribed a custodian to let us in."

"Let's go," said Jamie eagerly, reaching for the check.

"Hey, my treat," Cornette said, gently tapping the back of her hand. "I had the right side of the menu, and you only had a bowl of air."

They drove for almost half an hour before arriving in front of a two-story brick office building that looked brand new. There were only two cars in the lot when they parked. After entering the building, Cornette walked to the first room on the right and knocked on the door that was slightly ajar. A small black man in a brown work shirt and faded Levi's answered.

"Varnall, my man, I'm here for the tour," sang Cornette.

The man grinned. "Hey, bro, five minutes, no more. My ass is on the line. You have to get out when I tell you," he ordered sternly.

"Relax, pal. You're getting paid well for putting your ass on the line. We don't need a long time in there."

Together, the three of them walked up the stairs to the second floor and continued down the hallway until they reached the last office on the right. The custodian looked around before opening the door with his master key. He quickly disabled the alarm as Jamie and Cornette waited in the hallway. After turning on the lights, he began to chuckle.

"What's so damn funny?" demanded Cornette as he followed the custodian inside.

"This place was full yesterday. Looks like somebody was in a hurry to get outta town last night," said Varnall, his eyes sweeping around the deserted office suite with pockets of dust and a few discarded pieces of paper.

"Can you tell us anything about the people who rented this office?"

"Naw. I only saw two guys ever come in here. Never talked to them."

"What'd they look like?"

"Old. White. Rich."

"How do you know they were rich?"

"Hey, man, I heard one of them talk about his own plane. Ain't that rich?"

"Do you know his name?"

"Nope. Only saw him once or twice. He's from Grand Cayman, I think."

Cornette walked over to the far corner of the office and picked up a small scrap of paper that was wadded up into a ball. After unraveling it, he walked back to Jamie.

"What do you make of this?" he asked, handing her the scrap.

Jamie studied the three-inch piece of paper. It looked like the top of a document that had been torn into thirds before being discarded. The only two words on the sheet were "Dear Michael."

Shortly after eleven o'clock, David Whitney stared at the man across from him and wondered how he was involved in the destruction of Lee Harlow and his family. Austin Harlow was four months short of forty-two. He'd joined his father's clinic after his residency. His education, training, and experience made him a natural senatorial candidate. His family's political power would almost guarantee him the nomination. A scandal, on the other hand, would leave him ruined.

Whitney continued reviewing the documents in front of him before interrogating Austin. He had not looked forward to the meeting, because in Whitney's mind, Austin Harlow was a sniveling little shit who spent his whole life capitalizing on being Langley Mitchell's grandson.

Whitney looked into Austin's gaunt face. From the alabaster skin, to the thick, perfectly styled brown hair, his features were commanding. Austin was not a handsome man, but the aristocratic way he carried himself, coupled with his lean, wiry frame, served notice that he was a conspicuous force, albeit an annoying one.

"Austin, tell me what you know about the Sorenson case."

"I never even heard of these people before this case. Based on what you told me, it looks like someone screwed up on the semen exchange."

"What was your relationship with Lori Wegman?"

"I barely knew her. She was just another employee. I never paid attention."

"Have you ever had a mix up like this?"

"Of course not, but then, I'm not my father."

"You didn't think much of your father, did you?" asked Whitney, carefully studying Austin.

"He never was the man Grandfather is. I wanted to get close to him when I was young, but he kept trying to poison me against my mother and my grandfather. I think the fact that he knew that I loved my grandfather dearly made him despise both of us. I never knew why he stayed with my mother, because I could tell there was nothing between them."

Whitney was surprised at the emotion in Austin's voice, but did not let it show.

"What caused the rift between you and your father?"

"It started when I was a child and Grandfather insisted that I attend the same schools he had. I was still in grammar school, and I remember a violent argument when Grandfather demanded I go to Exeter. My father told him I needed to go to a school where I could learn something about character first. Grandfather yelled that I could never learn character from Lee because Trenton never taught him any. Lee tried to strike Grandfather, and the servants had to separate them."

"Is that it?"

"No. It was the accident I had that drove the wedge between us."

"Anthony Damon, right?"

"Well, I knew him as Speed. Most people called him that because he was a math genius and could calculate equations in his head before most people could blink. He had a full academic scholarship and a promising future as a mathematician."

"Was the accident your fault?"

"My father thought so. There were six of us in my car. We had all been drinking."

"How did the accident happen?" Whitney asked.

"We were driving to the beach in Maine. I was going too fast and lost control of the car and hit a tree. Speed was thrown out and injured his spine. My father blamed me for what happened."

"It was your fault, wasn't it?"

"No. Everyone else was drinking. We were all responsible."

Whitney laid his pen down and stifled the urge to reach across the table and smack the little prick.

"But you were the one who was driving. How could you possibly think you were not to blame?" asked Whitney, arching his eyebrows.

"I never forced anyone to get in the car. They all knew I was drinking and assumed the risk. Grandfather stepped in and said he would resolve the matter. Damon's medical expenses would be paid, and his family would get a cash settlement. The charges against me would be reduced, and I would only have to pay a small fine."

"How did Lee react when you told him about the senator's involvement?"

"He said he had made many mistakes, but always tried to atone for them. He told me some nonsense about how the Greeks have a saying, 'Character is destiny,' and it was a reflection of a man's character if he made amends when he was wrong. I said I didn't think my being punished would help Speed; he would still be a paraplegic."

"What was Lee's response?"

"My father called me a coward and a thief. He told me I was, quote, 'stealing from my soul.' He also said someday I would have a crisis that Grandfather could not cure. Lee called the senator a crutch I relied on to get by."

"Whatever happened to Damon?"

"He lost his scholarship and had to leave school because of his injuries. Someone told me he moved back to Canada."

"He was Canadian?"

"From somewhere near Montreal."

Whitney stared at Austin for a moment and thought. "You used the plane the day before your father went down, didn't you?" he quizzed, deftly switching subjects.

"Yes, why?"

"We'll you're a pilot, just like Lee. Did you hate your father enough to tamper with the fuel line?"

"Dammit, I resent that," shot back Austin. "Just because I didn't like him doesn't mean I would kill him. Jack Bartlett's a pilot also. Did you ask him if he killed my father?"

"You've got the most to lose if this other scandal hits, don't you?"

"What do you mean?"

"Your mother and grandfather and Jack Bartlett can all recover and go on with their lives whether or not I save the clinic. But if a scandal hits, your senatorial future is gone."

Jamie drove south on I-95 and exited west on I-75 toward Naples. Two hours later, she took the second exit, turned south, and followed Highway 41 until she came to a high-rise building overlooking the Gulf of Mexico. Using the security telephone, she called Harry Jacobs, but received no answer.

A custodian was cleaning the floor inside the building. A $20 tip got her escorted to the beach where Jacobs was taking his daily walk. Jamie had memorized Jacobs's features from a photograph she had. Instead of going off in the wrong direction, she decided to wait until he returned as she sat on one of the beach chairs under a cabana. Almost half an hour later, a portly, bald man of average height wearing red swimming trunks, a white T-shirt, and Panama hat, matching Jacobs's description, came walking from the northern part of the beach and turned toward the building.

"Excuse me. Are you Harry Jacobs?"

"Yes, I'm Dr. Jacobs. Who are you?"

"My name's Jamie Quintell, Doctor. I need a moment of your time."

"What about?"

"I'm a private investigator checking on the death of Lee Harlow. I believe he was one of your patients."

"A friend from Boston called me right after it happened. It's a tragedy."

"I work for Dr. Harlow's attorney, David Whitney. The FAA found that Dr. Harlow's fuel line was tampered with, and the coroner said he was hit on the head before the crash. It looks like foul play, and I'm checking out all the leads."

"I see," said Jacobs. "Would you like to go up to my place and talk? We'll have some privacy there."

Jacobs led the way to the front entrance and escorted Jamie to the elevator, which they took to the sixth floor. His condominium was located at the rear of the building, with an unobstructed view of the beach and the water. Jamie sat at a table on the huge screened-in balcony and watched flocks of seagulls swarm over the land and water, and boats with their sails unfurled passing by until Harry returned with two red plastic glasses of iced tea.

Jamie took a sip as Harry raised his glass, gave a short salute in her direction, and said, "Tell me how I can help."

"The body they found was unrecognizable and had to be identified by dental records. I understand you took care of all Lee's dental work for over twenty-five years," she began.

Jacobs nodded.

"The dental records that were used to confirm his death came from your office after you gave them to Lee when you moved to Florida, correct?"

"That's right. Lee was in the process of finding a new dentist, and I saw no harm in giving him the records."

"The coroner's office has lost Dr. Harlow's dental records. They claim the file is gone, and they are still looking for them."

"How could they lose the records?" asked Harry. "They would be the only means by which they could identify the body."

"They were probably just misplaced. The coroner made a positive identification and closed the case, but I can't do that without seeing the records."

"You mean you're still investigating whether it was Lee's body they found?"

"I have to until I get confirmation. That's why I was hoping you could tell me what you remember about them."

"Good Lord, young lady, I had thousands of patients. I can't remember the exact details about everyone's dental history. That's why we keep records, you know."

"Don't be offended, but are you sure you gave Dr. Harlow the right records?" Jamie asked carefully.

"Of course I did. Why do you think the body they recovered isn't Lee's?"

"I don't. There's nothing to suggest that, but I want to clear it up in my own mind in case the police missed something, especially since I don't have the actual dental evidence to see for myself."

Harry suddenly sat up straight as his eyes began to sparkle.

"Wait a minute. There is only one thing I remember about Lee's mouth that was distinctive. He had a bridge made out of gold, put in when he lost a tooth playing football in college. The reason that stands out is because we haven't used dental gold for years. But whoever did the work on Lee was a master craftsman. So see if the report lists the gold teeth. That might save you some sleepless nights," answered Harry, as Jamie continued to take notes.

Chapter Twenty-Three

Tuesday, November 4

It was barely six o'clock in the morning when Jamie was awakened by the sound of her fax machine. Forcing herself to become alert, she donned a turquoise terrycloth robe and went into the kitchen to make coffee as she waited for the transmission to cease. After several documents accumulated on the tray, Jamie retrieved the pages and began to read.

The documents were from the Pentagon personnel file of Andre Vellois. There was a report on a background check, Vellois's combat record, and an exit report. Several areas had been excised with a black marker. The final document was a photograph of Vellois taken in 1973. Although it was several decades old, Jamie studied the features and found several characteristics in the ruggedly handsome face that time would not hide.

The exit report showed Vellois was shot down over the Gulf of Tonkin in 1973, a few days after his wife's death in Boston. The downing of his aircraft was a ruse. He was sent to Germany on assignment. His assignment was of such high priority that he was denied emergency leave to return home for his wife's funeral.

The CIA arranged for his son to be cared for while he was away. The report said that Vellois left Germany and returned to the United States in 1974, where he found his son, Michael, in St. Lucy's Home, an orphanage located in Manchester, New Hampshire.

There were conflicting accounts about what happened to Michael. One report said Andre took Michael away from St. Lucy's on the morning of the great fire. Another indicated the boy perished in the blaze. CIA investigators were unable to confirm reports that both were seen the following day in Boston before vanishing. There was nothing in the official record to indicate anyone had seen Vellois or his son after September of 1974. They simply disappeared.

Jamie telephoned Cornette, who was on his way to Grand Cayman Island. He told her he was taking his copies of the documents with him. Jamie told him the money had been wired to his account the previous day. Cornette promised he would contact her as soon as he could compile a full report.

Afterward, Jamie called Paul Sweeney and gave him the information about Anthony Damon. Paul told her he would have a complete profile run before following up with a personal investigation.

At quarter to nine, Whitney drove to Marblehead to meet Katherine Harlow and Senator Mitchell. They were waiting for him in the study.

"Senator, you and your daughter are caught in a trap. Fifteen million dollars is relatively reasonable compared to what a jury could award," replied Whitney.

Mitchell began shouting and waving his arms wildly.

"Reasonable? Reasonable for a damn black bastard and his whore mother?" raged the senator as Katherine gave him a shocked look. "In a pig's eye. Exactly whose side are you on here, David?"

"Senator, I'm giving you the best legal advice I can. And fifteen million dollars is a reasonable figure."

"Of course you think that way, dammit. It's not your money!" sputtered Mitchell, his face turning the color of a ripe cranberry.

"You can always get another lawyer if you don't like my advice," said Whitney squarely.

"I just might."

"Father, David is not the enemy," declared Katherine. "The least we can do is hear his reasons."

"If you go to trial and lose, not only could you lose everything, but all of your financial dealings will become public knowledge. They can ask you anything about your assets, and you have to answer. And you'll be under oath. Mislead or fabricate and you could face perjury charges. Is that what you want, Senator, now that you're ready to pass the torch to your grandson?" asked Whitney.

"This couldn't come at a worse time. We're making the announcement on Friday. There will be two thousand people at a fundraiser for Austin, for Christ's sake. Can't you make this go away?" asked Mitchell.

"I certainly can. Give me the money, and I promise you it will go away."

"Don't you know what this means? In politics, timing is everything. We can't delay Friday's rally. And we sure as hell can't let word leak about what's happened at the clinic. Those vulture sons of bitches in the press will have a field day. I can't have Austin's political future tied to the incompetence of his father."

No one replied for a long moment.

"Tell us what you propose," said the senator finally.

"How much cash can you both scrape together?" asked Whitney, looking first at the senator and then Katherine.

"Four million, tops," answered Mitchell. "That includes liquidating everything and tapping into my campaign funds."

Whitney looked Mitchell directly in the eyes and shook his head vigorously. "You know it's illegal to use your campaign funds, Senator. As your attorney, I must advise you not to do that."

"I've got a fundraiser planned for next month. I'll use that to replace the money before anyone is the wiser," vowed the senator, nodding at Whitney, who again shook his head.

"If you decide to do something like that, you're on your own," said Whitney.

"If we agree, how soon do we have to get the money?" asked Katherine.

"Probably tomorrow. Friday, at the latest."

"Impossible," declared Mitchell. "It will take at least a week."

"Senator, if we don't produce the money right away, Ms. Sorenson's lawyer is going to call a press conference and blow the lid off everything. So start making calls today to get the money here by tomorrow."

Senator Langley Mitchell looked at Whitney for a long moment and made a decision. In his years in the Senate, he never ran from a fight. He felt dirty sitting there planning to give away everything he'd fought so hard to get. His blood grew fiery like the interior of a blast furnace. Gritting his teeth as he rose from his chair, Mitchell glared at Katherine before facing Whitney.

"Tell those two bitches to take that little spook baby and go buy some storefront in Harlem, for all I care. They'll have to settle for what they can get from the damned insurer," he said forcefully. "No Mitchell money is going to sweeten the pot."

"I think you're making a big mistake, Senator," answered Whitney, snapping his briefcase shut.

"Perhaps, but I'm going down swinging. We have paid you several hundred dollars an hour for years, David. Lee kept you because you were tough, smart, and ruthless. I'd like to see that side of you, unless Erica Payne is too much for you to handle," he said in a mocking tone.

White patches of anger formed at the corners of David Whitney's mouth. Stifling the urge to tell his clients he was through, Whitney thought of Lee and almost smiled as he considered the senator's words.

"All right, Senator, let's find out just how tough Erica Payne is."

At mid-afternoon, Jamie Quintell arrived at the clinic in Newton and found Ruth Oliver and Judy Davis waiting for her in Whitney's office. Both looked concerned as Jamie opened her briefcase and removed several folders.

"Ruth, do you have any idea how the semen could have been mixed up?"

"Absolutely none. I've gone over this a thousand times, and there's nothing to explain how it could have happened."

"What if Dr. Harlow made a mistake and delivered the wrong specimen to Dr. Bartlett for the in vitro?"

"Dr. Harlow never collected specimen containers. That was the nurse's job," said Ruth defensively.

"Did you know Lori Wegman?"

"Of course."

"She told me Dr. Harlow collected Mr. Sorenson's sperm and delivered it to Dr. Bartlett."

A look of anger clouded Ruth's face.

"She's a lying little bitch," she snapped.

"How do you know?"

The expression on Ruth's face turned into a scowl.

"Because she had an ax to grind."

"What kind of ax?"

"She came on to Dr. Harlow, and he turned her down. She'd say anything to try to get even. If you ask me, I'd bet she deliberately switched the semen."

"Can you prove she propositioned Dr. Harlow?"

"It's common knowledge," said Judy. "Lori and I were friends. She admitted it to me one night when we went for a drink after work."

"Are you sure Harlow turned her down?"

"She admitted that too. She fell for him hard. But he was not a philanderer. That's one of the reasons she quit. Because he rejected her."

"One final thing," Jamie said, reaching into her briefcase and removing the photograph of Andre Vellois. "Have either of you ever seen this man before?"

Ruth studied the picture for a moment and indicated no recognition before passing it to Judy, who shook her head.

"Who is it?" asked Ruth.

"His name is Andre Vellois."

Judy shook her head and shifted uncomfortably.

"What is it?" asked Whitney.

"Well, I accidentally overhead Dr. Harlow and Dr. Bartlett having an argument about a woman named Michelle Vellois. Is she connected?"

"She was married to Andre. What was the fight about?" Jamie asked.

"Dr. Harlow said Bartlett was responsible for her death. Dr. Bartlett screamed back at him that he had blood on his hands too," said Judy.

"Who is this guy?" asked Ruth.

Jamie stared at both women for a moment before she answered.

"Someone who holds the key to this whole mess. Someone we have to find."

Chapter Twenty-Four

Wednesday, November 5

Erica Payne arrived at David Whitney's office at mid-morning, and was escorted to the conference room to wait. After several minutes, Whitney entered through the rear door and then sat in a chair at the head of the table.

"I thought we'd settle this face-to-face," said Payne. "The telephone is so impersonal."

"I've just spoken to Rebecca Castle," replied Whitney.

"Is there a new offer?"

"She said seven million. Firm. I practically had to talk her down off the ledge to squeeze that out of her."

"Fine. Then Senator Blowhard and his debutante daughter can come up with eight million on their own."

"Not a chance. They are set in their position. I am authorized to offer you the seven million under the policy, nothing more. It's take it or leave it."

"I see," Payne said, congratulating herself for having anticipated this move. "Now you expect me to rave about bad faith dealing and how we're going to nail your ass in court, right?"

"If that's the way you want to play it," replied Whitney.

"This is the way I want to play it, David. The complaint will be finished today. Then I will call every newspaper and television station, and tell them to meet me at the Suffolk County Superior Courthouse on Friday morning where I will hold a news conference. On my way inside, I will give the media the details of this egregious action and inform them of how the senator has been using his influence to cover it up. Then I will have Ann Sorenson tell every woman in the world what it's like to fight nature to try to conceive and wind up having a baby who was fathered by some stranger who also managed to kill her while his semen was invading her body. My client and I will both be there to answer any questions. I think there might be one or two inquiries. What do you think?"

Whitney thought for a moment before he replied. Despite the bluster and bravado, Payne sure as hell had the truth for an ally. Then he had another thought.

This is one of those moments in life where Lee would tell me that my character is what will let me overcome this adversity, thought Whitney.

"Then I guess we'll have to go to war," he replied coldly.

Payne shot back at him like she was commanding a landing craft raiding a beachhead. "Fine. I'll come after your clients like a guided missile. From what my investigator found, the clinic is on the verge of collapse, the lead doctor is under indictment, the main shareholders in the corporation have been co-mingling their own funds with those of the corporation, and documents have been filed dissolving the corporation, so I will sue Senator Mitchell and Katherine Harlow individually. Also, I have scheduled the senator and Katherine's deposition for a week from tomorrow to find out the exact extent of their holdings. I will also tell them about the *ex parte* attachments I intend to place on all personal assets of Katherine, Austin, and Langley Mitchell and Jack Bartlett, as well as how one or all of them has been selling off corporate assets and stashing the money in a foreign bank account. Then I will sue the insurer and Rebecca Castle in her individual capacity because her actions in failing to offer a reasonable settlement where liability is clear were intentional as well as unfair and deceptive business practices."

Whiney stared at Erica to see who would blink first. Neither caved.

"You won't win that one," he said finally.

"I don't care. I can't wait to cross-examine Castle, who should be known as Attila the Hen with a law degree, who's been masquerading as a human being, in open court. And at the end of my press conference on Friday, I will issue a warning to all women who are currently getting treatment at the clinic to consider if they still want to do so given the fact that they could have anyone's baby, from Charles Manson to Bernie Madoff to the Boston Marathon bombers."

Whitney's face was beet red when she finished.

"I think that's what they called a counteroffer in law school," said Payne in a voice that seemed to be dripping in syrup as she rose to leave.

Whitney let her reach the door and open it before he spoke.

"What's the bottom line, Erica?' he asked forcefully.

A slight grin spread over her face, and her chest grew tighter with excitement before she turned.

"My demand is still fifteen million."

Whitney rose and walked toward her.

"For Christ's sake, be reasonable. My clients have not given me authority to offer anything besides the seven million. I've got one helluva tough sell to get an extra ten dollars."

"I don't care about how hard your clients will take the news. Maybe you'd better try explaining to them how serious their situation is," Payne said in a biting tone.

Whitney was silent for a moment.

"If I get the insurer to kick in the policy of ten and the senator to come up with another one, will that close the deal?"

Payne almost experienced a sexual surge as she considered the offer.

"I'll consider fourteen five."

Whiney let his emotions stir as he threw up his hands.

"C'mon Erica, dammit. This isn't negotiations 101. We're talking eleven million dollars here."

"The case is worth twice that. A courtroom is not the floor of the US Senate, nor a drawing room in Pride's Crossing where your clients would have home-field advantage. So tell those aristocrats with all that blue blood flowing to come up with a fair figure or face me under oath and find out my name is really spelled P-A-I-N," she spat.

They stood toe to toe for a long moment, neither flinching. Finally, Whitney broke the silence. "See you in court, Counselor."

Payne turned, ripped open the door, and left.

Something struck a chord with her, thought Whitney as he reviewed Payne's display of emotion. *There was true hate there, or maybe she was being a good actress. Guess I'll find out soon.*

Whitney opened his briefcase and shut off his digital recorder. At least he had accumulated some ammunition to take with him and play for the senator and Katherine.

Let them hear from Payne herself how she planned to dismantle them and everything they've worked for. He'd done his best to protect Langley Mitchell and his daughter. It was time for them to protect themselves.

At three o'clock, Jamie Quintell and David Whitney left Whitney's office for the drive to the Mitchell estate. Traffic was heavy on the way out of the city, even that early in the afternoon before the evening rush. Each welcomed the time to have a quiet conversation and to reflect on what would happen in the next twenty-four hours.

Forty-five minutes later, they entered the long, winding driveway and parked in front of the estate. Then they were admitted into the library for their meeting with Katherine and the senator. Katherine was sitting alone in the parlor as Whitney and Jamie entered.

"Hello, Katherine," greeted Whitney.

Jamie nodded.

"Where's your father?" Whitney asked.

"He said he has nothing new to say unless Ms. Sorenson agrees to take the money from the insurance company and move along," said Katherine, angrily gripping the armrests of her chair.

"I want you to hear a recording I made of my session with Ann Sorenson's lawyer this morning. Then you can decide if your position is still as clear as you think it is. But I'm not going to play it unless your father can hear it also."

The door opened and Senator Mitchell entered.

"I heard you from the hallway. What's on that recorder that you think will change my mind?" he demanded.

"It's an outlay of the plaintiff's case, Senator. And it's a pretty cogent one. Maybe if you hear from someone else how much trouble you are both in, it might influence your judgment," answered Whitney.

"Play the damned recording," barked the senator as he slumped into a chair.

Whitney turned on the recorder and the voice of Erica Payne filled the room. When the tape finished, there was an astonished silence. Senator Mitchell looked at Katherine for a long moment before he spoke.

"I've never run from a fight before. To hell with both of them," he muttered, before stalking out of the room.

Katherine stared straight ahead and no one spoke. Finally, Jamie broke the silence.

"Ms. Harlow, I realize this is a delicate time, but I have to ask a few questions."

Katherine remained stone-faced. "What?" asked Katherine as tears formed in the corners of her eyes.

"These questions are about your husband's body. Please understand that I wouldn't ask these things if I didn't have to," continued Jamie.

"Go ahead," snapped Katherine. "It can't make any difference now."

"Do you remember anything distinctive about his teeth?"

"His teeth? Why on earth would you ask that?"

"The medical examiner's office cannot account for your husband's dental records. I went to see Dr. Harry Jacobs, and he remembered a gold bridge in your husband's dental work. I need to know if that coincides with your memory."

"How can you expect me to talk about Lee's teeth at a time like this?" asked Katherine as her voice rose.

"Ms. Harlow, this is important. Please think," said Jamie.

"All I can remember is Lee lost some teeth playing college football. He told me the dentist in South Bend replaced them with a gold bridge. I don't understand why that's pertinent."

"Your husband's body was cremated, right?" Jamie asked, suddenly remembering a dramatic discovery she made in a world history course in college.

"That's correct. Why?"

"Did you receive the ashes?"

"No. They were interred with his parents in the family mausoleum. It was Lee's last request."

"Was the bridge removed before the cremation?" asked Jamie.

"Why would you ask such a macabre thing?" cried Katherine, sitting up straight and glaring at Jamie. "These are pretty sick questions, you know!"

"Please answer the question," commanded Whitney.

"I have no idea," replied Katherine.

"One final question, Ms. Harlow. Did anyone from the funeral home tell you that Dr. Harlow's gold bridge did not disintegrate when he was cremated?"

"Absolutely not," said Katherine angrily as she stared at both Jamie and Whitney. Then she got up and stalked out of the room.

"Why are you pressing this point?" asked Whitney.

"Because if the body was Lee's, his gold bridge would still be intact after cremation. It's another loose end."

Chapter Twenty-Five

Thursday, November 6

Just before ten, Ann and Speed entered the cemetery in Chelsea. After they exited the vehicle, Ann slowed the pace to accommodate Speed's crutches until they finally reached the row where Andrea was buried. Speed braced himself on one crutch and bent to place the bouquet of lilies on the grave. Ann slipped her arm through his as they stood in front of the marker for a few moments, concentrating on the inscription.

"They did a first-class job on the new headstone," said Speed.

"Ricki and I saw it on Andi's last birthday. It came out better than I expected," said Ann.

Ann opened a small black bag and removed a battery-powered drill and a small package. Then she reached for the chain around her neck and exposed her pendant. After removing it from its necklace and holding it up against the tombstone, she quickly drilled two holes, inserted anchors, and secured it. An inscription had been added to the pendant under the *sheng li*:

"The Eagle Has Landed."

Ann stared at her sister's grave for a long moment.

"I couldn't come back here until I knew Andrew was safe," she said.

"He will let us keep her alive," said Speed.

"If not, at least she can finally rest in peace," said Ann, as she reached over to embrace him before they began their drive downtown where he dropped her at the Hyatt for her lunch meeting with Ricki.

At the same time, Erica Payne was just finishing a call when her secretary told her Ritchie Carbone was on his way back. Seconds later, he entered and she could see he looked troubled.

"What's wrong, Ritchie? You look like someone took your last candy bar," she said lightly.

"Well, you remember I told you about the parking lot attendant who told me about the black BMW and the partial license plate number?"

"Yeah, why?"

"Well, I just got a report in from a friend at the Registry of Motor Vehicles. I had him get me a list of every vehicle that could fit that description. I had them run not only RAE in the plate, but RAF, FAE and FAF, because they're similar to RAE, and the attendant could have made a mistake."

"What did you find?"

"One helluva surprise. I've got the list right here. There are only fourteen possible names on it. Guess who the last one is?"

"I don't know," replied Erica, feeling her body grow tense.

"Steven Sorenson."

"How could that be?"

"Black Beamer 325i. License number 536 RAE. He also fits the description the guy gave me: six three, blond, and good looking."

"There are a lot of people who fit that description, Ritchie."

"Maybe, but they don't drive a black BMW with that license plate number."

"What's your next move?"

"I'm gonna show the attendant a picture of Sorenson. Get him to give me a positive ID."

"What if he identifies Sorenson as the man he saw with the black man?" Erica asked.

"Then you've got a problem. The black guy called him Clay, remember? You might be representing someone who's trying to pull a fraud."

"Wait a minute," said Ritchie, his voice rising. "I know how we can confirm this. The Sorensons signed a fee agreement form with you, and you have it your file, right?"

"Of course."

"Then we have their handwriting and fingerprints. That's definite confirmation of who they are," said Ritchie, shifting backward in his chair and putting his hands behind his head while smiling like he just won the Powerball.

Erica thought for a moment as she surveyed his face. She knew her next move would have to be precise and accurate to avoid arousing his suspicion. The fee agreement could cause everything to unravel.

"Great idea," she began. "Get a positive identification from the attendant first, OK? If he names Steven Sorenson as the man he saw, I'll give you the fee agreement and have you lift the prints."

Ann Sorenson entered the Hyatt Regency in Cambridge for an early lunch. Erica had already secured a window table and ordered a pot of coffee, which a waiter began to pour as soon as Ann was seated.

"How's the baby?" asked Erica.

"Great. He's the gift of a lifetime."

"Is he with Speed now?"

"Yes. We're getting ready to leave in the morning."

"A lot of people's lives are about to be altered. Mitchell and his crew for the worse. My brother and your sister for the better," said Ricki.

"The best part is that everyone gets exactly what they deserve," said Ann.

"Let's go over the plan."

"What do you think will happen tomorrow?" asked Ann.

"Whitney will probably offer a token sum over the policy. I'll reject it, and try to talk him up. I expect we'll meet somewhere in the middle between ten and fifteen million dollars."

"I will follow your lead."

"Let's talk strategy," said Erica.

"How do you think I should play this?" asked Ann, her face growing tense. "Like I absolutely won't take a cent less than fifteen million?"

"You have to come across as reasonable. You'll be into Whitney's clients' pockets for several million dollars. You can't act like you think they'll invite us to come over to their vault with a couple of suitcases to help ourselves."

"You know I don't care anything about them. It's certainly my right to hate them for what my husband and I have been forced to go through because of what they did."

"Expect a helluva fight," said Ricki.

"I think of that every time I look at the pendant you bought me," smiled Ann.

"Remember, we've already received five million, so we can afford to be a little reasonable on this one," said Erica.

Erica studied Ann's face carefully. Her facial features were unwavering and taut, and projected a look of brazen determination, one that seemed to shout that she would not accept anything less than what she decided was completely justified.

"I'll get as close as I can to fifteen million," said Erica, raising her glass to salute.

"Here's to your success tomorrow," answered Ann, clinking her glass with Erica's.

After paying the check, Ann and Erica entered the parking garage. As they were saying good-bye, a figure in dark clothing, walking at a brisk pace, approached the two women from behind with his head down. When he came within a few car lengths, he raised his right hand and aimed a large caliber pistol.

As the shooter drew his bead on Erica's back and prepared to fire, Steven Sorenson stepped from behind a support column several feet away. He raised his Glock semiautomatic, with the silencer in place, and emptied three shots in rapid succession into the man's rear upper torso and then shouted to Ann and Erica to get moving fast. The man pitched forward and fell to the concrete floor, dead on impact.

Startled, Ann and Erica turned toward the muffled sounds behind them as Steven rushed over.

"Get out of here right now," called Steven.

"Who the hell is that?" asked Erica in a husky voice, shaking as she struggled to open her door after inadvertently pressing the lock button on her ignition key.

"Probably a messenger from our friend, the senator," replied Steven.

"Jesus, are we going to make it?" asked Ann, as her voice broke.

"It will be over tomorrow," said Erica.

"Stay strong and focused," said Steven.

The women roared away in Erica's car, and then Steven ran to his BMW, slipped out of his Kevlar vest, and headed for the exit.

Jamie had just fallen asleep when the telephone startled her. Looking at the clock, she saw that it was almost midnight.

"Hello," she muttered, struggling to sound coherent.

"Hey, kiddo, did I wake you up?" giggled Mickey Cornette.

"What's up?" she asked, fully alert.

"What, no foreplay before we have investigation sex? Jesus, you're no fun," he cackled.

Jamie smiled. "Talk to me, Mick."

"First, I showed the photo of Vellois to the custodian at the address we got. He couldn't ID him."

"What else?"

"Well, I just got back from the Caymans and you ain't gonna like what I found. Our friend Andre has a place there all right, but it's a damn fortress. We're talking guards with guns and all the trimmings. I couldn't get close enough to do any good."

"What about bank accounts?"

"Oh, he's wired in with the big boys, all right. But it's with the Swiss, and they'd drive over their mother's bodies with a panzer before they'd betray a confidence. Some of the locals made it sound like he's got a lot of juice. I showed the picture around and nobody could identify him. I know it's several decades old, but the resemblance should be strong enough to make a tie-in."

"Anything else?"

"It's a lie that he died from being shot down in combat. He was CIA, but they would lie even if the truth made them money."

"Did you confirm the death?"

"His body was never recovered. His death is listed as unconfirmed because his body was supposedly left in the Cambodian jungle. It's a great cover story because it can't be verified."

"So the only confirmation is the word of the men who survived the mission?"

"Yeah. A search party went back a few weeks after the mission and found nothing."

"I don't think we have an extradition treaty with the Caymans, but I'll let David deal with that. Thanks, Mick. Do one more thing for me, OK? Go see Harry Jacobs and show him the photo. See if he knows anything about Andre Vellois."

"I'll go first thing tomorrow. My ass is dragging."

"Thanks again. Send me your bill."

"As Price once told Waterhouse, you can count on it," said Cornette with a chuckle.

Jamie was just about to get back into the bed when the phone rang again. It was Paul Sweeney.

"Sorry, I know it's late, but I received several things I thought you'd want to know about right away," he began.

"Go ahead," said Jamie, sitting up straighter.

"First, we tried to trace Hans Straussman. My contacts in Washington think he may be somewhere in Southern California. There's a report that he was a double agent for the KGB who came to the United States after being hunted for treason."

"Even if that's true, what the hell is the connection?"

"I don't know. I'll keep looking."

"What else?"

"Next, there is no trace of Michael Vellois. He must have changed his name and disappeared."

"OK. Is that all?"

"No. Remember the kid Austin Harlow paralyzed? Anthony Damon? My sources say he went back to a small town north of Montreal after the accident. I just got the address."

"Can you tie it in to anything in this case?"

"I don't know if it means anything, but he's black."

"Keep digging."

Paul promised to fax the reports to her as soon as they hung up. Jamie looked at her watch when they finished. It was almost 1:00 a.m. She had just turned out her light when the telephone rang once again.

Who could this be now? she thought as a strange area code splashed over the caller ID.

"Hello," she said hesitantly.

"Ms. Quintell, this is Doug Wegman, Lori's husband. Sorry it's so late, but I just got in, and Lori said you were desperate to talk to me. I'm calling you back on that photo you sent me that you said was Andre Vellois."

"Yes," said Jamie expectantly. "Have you had a chance to look at it?"

"I have. This picture is over forty years old, right?"

"Yes. Why?"

"That would make him at least in his early sixties now. Well, the guy I met was a lot younger, and he didn't have the same features. The man I saw is definitely not the same one in the picture."

Chapter Twenty-Six

Friday, November 7

Dawn was breaking on the following morning when a servant gently shook Langley Mitchell. He had been tossing and turning all night with wild thoughts polluting his mind and did not doze off until almost five o'clock. It took three tries before he was fully awakened.

"What the hell?" he began, almost shouting.

"Forgive me, sir. You are wanted on the telephone. An emergency."

"What time is it?" asked Mitchell angrily.

"Almost six."

"Who's calling me now?"

"He said to tell you it's Frederick von Steihl."

Langley Mitchell sat up straight with a look of terror on his face. He sat on the edge of the bed rubbing his right hand over his head as the servant waited for instructions.

"Do you wish to take the call, Senator?"

Mitchell stared off into the distance as his name was called twice. Finally, he had the courage to reply.

"Yes, I'll take it here," said Mitchell.

The servant left the room. Another moment passed before Mitchell reached for the telephone.

"Hello," he whispered tentatively.

"*Guten morgen*, Herr Senator," said the voice in a German accent.

"What do you want?" stammered Mitchell.

"Vat, no exchange of pleasantries after all zees years? No inquires regarding health or family? Ziss ees hardly ze way for old friends to speak."

Mitchell's anger grew like a brushfire, as he knew he was being taunted.

"Dammit, why are you calling me?"

"Very vell, right to business. Zey are closing in on us. I am calling to tell you to settle zess Sorenson case for every cent you have. If you do not, I vill tell ze authorities everything I know about you."

Mitchell's pulse began to race.

"Wait a minute, who's closing in?"

"Every cent, you evil, perverted bastard. Hold nussing back. You von't get a zecond chance."

"Who's closing in? I have power! I can stop them!"

Mitchell started shouting as the line went dead. After a pause, he hung up and stared at the ceiling. Suddenly, he snatched the telephone and dialed David Whitney's home number. He began shouting into the receiver before realizing he was talking to Whitney's voice mail.

A knock sounded and the servant reentered the senator's bedroom.

"You have another call, sir. A Mr. Graham," he said.

"What the hell is going on?" the senator shouted into the phone. His voice quaked from anger as well as fear.

"No go yesterday. My man got whacked, probably by Sorenson's husband. It's too risky to try again today. I'll find another time," said the voice before breaking the connection.

"Dammit!" shouted the senator, outraged at the news that his hit man had failed.

Mitchell also knew he was out of options. There was only one left. All he had to do was empty his bank accounts.

Meanwhile, Clay grinned as the connection was broken. He reviewed his imitation of Frederick von Steihl's German accent and congratulated himself for sounding like a member of Arnold Schwarznegger's family.

The old bastard won't know the difference until it's too late, he thought with a grin.

It was a quarter past eight when Ann Sorenson pulled into the parking garage at Suffolk General Hospital, driving a gray sedan. She found a space near the exit on the third floor. After she parked, a white SUV pulled up behind her, driven by Speed.

Quickly, Ann removed the plastic child seat containing her son, and approached the passenger side of the SUV, eyes darting from side to side to make sure no one was approaching. Opening the door, she placed the child and car seat in the rear of the vehicle and then secured it. She glanced at Steven, who was patrolling several rows over to make sure there would be no more assassination attempts.

"You ride home with your daddy, and I'll join you as soon as I finish my business," she said softly to Andrew before giving the infant a quick kiss.

"We'll be waiting for you at the Burlington Mall. You can leave your rental car there," said Speed before throwing her a kiss and pulling away.

"Good. I've been wanting to dump it since I totaled my car at the clinic."

Ten minutes later, Ann climbed into the back of a cab parked in front of the hospital and gave the driver Erica's Payne's office address. Erica had been in her office since seven o'clock making last-minute changes to the documents that she would use to bluff filing a lawsuit in the clerk's office of Suffolk County Superior Court in Boston. All corrections had been made, and Erica was reviewing the revisions. It was almost nine when her intercom sounded, and Erica's secretary told her Ann had arrived.

"How are you this morning?" asked Erica.

Ann's face held a look of complete confidence as she replied, "I'm ready."

"There'll be reporters peppering you with questions. You'll become a public figure if we have to hold the press conference. Your private life will be gone. Are you sure you can go through with it?"

Ann nodded vigorously. Erica continued, "Just remember to think about your answers before you reply. If you get stuck, look at me and I'll take over."

"I thought we couldn't have a press conference unless they refuse to settle. You said all our plans will have to change," said Ann.

"We have to prepare as though we won't settle before we negotiate. I can always take less at the last minute."

"I don't care about anything but justice. It's now or never."

"Don't worry, there's still an excellent chance that this will be resolved," answered Erica. "I've settled many cases at the last minute on the courthouse steps."

"Do you think they're forcing us to go to court just to make us take the offer?" asked Ann.

"Whether it is or not, we still have to go through with our threat to blow this case wide open."

"I'm ready when you are," vowed Ann.

"Is Clay watching our backs?" asked Erica.

Ann nodded.

Erica looked at Ann for a long moment. Finally, she grabbed her briefcase, stuffed the manila folder inside, and rose from her desk.

"It's time," said Ann, staring at Erica as her heart beat faster. She trembled slightly.

Erica reached out and grabbed Ann's left hand.

"No, it's about time, Emily," said Erica.

Ann's heart beat like a pedal on a bass drum at the sound of her actual first name.

Traffic on Route One was gridlocked. David Whitney stopped dead half a dozen times as he drove north. It took him almost two hours to extricate himself from the backup caused by two minor collisions. He did not arrive at the estate until almost nine o'clock. Katherine was waiting for him in the drawing room, and a servant told him the senator was on the telephone and would join them soon.

"We're almost out of time, so listen to everything I say," ordered Whitney in an exhausted tone. "If this thing blows up, you can kiss all of it good-bye. You and your father can always get more money. All the senator has to do is have a couple of fundraisers to become solvent, but without Austin, his influence ends. You'll be ruined."

David was waiting for her reply when Senator Mitchell burst into the room and hobbled toward him. His gait made him unsteady on his feet, and his rumpled look showed he had slept poorly. From the maniacal look in his eyes, David was almost afraid he was going to be attacked. Suddenly, the senator's eyes relaxed, as if they had been snapped open by a whip. He grabbed Whitney by the shoulders and spoke in rapid-fire bursts.

"Where have you been, David? No one answered at your office, and I couldn't get you on the car phone!"

Whitney broke the grasp and took a step backward. "I've been stuck in traffic. I came here to get you to reconsider settling the Sorenson case."

"Dammit, man, you're right. I've been so blinded by hate that I refused to see what needed to be done. Wait here," said Mitchell.

Mitchell turned and exited the room, leaving Whitney looking perplexed.

Von Steihl is alive! I have to give these bitches everything, thought Langley, as he reached the hallway.

He returned in less than two minutes, carrying a black canvas suitcase. After unzipping the bag, he tossed it at Whitney's feet.

"This is all we have, David. We liquidated everything, including my campaign fund. If they won't take this, then God help us all," Mitchell said.

Whitney stared at the open bag in disbelief. It was filled to the top with stacks of $100 bills.

"How much money is in here?" Whitney finally asked.

"Three million, nine hundred seventy thousand. We don't even have lunch money left."

Grabbing the bag while glancing at his watch, Whitney left the room and broke into a sprint to reach his car. He would call Erica Payne's office en route, have them get a message to her that he was on his way, and to put the media on hold. After starting the engine, Whitney looked at the dashboard clock. It read 9:22. It was thirty-eight minutes until Payne had her press conference.

But I'm forty-five minutes from Boston, he thought as he threw the car in reverse and backed away with the tires squealing like a flock of migrating geese.

Instantly, Whitney snatched up his cell phone and dialed Payne's office. The line rang once and then went dead. He called her office three more times on his way into Boston. Each time his phone dropped the call before he could leave a message. After throwing it on the seat, he drove almost eighty miles an hour down Route One, darting in and out of traffic, and miraculously avoiding detection by any law enforcement officer.

Several minutes later, Whitney was about to meet his first obstacle: a tollbooth on Mystic River Bridge. His dashboard clock said 9:40. Whitney was raging as he angrily laid on his horn and shook his fist at the elderly couple in the blue Dodge Intrepid parked in front of him in the exact change lane, casually looking for coins. Whitney shouted and pounded his steering wheel.

Finally, the Intrepid pulled forward slowly, and Whitney roared up to the booth. After throwing all his change into the wire basket, he gunned the car forward and sped around the Intrepid on his way to the courthouse. At that moment, a police cruiser pulled up behind him and turned on its flashing blue lights. Whitney's pulse raced as he continued to weave in and out of traffic. It was 9:47 when he reached the entrance to Storrow Drive and thought for a fleeting moment that he had a chance to make it, even with the cruiser bearing down.

Suddenly, Whitney's heart surged anxiously as a sea of brake lights merged into a single, cone-shaped lane. Cutting the steering wheel hard to the right, he had to pull all the way over and knew there was no way to get through. Another cruiser joined the first and tried to cut him off. At once, he knew the battle was over.

Out of nowhere, a red-and-white ambulance speeding toward Massachusetts General Hospital appeared on his left with lights flashing and siren blazing. Traffic squeezed to the sides to give the ambulance clearance, and Whitney knew his only chance had come. Tromping on the accelerator, he moved the Lexus forward, slipped in behind the ambulance, and followed it as it sped toward the hospital. He felt like he was racing at the Daytona Five Hundred while drafting behind the pole setter.

Whitney collided with a Ford Escort that had tried the same maneuver. The impact caused his car to ricochet and head back into line behind the ambulance. One of the cruisers also collided with the Escort and was forced to pull over because of the front-end damage.

As Whitney negotiated the rotary at Charles Street, his cell phone rang. Snatching it from the passenger side, he held it to his ear and listened in frustration at the sound of static. He kept shouting, "Hello," but there was no one on the line. The clock read 10:03. Traffic stopped on Charles Street as the ambulance took a sharp left onto Fruit Street, and Whitney continued racing up Charles Street toward the courthouse. Several police cars were chasing him with sirens and lights as he weaved a pattern in and out of traffic that forced him to ride on the sidewalk briefly two different times while pedestrians scattered.

The light at the next intersection changed to red just as David arrived, bringing traffic in his lane to a halt. Undaunted, he hit the accelerator and cranked the steering wheel all the way to the right, narrowly missing several vehicles from oncoming traffic and almost hitting a group of pedestrians who were forced to spread out in different directions. The sound of sirens and orders from police car loud speakers warned him that the cruisers were continuing their high-speed chase.

"Shit!" shouted Whitney, who refused to stop.

The dashboard clock read 10:06 when he drove the Lexus onto the sidewalk, threw it in park, grabbed the bag, and ran for the courthouse. A cruiser that had been following Whitney pulled up, and two Boston police officers stepped into David's path. The larger officer drew his service revolver and pointed; then he grabbed the bag and pinned Whitney's arms behind his back while his partner slapped on handcuffs.

Whitney's heart sank as he watched the rows of television trucks parked on the sides of the street. He was several minutes away from reaching Erica Payne, who was surrounded by lights as she stood on the courthouse steps. It was too late. He had lost and let down his old friend, Lee Harlow.

Instantly, hope appeared as he saw his chief media ally, Meredith Lacey, the lead news anchor from channel thirteen. She was standing in front of Erica, microphone in hand—cell phone clipped to her purse.

The Waringer Crematorium was located in the suburban town of Everett and serviced most of the local mortuaries in the Boston area. It was contained in a nondescript antique brick building on Front Street, and few of the town residents bothered to inquire as to what really occurred after a hearse arrived at the rear entrance and deposited its cargo.

Just before 9:00 a.m., Jamie Quintell found the last parking space at the corner of Front and Hamlin, two blocks from the entrance to the crematorium. After entering the building, she looked for the manager but found his office was empty.

"Excuse me," Jamie called to a man in the back room. "I'm looking for Ernie."

"He had to run out for a minute. He'll be back in about fifteen."

"We had an appointment. Where did he go?" she asked before glaring at her watch with a look of irritation.

"To buy a lottery ticket. The Megabucks jackpot is up to twelve million," the man said with a shrug, not comprehending her aggravation. "Why don't you wait in his office?"

Jamie sat in one of the metal chairs. She had slept badly and felt tired and cranky. She was troubled as she recalled the conversation concerning Lee's gold bridge.

Jamie remembered reading books in college about the Holocaust and how victims of the death camps had gold teeth plucked from their mouths after they came out of the ovens. That was immolation of the most brutal kind. If gold teeth survived heat that intense, they would probably not melt in today's modern crematoria.

Her cell phone rang. It was Paul Sweeney.

"What's up?"

"Every damn thing that could go wrong has!" screamed Sweeney.

Jamie moved the phone away from her ear. "Take it easy. What happened?"

"I drove up here last night. Just before I hit the Canadian border, I blew the thermostat on my car. I spent most of the night and morning trying to get it repaired. Naturally, it happened in a small town, and there are no rental car agencies close by. As soon as I can rent a car, I'll head for Montreal."

"Hurry, Paul. We don't have time to waste."

"I know. I'll talk to you later."

Twenty minutes passed, and Jamie began to pace around the office as she waited for Ernie to return. She left a message for David Whitney telling him she would call him as soon as she could if anything turned up at the crematorium.

If, on the other hand, she reached a dead end, she would not bother to call. If he did not hear from her by 9:45, it was safe to proceed.

At 9:30, Jamie grew more agitated and walked over to the filing cabinet to the left of the desk. Opening the top drawer, she came to the letter "H" and searched for Lee Harlow's records. They were missing.

Several minutes later, a man in his early forties, bald and slightly paunchy, entered the office. He was dressed in a flannel shirt and gray pants, and he was carrying a Dunkin' Donuts carryout bag, which he set on the desk. Jamie looked at the black plastic clock behind the desk. It read 9:39.

"Are you the manager?" demanded Jamie.

"Yeah, why?" replied the man, holding a donut between his teeth as he removed his jacket.

"Because you're late. We had an appointment at nine," Jamie said testily, "I'm almost out of time, and I need to talk to you."

"Sorry, I forgot and had to run out for a couple of minutes. What can I do for you?"

"You did the cremation of Lee Harlow. I need some information."

"That's confidential. I can't talk about it."

"Here's a release," countered Jamie, shoving a notarized document containing Katherine's signature toward him.

The man examined the document. "Let me make a photocopy," he said, rising and walking to a small portable machine.

Jamie jumped up to stop him.

"There's no time!" she said excitedly. "Keep the original and get me the information."

"Take it easy, lady. What do you want to know?"

"What happens to teeth during cremation?"

"Usually, we have to grind them down. Just like bones."

"What do you mean?"

"Well, the oven gets pretty hot, almost seventeen hundred degrees, but it still doesn't melt everything like it does flesh. Sometimes bones and teeth have to go through a machine called a pulverizer that grinds them up after the cremation is finished. Even then, we might have to use a little hammer to knock the leftover chunks into ashes."

"What if some of the teeth were gold?"

The man flashed a silly grin at her.

"Well, dental gold's not the stuff in Fort Knox, OK? But it's still pretty durable. In my experience, it probably wouldn't melt but would survive pretty much intact."

"Any way you could recover it?" Jamie asked between scribbles.

"Sure. We have a retort oven in the area in the middle to catch the ashes. It's supposed to catch everything after the cremation. See, the body is usually wrapped in a plastic sheet or pouch so fluids can't leak. Then it's placed in a cardboard and wood box so it will catch fire quickly and burn. The retort oven in the middle catches the ashes and the gold teeth would probably wind up there," he declared proudly, grateful for the infrequent opportunity to interest someone in his work who did not have a ghoulish streak.

"You gave the ashes back to the mortuary, right?"

"Of course."

"What happened to the gold teeth?"

"I'd have to check. Usually, we would place them in a separate bag for the family. Other times, we don't. Some people aren't real happy to see Grandma's teeth in a ziplock, you know," he said, grinning.

"Can you hurry and check the records and see if Dr. Harlow's gold bridge was recovered?" asked Jamie. She looked at the clock, which read 9:53.

"Sure," he answered, opening the bottom-right drawer of his desk and pulling out several manila folders that were waiting to be filed. He thumbed through them until he reached the one containing the records of Dr. Lee Harlow.

"That's funny," he said, after reading the first page in the file before handing it to her. "This report says there was nothing in Harlow's mouth except amalgam fillings. According to this, he never had any gold teeth."

Jamie snatched the telephone from the desk and furiously dialed Whitney. There was a buzz and the line went dead. For the next several minutes, she desperately tried to reach Whitney. Finally, she gave up, called the Mitchell home, and got no answer. She tried to reach David several more times. Twice the connection dropped and the other time it was busy, but with a signal as though the line was incapacitated instead of being occupied. After trying to text without success, Jamie looked at the clock again: 10:08. Her spirits sank as she realized it was too late.

Jamie felt a flash of anger because the time to reach Whitney had passed and he was still incommunicado. Quickly, the anger dissipated and turned to resignation. After picking up her briefcase, she looked at the manager and spoke softly.

"By the way, did you win on that lottery ticket?"

"Naw. I only had one out of six numbers. It was a loser."

Jamie smiled sadly and said, "You're wrong. It was worth fourteen million dollars."

Chapter Twenty-Seven

Erica Payne was standing on the steps of the Suffolk County Courthouse, talking with her friend, Meredith Lacey, the longtime news anchor. Lacey had covered all of Payne's biggest cases for years. She was only a rookie reporter when she was first sent to cover one of Payne's trials. The two women took to each other instantly, and Payne began to feed her scoops in exchange for favorable coverage.

"Hello, sis," Payne said confidently, giving Lacey a quick hug.

"Couldn't give me an exclusive this time, huh?" chided Lacey.

"Sorry. This one's too big."

"I thought you and I went back a long way."

"We do, but this case is in a class by itself," answered Payne. *All the way around the world*, she thought. *But not back again.*

"Ms. Payne, I've got a deadline," called a man on the second step down, looking at his watch. "When are you going to get started?"

"Just another moment," said Payne reassuringly. "Please be patient."

Payne was trembling slightly as she surveyed the crowd. She knew she couldn't file a lawsuit in the case. That would produce a thorough investigation, something she had to avoid. The entire plan would unravel.

Still, Payne knew she had to perform as well as she could at the press conference to convince Whitney and Castle to sweeten the offer. If neither showed up by the time she was finished, Payne planned to call Whitney and offer to meet him at his office. If everything else failed, and seven million dollars was all she could get, she would take it and run. The press conference was only a prop. If she needed to pretend she was filing a lawsuit, she would slip out of the courthouse before anyone could follow and discover her deceit.

Ann stood alone, waiting for Payne to begin. She grew tense as any hope of increasing the settlement offer dwindled with each passing moment.

Payne walked to the bouquet of microphones set up in front of the courthouse. Seeing neither opposing counsel made her uneasy. She never expected Castle to show, but she had been convinced that Whitney would make one final attempt at resolution. Her knees buckled slightly as the crowd quieted. Taking a deep breath, she began to speak.

"Ladies and gentlemen, I'd like to thank you all for coming. For those of you I do not know, my name is Erica Payne. I am an attorney representing the lady to my right, Ann Sorenson. In just a few minutes, I will be filing a multimillion dollar lawsuit on behalf of Ms. Sorenson, which alleges she is a victim of the most egregious negligence I have ever witnessed in all my years of practicing law."

"Is this a medical malpractice suit, Ms. Payne?" asked a man in the front row.

"It is. My client was forced to participate in a wrongful birth. We have made allegations that the defendants knew, or should have known, that they gave her the wrong—"

The persistent ringing of a cell phone interrupted the conference, causing Payne to look down at Lacey, who was standing only a few feet away directly in front of her. Meredith answered and then looked up and gave Payne a perplexed look before shoving her arm toward her.

"Ricki, you have a phone call. Says it's urgent." Meredith handed Payne her smoke-gray cell.

Annoyed at being interrupted, Erica reached for the phone.

"You have to stop the conference!" called out a breathless voice from the phone. "Look up. I'm standing here in handcuffs at the end of the building by One Center Plaza."

Payne looked up to locate the speaker. A tense smile covered her face as she watched David Whitney, who was surrounded by police and S.W.A.T. members who held his hands behind his back while he wiggled his shoulders back and forth in an effort to convince her he was captured. Three police officers restrained him while a fourth held a cell phone up to his left ear.

"We have to talk. I have a new offer!" shouted Whitney.

Payne felt a rush and then her breath began to gush out like a series of pyrotechnic concussions from a rock concert. The plan had worked. She turned back to the crowd with a look of triumph.

"Ladies and gentlemen, I'm told we are about to resolve this case," Payne said.

Ann squeezed her right arm.

A flurry of questions began as Payne held up her hands for silence.

"I have to meet with opposing counsel now. If this case does not settle, we will be back here shortly, and I will give you all of the details," Payne said. Then she led Ann to the entrance of the Suffolk County Superior Court as reporters continued shouting questions.

After David Whitney convinced the police he was not a road menace and accepted a citation for a slew of moving violations, he and Erica Payne entered the courthouse together. The security guards recognized them immediately and both were admitted without being required to pass through the metal detectors. Erica told Ann she would meet with Whitney alone and ordered Ann to avoid all reporters. The attorneys found an empty courtroom as the cadre of media representatives who were waiting for the press conference to resume milled around in the corridor.

Once inside the courtroom, the two lawyers walked to the plaintiff's table, located on the right side of the bench. Whitney placed the black bag of money on the floor next to Payne.

"Here's the bottom line. You've won. There's almost four million in cash in the bag. The malpractice insurer won't come up from seven million, but with that seven and this cash, you'll still get almost eleven million. Castle said she wasn't coming, but I'm sure I can get their check this afternoon. In return, we'll need a confidentiality agreement of nondisclosure from both you and your client. This is take it or leave it time, because there's nothing else."

Payne smiled faintly as she opened the bag and looked inside. She fought to keep her breathing even as she stared at the stacks of bills. Then she remembered her client.

"You said almost four million," she asked warily. "How much is it short?"

"Thirty thousand. It doesn't matter, you know, unless you want my clients to go out and sell their blood to get an extra hundred or two."

Payne chuckled. Whitney remained straight faced.

"Good line, David. I'll remember it."

"If the insurer kicks in their seven, do we have a deal?"

Payne was ready to respond when the door opened and Rebecca Castle walked in. She was carrying a large black bag and a briefcase.

"Hi, kids. Even though I'm late, I'm here now, so get the band warmed up and ready to play any song I request," said Castle in a voice lathered with sarcasm.

"How about if we just have Elton John sing 'The Bitch Is Back?'" asked Payne as she edged Whitney's bag under the table so Castle could not see it.

"As Norman Mailer once said, 'I have only two words for both of you and I guarantee you they are not "Happy Motoring,"' Rebecca said, shooting Payne a look of disgust.

What the hell are you doing here? I got word you weren't coming," said Whitney.

"You can stay if you have the price of admission," said Payne.

"What would that be?" Rebecca asked with a smirk.

"Ten million dollars."

"We'll see about that. Get your client in here and let's talk," ordered Castle.

"Why do we need Ann?" Payne asked as she folded her arms.

"Because lawyers are greedy bastards who would hold out for an extra subway token if they thought they could get it. I want your client to see for herself what we are offering, live and in color, before she turns it down."

Payne thought for a moment and then left the room. She walked down the hallway and approached Ann, who was still surrounded by reporters. On Payne's advice, Ann had refused to answer any questions.

"Counsel for the insurer is here," Payne said after moving Ann out of earshot of the reporters. "She is carrying a bag. I think it's filled with money. Don't be fooled when you see it. Let's find out how much it is."

"What do you mean?"

"If it's cash, it will seem like a lot more than it is. Be on guard."

"How do we know what to do?"

"Let's see what the offer is. Then we'll decide."

Ann's chest began to tighten as she and Payne returned to the courtroom where Castle and Whitney were waiting.

"Ball's in your court, Counselor," Payne said to Rebecca.

Castle looked at each person before she began. "Here's our offer, Ms. Sorenson." Suddenly, Castle picked up the bag and dumped the contents on the table. Hundred and fifty dollar bills spilled out and formed a huge pile. Everyone grew speechless as Castle smirked.

The sight of that much money caused everyone to breathe unevenly. Whitney reached forward and began to stack the bills into neat rows. Castle folded her arms and gave everyone a gleeful look of triumph.

"How much is here?" Payne finally asked.

"Seven million. I wanted your client to see what you've been turning down."

No one spoke for another minute. Rebecca reached into her briefcase and pulled out a file.

"I have the releases here. Sign them, and we can all go home. And we'll never have to see each other again," she said in a voice filled with victory.

Payne fought to keep from showing Whitney and Castle the joyous frenzy she was feeling. As Payne was about to accept the money, Ann Sorenson suddenly placed her hand on top of Erica's and then looked at Castle.

"Sorry, no deal. It's ten million or we let a jury decide."

Payne fought to stay calm as her chest tightened. She cast a frenzied glance at Ann. Her eyes opened wide and her mouth quivered slightly as she stared into Ann's eyes with a forlorn, pleading look.

She's blowing the damn deal! Payne thought savagely. *When we're so close. I might have to take her outside and beat some sense into her!*

Castle leaned forward. "Take a good look at that pile of cash, Ms. Sorenson. All that is yours. All you have to do is sign the papers. You've got thirty seconds or the deal is off the table, and you'll be in for the battle of your life," Rebecca said. She moved her hand in a sweeping gesture before it brushed against a manila folder on the table to her right.

Ann looked first at Payne and then at David. Each held poker faces. Turning back to face Castle, her eyes became fixated on a document that had been dislodged by Castle's hand as it stuck the folder. It was protruding almost two inches from the bottom of the manila folder on Rebecca's right. From its dimensions, it seemed to be the size of a check. Ann took a deep breath and folded her hands.

"What's that document for? The one sticking out?" asked Ann, raising her right index finger and pointing to the folder.

Castle looked down and then suddenly lost her composure. She panicked as she tried to stuff the check back inside to hide it in the file.

"Uh… er… That's for another case," stammered Castle.

Instantly, Ann reached forward and skillfully snatched the check from Castle's hand. She looked at it briefly before handing it to Payne with a look of triumph.

"Better use it for this one. A certified check for three million payable to us. Nice touch, Rebecca. It's too bad your haste to strong arm us didn't let you get away with keeping this check hidden along with all of the rest of the deceit," said Erica, smiling broadly as she stared at the composition of her favorite duet in the world: commas and zeroes.

Castle began to perspire. Her scheme had failed, and she was caught. She looked like a mark who had tried to finesse her loan shark, and now faced the prospect of cement-filled shoes and a long dip into the frigid Atlantic Ocean. Filled with rage, Rebecca snatched a document from her file and threw it on top of the money pile like it was a pipe bomb.

Whitney picked up the check and stared at it. It was made out to Ann Sorenson and Attorney Erica Payne in the amount of three million dollars.

"Take the whole ten million! I hope you get robbed when you leave here," said Rebecca. She snarled so loudly that her nostrils flared and her nose made a sucking sound, like a straw as it struggled with the last drops of liquid from the bottom of a cup.

Whitney handed the check back to Ann, who studied it for a moment before grinning and nodding. Rebecca angrily removed several documents from her file and shook her head in a gesture of disdain. David shrugged as he opened his briefcase and withdrew a manila folder.

It took several minutes to sign and notarize all the documents, including one binding each participant to secrecy and confidentiality. When finished, Ann and Payne shook hands with Whitney. They were barely able to hide their euphoria.

"This happened because of you, David. I owe you a bottle of champagne," said Payne.

"If the guilt starts to eat away at you, make it *Bollinger La Grande* 2004," he said.

The three walked directly past Castle toward the door, snubbing her as they quickly exited. Rebecca huffed and was preparing to leave the room when Whitney approached her.

"If you had the money to offer, why didn't you?" asked Whitney.

"Because it belongs to the stockholders," Castle replied with fire in her voice, "not to some tramp bimbo who had another guy's kid and her *Entertainment Tonight* Armani-infused attorney. Seven million was plenty of money for them. Ten is a downright windfall."

Whitney shook his head.

"If I live to be a hundred, I'll never figure out how you keep your job."

Castles slammed her briefcase shut and turned to face him on her way out. "I'm a winner," she spat.

Whitney's face dissolved in a mischievous grin.

"If you think you won today, you're in a dream world," he said with a snicker.

After Ann and Payne left, several reporters surrounded them, trying to squeeze out the slightest bit of information. Some tried to quiz Ann directly, but she referred all questions to Payne. As reporters shouted questions at her back, Payne refused to answer until she reached the microphones. She was carrying the black bag Whitney had brought. Ann carried the one from Castle.

"Ladies and gentlemen," Payne began, "I am happy to report to you that we have reached a settlement in this case. The lawsuit has been withdrawn. As we have all executed an agreement of confidentiality, we are bound by those terms and can say nothing more about this matter. Thank you all for coming."

"What's in the bags, Ms. Payne?" yelled a reporter as David Whitney arrived.

"Our lunch," Payne said as several people around her laughed.

"How many will it feed? The entire population of Beijing," yelled another scribe. The laughter grew more raucous.

"Mr. Whitney, you've been in the news as the attorney for the late Dr. Lee Harlow. Does this action involve him?" asked Lacey.

"I have hundreds of clients besides Dr. Harlow. As Ms. Payne just told you, we can't talk about any particulars in this case because all details are confidential and sealed," said Whitney sternly.

Meredith Lacey grabbed Payne by the arm and pulled her close.

"How much justice is in those two bags?" she whispered.

Erica Payne smiled broadly and pressed her lips close to Lacey's ear. "Not nearly what we deserve, but as much as we could get."

Jamie Quintell reached the front of the Suffolk Courthouse just before eleven as the last mobile camera crew was leaving. She'd double-parked on the street and quickly ran inside where she learned David Whitney had just left. She dialed his office on her cell phone and was told he had not yet arrived. Jamie ran back to her car and made a U-turn on her way to Whitney's office.

After parking, Jamie ran for the elevator. Her cell phone rang. It was Whitney calling from his office phone.

"David, I'm almost in the elevator. I'm losing the signal, so we'll talk when I get up there. Wait for me, OK?" said Jamie before breaking the connection. Five minutes later, she arrived.

"I've been trying to call you for a long time. What happened?" she asked.

"My damned phone is on the fritz," he said angrily.

"Did you settle with Payne?" she asked between deep breaths.

"I did. Why?"

"Call the bank and stop payment on the check," she said, picking up his phone and handing it to him.

"What the hell are you talking about? Why should I do that?"

"Because I have evidence that the body they found is not Lee Harlow's!" she sputtered.

Whitney grabbed her shoulders and shook his head in disbelief.

"That's impossible."

"Somebody got the wrong dental records, or Lee picked up the wrong ones from Jacobs."

"How can you be sure?"

"Harry told me about the gold bridge, right? Well, I just came from the crematorium and the body they cremated didn't have a gold bridge. It wasn't Harlow."

Whitney felt a wave of terror spread over him. "He can't be alive, Jamie, he was lost at sea. If he is alive, why hasn't he contacted me?"

"If that wasn't his body, that means the death can be reopened, and then you can fight all those transactions that have put the corporation in ruin. So what if Payne goes to the press then? If it wasn't Harlow's body, there's a slim chance he could turn up some day and defend this case, and Erica Payne will have to settle on our terms."

"Jesus Christ, I can't recover the money," Whitney cried suddenly, as a sinking feeling came over him. "The check from the insurer was certified and the rest was cash!"

"Call Payne and get her to stop the disbursement."

"I'm way ahead of you," answered Whitney as he picked up his phone.

Whitney's secretary knocked and entered.

"Excuse me, Jamie. Mickey Cornette is calling on line three."

"I'll take it in the conference room," Jamie replied. She walked quickly down the hall.

"Bad news, Jamie. Harry Jacobs never heard of Vellois and couldn't identify the photo. Want me to go back to the Caymans and keep digging?"

"No. I think that's a waste of time. Keep in touch, OK?"

After Jamie ended her conversation, Whitney burst into the room. He seemed flustered.

"Jamie," he said excitedly, "Erica Payne is gone for the day. Get over to Wellesley and see if you can find Ann Sorenson."

"I'll make some calls on the way and find out what bank she deposited the money in. Wait for me to find out so you can get a court order to freeze the money."

Chapter Twenty-Eight

At two o'clock, Senator Langley Mitchell and Austin Harlow walked to the podium that had been set up in the front atrium next to a large auditorium of the newly constructed federal building in Boston's West End. Most people were there to see the building dedicated to Senator Mitchell and to witness the ceremony naming the structure after him. As servers in black uniforms continued to offer *hors d'oeuvres* and champagne, several hundred people applauded wildly as the senator walked to the microphone.

The applause refused to die as Senator Mitchell held his hands up for silence. Finally, he gave up, turned, and whispered something to his grandson. They both laughed heartily as the noise rose to a giant crescendo. A tall blond man with a thick brown moustache wearing a black waistcoat finished placing a large frame covered with red velvet on an easel to the right of the podium, before walking to the rear of the room.

The man waited until everyone was seated. Chuckling, he softly fingered the ten $100 bills he had been given to deliver the easel with the campaign poster. It was a poster that would certainly get a response, but definitely not the one that Senator Mitchell and his grandson expected. Satisfied that his work was finished, the man walked to the back of the room and positioned himself at an angle where he had the podium in plain view.

"Thank you so much, ladies and gentlemen, for that magnificent Boston greeting. I come back home every weekend, and the only thing I regret about my time in the Senate is that I couldn't get the Capitol moved from Washington to Boston, where our country got its staht, heah in our beloved home state of Massachusetts!" boomed the senator to another burst of tumultuous applause.

"I am so happy to see all my old friends here today. All of you warriahs who have been through so much with me. I see people like Ted Dahling," continued the senator, pointing to the center of the crowd at a tall man who smiled broadly and waved. "A man who helped me rid this town of the smut merchants and morally devoid pornographers who are trying to ruin our nation's charactah by promoting acts so vile and repugnant that no civilized person could feel anything but disgust at being forced to see them."

Another ovation caused him to stop. After an appropriate pause, he continued.

"But like all old soldiers, I am growing tired. It is time to turn the fight over to someone else. Someone with youth and vigah. Therefore, I want to thank you for your support over these past forty-plus years, but I had to call you all together one last time to tell you that I will not be a candidate for reelection to the US Senate."

Pandemonium broke loose as people turned to each other. Suddenly, a cry of "no" filled the auditorium. It took several minutes before order was restored.

"Please, friends, let me finish," begged the senator, as the room grew silent. "One of the great secrets of life is knowing when it is time to move on. I have reached that time. I pray the country has acquired a small token from my devotion to yoah service," said Senator Mitchell in a voice choked with emotion.

"Many of you are wondering about my successor. I have been thinking of nothing else since I made my decision. There are many wonderfully qualified men and women who could take my place. I have consulted with party leaders to make certain that we pick someone who is the best qualified. So at this time, I want to bring our pahty chayah, Ted Darling, up to the podium to talk about the pahty's choice," he continued.

Frenzied applause accompanied Edward Theodore "Ted" Darling, a tall man in his middle years as he walked to center stage and stood next to Senator Mitchell and Austin Harlow. He had the look of a statesman, capped off by his shock of black hair, and was impeccably dressed in a charcoal suit and red-and-black striped tie. He grinned broadly, showing off his pristine white teeth, waving to the crowd while waiting for the noise to subside.

"Thank you, ladies and gentlemen," Darling began. "I want you all to know this was not an easy decision but one that we have spent many hours poring over and praying for divine guidance to confirm what we felt so deeply in our hearts. We have chosen a man who will pick up the fight where Langley Mitchell left off. Someone who is a physician and healer. A man with honor and courage and vision. Someone who will fight for what is right and decent, and lead the battle on the floor of the Senate to drive out all the purveyors of filth who are trying to destroy the things for which we stand. Someone who knows tragedy and devastation, and how to fight to overcome them. Someone who has recently lost his beloved father, but has demonstrated the endurance and fortitude to put this personal tragedy behind him and dedicate himself to the greatest calling of all: service for the people. Ladies and gentlemen, I am deeply proud and personally honored to give you our party's candidate for the US Senate, Senator Langley Mitchell's grandson, Dr. Austin Harlow."

A small stir turned rapidly into chaos. The senator had passed the torch. It would stay in the family. Austin Harlow might be an unknown, but if he had the confidence of the party and the senator himself; he was the candidate the people could throw their support behind.

Darling nodded to a uniformed aide who walked to the huge frame covered with the red velvet cloth positioned to the right of the podium at an angle where it could be seen clearly by all. The aide grabbed the rope controlling the cloth and waited for the signal from the senator to unveil Austin's first campaign poster.

Austin walked forward through the din and hugged his grandfather, who then reached for Austin's left arm and thrust it skyward in a victory salute. The applause reached a record decibel level as Senator Mitchell looked at the aide and pointed with his left hand, which was the signal to drop the cloth. The aide responded, the cloth fell, and the applause died slowly as the throng of people stared at the twelve-foot poster in disbelief.

Senator Mitchell looked confused at the crowd's reaction.

Suddenly, Austin yelled, "My God! No! No!"

Bewildered, the senator turned to face the poster and gasped loudly. He reached his hands up to his head and then pitched forward as he collapsed.

The man who had delivered the poster quietly slipped out of the room and exited the building through the kitchen. On the way out, he removed the blond wig and fake moustache, and tossed them into a trash receptacle on the corner.

Several people rushed forward. Austin ripped open the senator's shirt and pounded his chest.

The poster was a six-by-twelve-foot blow-up showing Senator Langley Mitchell, looking much younger and leaner, and standing over a body slumped on the ground. The man lying at Mitchell's feet had a gunshot wound to the head and lay in a pool of blood. His eyes wore the empty look of death, and the senator's face was contorted in an evil, angry scowl as he looked down at the man's body.

Langley Mitchell was holding a handgun and pointing it at the body. The scene in the background was the senator's home in Prides Crossing. The date was stamped at the bottom: July 21, 1974.

Jamie drove west on Storrow Drive, maneuvering toward the entrance to the Massachusetts Turnpike. Traffic was surprisingly light, and she made the usual fifteen-minute drive in less than ten. After entering the pike in Allston, she sped toward the suburban town of Wellesley and arrived in front of the condominium complex where Ann Sorenson lived. A huge Mayflower moving van was parked in front of her building.

Jamie fought off a sinking feeling in the pit of her stomach as she ran up to the open door. A young couple stood inside the living room while two small children played by the stairway.

"Hello," said the smiling woman as Jamie entered. "Are you a new neighbor?"

"No," said Jamie quickly. "I'm looking for Ann Sorenson."

"She doesn't live here anymore. We bought the condo last week," the man said.

A furniture mover entered with a huge white box, and the man directed him upstairs.

"It's important that I find her. Did she say where she was going?"

"No. She said her plans weren't certain and then asked us if she could stay here until today. Are you a friend of hers?" asked the woman, growing puzzled.

Jamie turned without answering. She was about to call Whitney when her cell phone rang. It was Paul Sweeney.

"Paul, where are you?"

"Still trying to rent a car. Then I'm headed over to Damon's place. I've been on the phone since I last talked to you. I've got the dope on Sorenson, Jamie."

"Go ahead."

"Well, the money she got last week is gone. She let the check from Payne clear and then had the balance transferred to Srotiart Corporation in Palm Beach."

"What about the funds she got today?" Jamie asked as her throat tightened.

"No record of any deposit yet."

"Didn't Payne deposit the money? The lawyer always puts the money in an escrow account and then gives the client their share out of the account."

"I ran Payne's escrow account. No deposit showed up."

"Maybe she hasn't gotten to the bank yet. Have someone call the airlines for me," Jamie ordered as she backed out of the driveway. "See if Sorenson is booked on a flight."

"OK. Wait a minute. The mechanic's yelling at me. Jamie, I just got news my car is fixed. I'm on my way north now. I'll call you as soon as I get something."

Jamie headed back to the office and drove quickly while fighting the urge to call Whitney because she didn't want to miss Sweeney's call. As soon as she pulled onto the highway, her telephone rang again.

"Jackpot time, Jamie. Ann Sorenson is booked on a flight to Rio at two o'clock. They found her car parked in the central garage at the airport," said Jamie's junior associate.

Jamie looked at her dashboard clock. It read 1:35. She didn't have time to make it to the airport. Quickly, she called David Whitney, who was standing in the corridor of Suffolk Superior Court.

"David, Ann Sorenson's on a flight to Rio at two," she yelled. "Stop the plane."

"Got it," replied Whitney, breaking the connection before opening the door to a crowded courtroom. He was on his way to petition a judge to halt the flight.

Fifteen minutes after his conversation with Jamie, Whitney left for Logan Airport armed with a court order to stop the flight to Brazil. A contingent of state police cruisers escorted him to the airport. After Whitney had presented evidence that there was probable cause for fraud, the judge ordered her clerk to call ahead and detain the plane. Passengers would be told there would be a slight delay. Ann Sorenson would have no chance to flee.

Whitney arrived at ten past two accompanied by two state troopers. The three men walked briskly through the International Concourse. After presenting their documents to the agent at the gate, the trio boarded the plane and searched for Ann Sorenson. Because her ticket was in coach, they walked quickly through the first-class section of the jumbo jet, paying little attention to the passengers seated there.

It took them almost thirty minutes to search the plane. They made each passenger produce identification in case Sorenson was in disguise. At the end of the search, they reached the only conclusion that was feasible: she was not on the plane. Their informant had been wrong.

Whitney arrived back at his office at a quarter past four and found Jamie waiting for him. After loosening his tie, David plopped dejectedly onto his couch while Jamie watched him from one of the burgundy leather chairs in front of his desk.

Whitney's secretary knocked and entered.

"Jamie, Chris Weeks just sent you this fax."

Jamie quickly scanned the document before handing it to Whitney.

"Who's Chris Weeks?" he asked before reading it.

"The woman who tested Evans's sperm for the AIDS virus."

Whitney finished reading and looked up. "What do you make of this letter?"

"She told me she found two foreign substances in the sperm specimen, so she ran some tests to determine what they are. Those are the results. Glutaraldehyde and a petroleum-based distillate."

"What the hell does that mean?"

"Antiseptic solution and lubricating oil."

"How could those things get in the sperm?"

"I don't know," Jamie replied.

"What does that have to do with the semen being HIV positive?"

"I'm not sure."

Whitney's intercom rang, and his secretary told him Paul Sweeney was on the line.

"What's up, Paul?" asked Jamie.

"I just got the final report on Hans Straussman. He's a German national who became a naturalized US citizen. He disappeared the day Trenton Harlow died. Speculation is that he went back to Germany."

"Didn't they confirm that?"

"Not enough time. They said there's also evidence suggesting that Straussman was a KGB double agent named Frederick von Steihl."

"Any connection to this case?"

"We haven't found one. I told them to keep digging."

"What else?"

"I'm about five minutes from Damon's place. I'll call you back."

There was a short knock and the Whitney's secretary entered.

"You just got another fax," she said, handing Jamie several more documents.

Jamie studied the documents carefully and then turned to Whitney.

"Here's another piece of the puzzle," Jamie said in a stunned voice. "See if you can figure out how this fits."

Whitney absorbed the documents. After a moment, he turned back to Jamie. "What the hell do you make of this?" he asked in an anguished voice.

"Maybe he found a miracle cure."

"Or maybe there was nothing to cure to begin with," replied Whitney, shaking his head and throwing the documents on the desk.

The documents were sent by Kenesha Evans, the widow of Maxwell Evans, whose sperm had been linked by DNA to Ann Sorenson and her son. The first page was a cover letter requesting help in deciphering the contents of the other two. Next was an application for life insurance dated six months ago. Following that was a letter from the prospective insurer explaining that Maxwell Evans's blood was sent to a laboratory to be tested prior to the policy being issued. Among the tests that had been performed on the blood was one for AIDS antibodies. The test was negative. Evans's blood was not infected with HIV.

Jamie reread the date of the report. It was barely four months ago. That was two-and-one-half years after he donated his sperm. There was no way he was infected when his semen was harvested. This was irrefutable evidence that Ann Sorenson did not get the AIDS virus from her insemination.

In the late afternoon, Paul Sweeney drove east on Canadian Route 10 until he reached the exit for the town of Marieville. Once off the highway, he stopped at a small market and was directed through the center of town to a house at the perimeter of the eastern city limit. He left his car a few yards ahead of the mailbox, walked to the door, and rang the bell.

After receiving no answer, he went to the side of the house and peered in the window. Suddenly, his heart raced as he focused on an eight-by-ten photograph on an antique desk next to an old recliner. In the picture, Ann Sorenson was hugging a black man who was seated next to her in a wheelchair.

After making certain there was no alarm, he grabbed a rock from the yard and quickly smashed one of the small windowpanes. Reaching to the top of the sill, Paul freed the latch, opened the window, and climbed inside. That was why he failed to see the white Blazer pull to the front of the house. Inside were Speed, Ann, and Andrew.

"Did you see that man go in our house?" asked Ann fearfully.

"Yeah, I did. That must be his car with the Massachusetts license plate," Speed replied, pointing to the blue Pontiac Firebird.

"What do we do?"

"Call the police."

As they pulled away from the entrance and parked, Paul began to rifle through the contents of the house. First, he found several letters addressed to Anthony Damon and another to Emily Damon, which he presumed was Ann's true identity. His eyes were also drawn to an old photograph of two teenage girls on the fireplace mantle. He could see from the photograph that Ann had an identical twin sister.

Paul walked over to the desktop computer and turned it on. He tried to hack into the e-mail accounts but had no success. Removing a flash drive from his pocket, he attached it to the computer's hard drive and typed in a command, and then the device began downloading all the files. He e-mailed everything to Jamie for her computer expert to decipher.

Walking into the spare bedroom, Paul was drawn to an old, two-tier filing cabinet in the corner. Instantly, he began going through the drawers. The top drawer contained only personal items, credit card information, the house deed, automobile records, and assorted correspondence.

It was in the bottom drawer where he hit the jackpot. The first file he opened contained several copies of yellowed newspaper articles concerning the automobile accident with Austin Harlow. Behind it were several files containing many pages of medical records. Paul skimmed through the contents.

The records showed that Anthony Damon's pelvis had been crushed and his spinal cord bruised in the accident, leading to paralysis from the waist down. They also indicated that he had suffered severe vascular damage to his penis, which left him impotent. Another file contained records of his extensive physical therapy and rehabilitation, and how, through self-determination and iron will, he forced himself to overcome his paralysis and regain his ability to walk on a limited basis through the use of leg braces and crutches.

The final folder of medical records detailed the extensive surgery Anthony had undergone in an attempt to restore his sexual function, all apparently without success. At the bottom of the records were several letters from an urologist named Dr. Jason Butler from San Francisco. The first letter was dated five years ago. It informed Anthony that new microsurgical techniques were now available and should enable him to become sexually active again. Several other pieces of correspondence confirmed that he was an ideal surgical candidate.

The final letter confirmed that penile function was restored, and Anthony's resulting sperm count was almost that of a normal male.

Paul snatched the next file from the drawer. He read the first document. It was dated two years ago, addressed to Speed, and told him how Clay and Ricki were ready to proceed immediately. Paul had just finished reading when a deep voice filled the room.

"Hold it right there. Raise your hands and don't try anything."

Instinctively, Paul thrust his hands in the air as two uniformed police officers approached him. After ordering him to place his hands behind his back, he was handcuffed. Then Ann and Speed approached him.

"This isn't what you think. I'm a private investigator."

"You are no longer in the United States. I suggest you stay silent unless spoken to," commanded the taller of the two officers, whose nametag read: J. Willis.

"Who are you?" asked the other officer.

"My name's Paul Sweeney."

"Why did you break into this home?" asked Officer Willis.

"Because these two just stole several million dollars."

"That's a lie," said Ann.

"She used the alias of Ann Sorenson and was the ringleader of a con game that netted her a fortune. Let me make a phone call. I can prove what I say," continued Paul.

"It doesn't matter," said the second officer.

"What do you mean?" asked Paul.

"You are a foreigner," said Willis.

"Let's clear this up right now," said Ann, handing Andrew to Speed and stepping forward while reaching into her purse. She handed her identification to one of the officers.

The officer read it quickly and then looked up.

"Her name is Emily Curtis Damon, and, unlike you, an intruder and a thief, she resides here," he said.

Paul winced and then began to panic.

"I'm here to take them back to the US to stand trial," insisted Paul.

"That's quite impossible. Unlike you, the Damons have done nothing wrong here in our country," replied Willis.

"Then we'll have them extradited," said Paul.

"No you won't," interjected Speed. "There's no extradition treaty between the United States and Canada."

"Bullshit," snapped Sweeney. "You two will spend a lot of time in a United States prison."

"I don't think so. But you, Mr. Sweeney, will see some time in our jail. We do not take kindly to foreigners burglarizing the homes of our citizens," said Willis.

"I want to speak to the American Embassy. They'll back me one hundred percent on this," he shouted.

"Don't count on it. Of course, if they don't, you can try to take it up with Parliament if you like. But I think you'd better let someone back home know you're going to be a guest of our corrections system for the immediate future," said Willis.

"What happens if we don't press charges?" asked Ann.

"We'll have to release him," replied the other officer.

"Can you escort him back to the border and release him there?" asked Speed.

The officers grinned.

"We certainly can," replied Willis. "But he'll need to stay in a cell for a couple of days while he's being processed."

"It will also give him a taste of what to expect if he ever returns to our country," added the other officer.

"I demand to speak with my embassy," yelled Paul.

"Sorry, it's closed for business today. If you are lucky, you might be released on Sunday night, but only on the condition that you be immediately returned to the United States. And we will circulate your picture at all the border crossings and issue an advisory to keep you out of the country as an undesirable," replied Willis.

"If you gentlemen don't mind, I'd like to put my son to bed. It's his first night home, and I know he's tired," said Ann.

The Damons watched from the window as Paul was led away and placed in the back seat of the police cruiser.

"Why did you tell him there's no extradition treaty between Canada and the US? You know that's not true," said Ann.

"Because I want him to think we're complacent and smug. That will give us time to catch our flight in two days, right after the movers get finished. The senator and his crowd will think we'll just be sitting here without a clue waiting for them to come and take us away any time they get ready," said Speed.

"That's brilliant," she said.

"As usual, it was Ricki's idea," he replied.

After the officers left, Ann picked up her son and approached the fireplace. Staring at the photograph of the two young girls, she gasped joyfully as a tear softly trickled down her cheeks. She moved closer to the picture of her and Andrea taken on their thirteenth birthday and began to speak directly to the photograph.

"I want you to meet your nephew: Andrew Anthony Damon. We're going to call him 'Andy' after you," she whispered, as feelings of joy and peaceful acceptance finally replaced all the years of torture.

Ricki and Clay arrived at the veteran's cemetery located west of Alexandria, Virginia, just before twilight. The graves were pristine and lined up in precise configuration. They walked quickly until they reached a headstone at the end of the fifth row and then stood in front of the gravesite for a few moments.

They focused on the inscription that read

Peter Unger Norwood

Corporal, United States Marine Corps

Born: August 19, 1981

Died: May 10, 2004, Battle of Fallujah

Awarded the Bronze Star Posthumously for Valor

Ricki pictured herself sitting next to her mother as she received the flag that had draped her brother's coffin. She could almost hear the gentle, haunting rendition of "Taps" from the lone bugler and flinched slightly at the memory of the twenty-one gun volley provided by the Marine Corps Honor Guard.

She reached into her pocket and produced a photograph. It showed her brother, Peter, next to Clay, standing at attention in their dress blues after they received orders for Iraq. Her hands trembled as Clay slipped his arm around her shoulders.

They stayed silent for a moment. Then Clay reached into a small black bag and removed a battery-powered drill and a package.

"It's against cemetery rules to affix anything to the headstone," he said. "So keep watch in case some pain-in-the-ass attendant tries to stop us."

Ricki reached for her necklace and exposed her silver pendant. In one quick movement, she detached it from its chain and handed it to Clay.

Underneath the *sheng li* were the words

"Marines Die, but the Marine Corps Lives Forever"

"When did you have this engraved?" he asked.

"Last week when I took it to the jeweler and had him add the clasp you requested."

Clay removed a military service medal dangling from a red, white, and blue ribbon.

"Is that your Silver Star?" Ricki asked.

Clay nodded.

"It should have been Punk's, but the CO only put him in for a bronze and me for the silver. I protested, but he wouldn't listen. So I'm taking matters into my own hands."

"It's the perfect addition," she said.

"Along with those words you added from *Full Metal Jacket.*"

"That was Punk's favorite movie," she said softly.

After Clay attached the medal to the clasp, he held it up against the tombstone, quickly drilled two holes, inserted anchors, and then secured it. Afterward, they stood silently for several minutes.

"Punk told me he was closer to you than anyone he ever met," said Ricki.

"Even though I used to make fun of his name."

A sad smile spread across Ricki's face.

"When we were kids, I tried to say Peter Unger real fast, and it came out P-Unker. He started calling himself Punk after that. Of course, the biggest reason was that my father told him he despised that name."

"Why did Punk and your father hate each other?"

"I guess they were too much alike. Dad and my brother were at odds for a long time. I never forgave my father for kicking him out. Later, I found out my dad never forgave himself after we got word that Punk died on the battlefield."

"Your brother told me that he planned to reconcile with your father. His dying wish was that I promise to find you," said Clay.

Ricki stared at the grave. They were both silent for a long moment.

"This is just like the day you and I met here," said Clay. "Right after his memorial when I was leaving the corps."

"That's when you gave me that disgusting photograph of Roger Newell that led to this scheme coming together," said Ricki.

"The key was Eddy recognizing Newell's photograph and telling you he was Langley Mitchell's chief of staff. Without that, none of this would have fallen into place," said Clay, shooting her a look of admiration.

"This case represents the thing I hate most in life: injustice and those who inflict it on everyone who isn't blessed with the kingdom, power, or glory. Speed's paralysis was the motivating force for me to act. It fit in with Emily having to stay infertile because they could never overcome his lost sexual function. All of that after her horrible childhood; you and my brother living on the streets of DC and being molested by that damn pervert Newell, who was protected by Mitchell; Austin Harlow never having to answer for his shortcomings; Langley Mitchell thinking he's God; and Katherine's betrayal. Those people demanded that we take them down because of their arrogance and cruelty."

"Still, the way you devised the execution of this scheme is absolutely brilliant."

"Not really. I just recognized exactly who everyone was. You can't fool yourself, and this outcome confirms that."

"How did you know everyone would behave the way you expected?"

Ricki squared her shoulders and took on a look of disgust.

"Remember that sign from Anne Frank in front of Lee Harlow's desk? Everyone was exactly who we thought they were. Actually, those people were sitting ducks for Sun Tzu and his battlefield theories. Not to mention your CIA connections."

Clay shrugged and nodded.

"Langley Mitchell deserved to be destroyed."

"At least Andrew's birth has given all of us a fresh start. Lee Harlow was right about character being destiny," said Ricki.

"And look at how things turned out for you. Finding the absolute love of your life."

Ricki smiled as though her heart was ready to burst as she reached up and gave Clay a prolonged hug.

"We'd better leave for the airport now so we can make our flights," said Clay.

"Where are you headed?" she asked.

"Back to Grand Cayman to help close up everything. Then I'll meet you all in Neum."

They shared a short kiss before Clay stepped forward to face the grave. He moved his heels together at a forty-five-degree angle, brought his body to rigid attention, and then swung his right hand up into a precise, perfectly executed salute that reminded her of a gate slamming shut.

They stared at the headstone for a long moment before each muttered a soft "good-bye" and then turned and walked back to the rental car. In less than an hour, they arrived at Dulles International Airport where they went to the overseas terminal and then headed off to board separate flights.

It was almost one o'clock in the morning when David Whitney was startled by the ring of the telephone, even though he was completely awake. Whitney reached for the receiver.

"Hello," he said hesitantly.

"Sorry if I woke you," Jamie Quintell said, "but this couldn't wait."

"Don't worry. I was lying here trying to figure this mess out."

"I'm glad you're lying down, because this may knock you out. I just got a call from my handwriting expert."

"At one in the morning?"

"I told you he was eccentric. He said he was going over the documents that transferred the real estate again and made an interesting discovery. Remember how he said the documents were forged by a woman? Well, on a hunch, he compared the signatures on the mortgages and deeds and guess who they match?" Jamie asked excitedly.

"Who, Jamie, for Christ's sake?"

"Erica Payne. My guy said her handwriting is identical to Robert Smith's signature. He compared them to documents Smith signed as the attorney for Andre Vellois."

"Why would Erica be a party to forgery and fraud?"

"I don't have a motive. But my expert is ready to swear to that under oath."

"What else?"

"You know the two banks that have mortgages on clinic property in Martha's Vineyard and Nashua?"

"Northeast Federal and East Coast Commercial. What about them?"

"They're the same banks that foreclosed on Lee Harlow's mother, Alicia, after Trenton died. I guess they were pretty nasty about it. Basically, they put her out on the street."

"Have you found a direct link to them on this case?" Whitney asked.

"Just that the presidents of both banks always contribute heavily to Langley Mitchell's senatorial campaigns."

"Have you heard from Paul?"

"No, and I'm worried something happened. We're never out of touch this long."

"Anything else?"

"I also got a fax from Mickey Cornette. He's got proof that Michael Vellois did not die in the fire. He's still alive."

"Where is he?"

"No one knows."

"Find him quick, Jamie. Pull all the strings you have to, but you've got to produce him."

"I also ran a check on the traces of lubricating oil they found in Evans's semen. It's pretty common. Hospitals use it to lubricate their surgical tools and instruments."

"How does it fit in here?"

"Someone added it to the sperm after it was used for insemination."

"Why?"

"To make it look like Ann and her baby had the AIDS virus. My source says oral surgeons use oil to lubricate their drills. Studies show that the virus can collect in the oil."

"How does the antiseptic solution fit in?"

"They also soak their drills in glutaraldehyde to help keep them in a cold, semi-sterile, disinfectant state before they run them through the sterilizer."

"Doesn't that kill the AIDS virus?"

"No. But there are other organisms they are concerned about besides HIV. So soaking drills in glutaraldehyde takes care of some of those problems."

"What about the AIDS virus?" asked Whitney.

"The only way to kill HIV is through heat sterilization. The CDC recommends that oral surgeons always use heat to make sure the virus is killed."

"What do you make of this?"

"Someone spiked Evans's sperm with the HIV virus from a surgical drill. That made the value of the case skyrocket. That would also explain why Evans's insurance test for AIDS came up negative, because he never had the virus. Ann and her baby were never infected."

Whitney was silent for a long moment as he considered what Jamie said.

"There's one other thing."

"Tonight's the night for it."

"I think I figured out what the corporation means."

Whitney stiffened, as if he had just been struck with a club. "What are you talking about?"

"Guess what Srotiart spelled backwards is?"

Whitney was silent as he did the calculation in his mind. He was almost ready to respond when Jamie blurted out the word.

"Traitors."

Chapter Twenty-Nine

Monday, November 10

After a restless weekend, David Whitney rose early on Monday morning, unable to lie in bed any longer. It was almost seven o'clock when his private line rang. It was Jamie Quintell.

"Did you hear from Paul?" he asked.

"He called me this morning just after two."

"Where the hell is he?"

"In jail in Canada. He was just released by the Canadian authorities. He should be back here in about an hour."

"Why was he in jail?"

"Breaking and entering."

"Where?"

"The home of Anthony and Emily Damon. Guess who Emily Damon really is?"

"Who?"

"None other than Ann Sorenson."

Whitney thought for a moment before he replied. "Is Paul sure?"

"Absolutely certain. She even confirmed her identity for the local police. He also sent me a bunch of files from her computer in Montreal."

"Whose baby is it?"

"Hers and her husband's. Her husband is Anthony Damon, and he's black. She was inseminated with her own husband's sperm. That means Steven Sorenson is an impostor too."

Whitney was silent. Jamie continued.

"Paul also found medical records about Anthony Damon and a doctor named Jason Butler who restored his sexual function after the accident."

"Are you running a trace on Butler?"

"As we speak."

"I wonder what's coming next."

"I'm having the computer files Paul sent me downloaded and analyzed now. Also, did you happen to listen to the news this morning?"

"No time. Why?" Whitney asked.

"It seems that Erica Payne has flown the coop. She has been missing since Friday, and the police have been contacted," Jamie said in an excited voice.

"She probably took a few days off, Jamie. She can damn well afford it."

"She didn't tell anyone at work she was leaving. The firm is in chaos."

Whitney was about to reply, when Jamie said her cell phone was ringing, and she would call him back. Less than a minute later, his line rang again.

"Damn, Jamie, that was fast—"

"Mr. Whitney?" asked a deep voice.

"Yes."

"I'm calling for Andre Vellois. If you want to find out why this happened, be at the Mitchell estate at nine o'clock."

Whitney's whole body tightened up into a series of knots.

"Who are you?" he asked.

The line went dead.

It rang a few seconds later. This time it was Jamie.

"David, I just got the strangest call. Someone said he was calling for Vellois. Told me to go to Langley Mitchell's place."

"I got the same call. I'll meet you there."

It was almost a quarter to nine when Whitney arrived at the Mitchell estate. Jamie and Paul pulled in behind him.

"Good to see you, Paul," Whitney said, extending his hand. "Never took you for the international fugitive type."

"It's good to be back. This was a conspiracy right from the beginning. The Damons were in on it with Vellois and his gang."

"Let's you and I meet when we finish here. We can go over everything then," Whitney said.

Together, they walked to the front door. The sound of another vehicle made them stop. Turning, they saw Jack Bartlett parking his vehicle behind Jamie's.

"Why are you here, Jack?" asked Whitney, puzzled.

"Because you told me to come."

"I did not."

"Someone from your office called me this morning and said you wanted to meet me here at nine."

Whitney started to protest when a red, white, and blue overnight delivery truck came up the driveway and stopped. The driver disembarked and walked up to the trio.

"Excuse me. I have several packages here that I have to deliver. Can you tell me who you folks are?"

"I'm Attorney David Whitney. This is Dr. Bartlett, Ms. Quintell, and Mr. Sweeney. Who are the packages for?"

"The first one is for you, Mr. Whitney. After you have yours, I also have deliveries for Ms. Katherine Harlow, Dr. Austin Harlow, Senator Langley Mitchell, and Dr. Jack Bartlett. I have been ordered to deliver them all at once after you have made sure that everyone's together," said the driver.

"Who sent the packages?" asked Whitney.

"The sender is the same on each package. Andre Vellois. Srotiart Corporation. Republic of Vietnam."

No one spoke for a moment. Bartlett began to fidget.

"Can I give you your envelope now, Mr. Whitney?" asked the driver, handing him an electronic device for his signature.

"Yes," replied Whitney and then signed where the driver indicated.

Instantly, he was handed a blue-and-white envelope. Inside was a single document. Whitney removed it quickly.

If Langley Mitchell, Katherine Harlow, Austin Harlow, and Jack Bartlett want to find out why this happened, you must have them assemble together. Each is required to sign before receiving a package. You must make certain that everyone stays together until the last package is opened.

If you refuse, the driver is under strict orders to return the packages, and none of you will ever know the answers. The alternative is for Langley, Katherine, Austin, and Jack to figure this out for themselves. That would be much easier, because each of them knows exactly what they are.

And why.

Andre Vellois

The driver waited until Whitney finished reading before stepping toward him.

"I have an additional envelope for you, Mr. Whitney, which I have been instructed to give you after the other deliveries have been made. If you agree to these terms, I'll need your signature again."

Whitney hastily scrawled his signature.

"What happens if these people won't follow the instructions?" Whitney asked.

"Then I have been ordered to return the unopened envelopes and to give you a message for the others."

"What's the message?"

The driver struck a pose and began speaking like he was reciting a speech he had memorized. "Tell them to remember their Shakespeare, who said, 'A coward dies a thousand deaths, a brave man only once.'"

The library was deserted when Whitney led the entourage inside. One of the servants reported that Katherine Harlow, Austin Harlow, and the senator refused to join the group. The driver said he would not disperse the packages until everyone came into the room, repeating that he was under strict orders from the company to follow the delivery procedure exactly as instructed.

Finally, Austin Harlow stormed into the room. He was indignant, and shouted in the driver's face to leave the packages because his grandfather was under suicide watch and too weak to appear. The driver continued to hold his ground until his instructions were followed. Servants were sent to bring Katherine and Senator Mitchell into the room. Katherine arrived momentarily, looking as though she had been crying for days. Another servant arrived, declaring Senator Mitchell was not coming, no matter what happened.

Whitney tried to intervene, telling the driver that he was the senator's lawyer and had power of attorney to accept the package, but still the driver would not budge. Austin and Katherine stalked out of the room. The driver declined to move, claiming he had been instructed to wait until the delivery sequence was followed to the letter no matter how long it took.

Several minutes later, Austin came into the room pushing his grandfather in a wheelchair. The senator wore dark glasses, his cheeks were sunken and hollow, and he looked as though he had aged twenty years.

"Let's get this charade over with," raged Mitchell, shaking his wobbling finger at the driver.

Unaffected, the driver had each member of the group sign in a predetermined order. After the senator scrawled a feeble signature, the driver continued undaunted until all packages had been signed for.

"You must open the first envelope together," the driver said and then handed one to each person.

Everyone complied and removed a single sheet of paper.

"What the hell is this?" demanded Bartlett.

Whitney moved to his side.

"Jamie, see if they're all the same," ordered Whitney.

"They are," Jamie answered, looking down at the pages she had collected from the others. Each contained the identical passage from the Old Testament.

Deuteronomy 28:7

May the Lord deliver up to you the enemies who attack you, and let them be put to rout before you. Though they came out against you by one way, they will flee before you.

"What is this, Bible study class?" screamed Bartlett.

Everyone looked at him.

"I'll kill the sick son of a bitch who's doing this," screamed the senator suddenly. He rose from the wheelchair and attempted to leave. Whitney caught him.

"You have to stay, Senator," Whitney said coldly, thinking of the picture that was made public last Friday.

"The next two packages are for Dr. Austin Harlow," continued the driver. He waited until Whitney identified Austin before walking over and handing him a long rectangular box.

Austin shook as he struggled with the box. Paul walked over and held it steady so he could open it. Austin reached inside and removed two pieces of light-colored wood. One end of each piece showed shattered edges that seemed to form a link.

When the two parts were fitted together, they formed a hospital crutch. The crutch had originally been a single component before being broken in half.

"What the hell is this?" he demanded, staring at each half and trying to fit them together as if to solve a puzzle.

The driver stepped forward and extended a small box to Austin.

"Maybe it's connected to the other package," Jamie said, nodding toward the driver's outstretched hand.

Discarding the pieces of the crutch in frustration, Austin snatched the box from the driver and slipped open the flap. Inside was a digital recorder.

"Is this some kind of sadistic prank?" Austin demanded.

Jamie examined the device before hitting the "play" button.

Several seconds passed before the recorder made a sound. The room grew silent as the sounds of country artist Clint Black filled the room. He sang the same chorus three times in a row, repeating the words to one of his hit songs. Over and over, the recorder played a line that said the singer was leaving here as: 'A Better Man.'"

"I don't understand," said Austin, bewildered.

"The next delivery is for Dr. Jack Bartlett," the driver sad.

"Well, I'll be damned if someone can scare me," thundered Bartlett, jumping up to meet the driver. He ripped open his envelope and extracted two sheets of paper.

"What the Christ does this mean?" he asked in a puzzled voice, but then his face clouded over as Whitney and Jamie arrived at his side.

"This is a report of a diagnostic procedure that was done on Lee Harlow. It's dated three years ago," continued Jack.

Whitney and Quintell looked at the report. It read,

Sperm count, non-existent because of a congenital blockage in the vas deferens.

"Congenital means from the time of birth, right?" asked Jamie.

"That's right," replied Whitney. "What's the other document, Jack?"

"It's a DNA report. A lab ran my DNA and Austin's to determine if there is any connection. It says there is a 99.75 percent degree of probability that there is a familial sequence," said Jack.

Bartlett pulled out a final document: a photocopy of Michelle Vellois's death certificate. Whitney moved next to him, and his eyes were drawn to two blocks: the one for the name of the decedent and the other listing the cause of death. The cause of death had been changed from cervical hemorrhage to murder.

Katherine Harlow was panic-stricken when she was handed the next envelope. She began to tremble so badly that it fell to the floor. Whitney walked over to her chair, picked up the envelope, and opened it. Inside was a photocopy of the birth certificate of Austin Harlow. In the block that said "father's name," Lee Harlow's name was whited out, and the name "Jack Bartlett" was typed in over the whiteout.

"That sperm count report means Lee Harlow couldn't have been Austin's father, and he couldn't have gotten Michelle Vellois pregnant, right, Jack?" asked Whitney as he folded his arms.

Bartlett slumped back in his chair with the documents dangling from his hand. He did not reply.

"That can't be why I'd be leaving here as a better man like that silly song we just heard from the recorder," cracked Austin. "Not with Jack the Greek here as my father."

"That document has to be a lie. There's no proof that Jack is Austin's father," screamed Katherine.

"The next two packages are for Senator Mitchell," the nonplussed driver said. He walked in Mitchell's direction and extended an envelope with his right hand, while retaining a small box in his left.

"The hell with you and everything you stand for, you incompetent fool," sneered Mitchell before grabbing the envelope and flinging it to the floor. He shook his fist at Whitney. "This is your fault."

"It wasn't me with that gun in my hand, you damn hack," cried David.

Jamie walked to the driver's side and picked up the envelope. After opening it, she reached inside and removed a navy-blue passport. Whitney approached and stood next to her as she opened the document. It was issued by the US government on December 1, 1973, in the name of Hans Straussman. The photograph was circled and Straussman's name had two lines drawn through it and the name Frederick von Steihl written in its place.

"What's this?" asked Jamie, extending the passport to the senator, who refused to look at it.

"There's another document under the passport," said Whitney.

Jamie reached down and retrieved it. She tore open the envelope and removed a one-page document.

"What is it?" asked David.

"An affidavit."

"From who."

"Roger Newell, Senator Langley Mitchell's former chief of staff."

"Read it," commanded Whitney.

Silence encompassed the room as Jamie read.

I, Roger Newell, upon being duly sworn and deposed, do hereby state as follows:

I am chief of staff to Senator Langley Mitchell.

I was present when Senator Mitchell shot Trenton Harlow.

I took the photograph of the senator standing over Trenton's body.

I state under oath that the events depicted in the photograph fairly and accurately depict the scene as it was on July 21, 1974.

I also recorded the conversation with the medical examiner about the cause of death of Trenton Harlow. The examiner agreed to falsify the cause of death in exchange for a cash bribe in the amount of $10,000 from Senator Langley Mitchell and appointment to a position as an assistant medical examiner in South Carolina.

I state under oath that the voices depicted in the tape recording are authenticated as belonging to me and the medical examiner in question, and that the conversation is fairly and accurately depicted as it occurred on July 22, 1974.

"Then it's signed and notarized. It's dated ten years ago."

Jamie turned to Whitney and asked, "Guess who notarized Newell's signature?"

As Whitney shook his head. Jamie took a deep breath and replied, "Erica Payne."

"Here's the other delivery," said the driver, extending a white cylinder toward the senator.

Jamie retrieved the oversized tube, ripped it open, and dumped the contents on the table. A rolled up poster slipped out. She unraveled it to reveal a photograph of Marlon Brando dressed in a tuxedo for his role as Don Corleone in the film *The Godfather*. He was pointing his index finger, and his eyes were fixed in a gesture of warning. Written at the bottom were the words:

Keep your friends close but your enemies closer.

"Here is the final package we discussed, Mr. Whitney," said the driver. He handed the package to the attorney and then left the room to hateful stares.

Whitney opened the box and removed another digital recorder. After it was activated, there was a twenty-second gap before the voice of pop singer Warren Zevon sounded as he sang the tag line to his greatest hit. Over and over it played the warning about sending "lawyers, guns, and money," because the shit just collided with the fan.

"I've had enough of this nonsense," thundered Jack Bartlett. He rose and left the room.

"How could someone destroy us all and then treat it like a sick practical joke?" wailed Austin Harlow before bolting through the rear door.

Whitney, Jamie, and Paul exchanged glances and then followed him out without a word to anyone. Senator Mitchell and Katherine were left alone, staring in opposite directions, in complete silence. Neither spoke for several minutes.

The doorbell rang. A servant went to the door to find two uniformed police officers and a man in a suit standing there.

"I'm Detective Briscoe," said the man in the suit. "We have a warrant for the arrest of Senator Langley Mitchell for the murder of Trenton Harlow."

Katherine began to sob as the officers entered the room and placed a quivering Senator Mitchell in handcuffs. They led him to the waiting cruiser.

As the officers headed to the station, they passed the parked delivery driver who was sitting by the side of the road, looking at a check in disbelief. It was the bonus he had received from making the deliveries at the Mitchell estate. His heart rate returned to normal as he remembered how nervous he felt in the company of such powerful people.

It was all worth it, he thought, as his fingers touched the cashier's check for $2,000. What he did not know was that the company had received $3,000 as payment for making sure the sender's wishes were followed to the letter.

Erica Payne was the first one off the plane and walked to baggage claim. It was her lucky day, because her bags were the first to arrive on the carousel. She identified her luggage for the porter, who retrieved it before escorting her to customs.

"*Dobro jutro, gospado*, for what purpose do you come to Bosnia?" asked the fat customs inspector.

"A vacation," she replied pleasantly, reaching for her new passport.

"And how long do you intend to stay?"

"Two weeks."

"At what hotel will you be staying?"

"Copacabana for today. Then I will be with friends."

"*Hvala, Madame*, enjoy your time here," offered the customs inspector.

Erica smiled back at him. "*Dobro dosao*, I shall."

After the drive from the airport, she checked into the hotel located in the heart of the city. She was given the best suite available and went immediately to her room to soak in the luxury of a hot bath and wait for the call. She was sipping champagne when the telephone rang. Erica jumped.

"Yes," she whispered.

"I will arrive in the harbor within the hour. I can't wait to be with you. Did you send the packages?"

"Yes, just like we planned."

"I am leaving as soon as I finish mooring the ship. I should be there by four," he said.

"Till then, my love," she said huskily. Erica did not think her heart could wait until they were together. It was ready to explode with joy.

At a quarter past four, Jamie Quintell was sitting in David Whitney's conference room waiting for Mickey Cornette to return her call. Sweeney had gone to Erica Payne's former law firm to retrieve the medical records of Anthony Damon from his accident with Austin Harlow.

Paul was unable to reach Dr. Jason Butler. The manager of Butler's office had told him they could not comment on medical treatment received by any patient because of HIPAA confidentiality requirements. A search confirmed that Butler had been a classmate of Jack Bartlett and Lee Harlow's in medical school.

Sweeney also told Jamie about a call he'd received from a friend in the Boston Police Department. After Payne disappeared, an investigation was started. Two detectives interviewed Payne's private investigator, Ritchie Carbone, who disclosed to them that he identified Steven Sorenson as a man named Delbert Clayton. Although Carbone insisted Payne was unaware of his discovery, the detectives were pressing him for more details. The only thing Carbone was able to learn was that Clayton was a former Central Intelligence Agency operative.

Jamie had immediately called Mickey Cornette, who agreed to use his contact to see what he could find out about Clayton. Three hours had passed since they'd talked. Jamie was growing restless when her phone rang.

"Hello, Mick. What's up?"

"Hey, kid. If you aren't sitting down, you'd better find a chair and plop in it pronto."

"Why?"

"I just heard from my guy at the Pentagon who made some interesting discoveries."

"Like what?"

"Clayton had a reputation as a top CIA agent. Before that, he was in the marines. Guess who was his best friend and served with him?"

"Who?"

"A kid named Peter Norwood. Erica Payne's brother."

Jamie grabbed the armrest of her chair with her left hand.

"Christ, Mick. Are you sure?" she asked.

"It was confirmed. Norwood died on a mission after saving Clayton's life, and then Clayton went into the CIA. With his background and training, he sure as hell could have pulled this deal off."

"Think he's posing as Andre Vellois?"

"No. I think he has an accomplice."

"Who?"

"The real Andre himself."

"But how did Vellois get all that money? You came back from Grand Cayman convinced that he was rich."

"Vellois could have stashed a fortune from his days with the agency. There's a helluva lot of money missing from Harlow's clinic. Plus, the insurance proceeds and the phony mortgages. All Vellois needed was a foreign account as a front to get him going until he could collect the funds from the clinic."

"How could Vellois steal from Harlow's clinic?"

"Maybe Harlow was in on it."

"What do you mean?"

"They could have been blackmailing him. Or maybe he got cold feet after raiding the clinic's accounts and that did him in."

Jamie's mind was desperately trying to figure everything out as Cornette continued.

"Andre's not the only one with a motive," she replied.

"Who else?"

"A boy whose father and mother were stolen away from him. Someone whose life was turned upside-down because of these men and who now wants to get revenge. Someone who became a man but never had a chance to be a boy."

"You mean—"

"This could be the work of his son."

Chapter Thirty

Tuesday, November 11

When Whitney reached his office, his secretary handed him a stack of messages, an overnight delivery envelope, and told him Jamie was waiting in his office.

"Most of those calls are from Senator Mitchell," she said. "He keeps demanding that you to call him back immediately."

"I've resigned as his counsel. If he calls again, tell him I'll get a restraining order to keep him away from here," answered Whitney as he tore open the flap on the overnight envelope. He quickly read the documents inside while walking to his office.

Jamie was on her cell when he entered. She nodded as he removed his suit coat and sat behind his desk while she finished her call.

"My expert went over some of the e-mails Paul sent me from the computer in the Damon home."

Whitney took a sip of coffee. "Why only some e-mails?" he asked.

"Because the others have a higher level of encryption. We're still working on them."

"Tell me what you have."

"There was a lot of traffic between the Damons and other people about the baby and the birth. We haven't been able to trace the IP addresses, but an analysis of the contents let us draw quite a few inferences. We're convinced one account belongs to Erica Payne and the other we think belongs to Delbert Clayton. There are multiple references to setting this up with the baby and Clayton getting together with Emily when she moves to Wellesley."

"What else?"

"Erica Payne was the ringleader. We think they met when she was approached by Lee Harlow who expressed genuine remorse over how Anthony Damon was treated after his accident."

"That's strange," said Whitney. "Lee told me he was not involved in Austin's case."

"The Damons wanted a child but could not conceive. Lee got in touch with Dr. Butler, who was able to restore Anthony's sexual function. When Ann did not get pregnant, Lee took her in as a patient and discovered her fertility problems."

"What does that have to do with ruining the clinic?"

"Before Payne's brother and Clayton went on active duty, they were kidnapped and sexually assaulted by Senator Mitchell's chief of staff, Roger Newell. Erica discovered the senator knew about Newell's actions and let it go on because Newell could blackmail him about Trenton."

"What a low-life prick," said Whitney.

"The e-mails also said this was planned for the spring after Ann had her baby. But when the announcement got moved up, it was the perfect time to create a sense of urgency, because Mitchell wanted everything kept quiet for Austin."

"But why would someone want to take down the whole clinic?" asked Whitney.

"The biggest bombshell is an e-mail that says 'AV death confirmed.' Andre Vellois is dead, and no one could blow the whistle if someone stole his identity."

"What's the evidence?"

"Medical records from a military hospital in Germany where Vellois was treated after being shot. Clayton confirmed his death through his contacts."

"What about the son, Michael?"

"No one can find out what happened to him."

"Anything else?"

"We think Lee Harlow is involved," Jamie said.

Whitney shook his head.

"How could it be Lee? Is there evidence that shows he is involved in anything besides doing the insemination?" asked Whitney.

"I've never been convinced of his death," said Jamie.

"This Federal Express letter just came. It might change your mind," Whitney said, handing her the red-and-white envelope.

Jamie removed several documents and a series of small x-rays. She read quickly before looking up.

"This is from the coroner's office. It's Lee Harlow's dental records," she said, looking puzzled.

"The coroner admits they were misfiled and that he sent the wrong ones to the crematorium. This proves the body on the beach was Lee's. Those are the same records that Lee got from Jacobs along with those from his subsequent dentist," said Whitney.

"Wait a minute. Katherine said Lee had a gold bridge that would not have disintegrated in the fire. How do we explain that?" asked Jamie.

Whitney pointed to an entry in the records.

"Lee Harlow had his gold bridge replaced with porcelain last spring by another dentist after he left Jacobs's care. There was no gold in his mouth when he was cremated."

The sun was shining brightly and the winds were brisk in the Southern California town of Barstow as the dark-green Ford carrying two men in dark suits arrived shortly after two o'clock in the afternoon. Both sides of the street were filled with vehicles. The men had to park almost two blocks away. As they disembarked and began to walk back to the modest white ranch on the corner, a black-and-white police cruiser arrived, and two officers stepped out of the vehicle.

All four approached the door of the ranch where they were greeted by the sounds of laughter and music. They rang the bell twice before it was answered by a woman of middle years with a plastic glass of amber liquid in her left hand. She smiled broadly at the men as a huge birthday cake covered with lighted candles was being carried to an elderly man in a lounge chair.

"Yes?" asked the woman pleasantly.

"Good day, ma'am. I'm Special Agent Jamison of the FBI. This gentleman is Mr. Rauff, a law enforcement agent from the West German International Intelligence Service. Is this the home of Mr. Joseph Rhodes?"

"Yes," answered the woman, her smile fading. "I'm Mr. Rhodes's daughter, Shelia. What do you gentlemen want?"

"To see your father," muttered Jamison, brushing past Shelia as the others followed.

Everyone turned to watch the men approach Joseph Rhodes, as one of the party guests turned down the music. Jamison stopped in front of Rhodes and opened a leather case, showing his identification. The old man sat in a dignified pose with his back straight and his eyes almost ripping holes through the intruders.

"Sir, we're from the FBI. Are you Joseph Rhodes?"

"Yes," replied the old man in an even, almost challenging voice.

"Also known as Hans Straussman?" pressed Jamison.

The old man remained silent.

"Also known as Frederick von Steihl of the KGB?" demanded Rauff as his face grew into a cold sneer.

Rhodes's face took on a momentary look of terror and then quickly changed to proud defiance as he replied, "You haff me confused veeth some-vonn else."

"We have a warrant for your arrest, sir. You'll have to come with us," said Jamison evenly.

"And we have an order requesting your extradition to Berlin to stand trial for murder and treason," said Rauff.

Bedlam broke loose as the party guests began to gasp. A man in his midforties came over to the officers.

"Wait a minute. What the hell are you trying to do to my father?"

"Your father was a double agent in the 1960s and '70s. He sold secrets from the Russians while acting as a KGB agent," replied Rauff. "He was discovered by the Russian ambassador's *Charge d' affaires*, and he wound up murdering him. Afterward, he bought a passport on the black market and came to this country under the name of Hans Straussman. Then he changed his name to Joseph Rhodes and moved to California."

"This can't be true," screamed Shelia. "Our father changed his name from Straussman so his family would have an American name. You've got the wrong man."

"You can't prove any of those charges," cried Rhodes's son.

"We don't have to. The FBI is not arresting him for espionage. The West Germans will see to that. I'm taking him in to face charges in an American courtroom," replied Jamison.

"What are the charges?"

"Conspiracy and accessory to murder in the first degree," answered Jamison.

"Murder? Of who?" asked the son with a look of horror on his face.

"His business partner from many years ago. Trenton Harlow."

The clock showed almost three thirty as the meeting in the local bank in Naperville, Illinois, a suburb of Chicago, concluded. The bank officer seemed irritated as he addressed the potential customer seated in front of him who was dressed in soiled work clothes and boots.

"I'm sorry, Mr. Goodman, but we can't give you an extension," said the banker sourly, looking out over his reading glasses. "The terms of your mortgage clearly call for timely payments. If you cannot comply with the payment schedule, the bank has no choice but to foreclose."

"But all I'm asking for is a month, can't you see your way clear to give me a break, Mr. Potter?" asked Goodman, staring at the nameplate at the front of the desk.

"This is a bank, not McDonald's," huffed Potter.

"My family will be homeless," said Goodman carefully.

"The law is the law. Now, I need to return to other business."

"You bastard," said Goodman angrily.

The bank officer grabbed his phone and said quickly, "Get security in here right away," as Goodman started around the desk.

Instantly, two burly guards stormed through the door and escorted Goodman to the street.

"You better come with a raiding party if you try to get me and my family out," he hissed at the guards.

Straightening his clothing, Goodman turned and almost bumped into a man carrying a briefcase. Too angry to step aside, he began to storm past him when the man called his name.

"Are you Michael Goodman?"

"Who wants to know?"

"My name's Santos."

"Whaddya want with me?"

"I have something for you. I just need to see an ID."

"For what?"

"A package."

"Who's it from?"

"Someone who wants to remain anonymous."

"Why?"

"Hey, pal, I only get paid to deliver things. So just show me the ID, and you can open the briefcase and look to your heart's content."

Michael muttered to himself as he reached for his wallet. Removing his driver's license, he tossed it to Santos who studied it for a moment before handing it back.

"Here's the key," said Santos. He handed Michael the black leather briefcase and then walked away.

"Hey, wait a minute. Who sent me this?"

"Everything you need to know is inside," called Santos.

What the hell is going on? wondered Michael as he turned up the street to where his worn-out Chevy Blazer was parked. Twenty minutes later, he pulled up in front of his dilapidated home, and a small blond boy wearing ragged clothing came out to meet him.

"What's in the briefcase, Dad?" asked Billy Goodman.

"Probably some stupid magazine or advertisement," replied Michael. He walked inside and headed to the tiny kitchen to see his wife.

"Can I open it?" asked Billy from the living room.

"Sure," answered Michael dejectedly, tossing him the key.

Goodman entered the kitchen where his wife was making a pot of coffee.

"What happened at the bank?" she asked.

"What do you think? That little bastard said they're going to foreclose if we don't get the money."

"Any luck on that job in Chicago?" she asked as tears formed.

"Only bad luck," he answered, as he turned and opened the refrigerator. There was only a single Bud Light on the second shelf next to two cans of Pepsi. Repressing his anger, Goodman reached for the beer before turning and walking back into the tiny living room. Billy was sitting mesmerized in front of the open briefcase.

"What did you find, son, a bomb?" he asked sarcastically, reaching for the newspaper.

Billy didn't answer.

"Hey, son, you can tell your old man. What's in the bag?" he asked again before turning to the sports section.

"It's a million dollars, Dad!" shouted Billy. "There's a letter on top of it!"

Right, and I'm the president of Disney, thought Michael.

"Dad," called Billy, as his voice began to rise. "Please come here, Dad!"

Billy's voice was so intense that Michael jumped. Quickly, he rose and walked over to the floor where Billy was sitting. Peering into the open briefcase, Michael's skin tingled as he stared inside. Sitting on top of several rows of $100 bills was an envelope addressed to Michael Goodman. Michael reached down and snatched one of the stacks of bills. He brought it up to the light to examine. At once, he could see the bills were real.

"Linda, come in here quick," shouted Michael to his wife as he quickly tore open the envelope and began to read the letter.

Dear Michael:

You do not know me. My name is unimportant. What is important is that I was a friend of your mother's and an admirer of your father's. I do not mean the people who raised you, Mr. and Ms. Goodman, but your biological parents, Michelle and Andre Vellois. Your mother was a very brave lady and had more courage than anyone I have ever met. I was devastated when she died and have thought of her since that time. Your father also died a very courageous death as an American hero serving his country. You came from the kind of parents that are rare in today's world, and I wanted you to know that they were appreciated and loved.

Many years ago, your mother was kind enough to loan me some money. As I never had the chance to pay it back, I invested it in the hopes that someday I would find you and give it to you and your family. I have enclosed the proceeds of that investment.

Please accept this in loving memory of Andre and Michelle Vellois.

A Friend

Michael Vellois stared blankly at the rows of bills in the briefcase as Billy began taking them out. It took them almost thirty minutes to count the money. When they finished, there were over 20,000 $100 bills lying on the floor: $2.1 million in cash. The exact amount that Jack Bartlett was alleged to have stolen through insurance fraud.

"Who could have sent this?" asked Linda Goodman as tears flowed freely down her face.

"I don't know," answered Michael, holding her tightly.

Michael began to cry tears of joy as he held his wife and son close to him. He took a deep breath as he remembered the telephone call he had gotten from a man who refused to give his name, but told him that his father died as the leader of a special forces team that was trying to help smuggle Americans out of prison camps in Cambodia.

Michael should be proud of his father, he was told. Andre Vellois was a genuine hero.

At the end of the afternoon, Jamie was on her way into Whitney's office when his telephone rang. After waving her into a chair, he held a short, animated conversation. After hanging up the receiver, he looked at Jamie and began to laugh.

"That was a good friend of mine, Jake Skylar of Evans and Skylar. Guess who's in the unemployment line?"

"Besides Senator Mitchell, I don't know," Jamie said.

"Rebecca Castle, Esquire."

Jamie laughed aloud.

"You're kidding. What happened?"

"Seems the board of directors at Eastern Casualty weren't too fond of the way she settled the Sorenson case with cash. They think she should have used a check, so they could have stopped payment if anything went wrong. But she insisted on her old settlement trick, so the cash is gone. The board held a special meeting yesterday and told Castle she's out."

"Maybe there is justice sometimes. Get hold of yourself. I've got a potential case-cracking discovery for you."

"What?"

"The identity of the third party who was in the e-mail thread about the Damon baby and the conspiracy. We think it was Lee Harlow."

"Jamie, we've beaten this horse until it's beyond dead. It couldn't be Lee."

Jamie removed a document and began to read.

"This is addressed to Speed, who is really Anthony Damon. The sender says, quote, 'I talked to Lou today, and he told me everything is being done to make sure the baby gets through this.'"

Jamie looked at Whitney, who seemed deep in thought.

"We think Lou is Dr. Louis Carnevale. The only one I can come up with who would have talked to him about the baby is Lee Harlow," said Jamie.

"It could have been Sorenson or Payne."

"No. The e-mail calls him Lou. The tone indicates a familiarity that would be between friends or colleagues. There is no evidence any of the others except Harlow ever heard of Carnevale before this case, so it's likely they would maintain a formal tone."

"That's pretty damn thin," Whitney said.

"It's almost invisible until you factor in one more discovery. On a hunch, I had Judy Davis run Emily Damon's name through the clinic files. Each time Ann Sorenson was treated, Emily Damon's health insurance in Canada was billed. Lee Harlow had to be involved with that," said Jamie, nodding as her face grew into a thoroughly satisfied look.

Whitney paused before he answered. "But why, Jamie? Why would Lee destroy everything he worked for? What could he possibly hope to gain?"

Jamie pressed her fingertips together. "Revenge. The oldest and most volatile of all the emotions. He got even with everyone, took the clinic down, and made a fortune."

Whitney stared at her for a moment. "I can't believe Lee would let me struggle through this case if he were still here. He would have found a way to let me know he'd pulled this off, even if he never spelled out the details."

Chapter Thirty-One

Wednesday, November 12

Port of Neum, Bosnia

The ceremony was short, barely twenty minutes. In the garden behind the villa, the judge looked at Ricki and Eddy and pronounced them husband and wife. With smiles overflowing, they kissed and then turned and accepted congratulations from the others. The judge shook each one's hand and then returned to his duties.

Speed and Emily approached them first. Emily gave Andy to Clay to hold as she hugged Ricki and Eddy. Clay shifted Andy to his left arm and then followed them. After a champagne toast, they adjourned to the balcony overlooking the ocean. It was finally time to celebrate.

The sea was calm, and the air was sweetly scented. It was a day of splendor—one to be remembered as the perfect way to begin the next phase of their lives. Emily lifted her glass as Clay slipped his index finger around the baby's hand.

"This little guy gave us quite a scare. But he came back like a true champion," he said.

"His respiratory problems showed us that Mother Nature will always be the one in charge," said Eddy.

"Ricki, how did you know this scheme was so perfect?" asked Emily.

Ricki stopped and looked at each of them before she answered.

"This plan exploited one of the worst fears about infertility treatment. A white couple forced to have a black child. It appealed to the racist streak a lot of people have that tells them a child of color has less value than a white one. The defense couldn't take the chance a jury would come down hard on them. Not with Clay playing the perfect aggrieved husband," said Ricki.

"Thank God Speed trusted me enough to let me pretend to move in with Emily in Wellesley." Clay laughed.

"I was convinced she would never dump me as soon as she found out you can't do math in your head like I can," said Speed, as everyone chuckled.

"When did the teaching job come through?" asked Clay.

"Right after I completed my undergraduate work in Montreal. We're flying to Cape Verde tomorrow. I can teach while I finish my postgraduate degree," said Speed.

"And I can work on raising a healthy son while the memory of Andrea looks over us and go back to college next term," said Emily.

"Why Cape Verde?" asked Clay.

Speed grinned at Emily and his son.

"No extradition treaty with the United States," he said. "Just like Bosnia."

"What's up for you now, Clay?" asked Emily.

"I have a lot of friends with problems. I'll keep busy," replied Clay.

"My biggest regret is that we never stopped that evil bastard Langley Mitchell years ago. Maybe we could have saved someone's life," said Ricki.

"Too bad it cost Trenton Harlow his life when he found out Hans Straussman paid Mitchell for a phony passport, went to confront him publicly, and Langley shot him," said Clay.

"The only reason we linked Mitchell to Trenton was because Eddy identified Newell," said Ricki.

"Ricki and I confronted him, and Newell cracked like an eggshell because he only had a few months to live. We kept the confession under wraps so we could take the senator down when the time was right," said Eddy.

"I'm glad everyone in Mitchell's world wound up in turmoil, thanks to Eddy," said Clay before his face spiraled into a smile.

Emily reached to take Andy from Clay.

"I don't think I'll ever get used to calling Lee by that nickname," she said.

Lee Harlow's face broke into a wide grin.

"I got that name long before your time," said Lee. "When I first got to Notre Dame in 1968, the coach told me I ran the football like their All-American running back, Nick Eddy, who led the team to their last national championship a few years earlier, so he gave me the nickname, Eddy. Every time I have been in a clutch situation since then, I've remembered all the work I did to earn that name. That's why only my closest friends call me Eddy."

"Are you and Ricki ready to move on?" asked Emily.

"I'm going to take over as medical director of a clinic to help underprivileged women obtain a chance to have a decent life," said Lee. He stopped and looked at Ricki before continuing. "I can also spend whatever time I have left trying to make the only woman I ever loved happy," he whispered before reaching down to give his new wife a kiss.

"I have accepted a position here with the human rights coalition to help victims of domestic abuse. They are underfunded and understaffed. It's the kind of challenge that always moved me the most," said Ricki.

"You're a great man, Lee," said Emily. "We all owe you a debt we can never repay."

At that moment, Andy let out a prolonged giggle.

"See that," said Speed. "Even your newest godson thinks you're a hero."

"I'm not a hero," said Lee. "The people in their graves who got pendants were heroes."

Jamie Quintell arrived at David Whitney's office just before six. His secretary handed her a small package that had just arrived by courier. There was no return address.

She watched as Whitney opened it. Inside were three envelopes and a book that looked many years old, as well as a magnum of *Bollinger La Grande* 2004 champagne. Whitney's eyes lit up as he ran his fingers over the bottle.

"Is that from a secret admirer?" asked Jamie.

"I have no idea," he replied and then suddenly saw himself shaking Erica Payne's hand as he remembered their conversation.

Two envelopes were from the Vellois Foundation, while the third was addressed to Artemis Associates. Whitney opened the first envelope and found a bearer bond payable in the amount of $500,000. The attached note said it was payment for his legal services.

"Is there a name on it?" asked Jamie.

"None," he replied

His pulse increased as he tore open the next envelope. Inside was another bearer bond, this one in the amount of $1.5

million. Another note said the funds were to be used to provide a year's severance pay to each nonphysician employee of Harlow's three clinics who was now out of work because the clinics were all in shambles. It also directed him to use the funds to pay all back withholding and social security taxes to the Internal Revenue Service.

Whitney's hands were trembling as he opened the final envelope and found a check in the amount of $3 million and a note directing him to establish a foundation that would provide scholarships in the name of Andre and Michelle Vellois for underprivileged children who wanted to study engineering. Whitney was directed to pick candidates of his choosing and to award as many scholarships annually as he determined were deserved by the applicants.

Jamie pointed to the well-worn, leather-bound book.

"You act like that book is familiar. What's the title?" she asked as David held it up.

"It's called *The Art of War.* It was written centuries ago by a brilliant Chinese general, strategist, and tactician named Sun Tzu," he said. Whitney's eyes lit up as he remembered Harlow showing it to him. "Several years ago, I was on trial, and Lee was my lead witness. I was having a really tough time with the other side's expert. Every time I looked at him, I got aggravated. Lee said he had a book that would show me how to go after the guy as well as any other adversary I ran across."

"It looks like there are markers stuck between some of the pages," Jamie said as she stared at the white paper shards extending from the book's spine.

Whitney turned to the first bookmark. Opening it, he read,

If you know your enemy and you know yourself,

you need not fear the results of a hundred battles.

They exchanged glances and then Whitney turned to the next entry:

If your enemy is secure at all points, be prepared for him;

If he is of superior strength, evade him;

If your opponent is tempermental, seek to irritate him;

Pretend to be weak, that he may grow arrogant;

If he is taking his ease, give him no rest;

If his forces are united, separate them;

If sovereign and subject are in accord, put division between them.

"Lee said it was his father's book, and he used those last passages against all his adversaries. That's why he passed it down to Lee," said Whitney.

"Those words were written centuries ago and they still apply," said Jamie.

"There was one passage that Lee used to quote all the time about attacking your enemy by appearing where you are not expected," he said.

Jamie looked at Whitney as his intercom rang. His secretary told him Lizzie Emerson from the *Boston Globe* was on the line.

"Wait a minute," he said, after listening for a moment. "I want to put you on speaker."

Whitney pressed a button at the base before replacing the receiver in its cradle.

"OK," he began. "Repeat what you just told me."

"All right," said Emerson. "I'm calling you because you're the attorney for Senator Langley Mitchell. He will not return our calls. When I went by his home, the servants refused to let me in. We want your comments about a story we're running in tomorrow's paper."

"What's the story?" asked Whitney.

"Yesterday, we received documents that said Senator Mitchell is being investigated for procuring illegal passports for immigrants to come to America in the 1970s in exchange for hefty campaign contributions. And we've learned that a grand jury secretly indicted him on a charge of murder, and he was taken into custody. As the senator's lawyer, do you have any response to these allegations, Mr. Whitney?"

Jamie looked at Whitney, rolled her eyes, and nodded her head.

"Sorry, but I resigned as his counsel after I saw that disgusting picture of him standing over the dead body of Trenton Harlow." Whitney took a deep breath before he continued. "I will comment as his former attorney. You can quote me, only if you promise to print what I'm about to add word for word."

"Go ahead."

"I would not be the slightest bit surprised if it were all true."

"Are you sure you want to say that, Mr. Whitney?" asked Emerson. "I know you're a lawyer, but couldn't he sue you for slander or something?"

"Not only do I think it's true, but I hope that damn criminal sues me. I can't think of anything I'd rather do than cross-examine him in open court."

"Look for the story to run tomorrow. Thanks, Mr. Whitney," said Emerson.

After breaking the connection, Whitney turned to Jamie. He was about to speak when his intercom rang.

"It's Neil Armstrong for you on line one," said his secretary.

"Neil Armstrong? Who the hell…" He shot a puzzled look at Jamie.

"That's the name of the first guy to walk on the moon, right?" she asked.

"What did he say this is about?" Whitney asked in a tentative voice.

"Senator Mitchell," she replied.

"OK, I'll take it," he said.

Whitney took a deep breath and activated the line.

"This is David Whitney."

There was a short pause and then a deep voice spoke.

"Don't say my name in case the line is tapped."

Whitney and Jamie leaped to their feet as each recognized the voice of Lee Harlow.

"Understood," said Whitney as his pulse quickened. "Why are you calling?"

"I have a message for you. The eagle has landed."

Jamie placed her knuckles on the edge of the desk and leaned closer to the phone. Her heart raced as she looked at Whitney and mouthed the words, "Oh my God."

"Can you tell me where you are?" asked Whitney, nodding at her.

"I'm in paradise," the voice said.

Whitney's heart felt like it was going to shoot out of his chest. "I got a package this morning. Do I have you to thank for it?" he asked as his voice broke slightly.

A brief chuckle came from the phone.

"The book is from me. The champagne is from my wife. The envelopes are from both of us."

Whitney and Jamie looked at each other with wild stares of disbelief.

"Your wife?" asked Whitney as an image of Katherine appeared.

"Yes. We were just married. She also asked me to give you a message. She said you were the only member of the bar she has ever met who raised the standard for honor and integrity, both as a lawyer and a gentleman."

Jamie brought her hands up to her face and covered her mouth.

"It's Payne," she whispered.

Whitney pictured Lee and Erica together. Suddenly, it all made sense.

"That's very flattering, but please tell your wife I will need written confirmation that she was talking about me and not Rebecca Castle," said Whitney.

The voice on the phone broke into a deep, guttural laugh. Another laugh, this one softer but distinctly feminine, sounded in the background.

"They're both on this call!" said Jamie, bouncing up and down on her toes like a ballerina as her voice rose while she pointed at the telephone.

"What's in store for you now?" asked Whitney.

"I've finally found peace. An unexpected bonus came with it: happiness. It took me a long time to get here, and I intend to spend the rest of my life savoring it."

Whitney's eyes clouded over as he stared at Jamie for a moment before he spoke again. "There's something I have to know. Can you tell me why?"

"Destiny decided to throw a party to collect on some overdue bills. I had to make sure all those who were invited showed up with their checkbooks."

Whitney and Jamie exchanged glances as each pictured the scene at the Mitchell home several days ago when all the packages arrived.

"I guess destiny needed to make sure everyone got Anne Frank's message about character," said Whitney.

"I couldn't leave without you knowing the truth and me saying thank you. I'm a better man because I have known you."

"I have just one final question. How?" Whitney asked.

A long pause ensued, and Whitney could almost picture Lee's face breaking into a wide grin as he spoke.

"A theologian might say there was only one way to get an eye for an eye, and that was to give a tooth for a tooth," said the voice.

Whitney's eyes opened wide as he looked at Jamie while a wave of amazement passed over him. "I hope you find all the joy you deserve," he said in a voice choked with emotion.

"*Vaya con Dios*, my friend," said the voice. Then the call ended.

Whitney and Jamie stared at the phone for a prolonged moment before plopping down into their chairs.

"What did you get out of that 'eye for an eye' and 'tooth for a tooth' riddle?"

Whitney grinned and stared back at her.

"He got his revenge because he switched the dental records," said Whitney.

"How do you know that?" she asked.

"He must have had a body on the plane with him, probably an unclaimed cadaver. Dental records were the only way to identify whoever was with Lee. There were no hands so no fingerprints, and Lee's DNA was not on file. All somebody had to do was make new records from the body before it went into the bay and switch them with the real ones. Pretty damn clever."

Neither said a word for several minutes. Then David got up, walked to the valet, and retrieved his jacket. After donning it, he approached Jamie and then leaned forward and gave her a kiss. She felt a surge and then responded with the same passion.

"What was that all about?" she asked.

He looked deeply into her eyes and smiled.

"The fact that I'm not involved any more. I'm hoping we can talk about it over dinner. I just learned a lesson from that phone call on how to reach out and grab happiness when it's staring me right in the face."

Jamie slipped her arm as she smiled a wicked grin. She squeezed him tighter as they walked out together, while sneaking looks of admiration and disbelief in each other's direction.

Chapter Thirty-Two

After the yacht reached the edge of the harbor, Ricki and Lee arrived on the most forward part of the upper deck with a bottle of champagne.

"I think it's finally time to let go of the past," said Ricki, removing an old Polaroid photograph from her pocket and handing it to Lee.

"This whole plan fell into place because you showed me this photo," he said.

"You recognized Roger Newell."

"Katherine dragged me to a fundraiser years ago and I met him. I wasn't important enough for him to pay me much attention."

"He found out exactly who you were after we went to see him and you beat that confession out of him."

"Remember how he cried when he told us Mitchell found out about him and those young boys, and he started taking random photos to use as what he called 'unemployment insurance?'"

"The only good thing about that is the shot he took of Mitchell shooting Trenton. I hope that old bastard gets what he deserves in prison," said Ricki.

Lee held up the Polaroid picture she had given him.

"Clay gave you this photo when you met at Punk's funeral, right?" he asked.

She stopped for a moment to dab at her eyes.

"It was taken soon after my father kicked Punk out at sixteen. He wound up living on the streets of Washington, DC, where he met Clay, who was also homeless. Newell and his buddies used to cruise the streets and give hard drugs to boys as young as thirteen and then take them somewhere and assault them."

"And those evil bastards took pictures with an old Polaroid," said Lee in an angry tone.

"Clay said he managed to slip out of his restraints and free Punk. That photo fell on the floor, and Punk picked it up just before they escaped. He told me Punk was haunted by it and still had horrible nightmares even after they joined the marines," said Ricki.

Lee looked down at the picture and then turned back to face her.

"Anne Frank was right about everyone. This photo let us take revenge for your brother, the deaths of my mother and father, Bartlett and Katherine's affair, and Austin for all the pain he caused Speed."

"It also led you to making amends to Speed and Emily by giving them Andrew."

"I guess I can give thanks for the fact that you are such a superstar as a lawyer. That's why I asked you to meet me before Speed's case settled. I wanted to reason with you and offer to help Speed with his medical problems. Especially when I told you I would do whatever I could to make things right because of how Austin was being coddled by Langley Mitchell."

"That's when I fell in love with you. After I found out how you kept a sense of honor among all those thieves. Then you told me about your urologist friend and how you would do everything possible to help Speed and Emily have a child," said Ricki.

"Jason Butler was on the cutting edge of microsurgical techniques for restoring male fertility. He was more than happy to help."

Ricki looked at the picture one last time and then nodded. Harlow removed a small lighter form his pocket.

"Knowing we had this plan let me resolve my biggest regret. When DNA confirmed Bartlett was Austin's father, I got tested and learned it was impossible for me to have gotten Michelle pregnant, and that gave me some closure," said Lee, flicking the lighter.

Holding the photograph up over the side, he touched the flame to its edge. Instantly, the image of Ricki's brother Punk tied to a chair while bound and gagged with duct tape as he was being sexually assaulted by Roger Newell, disappeared. Lee let it go, and traces of ash flittered away in the soft breeze.

"May we all finally rest in peace," said Ricki, slipping her arm into Lee's.

The sun was about to set at the Perpetual Garden Cemetery in the town of Wellesley, just west of Boston. Santos drove through the entrance and parked at the Harlow family mausoleum. Remnants of fall foliage surrounded the driveway, and a flock of wild geese paraded around the lake that bordered the epicenter.

After his arrival at the gravesite, he opened a small bag and removed three silver pendants from the package, sized one against each headstone, quickly drilled two holes, inserted anchors, and attached them.

He stepped in front of Trenton's sepulcher first and read the engraved saying to make sure it was correct. After confirming the wording, he secured it in place.

Underneath the *sheng li* were the words,

The Supreme Art of War Is to Subdue Your Enemy Without Fighting.

Alicia's headstone was next. Her words read,

All Warfare Is Based On Deception.

As he moved quickly to the front of Lee's tomb, the sun was sinking. He read fast in order to complete his task with enough daylight left. After a final check, he sent pictures of each from his phone to Clay.

The wording on Lee's pendant stuck in his mind. It contained a saying to use in all future dealings and was a piece of advice so profound, yet so simple, that it would apply equally to legal battles, corporate fights, or governmental acts of aggression.

He brought up the picture of Harlow's pendant and then typed in the quote for attribution. All three sayings were listed together, and the author was identified as an obscure, ancient Chinese military tactician, Sun Tzu, who offered this completely straightforward, yet most tragically precise, observation:

Attack your enemy where he is unprepared; appear where you are not expected.

The End

About the Author

Tim Cagle is a practicing trial attorney in the fields of Medical Malpractice, Products Liability, and Personal Injury law. He has also served as co-counsel to other trial lawyers by conducting the cross examination of adverse expert witnesses during trials.

In addition, he was a law professor and taught courses in Torts, Evidence, Medical Malpractice and Negotiations. He is admitted to practice law in the Commonwealth of Massachusetts, State of Missouri, before the Federal District Court in Boston, and has been admitted pro hac vice for the trial of cases in the State of New Hampshire, the State of Rhode Island, and before the Federal District Court in the State of New Jersey.

He received a Bachelor of Arts Degree from Kansas State College and a Doctor of Jurisprudence Degree from Suffolk University, Boston, Massachusetts.

His memberships have included the American Bar Association, Massachusetts Bar, Academy of Trial Attorneys, Massachusetts Academy of Trial Attorneys, Nashville Songwriters Association, American Legion, Boston Pacemaker Club and Sigma Chi Alumni Association. He served as a First Lieutenant in the United States Army, was assigned to Military Intelligence and was honorably discharged.

After playing college football, he served as an assistant high school football coach. He has written over three hundred and fifty songs, played professionally in groups and as a single performer and spent time in Nashville as a songwriter. He is also the author of *Whispers From The Silence*, a novel based on his experiences writing songs and his career as a singer/songwriter. It was released in June, 2017.

Unexpected Enemy (Ultimate Revenge) is his second book. He is currently finishing a sequel to *Whispers From the Silence,* and also is writing another novel which deals with a nationwide scandal involving the implantation of defective cardiac pacemakers.